Talhan

Book Three of the Lissae Series

R. Lennard

Talhan

First published in 2020 by R. Lennard
Second edition published in 2024 by R. Lennard

All books in the Lissae Series are written in **UK English**.

Edited by Anna at CREATING ink.
www.CREATINGink.com

Published by Rebecca Lennard.
lissae.com

Check the trigger warnings by scanning the QR code below:

A catalogue record for this book is available from the National Library of Australia

To Jess.
Your encouraging words, talent, and fortitude in the face of everyday life
are only overshadowed by your brilliant smile.

PROLOGUE

Autumn 3958

Bent over the form of another broken body, Temira, now of Talhan, sighed. It was going to be a long night.

The left arm and leg were gone. Haemorrhaging. Crushed cheekbone. Skin and tissue removed from skull and torso. Breath and heart rate...

Stopped.

Prodding the wound on the victim's side, Temira sent her Innarn out to determine if it had damaged the lungs. They were intact.

Limbs first. Then the torso and head. Heart and lungs would have to be last, or he'd bleed out. Come to think of it, extra blood would probably be helpful.

Temira snapped her fingers. Xani slapped a disc of femto crystals into her hand. With skill, and a small amount of luck, this poor Lissaen would live.

After a quick glance at the crystal disc in her hand, she poured her Innarn into it. She told it what to heal first, showing the tiny crystals how to keep this man healthy for a long time. She reminded them what arms and legs, muscle, skin, and bone were.

Time was wasting. She sensed other patients were arriving.

Leg first.

She took the disc in both hands and twisted, activating the femto crystals on both sides. Slamming the first of the discs onto the leg stump, and ignoring the scream from the fallen man's comrade. The arm got the other half of the disc. A few of the femto crystals stubbornly clung to her fingers.

Temira chanced a glance at Xani. They'd have to work on the crystal's reluctance to say goodbye to the Innarnian who powered them.

With a grimace, she smacked the man's ribcage, dislodging the last of the crystals straight into his bloodstream.

A quick look at his stumps showed the limbs regrowing successfully. The skin reformed first, filling with the bones, muscles, blood, and tissue between one blink and the next.

A seeking tendril of Innarn told her the crystals were doing their job. The skin had started to repair.

In less than a minute, he would return to the living. But others would not be so lucky if she dallied.

"They said you'd fix him!" It was one of the patrollers, held back by his more experienced team mates.

The raw, anguished scream from behind her sent her mind spiralling back to a Realm covered in fires and ash. Back to her own voice, hoarse in her throat, as she shouted at the injustice of her burning home.

She swallowed her pain and turned to the healed man as he gasped the first breath of his second chance.

"I did." Turning, she then swept away, Xani by her side as they attended to the next patient awaiting a miracle. As she worked through the remaining patients, she ignored the whispers of 'technomancer'.

Stories of the technomancer grew, spreading across Lissae. Droves of sick and injured worked their way to Talhan, hoping for a cure.

Her success rate had become so high, the Ducibus diverted any patrols with dying members to Talhan upon their return.

Many who saw the technomancer were fixed. A rare few did not survive. Word spread farther, reaching the ears of every patrol on Lissae.

Whispers of what the technomancer could do became the stuff of legend.

Spring 4059

Tania shuffled the bundle of books in her hands, so the ones on crystal Innarn were at the top. As she lifted one to restock the shelves of Books 'n' More, there was a flicker of movement in her peripheral vision. Something metallic scraped over the wooden shelves.

Tania shivered as her gaze snapped to the shadows on the shelf next to her.

She sent a few soft lights out, illuminating the space between the books. As shadows faded away, she caught a glimpse of silver.

A dense presence behind her made the fine hair on the back of her neck stand on end. A heavy hand clamped down on her shoulder before she could turn.

Her Innarn burst out of her in a heavy wave as she shrieked, sending her attacker flying. Books leaped from the shelves, clattering to the floor.

Jonathan Buan, Guardian of Lissae, clambered off the floor, rubbing the spot where he'd hit his head on the shelf. "I was just going to say well met."

Tania was sure she heard something scurrying away, but a quick glance towards the shelf showed nothing. "Ever get the impression you're being watched?"

"Only since I stepped foot on Ronah." Jonathan gave a lazy wave of his hand, restoring the books to their rightful places.

As the *Guidebook of Protected Realms* and the *Portable Compendium of Distant Conjuration* streaked past her nose, Tania met Jonathan's gaze. "I thought I heard... never mind. Well met, Guardian."

He gave her a rueful grin. "Well met, Ronah's Linked. How are the plans for Talhan's joining?"

"There's so much to do!" Tania sighed. "Zana and I have split the tasks between Rakemyst and Ronah, but it's still a monumental job. So far, I'm trying to convince the Shansky Clan that dying the cloth they spin is an innovative idea. I'd love to have purple robes for Ronah's Elders."

Jonathan hummed and gave her an encouraging smile.

Tania bounced on the spot a bit, glad he didn't think the idea was as daft as her schoolmates had made it out to be. But they had said something which was playing on her mind. "A few girls at school today said something about a..." Tania's voice lowered. "...technomancer on Talhan."

"A technomancer?"

Tania nodded, worrying at her bottom lip as she hefted the next tome. "They said the technomancer uses crystal Innarn to bring back the dead and make the injured into her experiments."

Jonathan's eyebrows raised. "You can't be serious."

"That's what they were saying. They told me to avoid her at all costs."

"Stories of the technomancer are greatly exaggerated. When the 'technomancer' is mentioned, people are usually referring to the head of crystal healing. Temira may be many things, but she is a perfectly rational being." Jonathan's voice remained steady, but his eyes flicked to the side and he frowned.

With a huff, Tania shelved the last book. "I still say you shouldn't trifle with someone who plays with the dead."

Jonathan sighed as he pinched the bridge of his nose.

CHAPTER ONE

Spring 4059

A flurry of tiny wings beat against her unprotected skin. Shari Dawn, Altoriae of Lissae, laughed as she fell to the ground.

Soft grey grass cushioned her fall. Was it her imagination, or was the grass on Rakemyst softer than what grew on Ronah? Maybe it was the altitude of the clearing on the tiny island, hovering above the bulk of the Shifting Islands, which sprawled out below them? Either way, Shari relished in the feeling of wings continuing to beat against her skin as hundreds of tiny honeyhawks in all colours of the rainbow surrounded her. Her uncle laughed. The tiny birds startled, and spiralled into the air. Shari sighed and lifted a hand to wave goodbye.

A honeyhawk with iridescent green wings broke away from the flock, landing on her outstretched hand.

Eyes lighting up, Shari drew the tiny creature closer to her face. Its long, slender beak opened, and it warbled at her before flitting from her finger, as light as a single Ilutri feather. Shari looked after them in longing as it spiralled higher and higher before diving to rejoin its flock mates disappearing into the forest below.

"Told you the hike would be worth it." Her Uncle Wolf almost sounded smug.

"I still don't understand why you couldn't fly up here," Shari replied, picking a fallen leaf off the ground beside her.

"Because my smallest feather is bigger than they are. They're just as good at protecting themselves as you are, only they flee instead of fight."

Shari rolled her eyes at the jab and lazily rose to her feet. "Where to next?"

"Next, we'll go to one of *my* favourite places," Belfar, her uncle's mate, said, grinning at her. "And now the honeyhawks are nesting in the forest, we can fly there."

Wolf shoved Belfar with his shoulder. "*Some* of us like the exercise."

Belfar rolled his eyes and winked at Shari. "And some of us prefer to exercise our Innarn. Ready, Altoriae?"

Not waiting for an answer, Belfar sprinted for the edge of the cliff and leaped off. His whoop filled the air as he spread his wings and caught the current, flying above them with ease.

"Show-off!" called Wolf.

"He's your show-off." Shari grinned at him.

The line of Wolf's shoulders tensed for a moment, and then he melted. "He is mine, isn't he?"

Even as she shook her head, Shari couldn't wipe the grin from her face. She drew a twister of air into being and followed Belfar into the sky.

Her uncle sighed loudly, making the two in the air giggle. Wolf gave a mighty bound and joined them.

Together, the three Innarnians moved through the sky as if they had been doing it forever. Shari firmly repressed the niggling thought of how life might have turned out if she had said no when Lissae had asked her to be the Altoriae.

She followed Belfar's lead, and the three came to land on the lush lawn of her grandfather's garden.

"Time for lunch." Belfar announced with a grin.

"This is your favourite place?"

Belfar ignored the hint of scorn in Wolf's voice with the grace of practise.

"It is. This is where I come to be closer to the one I love." Belfar stared into Wolf's eyes. Her uncle flushed, and Shari suppressed a giggle as she slipped away from the oblivious duo.

"Ah, it must be lunch. Belfar's stomach always knows when it's mealtime." Her grandfather grinned at her as she slid through the doorway and into the dining room.

The delicious aroma of seared sun cake made her stomach growl, and Shari put a little of everything on her plate before her guides for the day entered, looking a little mussed.

The Ilutri had done their nightly dance. The sky was filled with Innarn and colour.

In the darkness, just before dawn, Shari rested her elbows on her grandfather's table, where dinner had turned into a friendly food fight. It had been a beautiful night, and Shari wasn't ready to go home to the silence of the empty house yet.

She steepled her fingers and propped her chin on them, staring out at the stars.

Shari was so lost in the beauty of the night, she startled when someone knocked on the balcony doors. She slid her chair back and pulled a stray bit of muffin out of her hair before opening the door to a glowing Belfar.

"There's something else I want to show you," Belfar said. His cheeks had reddened in the wind, and his hair was carelessly ruffled. The enormous smile on his face told the world how happy he was.

"Do tell," Shari said, trying to arch her brow. Her breath frosted in the cool morning air. With the sun yet to rise, tiny icicles carpeting the grass glittered in the light of the descending moons.

"Think you can keep up, Altoriae?" Belfar sprung into the sky, the down draft threatening to send Shari sprawling. He looped above her head and winged away.

"Cheater!" she called after him, and pulled the air towards her, creating a cushion to ride on. She zoomed after him, keeping the Ilutri in sight.

He led her on a chase through the changing clouds. As the sun rose, Belfar dropped like a stone, wings tucked in behind him. Shari dropped too, shivering as she passed through the cloud and whisking the water away from her clothes as they drew closer to the ground. Belfar's landing barely disturbed the grass.

"Oh." Shari stumbled as her feet hit the ground, too focused on taking in the view.

Oh, what a view. Golden trumpet flowers and silver-leafed trees circled a clearing of blue grass. The flowers chimed as Belfar fanned his wings, leaving Shari with her heart so full, it was in danger of bursting.

"What is this place?" she whispered.

"This is the Circle. It's where we come when we need to contemplate life, or if we've had a rough day, or when we've lost someone. Kinda looked like you could use some time here."

More and more, as the peaceful days crept on, Shari turned to share things with someone who wasn't there. Who'd never be by her side again.

"Do you want to talk about it?"

She sunk to the ground, digging her fingers into the grass. "I don't know where to start," she admitted.

"The beginning is best." Belfar sat down near her, close enough to be a comfort, but too far to touch. His actions were exactly what Shari hadn't realised she needed.

She raised a sod-covered hand and let the tears drip onto it. "The first time I lost someone changed my life, you know? I never, ever wanted to get close to anyone again. And then Mitch ruined it all." The last word came out as more of a sob, and Shari collapsed. She detected Belfar's calming presence in the back of her mind, but pouring out the months of pent-up grief over Mitch's death was all-consuming. "He... he started joking. Made me laugh. When we were fighting a gourhog, the tuzar made me snort so hard, a three-banded toe biter flew up my nose."

Behind her, Belfar chuckled.

"One patrol, he was sloppy. He'd been studying for his last school exams instead of resting, but still wanted to come with me. He got stabbed. His eyes went so wide, and for a moment I..." Her vision filled with the sight of Mitch, eyes wide, fingers splayed around the green, oozing wound, the dagger he'd pulled out of it in his other hand.

"I promised myself that I would always fight at his side to protect his sorry arse." She hiccoughed and scrunched her eyes up. "But... but then, Anriluka. He stood alone on the cliff, and I wasn't fast enough and she..." Shari started sobbing. Belfar used his Innarn to rub circles on her back.

Slowly, Shari came to her senses. The flowers in the clearing chimed, heads bowed as if they too remembered. "He could always make me smile," she whispered. Her thoughts turned to the crummy jokes he'd told whenever he'd pick up take-out, and how he'd proclaimed his glee because his father wasn't cooking that night.

Or when he'd tell her an anecdote as he bandaged her back or shoulders, praising her for taking down the latest foe as Jon berated her at the same time.

"What's your favourite memory of him?" Belfar asked, voice as low as the ground.

"He used to sneak out the back of Jon's store to practise. I'd leave shrunken things hidden around room, and he'd spend ages finding them and returning them to the right size. I love that I had been the one to show him how to enlarge objects. Mitch was the first person I ever taught, and he got it straight away. But whenever Jon would teach him, it would take him an age to get it right." Tears welled in her eyes again. "He still had trouble shrinking things when he…"

"He sounds brave," Belfar said. Shari noted the warmth of his Innarn, despite half the clearing being between them. Belfar made a handkerchief dance over to her.

"Almost as brave as you." Shari sniffled and blew her nose, wadding the handkerchief up and shifting it to the laundry pile at home.

"Brave? Me?" Belfar placed a hand on his puffed-out chest and fluttered his eyelashes.

Shari giggled and frowned. Feeling happy seemed so wrong when…

"Why call me brave, Altoriae?" The Ilutri's words pulled her out of her head.

"You'd have to be, to have put up with my uncle's nonsense for so long."

Belfar threw back his head and laughed.

Shari was careful to not let herself slip into her grief after Wolf summoned Belfar, who'd left with a quiet apology. At the moment, it seemed like it would be never-ending. She knew time would make living with her grief easier, but it didn't stop her from wanting to speed things up.

Flowers chimed gently, and Shari felt another presence enter the Circle.

"I wouldn't do that if I were you, Altoriae." The morning hum of insects faded away as the stern voice spoke from behind her.

Abruptly, Shari turned, and her gaze fell on Zana, Rakemyst's Linked. Ronah's Linked, Tania, was becoming a good friend, but the two Linked couldn't be further apart in looks or temperament. Ever since Tania had stepped foot on Ronah, she had been filled full of joy and bubbles and brightness. Zana remained as aloof as the wind and twice as likely to sting you.

"You have been traipsing around on my isle long enough, Altoriae. It's time you had a proper introduction."

From Shari's spot on the grass, Zana seemed to tower over her, even though she stood only a few fingers taller than Shari. The Altoriae rose to her feet and dusted off her behind. "I suppose you're right."

Zana blinked, and her wings ruffled out behind her for a moment. Shari couldn't stop the quirk of her lips. Apparently Rakemyst's Linked had been expecting more of a fight.

"Right. Good. Come with me then."

Zana sank into the ground.

Shari sent out a tendril of Innarn and waited until she sensed Zana come to a stop. She slipped into the Linked's mind and saw the enormous cavern with a towering ceiling. Shari shifted in, standing next to the unimpressed Ilutri.

The cavern was more majestic than Zana's jaded view gave credit to. If the vaulting ceilings were to be believed, only a thin crust of earth protected the heart of Rakemyst from the outside world. Air whistled through intricately carved rock pillars. Sunlight streamed in all around them. There must have been holes to let the light in somewhere over on the sides.

"This is beautiful," Shari whispered.

"Rakemyst knows you doubt his ability to protect his people."

Shari opened her mouth, but Zana held up a finger.

"Do not deny it. You must remember, Rakemyst is both older and wiser than Ronah. He knows how best to look after us."

Despite her desire to fume and rant, Shari buried her angry rebuttal. If she said anything now, while she stood in the heart of Rakemyst, it would be exceptionally rude.

Zana noted her tense form and nodded. "Perhaps there is hope you will become a diplomat yet," she said idly, and turned away.

For a second, Shari contemplated letting loose one of her blades. She was so glad Tania was nothing like the condescending Linked before her.

Zana raised her wings and beat them towards a rocky wall. Slowly, a face appeared, changing every now and then. A high brow here, a firm jaw next, then a pointed chin and hooked nose turned into narrowed eyes and a downturned mouth.

'*You're the Altoriae.*' The airy voice seemed to be the polar opposite of the strict countenance before her.

"I am." Shari stepped next to Zana and bowed her head. The Ilutri hummed in approval.

'*I have failed you, Altoriae.*' The face in the wall looked younger now, the voice higher, but the tears making tracks were the same.

"Rakemyst." Kneeling before the face, Shari dared to touch the wall. "You have not failed me, or your residents."

'*But so many died!*' The wail echoed through the cavern, bouncing off the high ceiling and bringing tears to Shari's eyes.

"And so many more lived. The Chirea were cruel, and we must," Shari stopped. She would not lecture an ancient island on battle etiquette. "It is why we must work together, like we did to overcome them."

'*You want me to fight.*' A crone stared her down, features drawn into a bitter snarl. '*Fighting and dying is all we're good for, is it?*'

"Hardly." Shari sighed. "I hope those who have trained will continue to aid you and the rest of Lissae in protecting our dear Realm, but I do not expect you or the other Shifting Islands to fight the battles yourselves. It isn't fair and would no doubt lead to the creation of weapons we cannot even comprehend."

The crone faded, and a middle-aged man with a goatee took her place. '*Thank you, Altoriae. Rakemyst can sense your belief that it is so. But we must warn you,*'

The man's face grew longer, his lips plumper, until a visage she'd recognise anywhere looked back at her. '*Shari.*' Her grandmother seemed entranced by her appearance.

Shari pressed her hand hard against the rough cheek on the wall.

'*You must know, dear one, that one of your guild is not who they claim to be.*'

Far too fast, her features were changing.

"Who? I can't have someone else lying to me." Shari wanted to cry as the face on the wall faded.

From behind her, Zana said, "The one who you have doubted all along."

Shari turned. Rakemyst's Linked looked serene, hands clasped together and disappearing in the long sleeves of her robe, as regal as a queen.

"Who have I doubted?" Shari frowned. Not Jonathan, not Tania, and not any of the candidates. She'd been so sure of Kodan, so it couldn't be him. Therdon was just as unlikely, seeing his remains had been sent adrift on the breeze as particles of ash.

"You set sights on him and decided him to be false. He refuses to tell you his proper name, yet flaunts his power to others when you are not around, hoping to keep them in check using their fear of his kind."

"Can't you tell me his name?" Something niggled in the back of her mind. Shari could almost picture the scene Zana mentioned, but if she was right... well, she didn't want the Linked to be right. Shari would prefer to live her days in ignorance and take out anyone who tried to hurt any of the members of her guild. "Are you aiming to make me suspicious?"

"Hardly, Altoriae. My aim is, as always, to draw the truth into the air and set it free."

"Is the being you talk about free?"

Zana looked down at her clasped hands. "He feels more freedom than he has ever experienced before."

"Is he an immediate threat?" Shari had to know. If Zana answered yes, then she'd do something about it, but if she said no, Shari planned on shoving the conversation down into the deep recesses of her mind until it was needed again.

"No. I... Before the battle with the Chirea, my answer may have been different, but I believe the changeling is true to you."

"Is... That's a good thing, right?"

"Not always." Zana looked off to the side and her eyes glazed over, turning white as she slipped into a trance. "His decision to be true to you means he will put your needs above all others—including what is best for our Realm. If you gave him a direct order to let you die to save Ronah, or Lissae, he would disobey."

Shari took a moment to relish in the thought of someone putting her safety first in a battle. But behind her eyes, she saw all the disastrous ways it could turn out. "I understand. Can I train him to think differently?"

"His culture is so different from ours, and I am not privy to all the ways which the world may fall. Out of all those he knows, you would be the one with the best chance of getting through to him."

"Does he have anyone else?" Shari had the sensation of being both small and inflated at the same time. She was glad he thought so highly of her, but she knew all too well what it was like to only have a friend or two by her side and no one else. For the longest time, it had just been her and Jon. And then Mitch.

Mitch.

A sob tried to escape, but she suppressed it. This was about the not-so-mysterious changeling guy.

She hoped he had someone like Mitch—someone to take him home for a dinner which smelled funny, someone who was surrounded by a loving family. Someone who could pull him out of his head when things got too stressful, and someone who was willing to do the unthinkable for him.

"It is our wish," Zana said, "that you are not the one to do the unthinkable. If you are, his reign will destroy our Realms and the surrounding ones. If you are to die when he is watching, so shall we all."

"Okay. Die when no one is around. Got it." Shari rose to her feet, ignoring Zana's stunned look. Shari's flippant words seemed to have pulled her out of her trance.

"Altoriae, I did not mean…"

"You must know how many of the Altoriaes who've come before me lived out their lives and died a natural death."

"I'm afraid not." Zana shook her head.

Shari ignored the impulse to grab her by the shoulders and shake them too. "One. One out of thirteen lived to retire. The other eleven died on the job. Then there's me. Fairly sure I'm part shem'ar, because I should have died a bunch of times already and I haven't."

Now Zana was frowning and shaking her head. "Just because a shem'ar has seven lives doesn't mean you do too!"

"It's better to think I can get out of it than to wonder if I'm stuck dying on a backwater Realm because I twisted my ankle and tiny squirming jalbovesi are eating away at my flesh." She rubbed at the still-healing wound on her thigh. Her position on the hard ground had pulled on the tender skin.

"What a horrible way to die!" Zana's hand flew to her heart.

Too late, Shari remembered the Linked did not go on patrol. With Rakemyst's unwillingness to fight, Zana had likely not seen any combat since she'd taken over from the last Linked. "Just an example," she said airily, waving it away, hiding her grimace by ducking her head and rubbing at her thigh again.

Wrung out and wanting the comforts of home, Shari shifted to the corner of Ronah's Town Square. Only a few people wandered through it at this time of the afternoon. Shari was surprised to see three of her favourite Ilutri. SilverCloud, Wolf, and Belfar were on the receiving end of awed looks from her peers as they stood chatting to each other.

Honestly, you'd think Ronah's residents would be used to the Ilutri by now. They've seen my father often enough.

As Shari watched them, she realised the three spoke as much with their wings as they did with words. Feathers ruffled and smoothed, wings quivered, and at one stage, Wolf's wings shook out, startling the palon Reanna was walking.

With a small smile, Shari figured she'd better break up whatever argument they were having. Perhaps she could introduce them to more of the wonderful things Ronah offered. She shoved aside her tiredness and pasted on a smile before she strode up to them.

"Where have you three been hiding?" she asked.

Wolf looked uncomfortable, blushing as his eyes flicked to Belfar and away. Belfar puffed his chest out, wings flared behind him.

"These two expert healers think I should stay away from the new medicine!" SilverCloud grumbled, wing tips almost dragging on the ground as he ignored the two younger men.

"Medicine? Am I missing something?" Shari asked, frowning.

"I'm just saying that not all the studies have been done yet. They shouldn't be using an elder as a test subject!" Wolf growled.

"Fill me in?" Shari asked. She tried to bury the thought that her uncle still sounded like he gargled rocks, but Belfar's lightning-fast grin told her she hadn't been quick enough.

'*Your grandfather is trying a new medicine which is being produced on Talhan. It's experimental, and Wolf is worried it's having negative side effects*,' Belfar sent her.

'*What side effects?*'

'*He's losing chunks of time. He woke up in the kitchen this morning, with no idea how he'd gotten there.*'

'*Did this only start after the medicine?*'

'*Yes.*'

Shari frowned. Losing time could be a dangerous thing. But it might not be because of medicine. "Would these side effects be left over from whatever Therdon was doing in your head?"

"Therdon was a traitor and a trusnuck of the highest order, but..." Wolf growled.

"Yes! Thank you." SilverCloud's wings flared as he cut his son's rant off, then fell limp. He wasn't up for a spirited debate.

"This is a serious matter, and we can't ignore it, but you look like you need some fun," Shari said. "May I?"

Wolf scowled at her, but nodded, worried eyes flicking over his father.

"Let me introduce you to Ronah's Town Square."

As if on cue, hanging lights flickered to life, and a troupe of Silverstone musicians started playing in a corner of the square where they had set up a temporary gazebo. The sun was dipping below the trees, casting a beautiful peachy glow over everything.

"The square is where we hold any festivals or celebrations, where kids and families come to play, and where the Silverstone Clan come to test out their latest characters in their ongoing saga."

A family passed by them. Shari noted, by the ink on their skin and lack of familiar faces, that they had to be some of the Returned. She needed to get to work on being able to identify all of them on sight.

"Sometimes, on muggy nights, the local restaurants will place tables on the outskirts of the square, and we can dine in the fading light, spending time with the other residents of Ronah."

"Is this something you do often?" Wolf asked.

"I'm usually too busy helping Mum and Dad to join the others." Shari admitted.

She would rather be holed up in the Quiver and Quill's storeroom, eating off a precariously balanced plate than sitting at one of the tables which were popping up around them.

Wolf smirked at her. He seemed like the type who would do the same.

"Looks like tonight we'll all be joining in," Calem boomed.

Startled, she glanced up as her father floating an array of dishes their way. Her mother followed with a basket full of cutlery and condiments.

"Collis is watching the store while we grab a bite to eat. He saw you on his way in and suggested we join you out here." Arilla smiled as she set the table for eight.

"Who else will join us?" Belfar asked.

"Well, I can always eat at home. Alone. Where no one will poison my food again."

"Sam!" Shari grinned at Jon's new apprentice. Hands in his pockets, Sam rocked on his heels. "Glad to see you up and about again." Zana's words tickled the back of her mind, but she resolutely shoved them away.

"Just because you left me in the dust yesterday doesn't mean I won't get out of it," he grumbled. The twitch at the corner of his mouth gave away his pleasure, though.

"And I suppose the last seat is for me."

"Well met, Jonathan! Glad you could join us on such brief notice." Calem smiled at the Guardian of Lissae.

"My thanks for the invitation." Jonathan Buan bowed his head, and Sam rolled his eyes at Shari.

She ran a hand over her mouth to hide her smile. Shari took her seat, surprised at the array of food on the table. It was highly possible her parents had had this dinner planned for longer than they would admit to.

"Don't look so suspicious, Shari. I cooked it all myself," her father said.

"It just smells so good. I can't decide what to eat first!" Shari tried to cover her faux pas. Her dad grinned to show he had no hard feelings.

Later that night, as she slipped into her bed, she couldn't help but mull over the day. Although it had been emotionally draining, Shari felt lighter, freer.

There has never been a more perfect day.

That was when everything went wrong.

CHAPTER TWO

Zac Hudson panted as the heat weighed him down. Taking in the tangle of vines ahead of him, he tried not to groan.

All the stories he'd heard about Atlantis growing up had been about a magical place where they used science alongside Innarn to do everyday things. Instead of creating a hollow trunk of ever-frozen water to store food in, they had machines.

Machines.

Mechanical things to do the jobs of an Innarnian.

And that was what he was after. It was hardly their biggest or baddest machine he wanted. In fact, the thing was small enough to fit inside a bag he could carry on his back. If he wasn't busy running from mechanical guards, he'd laugh.

Motors whirred behind him, and Zac rolled his eyes. The best thing about having machines guarding items meant they never slept.

When you stole something from a mad Atlantean scientist, it kind of made machines the worst guards of all.

The jungle on the outskirts of Meropis had slowed the machines down, but it slowed him more.

Vines with claw-like barbs were intent on rending the careless traveller six ways from Lissae if he moved the wrong way. There were insects whose bite could paralyse, and force you to feel every slow, agonising inch of being digested by the carnivorous flowers adorning the ancient trees.

And he couldn't forget the bears, boars, and wolves eager for a meal. He was practically a snack on slow-moving feet at this stage.

But he was almost at the doorway.

Ducking and weaving through the last vines, Zac came nose to chest with a white coat.

"Well met, lover," Nisethran purred at him. Lined up at the rear of the towering Atlantean were more mechanical guards.

From the beeps and screeches behind him, Zac had managed to get himself surrounded.

"Well met." Zac puffed at a strand of limp hair hanging in his eyes. He ignored the sweat as it slid between his shoulder blades. "Nice day for a stroll, isn't it?"

Nisethran's perfect eyebrows climbed high on his flawless face. "Nobody strolls through the Penemiota Wilds for enjoyment."

"Hey, it's just another one of my loveable quirks." Zac shrugged, one hand wrapped around the strap of the bag over his shoulder.

Eyes narrowing, Nisethran held out a hand, his perfectly manicured fingers extended. "I believe that's mine."

"T'isn't." Zac could do this all day.

Except for the whirring sound behind him.

"Oh, but it is." Nisethran didn't seem impressed.

"Look," Zac said, shaking his head and setting the bag down. For something so small, it was relatively heavy. "I wanted to see what this thing would do to the vines before using it on my eyes." He pushed his fake glasses up higher on his nose.

With that cruel smirk on his handsome face, Nisethran looked less like the perfect monolith of a man and more like the twisted, mad scientist Zac had been warned of. "You wanted a demonstration? You only had to ask."

Zac gulped as one of the mechanical guards swooped forward and grabbed the bag, depositing it at Nisethran's feet.

"Well, you know. You're always so busy." The perspiration dripping down his back was growing itchy. Every fibre of his being told him to get out of there. He couldn't. There was no way he would leave without the machine.

"I'm never too busy to show off one of my inventions." Nisethran was purring again, and for the first time, it sounded sinister.

As he rubbed at the hairs standing up on his arms, Zac debated shifting out. Surely, he would get another chance at snatching this machine? Nisethran's flawless green eyes pierced through him.

It was now or never.

"Do you know what this does?"

"Flashes a red light?" Zac tried for casual, but failed the second the words fell from his lips.

"Flashes a red..." Nisethran looked like he'd sucked on something sour. "What a plebeian way to describe the workings of this machine. Red light..." he muttered. "This dial shows the different settings. It is best to warm it up for the patient." His eyes cut to Zac and hardened. The Atlantean nodded, and two machines came forward and grabbed Zac's arms, holding on tight. He strained in their grasp, shaking his head and dislodging the fake glasses as he tried to get free.

Zac discovered fear had a taste. It was of decomposing jungle rot and sweat.

"Since you're so eager, we'll skip straight to the major event. Hold still." The thing in Nisethran's hands hummed as he turned it on, and the red light on the front blinked. Zac struggled with the machines pinning his arms.

If he shifted now, the guards would come with him, and he'd still have no machine.

"All you have to do is press it to the desired area and…" Nisethran stepped forward and held the device up to Zac's face.

Zac was not ashamed to admit that he screamed.

Burning like nothing he'd known before seared across his temple as he twisted his head. He pretended to collapse, forcing the machines to take his weight. The light scorched upward across his temple and sliced one of the machines holding him.

It gave a startled-sounding *beep* and loosened its grip. The other machine was still holding on tight.

If this was the only chance he had, he was going to take it.

Supported on either side, Zac slammed both feet into Nisethran's chest, kicking the Atlantean back.

Nisethran dropped the device onto Zac's outstretched legs. Thank the Deities the red light was pointing up.

Both machines dropped him like a sack.

Mid-air, he shifted just outside the Lissaen gate, leaving the machines and one angry scientist behind him.

Fire consumed his senses like it was burning through to his brain as he came out of the shift. He fumbled with the device, cursing as pain made his fingers clumsy. Viciously, he twisted the little dial to stop the light from working and it blinked off.

Zac stumbled through the gateway and back to Lissae. He couldn't stop there.

He had stolen tech.

With a final lurch forward, Zac made it to the other side of the double doors of the museum, letting them swing closed behind him as he collapsed.

Falling in and out of consciousness, he wasn't sure how long he'd been there when there was a metallic tapping on the stone floor.

He cranked open one eye and saw a silver glint.

As he passed out again, he sensed a tugging on the device in his hand, but didn't have the strength to do anything about it.

'*Jon.*' Then he knew no more.

Jonathan Buan was about to head home for the night when he heard a whisper of his name.

He peered around the empty bookstore and shook his head. His mind had to be playing tricks on him. He waited a few more moments, but didn't hear anything else.

Continuing to close up the shop, he wondered if there was any point in keeping it open. Lissae seemed to be under constant threat these days. He needed to find someone to run the store who wouldn't become part of the guild and have to rush off at a moment's notice.

Perhaps one of the Returned might like a quieter challenge than the living nightmare they'd been trapped in?

Musing over his options, Jonathan stepped out the front door and turned to lock it.

Metal scraped on stone.

The peculiar noise had him snapping his gaze towards the town square. A red light lit up the night, hitting one of the orange pillars which acted as the fencing for the shop across the road.

The crystal pillar *shrieked*.

Hands clamped over his ears, Jonathan ducked as the red light continued its arc, heading straight for his face.

Something snagged onto the back of his coat and dragging him backwards. The wards around the shop door flared white-hot as they activated to defend the store.

Gasping, Jon turned to see who'd saved him, only for a dark form to launch itself at the metal beast with the red light.

"No!" Jonathan cried. Something was tickling in the back of his mind, and he didn't like what it meant at all.

The metal creature took no notice, clacking up the street.

The being who had saved Jonathan tripped over their feet and fell just short of grasping it.

From the tone and the curses, he knew it was Amara. Jonathan found himself more thankful than ever that she had chosen to stay after he had released the name of his new apprentice.

The laser flicked around and started cutting through the street.

If he thought the crystal screaming had been bad, it was nothing compared to the agony of Ronah's groan. Cutting deeper than bone, it was soul-felt, going on until the end of time.

Voices cried out, and every Innarnian sent a flurry of messages, trying to discover what was going on.

Shari shifted in beside him, taking in the scene. "Well, aren't we going to stop it?" She pulled a crossbow from her pocket-Realm, took careful aim, and shot. The tip glanced off the metallic body and Jonathan resisted the urge to curse when the thing seemed to turn and size them up.

A direct beam of red light came for his face, and Shari pushed him aside with her Innarn, the force knocking his glasses askew.

For a moment, the machine seemed to dither, the red light flickering. Metallic legs clattered against the stone as it as it headed closer towards the town square.

Samuel stepped out of the shadows and stomped a hefty boot down on the device. When it whined and rumbled, he blasted it with pure Dark Innarn.

"Did you forget that you're an Innarnian?" he grumbled. The thing whined again, and he lifted his boot and stomped harder. The metallic legs went limp. "Where did this come from?"

Shari took in the smouldering hunk of metal and shrugged. "It kind of looks like the thing I brought back from Atlantis, but that didn't have a red light."

"You brought something back from Atlantis?" He was growling now. Jonathan rolled his eyes as his new apprentice tried to use his height to loom over Shari.

Shadowy wings threatened to drown out the light from the two moons. Jonathan scrambled to his feet and pointed needlessly to the museum. "It would have come in through the hallway."

Samuel looked at him like he'd lost his mind. For a moment, Jonathan sensed the scrape of razor-sharp claws on the back of his neck. He shivered and rubbed the sensation away.

"I suppose we should return it then." Still scowling, Samuel scooped up the machine and started towards the museum, Shari and Jonathan falling in step behind him. As they walked, Jonathan sent out a broadcast stating that Ronah was safe, and there was nothing to worry about.

They arrived at the museum before he realised it. Shari's breath caught as she stepped through the doors.

Shari had been expecting Anna to greet them.

But it was Tania.

Face streaked with tears, Ronah's Linked wrung her hands. "Jonathan, someone is demanding entry to Lissae. And I think they did this!"

"Where are they?"

"The Ducibus are holding them at the double doors."

Before they moved to the next room, Wolf and Belfar joined them, wings flared out and wearing matching scowls. "Rakemyst sent us. He wants to understand what hurt Ronah."

"We're just about to find out," Shari said.

The group strode through the museum. Jonathan sensed that, for once, Shari wasn't paying attention to the treasures and priceless memories surrounding them. Instead, her entire focus was on the being who wanted to hurt her home.

As they stepped into the last room, his gaze fell to a dark heap resting just inside the double doors.

A weak hum flashed across his Innarn as he hurried to the body. Jonathan fell to his knees next to it. He sensed the others crowding around, could tell Shari had her blade out, but all he focused on was the coppery gaze which stared up at him.

'Jon.' The man grinned, then grimaced.

"Jon?" Shari asked behind him.

"Zac," Jonathan whispered, taking in the recent wound which was still bubbling on his friend's face.

"Better move him." Shari looked grim. "We've got incoming."

"They don't like the Dark," Zac said.

"We got it," Samuel dismissed the concern.

Jonathan used his Innarn to move Zac farther into the room, sending out gentle pulses of healing as the doors opened.

Zac levered himself into an upright position with a soft moan. Jonathan doubted he would have noticed if his hand wasn't resting on the other man's chest. Guilty, he tried to snatch it away, but Zac caught it and put Jonathan's hand back where it had been.

He gave the other man a fond grin before his eyes were drawn to the monolithic man standing in the middle of the double doors.

Nisethran strode up to the museum doors, furious. Scanning the ragtag group on the other side, he spotted his traitorous lover curled in the arms of another man.

"You have something of mine," Nisethran snarled.

Zachariah's eyes rolled into the back of his head, the burn line on his face puckering and twisting. No one would fall for his pretty lies and his prettier face ever again.

"Give it back," Nisethran commanded. The Ducibus had allowed him only one unarmed mechanical guard. It was not the intimidation factor he had been hoping for.

A man dressed all in black tossed the smoking, crushed hunk of metal at him. A grabber from the guard shot out and snatched it before it could hit him.

"What is this?" he demanded.

"Your something," the man in black scowled. His golden eyes reminded him of something else.

"This is not all mine! You've changed it!" After taking it from the guard, he peeled away the foreign parts, nicking his finger. His internal healing bots took over, sealing up the cut before anyone else noticed it. He tossed the foreign part back onto the floor and scowled at the group before him.

Zachariah moaned, his eyes fluttering open.

"Why don't you come see me again, lover?" Oh, and when he did...

A tiny female stepped forward, glowering. "Why don't you crawl back to where you came from? You got what you wanted."

"I should be recompensed."

"What? For being a..." the one in black started. He mouthed the last word and shot a dirty glare at the female in black leathers.

"What do you think would be satisfactory?" she asked. The blade tapping against her thigh was cute, if not outdated.

"I lost a lover. Maybe I should take another," Nisethran teased.

"I don't take well to kidnappers," the one with the blade snarled, stepping up to him. Her eyes dared him to try.

"No? You're such a primitive little Realm. I thought you'd still be auctioning your people off to the highest bidder." He took in the disgust on the faces before him and smirked. One at the back ruffled his wings, and Nisethran fixated on him. "Oh, but if I could choose, it would be you," he breathed.

A shorter, winged man, with the same dark hair as the tiny female, stepped in front of the other. "Go home, Atlantean."

"The Ducibus said I was forbidden from entering your hallowed halls," Nisethran said, pacing along the very edge of where he could go.

Glaring, the female in the leathers matched him stride for stride. His mechanical guard stayed still.

"They said it was because only the invited are welcome on Lissae. They said nothing about my friend here." He punched a button on the remote in his pocket, and the guard's chest exploded out, releasing the little drone he used to capture things. Controlled by the remote, it zigzagged around the room on the other side of the doors. "Don't worry. I only need one. I'm sure even your archaic healers will be able to stitch something together for you."

"Sam! Get it!" the female growled, not taking her eyes off him.

The male in black, Sam, apparently, started shooting off blasts of magic. Oh, if he could harness Innarn, he'd make a fortune! But he wasn't here for magic. Not today. The drone swooped lower, looping around the heads of the protectors until it got to the auburn-haired one with the wings.

"I'm sure you'll take to the skies again sometime," Nisethran said, activating the laser. Before he could press the next button, a beam of magic shot out and mangled the drone as it hung in mid-air.

Nisethran scowled. "Fine. I'd say we're even now." He turned to walk away. The tension drained from his shoulders when the doors slammed closed behind him.

The Ducibus guide was glaring at him from under the hood; he was sure. "It's just business. The things I could do with a set of wings!"

"Just business, hey?"

Nisethran swung around and sneered at the man who'd been holding his lover. "You get my lover, and I get my prototype back. It is hardly fair. Although, he is defective now, so I suppose his value has gone down."

"He is a *being*. His value is infinite." The man's glasses glinted in a way that reminded him of the lasers in his machines.

Nisethran stepped up to the man, but something inside him warned him there was no chance he would win. "He's your problem now."

He turned away with a snarl, ignoring the Astral Projection as he stalked back to the gateway.

"I need someone to make sure he leaves and doesn't come back," Shari growled.

"I'll go," Sam offered.

"Thank you for the save." Belfar nodded to Sam. "But he's from a Realm even lighter than Lissae. You wouldn't be able to function."

"We'll go," Wolf said, nudging his partner.

"Off to canoodle," Sam scoffed.

"What?" Shari had never heard that word before, but Sam's meaning was clear. "No. Look, Belfar's right. You'd burn the instant you walked through the door. Wolf and Belfar can go. Although, perhaps hide your wings. It was like he was obsessed with them."

"Very well." Belfar's wings shimmered, then disappeared.

Wolf looked at her and sighed. "We'll report back when we can."

They slipped through the double doors. Shari hoped it wouldn't take them too long.

Longing for her bed, she turned with a sigh. "I suppose we'd better clean up the mess."

Jon was still cradling the man they'd found slumped on the floor.

"Do you need a hand?" She frowned. Even without the scar, she didn't remember this man, but Jon was holding him as if he were precious. His eyes flicked open and Shari frowned harder. She was sure she recognised him, but she didn't know where from.

"I think it would be best if we got Zac to the Healers Centre."

"Zac? You know him?"

"Yes. We... I... Zac used to be on my patrol team."

"We don't have patrol teams." Shari frowned.

"Who's on your team now, Jon?" Zac slurred. His hand rose up as if to caress Jon's face, but it fell limply onto his chest.

Jon looked guilty for a moment. Just what had her Guardian so spooked? "We don't have set teams anymore."

Something twisted on Zac's face, and he crumpled.

Shari said, "I think having a set team would be handy. Get to know each other's strengths and weaknesses, fighting styles and—"

"It's all good until someone leaves. Or dies." Jon cut her off.

Shari closed her mouth so quickly her teeth clacked together. "Yeah."

Without another word, Shari shifted Jon and Zac to the middle of the waiting room at the Healers Centre.

She took a deep breath and tried not to fume. When she turned, Sam was leaning against a pillar, smirking.

"Shall we?" She tried not to snap. Shari couldn't believe Jon had thrown Mitch's death in her face. *It wasn't my fault... it wasn't.*

But the words sounded hollow in her mind.

"Want to spar, Altoriae?"

Shari straightened her shoulders before she forced a grin. "Oh, I do. But we have some clean-up to do first."

"I've got the clean-up," Tania said. "I won't be able to sleep if I don't do it. The biggest wound is where the machine cut Ronah open. Why don't you go patrol or something, and I'll see you in the morning?"

"Sounds like a plan." Sam pushed off from the wall and strolled over to Shari, grinning down at her.

"Just don't wreck anything else. Is there somewhere off-Realm you can go? Or off Ronah, at least?" Tania threw over her shoulder.

"Sometimes she sounds just like my mother," Shari joked.

Eyes flickering in the light, Sam looked away.

"Well, off-Realm wouldn't hurt," Shari said.

"It wouldn't hurt you." Sam seemed coated in shadows tonight.

"What do you mean?"

"I can't leave without the Guardian's permission."

Shari's chin dipped down, and she glared into the distance. "Really." Her voice was crisp enough to make him shiver. *'Will you let Sam leave without needing permission now he's your apprentice?'* Shari sent to Jon.

'What? Yes, sure. If that's what you want.'

She ignored how distracted her Guardian sounded and rounded on Sam instead. "Come on then, apprentice. Let's go spar."

CHAPTER THREE

The next morning, Shari woke to her mother sitting on the edge of her bed, humming. Filtered sunlight lit the pale walls of her bedroom aglow.

"G'morning," Shari mumbled around a yawn. The temptation to snuggle under the covers and not get up was strong.

"Breakfast time, sleepy," Arilla crooned.

Shari groaned.

Arilla grinned as she leaned over and kissed Shari's forehead. "Late night patrolling?"

"No. Sparring. Everything aches. My bruises have bruises," Shari complained, levering herself up bit by painful bit.

"I don't think I've ever seen you so sore." Her mother pulled the blankets back, helping Shari get her battered legs over the edge of the bed.

"I haven't sparred with Sam before."

Arilla choked on her laugh. "Think you can make it down the stairs?"

Shari glowed green for a moment, making Arilla shade her eyes. "I should be alright now."

"Your grandfather is with us this morning, seeing as Wolf and Belfar are off patrolling."

"Okay. I won't be too long."

"And you have class today, missy. You can't skip so much school!"

"It was only to save the Realm." Shari wanted to put more effort into her defence, but it was far too early.

"Well, that can wait until you've caught up with your schoolwork," Arilla said as she closed the door behind her.

"I'll remember that next time Lissae needs saving. 'Oh, sorry. Don't take over the Realm just yet. I've still got one more class to attend.' It's not going to work," Shari grumbled as she staggered into the bathroom.

Despite the intensive healing Ronah had thrown her way, she was still sore. She'd never sparred with anyone who'd tested her as much as Sam. He'd got her to the mat more times than she'd been able to knock him off his feet. When she'd been ready to call it a night, he'd scoffed at her, and called her weak.

Her. *Weak.*

But the comment meant she'd stayed. She had set aside the pain and tiredness and knocked him on his arse before he'd let her go.

For the first time since she could remember, she'd been able to sleep. A proper, restful sleep. Even though she was a walking bruise, her mind was ready to go, spinning out ideas about how to revise the patrols, and putting together things she was still trying to ignore.

Intentionally focusing on getting to breakfast, rather than on discovering the reason why Jon had a ban on Sam going off-Realm, she settled at the table in time for SilverCloud pop a glowing orange tablet in his mouth and chase it with a sip of water.

"What are you taking?"

"LoneWolf made me promise not to take the 'experimental medicine' until he got back."

"Dad," Calem groaned.

"He should know me better!" SilverCloud protested.

"So, you promised not to take it, and now you're breaking your promise?" Shari pouted.

"Oh, don't you start on me too, Altoriae! I may be an old Ilutri, but I know what's good for me," he grumbled, stabbing the eggs on his plate.

"And if you know what's good for you, you'll eat up." Arilla grinned at him, refilling his mug with xobrac, a sweet, purple juice.

"With the convergence happening, perhaps Wolf can check out Talhan's healers and talk to them. It might help to set his mind at ease," Shari said, idly using a shaft of Innarn to steal a piece of toast from the counter and slip it onto her plate.

Calem raised his eyebrows at her and she flushed. Apparently, she'd lost her manners while they'd been away. She knew better than to grab things with Innarn.

"Will you be staying on Ronah while they're on patrol?" She tried to change the subject.

"Perhaps we should." Calem pointedly glanced at her.

Shari ducked her head, looking studiously at her toast.

"But it's up to SilverCloud, really."

"Oh, you lot stay in your own home, where you're comfortable," SilverCloud said, popping another pill into his mouth. "I'm happy fluttering about on Rakemyst."

Arilla and Calem looked at each other and sighed.

"You know we'll be checking in with you all the time." Arilla poured another glass of xobrac and handed it to her daughter.

Shari couldn't make her mouth smile in the way it was meant to. "I know you will."

"I'd feel better if you were living with someone else, though. Doesn't Jon have a spare room?"

"Probably not now." The corner of Shari's mouth quirked up. "He ran into an old friend last night."

"Oh, how lovely!" Arilla smiled.

"Do you know a Zac?"

"Zac?"

"He came through the hallway last night. He was pretty out of it, but he latched onto Jon and wouldn't let go."

"Zac... Not Zac Hudson?" Calem mused.

"I'm not sure." Shari shrugged.

"Oh, he was always sweet on Jon. I haven't seen him since Jon was injured." Arilla joined them at the table and started putting fruit onto her oats.

"Jon was injured?"

"Not long after he became Guardian. He was scouting, and something went wrong. He almost lost his eyes."

"You mean his sight?"

"No... He was in awful shape when Zac brought him back. He sat by Jon the whole time he was in the Healers Centre, but the second they let the Guardian out, Zac up and disappeared. No one knows where he went."

"I bet he's got plenty of stories to tell," Shari said. She shoved the last of the toast in her mouth and slid out of her chair. "And I'll find out where he's been. After school." She gulped the glass of juice, blew her parents and her grandfather a kiss, and slipped out the door.

Belfar huffed as he ran into Wolf's back, getting a mouthful of hair for his efforts. *'You need to tell me when you're stopping.'*

Wolf didn't even grin. He was staring at something in front of them. As he peered over his mate's shoulder, Belfar held in the curse which threatened to escape.

They'd been tracking the mad Atlantean since they'd left Lissae, and he'd led them on a merry chase. Belfar was half certain the Atlantean knew they were following him. He was either careless, or leaving crumbs showing where he'd be going next.

Now, under the watery light of a pale blue moon, they stood outside a white marble cube-like building. The material was similar to the buildings on Rakemyst, but the angles were foreign.

Almost as foreign as the phalanx of mechanical guards ringing the base of the building.

'*We could fly up and in,*' Belfar sent, pointing to a window in the impossibly smooth wall.

'*We wait. Our job is to ensure he doesn't return to Lissae. Nothing else.*'

'*We don't even know if he's in there.*'

'*You saw what he did to the Innarnian. I'm not taking the risk.*'

'*Aww, I won't care if you get a few more scars.*'

'*Belfar...*'

There was a whinging noise behind them. Turning, he glimpsed silver, then all Belfar knew was darkness.

Tania yawned. Ronah was not coping well, and the island had been having nightmares. Or maybe *she'd* been having nightmares and had taken Ronah along for the ride? Either way, if the bags under her eyes got any bigger, she'd be able to carry her schoolbooks in them.

She struggled to stay awake as she stumbled along after her siblings on the way to school, shivering in the cool morning air. As they passed the bookstore run by the Guardian, Tania drew to a halt. "I just have to get my jacket," Tania said.

Christopher waved at her in acknowledgement, not looking up from his heated discussion with Alistair about how Innarn could move molecules around. Jessica skipped ahead of them without a care. Caleb nodded at her before slipping away, no doubt on his way to his job at the fruit market.

She rested her hand on the front door. The lock clicked, and she turned the handle. A skittering noise had her snapping her head to the side, but there was nothing there.

As she stepped into the store, she ignored the extra lump in her shadow. Out the back, she found her jacket draped over a chair, right where she'd left it. Just as she was about to pick it up, something stirred in the shadows and she flinched, flicking her eyes to the side.

"It's not real," she muttered. "Just a leftover part of a nightmare."

"What's not real?"

Tania screamed, and her hands shot out, sending a blast of air Innarn at the intruder. The force of the blast slammed him up against the door. Amongst the gusts of air blowing the man's hair away from his face, she recognised Jon.

"Oh no! I'm sorry!" Tania squeaked, lowering her hand. Gentle wisps of Air wafted around the back room, setting things to rights.

"Twice in two days, Ronah's Linked." Jon straightened his clothing and cleared his throat. "Bit jumpy this morning?"

"I thought I saw something." Tania stared at the spot where the shadow had been and found nothing out of the ordinary.

"I used to have the same trouble after a battle." Jon crossed to the desk.

Tania looked at him, head tilted to the side.

"I would see things which weren't there," he clarified.

"You don't talk about your training much. Even when you were looking for a new apprentice." Tania tried to be subtle. She'd been caught up in Jonathan choosing her brother as his candidate, but what Jon's training had been like? Had his mentor had been anything like him?

"You'll be late for school if you linger."

"Avoiding!" she sang over her shoulder, laughing when he grumbled. She grabbed her jacket and skipped out the back door.

She let Ronah pull her through the earth, popping out behind her siblings as they stepped through the gate and onto the grounds of

Ridden Hall. Her gaze drawn to the ring of nine bereni trees, she grinned and hugged her books closer to her chest. Ronah's school really was one of her favourite places.

Shari settled into a seat in the back row of the classroom as quietly as she could. It was possibly not her best idea, as she was the first thing all of her classmates saw as they came through the door.

'*Shari! Praise Nar'eh! I'm so glad you're back!*' Elizabeth Ribeck sent to her.

She grinned at the friendly girl and started to reply, but a flurry of sends came her way.

'*Hey, if you ever need an extra being on patrol, I'm your guy,*' Eli Thorne sent as he leered in her direction.

'*If you're free after school, I think we should go shopping.*'

'*Did you really defeat a Q'Aralide? Maeve is saying you did.*'

'*How can I get better at throwing fireballs? Mine are so weak.*'

'*Can you go over shielding again? I think I need more practise.*'

Shari blinked and took a deep breath. The voices overlapped and merged into one. The flurry of words swirling in her head made her wish she'd had more than just a piece of toast for breakfast.

Was this something else she needed to get used to?

Tutor Boyce stepped into the room, and a blanket of blissful quiet settled over her mind. Shari studied the Innarn net which stopped the students being able to send to each other and subtly added to it. She'd always been free of its effects before, when the tutors had thought they didn't need to worry about her. It may be something she'd have to adapt and add to her personal shield.

"Glad you could join us again, Shari," Tutor Boyce said. "Come on, everyone. Leave the Altoriae alone. We have some serious revision to get done before you'll be ready for the test next week. Now, who can tell me—"

A knock on the door interrupted the lesson before it could start. "Excuse me. Could Miss Dawn please report to the headmaster's office?"

The usual chorus of "Ohhh…" followed Shari out of the room.

She found herself almost grateful to pack her books up. But dread filled her gut at the thought of going to see Headmaster Hollingsworth.

She'd spent so little time with Tania's mother, despite her promise to General Morrow to look after his daughter Liza and her family. Not to mention the last time she'd been called to the headmaster's office had ended with her committing genocide. She doubted General Morrow would take kindly to that thought. Shari hugged her books tighter and hung her head.

At least it was unlikely an Eni that had taken over the leader of the school again.

She ignored the churning of her gut. It was easy compared to the weight on her chest. When she opened the door to the room, for a moment, all she saw was the high-backed chair and a balding, age-spotted face smiling at her with death in its eyes.

Her breath froze. Chin quivering, she looked down, struggling to bring herself back to the present.

"Come in, Shari," a gentle female voice said.

She took a shaky breath, and she looked up. The room had changed.

The new headmaster had moved the desk, and there were comfortable chairs which looked like you could lounge in them. A short piece of timber acting as a desk sat over a chair in the room's corner, with a few scattered papers, a pen, and a vase of unusual flowers on top.

"Please, take a seat," Liza gestured to the low seats in front of the window.

Shari took the closest one to the corner, prodding at it with Innarn first to make sure it was just a seat.

"Cookie?" Liza asked, offering an open tin.

She blinked a few times and took one. The headmaster picked out one and nibbled on it. She couldn't hide a smile when she realised Liza had her hair out. The headmaster wasn't trying to hide her heritage as she had when she'd first arrived on Ronah.

"So, I'm sure you're nervous about being called into my office. But it is for good reasons only."

Shari nibbled at her cookie and said nothing.

"I know you met with Jordan to discuss your teaching duty, and it was all very informal and rushed. I'd like to discuss how we can handle the rest of your last year at Ridden Hall."

"Okay…"

"If I may be blunt, I've spoken to your parents and the Guardian about your extracurricular learning, and I see no point in you taking History of Lissae, or any of the Innarn classes we offer. You're far more advanced in those areas than the other students. I'm not sure why you chose history."

The question was rhetorical, but Shari decided answering wouldn't hurt. "I use the time to add to the wards of the school. It helps to learn what the rest of Lissae thinks our history is."

Cookie halfway to her mouth, Liza paused. "You add to the… well. Would it be easier if you could do it without being in a class?"

"I've been adding to the wards so long, it only takes about ten minutes. I adjust them and try to practise different Innarn exercises when in class."

"Such as?"

"I throw my Innarn, so it looks like someone else is doing it. Anything so I can exercise it, but won't get caught."

Liza smiled. "A wise person once said to me: you don't have to hide who you are or where you come from on Ronah."

Shari blinked, hearing her own words echoed back at her.

"I think you can show your Innarn now."

She took another bite from the cookie and nodded.

"As far as teaching goes, I think it best if you and Samuel continue to work together. I'd much prefer you teaching one class a week to the younger grades, rather than a few one week and none the next. Even if you and Samuel swap out, or only one of you is there at a time. I understand saving the Realm comes before any classroom activities."

Nodding again, Shari couldn't help the relief sliding through her veins.

"There's a few short months to go for the schooling year, and I'd like to see you take the time to come up with a cohesive lesson plan for next year, instead of your history class. Are you able to work warding into that time?"

"Yes," Shari said firmly. It'd be nice not to have to sit through another yawn fest. *'Jon, did you talk to the headmaster?'*

'Yes. She seems reasonable. And is herself, so no need to worry.' Jon sounded distracted. She smelled the herbs used in the Healers Centre and had a suspicion he was still visiting his old friend.

'Brilliant! No more history for me!'

'Your wish came true.' Even distracted, Jon was still good for a sarcastic remark.

"I also see little point in you taking the Realms class. Your records show you fought bitterly for it. Was there a reason?"

"The Realms class is interesting, but the one we're studying is one I've been to a few times."

"I'm sure I can convince the teacher to let you take the test early, and you can also use that time for lesson planning, or Realm saving, depending on the day."

Shari wavered. Jon had desperately wanted her to study the Realms, but she was finding the last unit boring. She'd thoroughly explored Mid-Canak and its features, and the thought of the field trip at the end of the unit held no appeal. There were typically interesting bits scattered amongst the rest. She would never have known the Realm of Earth had ley lines like Lissae if it hadn't been for that class.

"I'm torn," she admitted. "But I don't think I'll learn much more about Mid-Canak."

"Your mapping teacher has also offered to let you take the exam early."

Mapping was something she enjoyed. She half wanted to keep the class, it but knew the value of having more time. "All right," she sighed.

"There's one thing your maths teacher wanted me to ask," Liza said.

"Tutor Boyce?"

"Yes. She's asked if you can please stop using your time Innarn to make the lessons go faster."

Shari wrinkled her nose. "Okay. If I must. No chance of dropping maths?"

"Not even for you, Altoriae." Liza smiled to soften her words.

"Worth a try," Shari said with a grin.

"Teachers also have an office. The two of you are quite unexpected, so I'm afraid it's a bit squishy, but let me show you where you'll do your lesson planning." Liza rose, heading for the door.

Shari hastily joined her, dusting cookie crumbs from her fingers and shirt. They travelled down the branch and across to the next tree. Right near a spare classroom was a door which looked like Sam would have to duck to get through it.

Swinging the door open, Liza let Shari glance inside. Two desks butted up against each other in the tiny space, each with just enough room for a chair to slide back. The wall nearest to the corridor held dusty filing cabinets.

Wishing she was better with earth Innarn so she'd be able to enlarge the space, Shari held back a sigh. Instead, she flicked out a tiny air twister, instructing it to gather all the dust and take it outside.

The headmaster coughed as the dusty twister went passed her.

"Welcome to the teaching staff." She grinned at Shari and turned back towards her office. "Brilliant. Now, I believe we've dallied long enough for your maths class to be over. Science next, if I'm correct?"

Shari gave a guilty smile and nodded. She paused at the door and looked over her shoulder, trying to commit the new office to memory. "Thanks for the cookie."

A skip in her step, she was decidedly more excited to return to class. With only maths, language, and science, school seemed more like something she could do—and she hoped it would remain that way when the next lot tried to invade Lissae.

Chapter Four

After the severe culture shock Tania had experienced attending Ridden Hall as a student, she'd thought she was prepared for anything. But this...

Rakemyst's answer to a school was like nothing she'd ever seen before.

Students of Thistlewood Institute were winging their way through the air, playing some game with a ball. It seemed to involve far more death-defying diving and screaming than Tania thought her mother would ever allow at Ridden Hall.

On the ground, kids were sprawled out, wings and limbs akimbo, reading poetry out loud. Tania caught snatches as she passed through the distinct groups.

"Midnight eyes searching darkened skies..."

"Malcontent, he would not see..."

Tania tried to step around outstretched legs.

"The winged ones are nigh!"

A boy, not much older than her, leapt to his feet, silvery wings gleaming as he almost toppled her over.

"Sorry!" He grabbed onto her pinwheeling arms to keep her steady.

A little voice in the back of her head, or possibly the smirk on his face, told her he was far from sorry.

A shadow emerged over him, blocking the Ilutri's face from the light.

"Sorry," he said again. He dropped her arms and shot into the air, leaving his books behind on the grass and his friends laughing at his abrupt departure.

"Almost sounded like he meant it that time." Collis leaned low enough for only her to hear.

Tania chuckled. "You don't have to loom over everyone who's being ridiculous, you know."

"What should I do instead?"

She slipped her arm through his and led him forward. "Try walking next to me?"

Collis said nothing, but he smiled as they approached the closest building.

Tania pushed open the doors.

The inside looked remarkably like the outside. There was no discernible ceiling, and the walls mimicked a forest, with trees and moss painting them a beautiful green. She supposed it would stop the students from flying into them. The massive cylindrical walls rose up... and up. It was only by craning her neck that she was able to make out the tops of the wall where the students were flying. There seemed to be no rooms, but students grouped around teachers, the muffled noises indicating barriers of some sort.

"This is..."

A chime rang out, and the doors behind them opened. Collis spun her out of the way with ease as a hoard of Ilutri swarmed to their next classes.

Two collided mid-air, sending feathers and laughter everywhere. They sheepishly collected themselves amidst the mockery and hurried away, lowering their heads to hide blushes.

"Beings are the same everywhere, aren't they?" Tania said, a bitter twist to her mouth.

Collis grunted. When she looked up at his face, he was looking into the distance, thinking of something else.

"Collis?"

"Sorry."

Before she had time to question him further, a younger-looking teacher arrived. "You must be the Linked. This way." He turned and flew off to the right.

Tania blinked. "He has to be kidding," she muttered.

After a minute, the teacher came back, frowning. "You need to follow me, or we'll be late. We *are* late."

"Yeah, significant lack of feathers here. And new Innarnian who doesn't want to rip your school apart. Got another way to get me up there?"

"Oh. I... oh. This is highly irregular," the teacher grumbled.

"Okay, well, I can give it a go." Tania gathered the surrounding air, using it to power her Innarn. She corralled it into a cushion under her feet, but the sheer power of the other Innarnians in the area had her little cushion whipping around them. A door creaked ominously as the bottom set of hinges came loose.

"Oops," Tania muttered, and released the air, flopping to the ground.

The teacher adjusted his skewed glasses, and his feathers fluffed out for a moment before they settled into the glossy smooth wings. "Perhaps we should hold the class outside."

"Great idea!" Tania beamed.

With a slight growl, he said, "Stay here."

Belfar woke with a groan. He ached all over. He tried to stretch and found himself unable to move.

It took him a long moment to register that he was unable to move his arms. He was lying, belly down, on an uncomfortable metal table.

Struggling to roll over, he figured they'd strapped his legs as well. He beat his wings, and a ferocious pain fired along his nerve endings.

'Be still. Belfar. Belfar. You must be still. He's coming. He wants to see you in pain. Please, don't struggle. You'll make it worse.'

By raising his head at an awkward angle, he could just make out Wolf, crouched in a cage barely big enough to hold him. His wings weren't on display, and Belfar tried to figure out why. Wolf reached out and touched the bar with the tip of his finger. Blue sparks skittered around the metal of the cage.

A chuckle came from behind him.

"Still trying to get out? Thought you would have learned by now."

Footsteps. And a face with pure green eyes peered into his own. "Our star is awake! Brilliant. The procedure can begin."

It was the Atlantean they'd been following.

He kept a running commentary as he clattered and banged metal on metal somewhere behind him.

'Wolf? What's going on?'

'He... he wants your wings.'

'But they're mine.' Belfar felt foolish the instant the send left his mind. His head felt like it was separate from his shoulders.

'I know, Belfar, I know. But no one taught this guy he can't have whatever he wants.'

'Did he take yours?'

'He tried. I bit him.'

'Bit him?' It didn't sound like something Wolf would do. He was the best Innarnian fighter Belfar knew. Why would he have to *bite* the Atlantean?

'He gave us something which mutes our Innarn.'

'Well, that's just rude.' Belfar had never had to deal without his Innarn. He was in awe of the Altoriae and how she'd kept her skills a secret all those years. And Arilla impressed him by not letting her lack of Innarn stop her from doing anything. In the privacy of his own mind, he could admit he also

pitied her a little. To not experience the freedom of winging through the skies, or have the buzz and hum of the Innarn all around was unfathomable.

He wished he could borrow a little of their courage, and their know-how to get out of this mess.

"Perfect! And now, we shall begin."

Wolf's eyes widened. For an instant, it was all Belfar could focus on.

Then the pain began.

'*Wolf? What?*' He couldn't even finish the question. Belfar slammed his head down on the table and saw stars.

Wolf wouldn't answer him straight away.

When he did, it was with an image of the mad Atlantean standing over the top of him. His wings were held up by hooks through the meat of them. The being who'd been their prey was clinging to his left wing with one hand and using a metal saw to cut right through the joint.

Belfar gagged, then threw up. The grating on the metal table was the only thing stopping him from drowning in his own vomit.

The pulling, sawing pain stopped, and the Atlantean moved. Belfar saw feet standing just to the side of the bile he'd expelled. "Ah, that's the spirit!"

Then the feet disappeared, and the pain started again.

'*He's happy...*' His send was shaky.

'*Not for long. Close your eyes.*' Wolf sounded like even his mind was chewing on rocks.

Clenching his jaw to stop his chin from wobbling, Belfar did as he was told.

With his eyes closed, the sounds around him seemed to amplify. He tried to concentrate on Wolf's pounding heartbeat, rather than the noise of the saw cutting through flesh, feather, and bone.

A final twist, and his back was lighter than it had ever been before. He was lopsided, the left side of his body hitting the table.

Footsteps drowning out the thundering of his heart.

His right wing was gripped, and he couldn't help the scream when the saw bit into him.

'*Eyes closed, love,*' a voice whispered in his mind.

Belfar whimpered.

There was a sizzling sound, and the smell of burning flesh. The Atlantean tutted but kept sawing.

Wolf's heartbeat was a stampede.

His mate gave a guttural roar, and something metal snapped. Through a haze of pain, Belfar's world tilted wildly, and he wondered if the legs of the table had broken.

"Well, that won't do."

There was another sizzle, a thud, and a groan. Flesh hit flesh, and metal clattered against stone.

Gentle hands were removing the hooks, and the saw still stuck in his wing. There came a groan from behind him, and heavy footsteps. Flesh hit flesh again. There was a pause, and Wolf was by his side, panting.

'*Someone is coming,*' Wolf sent as he unbuckled the restraints. '*We've got to–*'

The door burst open before he could even finish the thought.

Wolf stood over Belfar, snarling as a group of Atlanteans in pristine white coats entered the room.

One of them gasped, hand flying to her chest as she took in the room.

The Atlantean they'd been following lay slumped against the wall closest to them, one of his hands missing.

It wasn't Wolf's fault—the trusnuck had tried to touch him when he'd had plasma coursing through his body. He couldn't help it if the hand had obliterated. It was pure coincidence that it was the one which had wielded the saw.

Wolf was still unstrapping Belfar from the table as the group watched on. He used the excess plasma to melt the restraints around his mate's ankles as he undid the one on his wrist.

His wing. His beautiful wing was hanging like a slab of meat from the hooks the madman had put through it.

Eyes tearing at the thought, Wolf pushed it away. If he'd taken out one of them, he could take out more. As gently as he could, he helped Belfar up from the table, making an Atlantean cry out.

"Don't move him!" One of them stepped forward, tears in her eyes, hand outstretched.

Growling, Wolf pulled Belfar closer to him, his arm wrapped around his mate's waist.

A male stepped in front of the female, hands up, showing the backs to the scared Ilutri. "You have no reason to trust us, but we're here to help. Nisethran is sick. What he's done to your friend…" The male was pale, his eyes flicking to the wing hanging on the hook.

Belfar groaned weakly, head lolling on his shoulders. Wolf sensed the blood from the stump of his wing making his arm slippery. He adjusted his grip and let the final pulses of plasma rest in his other hand.

A regal-looking woman stepped forward, her grey gown shot with silver. "Nisethran will be dealt with. Harshly. We wish to help you. To heal your friend."

'*Can we trust them?*' Wolf sent to Belfar.

'*So… cold…*'

With his mate pressed tightly against him, Wolf could feel each thud of Belfar's heart getting slower. He clenched his jaw. "You will heal him. Or I will level your civilisation until it becomes a forgotten memory."

The woman nodded.

The male stepped forward to help Wolf carry Belfar. He paled when Wolf snarled at him.

"This is a skipstep." He held up a small, clear disc with two embossed serpents entwined. "It will take us to our physicians. They'll be able to heal your friend."

"He's my mate," Wolf growled.

"Then we'd best hurry." One arm already around Belfar, the Atlantean reached out, and Wolf grasped his forearm. The male did something to the skipstep, and they vanished in a twinkle of lights.

Shari was glad to see the end of the school day. The lessons were fine, but the other students!

Every class, they had bombarded her with sends until the teacher dropped a blissful net of silence. Once she'd stepped out of the classroom, it was a free-for-all. She'd had to hide in the highest branches amongst the shadows of the leaves during the breaks, although she'd been half tempted to shift away.

Ripping a hole in the school's wards was not on her to-do list, so she suffered, and longed for the days of anonymity.

She was sure her classmates would settle down. Eventually.

They had gotten used to her not having any powers; they'd get used to this, too.

As she made to leave the school, students swarmed towards her. Out of nowhere, students with ink on their skin created a wedge formation, with her at the centre.

'Where do you wish to go, Altoriae?'

Shari realised Collis was leading the group away from Ridden Hall.

A thousand and one comments about being able to protect herself and noting the other students meant no harm ran through her head. The Returned saw it as a blatant lack of disrespect. They were upholding sworn oaths. Who was she to dissuade them? *'To the bookstore, please.'*

The wedge turned with military precision. What the Returned had gone through to ensure such synchronisation? When was the last time they had enjoyed themselves? '*Have you ever been to a beach bonfire?*' she sent to the group surrounding her.

There were one or two affirmative comments, but most were shyly negative.

'*I think we need something fun to do. Would you like to join me for one tomorrow night? Meet me at the point of Beach Street—and bring your friends. I'd love to get to know you all.*'

Shari slipped through the ranks and into the bookstore, tossing a grin over her shoulder at the excited whispers running through her escorts.

For a moment, they looked like any other group of teenagers on Ronah.

She hoped they would find their places on the island again.

For a moment, Samuel mistook the knocking noise for the war hammer currently doing its best to smash through this skull.

It took him an inordinately long time to realise it was coming from his front door.

"Well met, my friend."

He recognised the voice, but didn't think he had the energy to get out of the chair.

However pleasant sparring with Shari was, it had set his recovery back. He half wanted to test out his newfound freedom and get off Lissae long enough to change into his natural form.

But he needed to summon the energy to get out of this surprisingly cushy seat first.

"Stop brooding away and come open the door!"

Samuel groaned as he rose, holding out an inefficient hand to steady himself. Bipedal forms were ridiculous. He made his way over to the entry, keeping up a running mental commentary about uninvited guests and how good slow-roasted Lissaen would taste.

It didn't taste pleasant. He was ashamed to say he knew from first-hand experience. To be fair, he had changed a lot since then.

Wrenching the door open, Samuel hoped his unexpected visitor had given up on him.

Instead, Lizbeth beamed from the front step, holding aloft a basket. Despite the stasis charm she'd applied to it, he could tell the contents would be delicious.

"Well met, grumpy. Thought I'd come visit the invalid."

"I suppose you can come in," he groused.

"You're ever so charming." Lizbeth swept past him and into the house. "Oh, this is lovely. Ronah makes such pleasant homes!"

Samuel looked around the space. It catered to all of his creature comforts. There was a place to eat, sleep, and bathe. He'd figured out the ludicrous biological waste-removal system at Jonathan's, and he had a similar one here. There was even a soft spot to sit. What more could he want?

"A bit of colour, and a few things to mark it as your own, and this will feel like home in no time!"

"Doubt that."

"What does 'home' mean to you, Samuel?" Lizbeth asked as she set her basket down.

Gilded walls and a pervy queen? Had he thought of it as home for so long? He blinked, leaning back and hissing as his ribs protested. "I don't understand."

"Home," she breathed, "is where you feel safe. It is the place you dream of returning to after a long day, or a tough time patrolling. Somewhere you can have your friends over and make happy memories. It's where your heart lies."

He had been with her, right up to the last bit. "My heart stays in my chest, thank you."

Lizbeth laughed. "I meant that in a metaphorical sense!"

"Ah." He wasn't sure he understood, but he'd readily agree if she'd hand over one of the rutenberry cookies from the plate she was uncovering.

"Why don't you offer me something to drink and find some plates to put these on?"

In the recesses of his mind, he could be an exceptional host. Even if it meant something different here than it did back home. Less acid and more water, perhaps? The poison from the Chirea was still affecting him, making his thought processes sluggish and his healing take an abysmally long time.

Still, he shuffled to the sink and retrieved two mugs and two plates. When he turned back to the table, Lizbeth had laid out a veritable spread. But in the spot he usually sat was a cheery yellow bowl.

Poison.

Samuel could hear her, bone armour clicking as she moved, and his vision clouded. Seconds from lashing out, he heard another noise.

She was humming.

Breath coming in pants, Samuel narrowed his eyes in an attempt to focus. The bone armour disappeared, and the yellow bowl turned into a burnished copper. It wasn't soup or stew inside it, but a bushel of juicy-looking sand pears.

He took a breath too deep for bruised ribs and let the pain settle his senses on the present.

"I almost attacked you," he blurted.

Her hands were shaking as she placed the last plate on the table. "I am aware. You might want to put those scales away before someone sees."

Startled, Samuel looked down at his arms and swore. "Lizbeth, I'm sorry."

"Don't you dare," she snarled.

Funny, I thought snarling was my job.

"Don't you dare apologise. I should have been a better friend. Should have checked in more often. Should have..." She broke off, a sob strangling her words.

Samuel opened his mouth and closed it with a snap.

Lizbeth shuddered and drew herself taller. "Now, where's that drink?"

"Only got water. I'm not sure how to get sustenance."

"Not sure how to... Oh, Samuel."

Apart from gut them, he wasn't sure what to do with weeping females. "What should I do?" She hadn't steered him wrong so far.

"Look at me, crying all over." Lizbeth sniffled. "Do you know how to hug?"

He wrinkled his nose. What torture did she want to inflict on him now?

"I'll take that as a no." She laughed. "You wrap your arms gently around another person."

"Why?" Visions of knives and the correct angle to puncture both kidneys at the same time filled his head. Or perhaps a longer garrotting wire, to cut the body in half?

"To show trust. To provide comfort, and because sometimes, all you need is a hug."

He took in the one person who'd been kind to him since he'd stepped foot on this too-bright Realm and held out his arms.

She stepped into them, wrapping her arms around his waist and resting her head on his chest.

He stood, stiff in her embrace.

"I'm sorry I haven't been a better friend," she whispered.

"At least you have some experience in how to be one." He shrugged, and she let go, stepping away from him.

Face shiny with the tracks of her tears, Lizbeth served them both, shifting in some tea leaves to flavour their water.

"Let's get you sorted on how to get some food into these cupboards, shall we?"

Samuel nodded, but his thoughts were on how he could put a lock on the cupboards so only he could open them. No one would poison his food again.

"I almost died in front of Shari," he said.

Lizbeth sat back in her seat, eyes welling with moisture. "I heard rumours."

"I feel... at fault."

"Why?" She took a sip from her cup. He politely ignored her trembling limbs.

"It upset her. I think if she lost someone again, it would not be good for her health." Or anyone else on the Realm when she went after the tuzar who took out the ones she loved.

Wait? Does it mean she loves me?

He shook his head and pushed the thought aside. "I carry the same title as Mitchel did. To lose anyone in this position would be difficult for her."

"You can't stop someone from trying to kill you. You're rather notorious, you know. Word is getting out about where you are."

Samuel growled into his mug. The last thing he wanted to do at the moment was cause Shari more distress. "Well, that needs to change."

"You can't control the actions of others, Samuel."

"But I can control my reactions."

Had Lizbeth been able to see, she would have shivered at the grin on his face. As it was, she calmly sipped her tea, ignoring the hairs standing at attention on the back of her neck.

"There's so much to d-do!" Tania yawned.

She wanted to sleep for a week. Ronah was tired. She was tired, and she was sure if she reached out enough, Lissae would be yawning too.

"And plenty of time to do it in," her mother soothed. A shawl dropped around her shoulders as her mother coaxed her to rise from the garden bed she'd been sitting in. "Come eat something, and then it's off to bed with you. I bet Ronah would prefer you well rested, rather than reeling where you stand."

Tania heaved a sigh and nodded. She let herself be guided through their yard. "I wish there was someone else who could help."

A throat cleared behind them. "Forgive me for the intrusion, but I wish to repay the kindness Ronah's Linked has shown me."

With a fond roll of her eyes, Tania turned to see the inked boy standing by their fence. "Well met, Collis. Mum, this is Collis. Collis, meet my mother, Headmaster of Ridden Hall."

"I'm afraid I overheard your plea for help, Tania."

Despite her tiredness, Tania smiled. "I'll be okay. Some food and some sleep. Just like Mum ordered."

Collis's throat bobbed. "When we were... away, we had to create a place to live. There are a few of us left who are Innarnian architects. They would be happy to lend their skill should you require it."

Tania yawned again.

"Why don't you join us for dinner, and you can tell us some more?" her mum offered.

"But... I... no, that's not..."

"Collis, we're not big on formalities around here. Come inside and eat." Tania reached across the fence to grasp his hand. As soon as their skin touched, a jolt of plasma shot straight to her spine.

If Collis's expression was anything to go by, he'd sensed it too. Despite the sudden mental clarity she was experiencing, she would unpack what had just occurred later. "Come in," she repeated.

Silent, he followed them inside.

Chapter Five

As the first bell of the day sounded, Shari leaned against the trunk of a bereni tree and munched on a sand pear as she watched the other students file in. She'd had to put up a shield to prevent the anyone from noticing her.

Mentally going over what she knew of the current patrol roster, she tried to match up who would work best together. Faces and abilities danced behind her eyelids as she stared off into the distance. Shari had almost come up with three groupings she was happy with when someone tapped her on the arm.

Flinching, she glared at Anika.

"You're so touchy." Anika tossed her hair and forced a smile. "We're joining with Talhan soon! Aren't you excited?"

"I'm super keen," Shari said, deadpan.

Anika patted Shari's arm again and huffed. "Don't be like that. The Shifting Islands joining up is such a big deal! Three of them together at once" Anika sighed. "The colours and sights of Rakemyst are so not what we're used to. And Talhan—they're like, the tech centre of Lissae! There's so much to see." Anika lent in. "I hear they even automate their clothing manufacture. I'd love to get a close look at that. The joining will be amazing."

"It's not like the last joining was smooth sailing. If we go through a fight every time, when the Shifting Islands join with Vannali there'll be no one left." Shari wished she had the same positive outlook as Anika. After the bloodbath when Ronah had joined with Rakemyst, she wasn't really keen for a repeat.

"There's a convergence?" Anika's eyes widened and her grin was blinding. "Oh, just think. I will be regarded as *the* foremost stylist on Lissae. *I'm* the one dressing the Altoriae!" Jumping up and down, she clapped her hands.

Shari fixed a grin on her face. She'd forgotten about her deal with the self-declared stylist.

"You won't back out, will you?" Anika narrowed her eyes.

"No." The Altoriae was all innocence.

"Good. I'm going to make you into the most stunning version of yourself! Oh! Another five outfits! I need to get planning!"

Shari sighed in relief as Anika teetered away on spindly heels, muttering to herself. What she was in for? So long as Anika didn't light her up with plasma and say it was for artistic effect or something, she'd be fine.

As she stepped into the science classroom, Shari's head snapped to the side. Something scuttled off into the shadows. She couldn't shake the sensation of being watched.

"Nice of you to join us, Miss Dawn. Take a seat, please."

She mumbled an apology to Tutor Heath-Ribeck as she slid into her chair. Shari tried to be grateful that the net which prevented sending was already in place. *It would be so much harder to teach the kids in my own year level.* The thought had her sitting up in her seat, eyes wide.

"As you know, the only place on Lissae to gather crystal which resonates at the right frequency to accept Innarn is Talhan. To prepare for our joining with Talhan, today we will discuss crystals and their various uses."

Shari reminded herself she didn't need to slump in her seat and pretend she knew nothing anymore.

"We are all aware that certain crystals have specific uses." On the board behind Tutor Heath-Ribeck, a list appeared:

Blue Crystal	*Purification—Air and Water*
White Crystal	*Communication*
Orange Crystal	*Fences/Technology*
Green Crystal	*Water conversion—Salt to Fresh Water*
Red Crystal	*Anchor Point*
Black Crystal	*Energy/Power*
Opaque Crystal	*Used by non-Innarnians to command other crystals*

"Now, as you know, we can't just pull a crystal out of the ground. Such an action would be detrimental to Talhan, and to the occupants' way of life. To harvest crystal, you have to use Innarn to call forth the bits which are ready to leave the ground. Otherwise, you risk the crystal acting in ways which you did not intend, or opposite to the intended purpose. They must follow a certain rotation so the crystal regenerates. If not, the balance of life those on Talhan have strived so hard to achieve would be negated."

The class murmured for a moment, talking about what it would be like to harvest crystal directly from the ground. She'd only ever seen it in pre-cut pieces, ready to imbue with Innarn and purpose.

"There are some exciting things happening with crystal uses on Talhan at the moment. The head of the technology centre has discovered a way to merge orange, black, and opaque crystals to create an alternative method of healing."

Was that the miracle medicine her grandfather was taking?

"For the rest of the year, I want you to work in groups to figure out how to adapt crystals which are used in our everyday lives."

Group work wasn't her idea of fun at the best of times, but looking up and finding her desk surrounded by her classmates made it even less so.

"Sit down." Tutor Heath-Ribeck looked exasperated. "I've assigned you groups. No swapping or changing allowed."

As the rest of the class reluctantly returned to their seats, Shari sighed. Disaster averted.

"Jon!"

One day, he'd miss Shari storming into Books 'n' More and bellowing his name, but today was not that day.

"Jon!" The call came again.

From experience, Jonathan wouldn't make it out the door and away before she caught up with him.

"Why is there a group assignment in the last term of school?" Shari asked, shoving the back door open.

Maybe I should just get a curtain installed instead? One day, she would open the door so fast, the hinges would come clean off.

He ignored her unimpressed look and shrugged. "Not my idea. But working with a group isn't a terrible thing, Shari."

"Says the man who abolished patrol teams."

Jonathan flinched and gazed at his desk.

"I'm sorry, Jon." Shari's voice was soft, and he had to resist reaching out to see what she was thinking.

"Zac is recovering," he said instead. "I visited him today."

"How well do you know him?" Shari fiddled with a smooth round rock he had brought back from Dansua.

He'd patrolled Dansua with Zac. A long, long time ago.

"He's a few years older than me, but Joshua put us in the same patrol group."

"Did you go to school with him?"

"I didn't go to school on Ronah."

Shari blinked, but before she could voice the question dancing on the tip of her tongue, he said, "Actually, you'd work well in a patrol group. A select few people to help you who you could grow to trust."

"Why'd you stop them?"

"The patrol groups? Because mine fell apart."

"What do you mean?" Shari prodded.

Jonathan gulped. Maybe it was time to reopen the old wound. "I scouted ahead of the others and was severely injured. They came through later, but the injury of the Guardian's apprentice was enough to shake even the most senior members."

Shari tucked her legs under her as she slouched in the chair and chewed on her lip. "What if the major part of the patrol groups were the same, but the leaders rotated out? It would help to stop any attachments and give members some stability. Even if the leaders rotated around say... five or six compatible groups, it would still be preferable to having to learn how to get a load of beings to work together night after night."

"Good idea. It's worth looking at," Jonathan admitted.

"Don't think I'll leave the whole 'I didn't go to school here' thing alone," Shari said. "For the moment, you're off the hook. Have you learned any more from the *Hekkor Mafae*?"

Jonathan shook his head and sighed. "It's painful to even be in the same room as it. I'll keep trying though."

"If only we had someone Dark on Lissae who we trusted."

Shari is picking up on some of my more unfortunate traits.

"Tania almost fell asleep in class today." Shari's abrupt change of subject was welcome. "I think she and Ronah have been working too hard. She was only partially able to clean up after the machine attack earlier in the week. Are you able to give them a hand?"

"Good idea. Shall we?"

They rose and went outside.

The worst of the damage done by the red light had been cordoned off with a temporary fence of orange crystals. A deep scar in the ground was yet to be healed. The shattered crystal from the shop across the road was receiving specialist care as they watched.

"How's your Earth Innarn?"

Shari wrinkled her nose. "How about I add my Innarn to yours?"

With a nod, Jonathan stretched out his hands. He let himself float in the sensation for a moment before pushing his consciousness down. The surrounding earth was hard and unyielding. He moulded it with his Innarn until it became warm and welcoming again. Jonathan pulled the edges of the gash together and soothed a hand over it.

Allowing Shari's Innarn in, and breathing it out, he reached into the rubble which had been cobblestones and reminded them what it was like to be whole again.

The aching wound on Ronah's surface healed, the duo turned to the looming mass of the castle.

"Wards?" Shari asked.

"Wards."

He allowed Shari to shift them to the top of the castle, and together, they pushed their Innarn out, adding to the wards which kept Ronah safe. Even if he had to alter it so his new apprentice wouldn't be burned.

Wolf paced along the hallway outside Belfar's room. It had been a week since his mate had been carved up. The Atlanteans had done everything they could to reattach the wing, but there were so many anatomical differences between their species, they weren't sure how to.

Belfar had almost died from blood loss twice before Wolf had ripped the tiny metal straw out of the bag of clear liquid and shoved it into his skin.

The healers had been horrified, until one rushed forward and exclaimed, "You can't do that with a needle!" and moved it to a different spot.

Wolf had watched as his blood reached Belfar and the colour came back into his mate. With Wolf's blood pumping through his veins, Belfar had made a remarkable recovery.

Now, Wolf was relegated to pacing. They were finally ready to reattach the wing. If the healers failed, Wolf had been assured they would be granted safe passage back to Lissae.

He hoped the prattling healers were able to actually help his mate, but the nervous glances they'd exchanged before entering the surgery were not reassuring.

"I cannot apologise enough for Nisethran's actions and behaviour."

It was the lady in the silver gown. She was the Atlantean equivalent of an elder. The drapes of her gown were tinged gold at the edges, and a delicate silver torque adorned her neck.

"I hope he's obliterated."

"We have given our ruling for his behaviour. I wondered if you might like to watch the judgement be enacted so you may share it with your partner?"

Wolf looked at the closed doors and nodded. He'd do no good pacing the hallway.

The lady beckoned him closer.

Grumbling, Wolf laid his hand on her forearm. They disappeared in a dazzle of lights, only to reappear in a high balcony, looking down into an arena.

Crowds filled the seats around the balcony they landed on, sneering and throwing rotten fruit at the docile figure kneeling in the middle of the arena. He had his head bowed, but his missing hand gave away his identity.

Wolf grinned savagely.

A gentle, persistent bell started peeling. Every eye turned to the lady in silver.

She waited until the restless crowd was silent before announcing: "Nisethran has been charged under the law of Furtum. His sentence is punishment four times over what he did to his victim."

How could such a thing even be possible? The trusnuck didn't have one set of wings, let alone two.

A metal bed, reminiscent of the one Belfar had been strapped to, was wheeled out. Nisethran was heaved to his feet by two burly men. He seemed to not have control of his faculties, his head hanging limply before he was dropped onto the bed and strapped in, face down.

"Children may wish to leave," the lady in silver warned.

A few in the crowd looked startled, and some parents began to guide their complaining children away.

"Wake him up." Her voice rang out through the crowd, clear and harsh.

Wolf had the distinct impression that this woman was not one you wanted to annoy.

A guard did something, and Nisethran jerked in his restraints.

"You have been charged under the law of Furtum, Nisethran. Hold still for your punishment."

Wolf, caught up in fascinated horror, couldn't look away as two more men strode into the arena. They handed the first two saws, and then they each started work.

Mouth dry despite the bile in his throat, Wolf took in every moment.

When Belfar had nightmares about his time on Atlantis, he'd be able to share the grisly end of the trusnuck who had stolen his wing.

Jonathan turned the page with a flinch, trying to read through the tears blurring his eyes.

Blowing on burned fingertips, he wiped the tears away and squinted in a futile attempt to make the words jumping around on the pages of the *Hekkor Mafae* stay still.

Sniffling as a tear dripped down his nose, Jonathan hunted on his desk for the handkerchief he'd put there a moment ago. The stacks of books had been cleared off and moved onto trolleys ready to stock the shelves of the store. Not to mention that he didn't want to risk the Dark book corrupting any of the others.

"I don't think it likes you."

Jonathan blinked a few times to clear his vision and sniffed again. "You might be right."

Samuel leaned against the doorframe, smirking at him. "You know I'll have more luck with reading the book than you."

He wanted to scowl, but knew his apprentice was right. "Why don't you take over then?"

"It must really be hurting you." Samuel crossed the room and nudged Jonathan out of the way.

"The Dark Realms are forever knocking on Lissae's door. There has to be some information in here to help negotiate, or on how to better meet their needs so they'll leave us be."

"Or how to get them to go back home and never return," Samuel murmured as he flicked through the pages with ease.

Jonathan tried not to be jealous. The book was so saturated in Dark Innarn, his fingers were covered in tiny, page-thin burns. He'd been trying to read the book for a measly quarter of an hour, and his eyes were blurry and itchy as if he'd been up for days.

"Well, this is interesting," Samuel hummed.

"What is it?" Jonathan tried not to sound too eager. He crossed the room, away from the book, which was giving him a headache just by its presence.

"A recipe on how to cook a Lissaen for the ultimate culinary experience."

Jonathan glared and shook his head.

Samuel laughed as he flicked through the pages. The Guardian wasn't entirely sure he believed it was a joke.

The merriment fell from his apprentice's face, and he appeared genuinely worried. "Thrice-damned, tuzar-loving buzzard."

"What?" Jonathan wanted to see what Samuel was looking at, but the push of the book was strong enough to make him stay where he was.

Samuel swore again as he slammed the book closed and breathed hard out of his nose. Shadowed wings rose behind him, and the skin on his arms rippled as scales tried to force their way out. Eyes shut, and breathing deeply, he slowly regained control of himself.

Jonathan waited until the wings receded and the scales disappeared. "What did you find?"

"I'd forgotten. What is this Realm doing to me?" He slammed a fist into the table and pushed himself away, turning his back to the room. "I'm to chair the next Dark Conclave."

Jonathan sucked in a shaky breath and swore softly. "How soon is it?"

"Three of your moons? Maybe less. Time moves as it will on my home Realm."

"So it will be held on Altum," Jonathan said, sounding distressed.

Samuel shot him a withering glance over his shoulder and snorted. "Things are brewing in the Realms. It's where the Queen feels safest."

"What happens if you don't go?"

"Have you heard of Mishone?"

Jonathan frowned, trying to recall if he'd ever caught a mention of it. "No."

"During one of the first Dark Conclaves, before I was a hatchling, the Chair didn't show up. The Queen burned down the entire Realm he'd been on, with him on it. Erased it from the history books. Only the eldest of the Ducibus would remember even the name. *I'm* the missing Chair's replacement. If I do the same, Lissae, and every being and creature on her, will die."

Samuel was difficult to read at the best of times, but Jonathan saw the genuine loathing at the thought of Lissae being no more. How different would it be if Shari was not of Lissae?

"Are you telling me you have to go, or we all die?"

"I'm sure your brain wasn't that scrambled by the book." Samuel scowled at him. "Yes. Essentially."

"How are you going to explain this to Shari?" Jonathan kept the idea of Shari going with him hidden for the moment. Samuel wouldn't exactly agree.

His scowl deepened. "A lengthy patrol?"

"Lengthy? How long does the conclave go for?"

"Anywhere from three days to three moons. It depends on the discussion, and how willing everyone is to agree."

"What would you guess?"

"The topics which will be covered would indicate a longer conclave than normal." Samuel sighed and bowed his head, tension dropping from his frame. "I'll not put Lissae in danger if I can prevent it."

"Have you grown fond of my Realm?"

There was a snort, and he turned around. "There are parts of Lissae which are tolerable," he admitted.

Despite the seriousness of the situation, Jonathan grinned. Samuel sounded so disgruntled to admit such a small thing. The glare the other man shot him sobered Jonathan. "If the fate of the Realm rests upon it, then I could consider it. It's because *your* fate rests on it that I'll tell you to go."

Samuel scowled, narrowing his eyes. It seemed to take him a moment to realise what had been said. "It's decided then." He brushed past Jonathan to leave the back room, but not before the Guardian saw the softening of his friend's expression.

Slumped in his chair, Jonathan ran a hand over his face.

Zac had left his insides tied in knots. He'd thought, way back when Zac had gone, that he had left all those feelings behind. Apparently, he was just as fallible as anyone else.

The slight possibility of Samuel's fondness for Shari may be the reason their Realm would still stand after the Dark Conclave didn't hurt either.

'*Altoriae!*'

The deep, rocky scream came in the middle of mapping class.

Shari shot to her feet so fast, she banged her knee on the desk as she rose. '*Wolf?*'

'*Healers. Now. Belfar...*'

An agony Shari understood all too well was tearing his soul. Grief, and loss, and pain.

Heart in her mouth, Shari ripped apart Ridden Hall's wards as she shifted out. Arriving at the doors of the museum, she sent for healers from Ronah and Rakemyst and fairly flew through the rooms to the double doors.

Her connection to Jon kicked in just as the doors opened. Wolf came through with Belfar leaning heavily on him.

Shari paused. Confused. She'd thought Belfar had died.

Wolf locked eyes with her and pushed images of their time on Atlantis toward her. Tears threatened to drop from her damp lashes, but Shari rallied and shifted them all, as gently as possible, to the Healers Centre on Ronah.

There was no need to state the injury. The healers started work immediately. They set Belfar up on a bed tutting at the way the Atlanteans had sewn the wound closed while they began the blood transfusion. It was a much more sophisticated way of shifting the new blood in, with none of the metal tubes or risk of infection they'd experienced off-Realm.

As Shari stood by her uncle's side in the corner of the room, the two watched as the healers worked to regrow Belfar's wing. Three times the team tried before another team replaced them, then another. Something seemed to block the healing from taking.

Shari had never seen someone return from the battlefield stitched up, and she ached to add her healing to the others' but was unsure how useful it would be. Wolf, with his eyes locked on his mate, sent her everything of their time away.

She'd never been gladder to see someone sawn apart.

As the last team left, heads drooping, she looked at Wolf. She knew what Wolf wanted her to do without him having to ask.

'Shall I try to heal Belfar?'

'Please, Shari.'

She stepped up to the bed and held her hands just over the jagged slice where Belfar's wing used to be. Shari pushed her Innarn into the wound, seeing the shape of the wing in her mind and willing it into being. It hovered like a spirit for a moment, before the green healing Innarn scattered through the room like dust motes.

"Wha...?" Belfar turned his head, taking in the room through blood-shot eyes.

Shari tried again. Same result.

'No...' Belfar groaned.

'Knock him out,' she commanded her uncle.

Wolf looked at her for a moment and passed his hand over Belfar's temples. His partner slumped, and Shari tried again.

Again, the healing Innarn dissipated.

"Wolf, I'm..." The words caught in her suddenly tight throat. "It's been too long. There's nothing I can do. I'm so sorry." Shari lowered her head, but not before she met Wolf's gaze through her tear-filled eyes.

"There has to be something we can do." Wolf looked desperate. "The healers on Rakemyst?"

"I'll shift you both there."

Her uncle inclined his head and gathered Belfar close, and Shari shifted them away.

Once they were out of sight, she slumped over the bed and let the tears fall.

"There is nothing we can do."

What was the point of coming home if the healers here were no better than the ones on Atlantis? Wolf scowled, and the healer flinched before scurrying from the room.

At least Rakemyst's Healing Centre had rooms more comfortable than the ones on the accursed Realm that had cost Belfar his wing.

"Well, I'll just have to get used to a lopsided life," Belfar joked weakly from the bed.

Wolf scowled harder. He couldn't get over just how badly he'd failed Belfar. "I shouldn't have let you come with me."

"Yeah. That would have gone over well. The Altoriae's uncle, trussed up like a chicken, then released back into the wild, wingless."

"Better me than you," Wolf rumbled.

"My thoughts exactly."

Wolf flinched, thinking Belfar agreed, but scowled even harder when he realised what his mate was saying. "No. Never. I..." Fists clenched, he turned away. "I'm not good enough for you. Never was."

"Funny thing is..." Belfar's tone was light, but Wolf saw in the window's reflection that their scowls were matching. "I get to decide who's good enough for me. Although, I'm only three quarters of the Ilutri I once was."

Teeth grinding hard enough to crack, Wolf shook his head. He'd never be able to repay Belfar for waiting for him to come to his senses. Never be able to show him exactly how much he was loved. If he could find a healer... Casting his mind back over the most horrific injuries he'd seen on patrol, there were only two which had been handled off Rakemyst.

It was right after Calem had left. They'd both been almost dead when they'd returned from patrol. The Ducibus had refused to let them return to Rakemyst and had, instead, pushed them to Talhan, where a tall blue-skinned Innarnian had healed them.

"The technomancer," Wolf whispered.

"Why don't you come help me up, and I'll show you how much of an Ilutri I still am?"

"Stay here," Wolf said, and strode to the doors leading to the balcony.

Belfar whispered something. Wolf paused and looked back at his mate. The stricken expression on his face made him reconsider briefly, but Wolf knew what he had to do.

'*I love you,*' he sent, and jumped from the balcony, allowing himself to plummet downwards before snapping his wings out.

CHAPTER SIX

After her failed attempt to heal Belfar, Shari headed down to the beach.

The stitches on the stump of his wing were plastered across her mind's eye.

A half-baked wish for a distraction appeared in the form of something rustling the tall seagrass lining the dunes.

Plasma flared to life in her hand, shooting up the length of her arm. It rested, crackling and ready to strike if she willed it.

A slight brush of sea breeze, and the seagrass rustled again. Turning, she almost missed the glint of the dying sun reflecting on something hiding in the long green blades.

A chorus of 'Well met, Altoriae,' had her looking up, away from the last of the rustling.

Hastily, Shari aimed the plasma curling around her arm at the stacked wood of the bonfire Tania had prepared. It shot from her fingers, the taste of ozone lingering in the air as the first of the Returned teens stepped foot onto the sand.

'Tonight, I'm not the Altoriae. I am just like you—a teenager attending my first ever beach party. There's food and drink and a fire. What more could we want?' Shari broadcasted.

The nerves fluttering around the group seemed to dissipate. People laughed, groups heading for the fire or the water. There was a low-level humming which reminded Shari more of a group of people sending than of Sam's singing.

It was because they *were* sending, she realised. All the Returned seemed to be so connected. Not exactly like a hive mind, but as if they constantly shared their thoughts. What was life was like before they'd been... Was there a polite way to ask how they'd lived before Anriluka had eaten them?

"What do we do now, Altoriae?" Collis asked, bowing to her.

"Have fun?" Shari winced as it came out as a question.

Collis looked at her seriously. "It is hard for us to have fun if you are not."

Opening her mouth to say something smart, she snapped it closed. "True. I guess... well, it's been a long time since I was at a party." *One which didn't end in U'tan guts*, she reflected.

"Even longer for us, I'd wager," Collis said easily.

"Well met!" Tania trilled, a line of floating lanterns drifting behind her. "I thought we could decorate the dunes a bit. And Mum made some punch!" A large jug at the end of the procession tilted wildly when Tania accepted Collis's arm.

'*Lead by example, Altoriae,*' Collis sent as he walked away, every fibre of his being focusing on Tania.

Just how am I meant to do that? Shari attempted to keep the scowl from her face as she walked towards the sea, awkwardly waving at a group standing ankle-deep in the water.

"Well met," she called out. They waved back, looking wide-eyed. Hurried whispers and the quick fizzle of Innarn let Shari know they were hiding something. It made her want to turn back around and retreat into the deepening shadows. "It's nice out tonight, don't you think?"

Please, please, can someone just jump out and stab me?

"The water is... wet," a girl with an intricate ink flower blooming across her cheek said.

"Funny that." Shari's voice was drier than the sand, but she hoped her smile made up for it.

"The water is wet? Really, Daivi?" One of the boys nudged her in the ribs. The claw marks on his face were covered with looping, whirling designs that disappeared into the collar of his shirt. "The..." He snorted loudly, and the group started laughing.

Shari joined in, grinning at Daivi. When she tentatively smiled back, Shari winked and flicked a finger out.

A line of water rose behind the boy with the loops of ink and tapped him gently on the shoulder. When he looked around to see who it was, Shari let go of her control, and it splashed him in the face.

The group drew a collective breath for a moment, and Shari sensed an edge which she hadn't been expecting. "Just checking if it's wet," she said easily.

Daivi snickered, and the tension dropped. Shari wasn't sure how, but they all ended up splashing and playing, pausing only to dive under or to ride a wave away from the main group in search of a better position to attack from.

Shadows from the dual moons crept over the sand. As the night grew darker, they started a different game.

Their playfulness gave Shari hope that she would be able to have a normal life—if the fighting ever stopped.

Tania smiled fondly at Shari playing with the Returned. What Mitch would think if he saw her now, and knew that wherever he was, he'd be smiling.

"Who are you thinking of?" Collis asked.

"Shari's friend. The Guardian's previous apprentice. His name was Mitch. He... Shari's taking his loss hard."

Collis frowned and turned to place another of the lanterns.

"What are you thinking?" she asked, pitching her voice lower.

It took him a long time to answer, but Tania was attempting to be patient. Ronah had taught her that sometimes, the right words were scarce.

"Loss is so... was so different. Where we were. Every time you stepped outside the walls, you were almost guaranteed to wake up dead."

"Wake up dead?" Tania frowned, shaking her head, trying to make sense of it.

Collis laughed, but it was a hollow sound. "In the pocket-Realm where we were stuck, lots of things wanted to kill us. And plenty did. I lost count of how many times I died. There was something about the way the U'tan structured the Realm. Nothing truly *died*—not in the same sense that it does here. But, now and then, people would succumb to the horror and just fade away."

Attempting to wrap her mind around it, Tania set out the next few lanterns in silence. She tried to envision stepping foot off Ronah and waking up knowing she had died. "I can't imagine... Do you remember any of it?"

With a nod, Collis set down the last of the lanterns. With his face hidden in the deepening shadows, Tania had the sense that he'd much rather hide than talk about what happened.

"And fading away?"

His Adam's apple bobbed. "My mother was the first."

Tania made a noise of dismay. She wanted badly to hug Collis, but was worried he would take it the wrong way. She wrung her hands and said, "I'm sorry."

"It was a long time ago," he murmured.

It was taking a while, but Tania now knew better than to believe the stoic act he was putting on. "Still miss her?"

He nodded and turned to the group having the water fight. "It's good to see an Altoriae who knows how to have fun."

"Who was your Altoriae?"

"Muran. He was strict. Fair. Interested in keeping us safe, but not so much in having fun."

"And he didn't make it?" Tania didn't want to spell it out. Collis didn't need to be reminded of another loss.

"He was amongst the Returned. But he gave his life fighting off the fulni."

She snapped her gaping mouth shut at the look he gave her. A different topic was called for. "You said something about being able to help with the new houses?"

"Ronah has changed a lot since we were last on her shores."

"How do you mean?"

Features alight with mischief, Collis waved his arm over the sand and parts of it fell away. She was left looking at a vaguely familiar outline. As she settled next to Collis, Tania realised it was an aerial view of Ronah. It changed before her gaze. Houses grew, shrank. Streets widened, narrowed, vanished. Farms sprung up, crops grew, were harvested, and disappeared. The occasional house leapt up here and there, and the castle in the middle was added too, until the sand sculpture became closer to what she knew.

"Hey! There's my house!" she said, pointing as the tiny bereni seedling grew impossibly fast. Then, the island started changing again. Tania recognised some of her own plans for the streets and the houses she had helped Ronah make.

It slowed down and stopped. She was looking at the view of Ronah as the island was now. "Beautiful," she whispered.

"Where we were, we had to make our houses out of nothing. We fortified the walls of the city we made by shaping Innarn with pure will. I believe you're trying to make the houses for us the same way, only you are doing it alone."

"No, oh no. Ronah helps so much." Tania couldn't believe someone would be able to do that—to build a city with just their mind. Then again, before she'd come to Ronah, she hadn't been able to believe herself capable of the things she'd achieved so far. "Could you show me what you built?"

The sand version of Ronah collapsed. Collis's eyes looked harder than any teen had a right to look. Tania was about to tell him it was alright, that he didn't have to, when he waved his arm above the sand again.

The first things appearing from the flattened sand were spiralling towers, some spindly, others sturdy, all reaching for the sky. A wall appeared next, tall and thick. It looked strong enough to withstand the longest siege. Houses, markets, and smaller buildings sprung up. The streets were closer than the ones on Ronah, the twists and turns no doubt making it easier to defend. With another wave of his hand, tiny lights twinkled in the windows of the tower.

"I lived right there," he said, pointing to a tower in the middle.

"It's beautiful," Tania breathed.

Collis let the sand hold its shape for a moment longer before it turned into a lumpy pile again.

"You're so talented," she exclaimed. The smile lighting his face was worth her embarrassment.

"Can I show you something else?" he asked as the group by the water started heading towards the flickering purple bonfire.

Tania nodded. How different had Collis's lessons in Innarn been compared to what was being taught at Ridden Hall now?

The shadows made his features hard to read, but the intense concentration was still evident. He tipped his head; a hum seemed to surround him. Then, silver lights shot out, snapping up against the other Returned.

The lights seemed to be contagious. They spread from one Returned to the next, weaving them together like knots in a net. In the blink of an eye, the silver net lit up, and the sky flashed bright.

Shari thought everything was going well. The water fights had been fun, and she'd been laughing along with the others as they'd traipsed up to the bonfire.

As she looked down, wringing the last of the water out of her hair and contemplating if it would be in good spirits to use the droplets to splash some others, the humming caught her off guard.

It took her a moment to realise the noise wasn't physical. It was the sheer weight of the sends zipping through the air. She shivered, blaming it on the cooling water dripping down her back. When the first bolt of silver shot straight through the boy with the loops of ink and into the girl with a dragonfly on her neck, Shari didn't scream.

It was a close call though.

Her glove appeared. If Anika could see her now, she'd probably get a lecture on how ridiculous she looked wearing a green bikini and a black, two-bladed glove.

The humming intensified, and she found herself trapped between four lines of silver thread. Her breathing came in harsh pants. She had wanted so desperately to think she'd found some people her own age who would like her for herself. She struggled to breathe, and a frantic thought filled every corner of her mind:

Is this really how I will die? Surrounded by the people I freed?

'Melodramatic?' Collis's voice was a gentle tap on her mind.

'Where are you? Something's happening, but I...'

'You asked how we have fun. Just like your relatives, we burn off our excess Innarn. We are...'

Shari sensed him ruffling through the edges of her mind, and she batted him away.

'We are like you, in a way. Spent most of our lives fighting, and not sure how to do anything else. Desperate to learn how to have fun. To not be violent. I thought some fireworks would be welcome?'

She attempted to curb her harsh breaths as she nodded. Now she knew a little of what to look for, she sensed the links between each of the Returned. They were literally sharing the load of their Innarn so no one being had more than the others.

'*Care to join us?*'

Knowing he couldn't see, Shari nodded again. She'd worked with Jonathan before, adding her Innarn to his in layers. Surely, she could…

The world went white.

'*Too much!*' Collis cried.

Guilty, her shoulders rose as she pulled her power back. 'Oops?'

Around her, the Returned whooped and laughed.

The sky lit up. Colours of all types flared and burst, drawing patterns which mimicked the ink of their skin in the dark of the night.

She became lost in the awe of it, searching out the next person who'd light up the sky and match the patterns.

Her glove melted back into her skin as a small part of her wondered at the potential for weaponizing such a network. As other teens, along with their families, arrived at the beach and joined in the party, Shari pushed the thought to the back of her mind.

"Amazing!" Daivi turned to her, face reflecting the lights in the sky.

"Thanks for the invite," a voice said as Shari summoned a blanket large enough for a group to sit on. The hesitant words carried a weight of hope.

Her gaze fell on the group of former candidates who had remained on Ronah. Amara, Talofa, Raven, Dealon, Lira, Mu, Elani, and, of course, Alistair and Samuel.

"You are always welcome," Shari said, smiling. It was an oversight, she realised, not inviting the others.

"And what are we? Boiled buta sprouts?" a snippy voice said. Anika was heading the delegation of teens Shari had grown up with.

"You absolutely are," Shari agreed.

Anika huffed and rolled her eyes, but didn't storm off as she would have before Shari had saved her from Anriluka.

Shari lowered her face to hide a blush. With a flick of her hand, she enlarged the blanket even more. She was not entirely ready to admit to such a large crowd that she wasn't good at this. You could throw her a blade and call her into battle, but socialising was a skill set she struggled with.

"At least the food will be good." Anika flicked her hair and started to lead the others away.

The crowd moved farther onto the beach, but Shari knew she should say something. She just wasn't sure what. "I... you *are* welcome. Everyone is. It's taking a while to get used to people wanting to spend time with me." *Outside of battle.*

Amara's mouth fell open. "People are idiots if they don't want to spend time with you! You're amazing, and not just because you can blast fire from your hands." She stepped forward and tripped over the edge of the blanket. Shari and Raven reached out together with their Innarn, setting Amara to rights amongst the laughter of the others.

"It's easy to forget, sometimes." Shari fiddled with the edge of the blanket, struggling to keep her head up.

Anika's face pinched, eyes tight and worried. Shari knew why and tried to smile at her to lessen the sting. Anika gave a small smile back, but still led some of the others to mingle with the rest of the partygoers.

"Well, perhaps you need us around more so you remember." Lira slid gracefully to the ground near the corner of the blanket. She held up a bowl in invitation.

Shari gratefully took a handful of sweet osin berries. "I'd like that."

The group started a happy, light-hearted discussion, and Shari fell into it easily. At the end of the night, she hoped the feeling of easy inclusion was the same for everyone.

Wolf had been flying all evening. He'd passed the point where he'd be able to turn back hours ago.

Even with the aid of his air Innarn, he could still be hours, maybe days away from Talhan's shores. But he had to get to the technomancer. He couldn't fail Belfar again.

An endless expanse of water slid by under his wings. The morning sun was rising behind him, but the glare on the water made him want to shut his eyes.

He yawned. Maybe it wouldn't hurt to rest for a while.

His eyes slipped closed for a moment, even as his wings kept beating.

Just for a while...

Sea spray splashed his face in a rude wake-up call. Wolf jolted, the tips of his feathers brushing the waves below.

So tired.

But he had to keep going.

Belfar needed him.

Steeling his resolve, Wolf reached down and scooped up a handful of the morning-cold water, splashing it on his face.

Pumping his wings harder, he rose.

Gulls cried in the distance, and Wolf turned his head. Shimmering in the pale light of the sun, he could just make out a hard shape in the water.

Talhan.

When Shari woke the next morning and realised her first class of the day was a 'planning session,' she was tempted to sleep in and skip it.

The Ducibus had mentioned a disturbance near the gateway of Lioccanor, and Shari had patrolled the section after the beach party with the rest of the former candidates.

She couldn't get the idea of concrete groups with rotating leaders out of her head. It was becoming more and more appealing. But for now, she wandered towards the tiny office Headmaster Hollingsworth had said she was to use.

As she opened the door and rubbed at tired eyes, she walked straight into someone.

Shari bounced off a hard back. She didn't even have to look to know it was Sam. His leather, mint, and Dark Innarn scent gave him away.

"Well met, little Altoriae," he said.

"Well met, Sam. And if you—" she yawned— "call me Altoriae again, I will stab you."

He gave a surprised laugh and stepped out of the gateway. "I knew there was a reason I liked you."

"Because I threaten you with violence?"

"Kinda reminds me of home." He shrugged as if he had said nothing important.

"You don't mention home a lot," she hedged.

"I haven't been back in a long time. Looks like I'll be seeing some of my kin again soon." His mouth twisted.

"Are you not looking forward to catching up with your family?" Shari asked.

Sam plonked himself in the chair closest to the door, and Shari gratefully set her box on the other desk.

"My kin are difficult." Sam ran his hand over his face. Had he picked the habit up from Jon? "Most of them are..." he rubbed his fist along his jawline. "Unrepentant. Irredeemable. Have committed atrocities... well. They aren't good."

Shari took a breath. "And the others?"

Sam smiled, his features soft in a way she hadn't seen before. "The others are more like me—willing to escape to be who they are. But we always seem to get drawn back into the fold." His features darkened again.

"Can I help?" Shari asked softly.

"My thanks, but this may be something I have to do alone."

"If you ever need a hand with your family, I'm here."

Finally meeting her eyes, he tilted his head slightly. "Of everyone in the Realms, you're probably the only one capable of helping me with them." He held her gaze for a long, charged moment.

Breath caught in her throat, Shari shivered as Innarn sparking between them.

"For now, we should probably figure out what we will teach these kids."

"Good idea," she said.

After school, a group of Returned teens escorted Shari to the bookstore. It felt more like being surrounded by peers than bodyguards.

Or it did, until they bowed, Daivi throwing in a wink before they turned as one and strode off.

Jon was actually in the main part of the store this time, arranging a display to put in one of the bay windows at the front.

"Well met, Jon."

"Well met, Altoriae," he said as Sam walked in too, the bell above the door trilling.

"Why doesn't he get threatened with violence?" Sam muttered.

Jon blinked, head rearing back.

"Because he's Jon. My stuffy, formal, mentor, who I can only change so much. You, I can tell to quit it before you start."

"Stuffy?" Jon grumbled.

"You're a product of your training." Shari shrugged. "Oh! We need to sort the schedule out."

"Sort out what?"

Shari picked up a clear, crystal globe to fiddle with. "I have school, teaching, patrolling, and training with both of you, and the patrol groups.

And I wouldn't mind spending some time with my family and getting to know the Returned. And I need to find a way to fix Belfar's wing." She huffed. "I feel like pulled taffy."

Sam looked at her in confusion.

"Stretched thin," Jon clarified. "I'm much the same, actually. We need to sit down and plan. Why don't you spend some time with your family now, and we'll all meet over dinner at my house?"

Shari looked at Sam, who nodded.

"We have a plan." Shari grinned, and bounded out of the store.

CHAPTER SEVEN

olf fumbled his landing.

He gathered himself from a tangle of feathers and limbs and shook his wings out. *If no one on Talhan saw me crash, did it really happen?*

A mechanical bird flew towards him, squawking, "Injured! Injured!"

Wanting to growl a denial, Wolf resisted. If the thing thought he was injured, maybe it would take him to the technomancer.

The bird nudged him onto a crystal disc. Trying to remember he was back home, and that there was nothing to worry about, he stepped on. He gasped as the disc sped through the air, depositing him directly into what he was coming to recognise as a healer's office.

Slumping against the wall, Wolf looked through bleary eyes as a blue-skinned woman entered the room.

"State the nature of your injury."

"It's not me; it's my mate. They took his wing. I need the technomancer. She's the only one who can fix it."

She gave him a supremely unimpressed look. "Your mate is not here. You are. State the nature…"

Growling, Wolf pushed away from the wall and tried to turn anger into energy. "He's not here because a mad Atlantean sawed his wing off! He can't travel! He's…" he sobbed and collapsed.

Strong blue hands caught him before he reached the floor. He was firmly pressed into a chair.

He reached up, grabbing at her arms, fingers brushing against a red studded leather cuff on her wrist.

Large, purple eyes looked at him, assessing his condition.

Something was shoved into his hand and he glanced at it uncomprehendingly. The gelatinous cube was small and green.

"Eat it. Or I won't help."

Wolf crammed the cube in his mouth. It was surprisingly tasty. Something akin to salted, tangy fish burst across his tastebuds.

"Show me what happened."

He offered his hand, and the healer took it. He showed her everything that had transpired on Atlantis, and how the healers on Ronah and Rakemyst had been unable to help. How even the Altoriae couldn't heal Belfar's wing.

The blue-skinned face smirked at him.

"If you can get your mate to me before the half turn of the moons has passed since the separation of his wing, I can heal him. After that, it will be too late."

"But the technomancer…"

She rolled her eyes. "I am the one they refer to as the technomancer."

She grumbled something that was drowned out by the roaring success filling Wolf's ears.

Or maybe it was whatever had been in that cube finally starting to work. He felt renewed, and hopeful. Maybe he would be able to prove to Belfar that he could be a good mate after all.

Suddenly, he sobered. "That's in three days."

"Then you'd better get moving. See the guards out the front. They will ensure you get back to Rakemyst. *After* you've eaten something. And rested."

"But he can't travel."

The technomancer's face was impassive. "You got here. I'm sure you can figure out something for him."

After school, Tania was intending to walk home with her siblings when a chime sounded in her mind.

'*Are you prepared for today's training?*' Zana sent.

Tania yawned. It had slipped her mind, but she sent back an affirmative answer and hurried to just outside the gate where Zana was waiting.

'*Shall we?*' Zana sent.

Tania nodded, like she hadn't spent half the night constructing the outer walls of the next rezem on the list, been up early to help her siblings in the garden, and almost bonked her nose on the desk in her last lesson when she'd nodded off.

Still, the imposing Ilutri raised her brows and pushed something into Tania's hand.

'*What's this?*'

'*Gilfress elixir. A drink of my making. It helps when I'm tried or stressed, without the disadvantage of having to sleep.*'

Tania blinked, eyes widening. '*You made a joke.*' She hadn't thought Zana had a sense of humour.

'*I do that occasionally.*' Then she was in the air, her wings beating steadily.

Curious, Tania looked at the drink. It looked like honey but moved like water. She uncapped the lid and sniffed. The spices tickled her nose. She took a drink, and as soon as she swallowed, her entire body tingled like tiny bolts of lightning were zapping under her skin.

"Oh!" She shook her hands out, and carefully cast a twister of air, lifting her to Zana's level. "Shall we?"

Zana smiled and winged her way across the sky, gliding over the Innarn bridge which joined the two Shifting Islands and right to the heart of Rakemyst, on the very top of the tall white tower.

They weren't alone.

Shari's uncle was waiting for them.

"Please, help me." His voice rumbled across her skin.

Tania saw what he'd been through play out like a show on the screen. Their traumatic trip to Atlantis. His journey across the sea to Talhan, and his meeting with the imposing blue-skinned Innarnian who offered her aide. His return to Rakemyst, and Belfar's healers saying he was still in no shape to make the journey.

"She said if he's been separated from his wing for a half turn of the moon, she can't help. That's—there's three days left." He looked even tireder than she felt, and his voice broke on the last word.

Tania had tears pouring down her face. "I'm so sorry."

"You want us to speed the joining up?" Zana said incredulously.

"Please, it's the only way."

"What you're asking has never been done before. Ronah, Rakemyst, and Talhan would all have to agree. The shielding on all three Shifting Islands must increase along with their speed, else the residents would fall off, or be compressed into sheets as thin as paper by the forces at play."

"I'll do it. I'll shield them all. Please, please." Wolf dropped to his knees.

Tania dropped too, reaching out to clasp his hands.

"You can't shield the islands, Wolf," Zana whispered. "Only the Linked can."

"I'll shield Ronah," Tania offered without hesitation. The houses would have to stop, but the Returned might continue the work instead.

Zana sighed. "I feel your pain, Wolf Dawn. I am happy to shield Rakemyst. But we must speak to Talhan's Linked and ensure they can protect their island."

"Then what are we waiting for?" Tania bounced to her feet.

Wolf bowed his head. Tania pretended not to see the tremors wracking his frame.

"Talhan's Linked cannot send," Zana said.

"Well." Tania looked around for inspiration. They were high enough that the cumulus clouds seemed close enough to touch. A bit of cloud broke off and joined another one. "That's it! We can travel to Talhan and ask ourselves!"

Zana sucked a breath in. Tania gazed up as the older Linked's eyes fall on Wolf's hunched form. "Very well."

When Shari's uncle lifted his head, there was a sheen of tears in his eyes. She just hoped she could convince Talhan's Linked to shield their island.

"Ask for the Head Healer. She might help convince him," Wolf said. "I need to check on Belfar."

"Go. We will do what we can."

Wolf stumbled to his feet and winged away.

Tania rubbed her hands together, trying to ignore her sweaty palms as a hand reached out and touched her arm. Zana sent a soothing thought.

In the next blink, they were elsewhere.

A broad street was bustling with people, and it took Tania a few moments to orientate herself. The white tower they had been on couldn't be more different from where they were now.

Talhan was like nothing she'd ever seen before. Hard lines and angles were everywhere. The building walls were smoother, more uniform in architectural design, although the Elements seemed to coexist just as easily as they did on Ronah. A funny, straight-walled building of water sat against a crackling plasma structure. After Ronah's curved walls and Rakemyst's disdain for straight lines anywhere, Talhan's buildings were a shock to her system.

The only soft things in sight were the beings.

The people of Talhan were something else altogether. All races and creeds seemed to walk the streets here. Dressed mostly in the colours of dusk, their loose, baggy pants and flowing asymmetrical tops seemed to be in direct contrast to the environment.

Tania shuffled on the spot, self-consciously playing with the hem of her shirt.

Almost every head had some sort of covering—scarves, oversized beanies, close-fitting hats with narrow brims, or flowing head wraps. The purpose seemed to be keeping their hair safely hidden from the tiny mechanical birds hovering by their heads.

Everyone moved with a purpose. From the young mother wrangling three reluctant children, chiding them for being late to school, to the twenty-something-year-old guy carrying a stack of hefty textbooks.

People didn't just walk in Talhan—the favoured form of travel was the continuous slip stream. A man dressed in loose clothing, his head wrapped in a scarf, stepped onto a platform and *whoosh!* He zoomed away, idly glancing at a crystal slab as if it were something that happened every day.

The few people who were walking had their heads were down, focused on tiny hand-sized slabs of crystals. Tania couldn't figure out how they weren't running into each other when many of them weren't looking where they were going. Maybe the birds were guiding them?

A stray bird came to hover next to Tania.

"Welcome, visitors. Please state your purpose." Something trilled at them.

The bird thing was speaking.

Tania tried not to gape at it—she really did. A wave of amusement washing over her from Zana showed she hadn't been as successful as she'd hoped. The bird was comprised of lots of overlapping metal circles.

The studded wings glinted with tiny yellow crystals as it flapped. Tania stared, mesmerized.

"I am Zana, Rakemyst's Linked. This is Tania, Ronah's Linked. We are here to speak to your Head Healer."

A glowing orange crystal in the centre of the bird hummed, and the tingly sensation of being scanned by Innarn flowed over Tania.

"You are not injured. No healer required." The bird, apparently done with them, made to fly away.

In a desperate lunge, Tania grabbed the bird by a wing.

Instantly, she regretted the decision. A harsh jolt slammed through her body, leaving her fingers and toes tingling, and her hair standing on end. There was a high-pitched scream. It took her a moment to realise she was the one making it. The shock subsided, and she wrenched her hand away, cradling it to her chest.

"Wait! Please!" her voice shook as she cried out.

When the bird swung back around, triumph quickly turned to dismay. One of the metal circles had cycled open, and she was facing a super-heated container of lava.

Oh, Talhan was going on her no-go list.

"Someone has hurt our friend. He had his wing cut off. Our healers haven't been able to grow him a new one. We were hoping your healers would help," Tania babbled

Tania kept Wolf, Belfar and Shari's faces clearly in her mind. She was here for them.

"The best way to ask for help rarely involves assaulting one of my creations." The clipped, curt voice came from behind her.

A chill skittered up Tania's spine.

The metal disc on the bird cycled closed. The noises of the others on the street fell away. Tania gulped as she turned.

The tall being before her wore purple, which nicely offset her blue skin, enormous eyes, and bald head.

Another accompanied her. A being seated in a hovering chair, who looked, in comparison, rather grey. She had all four arms were crossed.

They were both glaring mightily.

The fierce looks didn't wipe Shari's expression from her memory. "Please, I meant no harm. Our friend needs help."

"So do all who come to Talhan's shores." The tall one leaned in and stared, uncomfortably closely to Tania's face. "Few are willing to pay the price." She gestured to the being in the chair. She had slumped over, drool gathering at the corner of her mouth.

Tania stepped back and crossed her arms. "Really?" She sent out her Innarn to lift a pebble she'd pocketed from the garden. It hovered next to her head for a moment before shooting it directly at the being in the chair.

Zana gasped.

The surrounding beings echoed the noise as they finally lifted their heads from the screens to watch the drama.

Flashing through the distinct colours of Innarn—the brightest of purples, clearest of yellow, sunset orange, fiery red, clearest green, brilliant blue, shining silver—the pebble sped through the air towards its target.

It got closer without the two making a move to stop it. For an instant, Tania regretted her actions and was just about to call the pebble back when the being in the chair snatched it from the air.

'I hate playing the victim.'

The tall one laughed, and Tania's sigh of relief faded into the noise of the crowd.

"You have heard of me?" the tall one asked curtly.

"You must be the technomancer." As soon as the word fell from her lips, Tania wished the ground would swallow her up.

The technomancer's face did a funny scrunching thing, which looked like she wanted to scream, laugh, and glare at the same time. Instead, she yipped as the one in the chair came forward and poked her in the ribs.

'Told you the theatrics would come back to haunt you. I'm Xani, and this is Temira. We're the heads of the techno Innarn centre on Talhan, also known as the technomancers. Why don't we find somewhere to talk?'

Bravely ignoring the scolding she was getting from Zana, Tania graciously bowed her head–'Like you didn't just threaten to assault the head of the Techno Centre with a rock!'–"That would be lovely. Thank you."

With Zana muttering in her mind about diplomacy, and Temira grumbling out loud about technomancy, Xani and Tania led the way, Tania trying to tune out their complaining the whole time.

When they stepped into the shade of a hulking, cubic building, Xani turned. 'You must be here on behalf of Wolf Dawn. I've sent word to Talhan's Linked. I'm afraid he has failed to respond.'

Tania's shoulders slumped.

'We do, however, have a screen you may use to talk to him.' Xani added.

"Brilliant! Thank you."

Temira led them to a room off the side. Plush, white stools surrounded a clear crystal table.

'Please, take a seat. We shall call him and then leave you to speak,' Xani sent.

Tania looked at Zana for the correct etiquette, and followed the Ilutri's lead, sitting primly on a stool next to her.

Temira did something, and the form of a man rose from the table. He wavered slightly, like they were on the opposite side of a pool of water. Xani sighed and tapped what must have been the controls. The image cleared up, and they were looking at the back of his head.

The blue-skinned healer cleared her throat, and the man whipped around as if he'd been stung.

"Healer Temira! Well met," he said, an amiable smile on his face. "And you brought friends! Didn't know you had any."

The death-promising stare the healer levelled at him didn't seem to faze him at all. Tania had the impression he'd seen it too many times.

"Cyrus, it is my pleasure to introduce Ronah's Linked, and Rakemyst's Linked." Temira bowed her head slightly, then slipped out of the room with Xani.

"So, you're Talhan's Linked." Tania lent forward, ignoring Zana's sigh at her lack of decorum. "We have a favour to ask."

Shari sat at the Guardian's kitchen table opposite Sam and Jon. Platters of roasted vegetables were scattered along its length, and a glass of chilled rutenberry tea by each plate.

Sam looked slightly tense and kept eyeing the yellow bowl containing the bread rolls.

"Are you okay?"

His head snapped towards her, fist gripping the handle of the knife in his hand tight. "No."

"How can we help?"

"The yellow is... the poison..."

Jon flicked his fingers. All the bowls changed to blue.

His apprentice took a deep breath and relaxed. "Thank you."

"I'm not here to make things harder for you," Jon said, scooping up some roasted carrots. "I'll beat you down in training often enough as it is."

Sam smiled as he narrowed his eyes in the Guardian's direction. "You sound so sure."

Even though Shari could tell he was teasing, she cleared her throat and said, "So, how should we set this up?"

"What do you mean?"

"I need to train, patrol, teach, go to school, see my family, get to know the Returned and the former candidates, and fix Belfar's wing." She paused the motion of spooning more grilled green spears on her plate. "It's a lot."

"They're all important," Jon admitted. "School and teaching are taken care of—you have hours allocated to those tasks. Patrolling you do at night. We can do training on the weekend, and spend time with the Returned and former candidates then too. It may help if we all move into the castle."

"Why do I need school when my job is protecting the Realm?"

Jon sighed. "You only have a few months left. The Altoriae is a lot more than just fighting. You need an understanding of the people you're protecting, how they act and react. A straightforward way you can learn this is to finish school."

Shari sighed. "After I finish school, I just end up going back again to teach. And to move into the castle at this stage..." She shook her head.

Fork halfway to his mouth, Sam shook his head too. "I've found that I rather enjoy having my own space."

"The former candidates and those of the Returned who have yet to find a house are still there. There are a lot of bodies to add three extras to the mix," Shari added doubtfully.

"I'd prefer you did at the very least, Shari. You need someone to keep an eye on you, or you wouldn't sleep at all."

Shari wanted to refute him, but found she wasn't able to deny the truth. "Can we leave the moving until after we've joined with Talhan? It's not that far away now, only a few weeks. Or maybe wait until there's more space?" She hated how desperate she sounded.

Jon sighed. "I can understand wanting to wait." He took a bite and chewed thoughtfully. "Has there been any luck with Belfar's wing?"

It was Shari's turn to sigh. "No. All the healers on both Ronah and Rakemyst have tried. Wolf's back though, and he said if we can get Belfar to Talhan in time, there may be someone there who can help."

"Temira. Of course."

"Who?" Sam frowned.

"Temira. She's originally from Ulnan."

Sam started coughing, choking on a bite of food.

Shari frowned, but he waved away her concern, taking a large drink instead. "How can she?"

"She's skilled at combining healing and technology. She's made more advances in the healing field than anyone else. Temira might have something for Belfar's wing."

"I hope so," Shari speared another potato. "If she can fix Belfar's wing, perhaps she can fix your friend's burns. And make sure you're all clear from the poison, Sam."

"Are you suggesting I'm still under the effects?" he asked coolly.

"No. But sometimes poison can slow down your healing or your reflexes, and it makes our job so much harder."

"You speak from experience?"

"Yes," Shari said. "I think I'm up to twelve times now?" She looked at Jon.

"Thirteen. I still say the bite from the ekrix on Flachaeus was green."

Shari rolled her eyes. "It'd been eating plant matter. It would be green."

"And swollen?"

"Well..."

"And leaking..."

"Can we not talk of green pus over food?" Sam interrupted. The quirk of his lips gave away his mirth.

Despite the lightning-quick sending between the two men that ended with Sam smirking and Jon looking about the colour of her ekrix bite, Shari played along. "Back to training!" she said brightly. "How about we rotate out and each take two nights off a week to train with Sam?"

Jon seemed to take an extra-long time to chew his food. "Two nights each? Would you be okay with that?"

"I think," Sam drawled, "it would be best if I learn how you do things."

Shari had a funny feeling as Jon gave his new apprentice a sharp look, but shoved it down in favour of finishing the last morsel on her plate. "Brilliant," she said happily.

Jonathan noticed the change in his wards the instant before his front door burst open.

"Great news!" Tania said, ducking the plasma bolt from Shari and dodging the blade Sam threw. Eyes wide, she looked at the knife sticking out of the hanging plant by the door. "Alright, already! I promise I'll knock next time."

As he rose from the table, Jonathan was grateful the knife hadn't stuck in his door this time. "You say you have news?" he asked, pulling the blade from the trunk of the plant and gently encouraging the wound to heal.

"Talhan's Linked agreed to the quicker joining. We should meet tomorrow."

Jonathan handed the knife back to Sam, who looked mildly shame-faced.

"Talhan's Linked is quite accomplished. It'll be a long day for you though, won't it?" he asked.

Tania shrugged. "It's worth it."

"Brilliant. I'll let Wolf and Belfar know. We can spend get him to the meeting point so he's the first across," Shari said, rising from the table.

"We still have to have the ceremony," Jonathan said. He winced as he reminded her, but it was necessary. If they skipped even one ceremony, the conjoining would not end well.

"We've figured that out, too. There is an ancient ceremony where only the Linked are involved in building the bridges. I'll create Ronah's, Zana will create Rakemyst's, and Talhan's Linked will meet us halfway. He says he's happy to do both, but if the Altoriae wants to stand by his side to do one, he'd be grateful. Personally, I think he just wants to meet you, Shari." Tania winked.

Shari wrinkled her nose. "If meeting him means Belfar gets help sooner, then so be it. When is this meant to happen?"

"Tomorrow, at dusk."

All three spoke at the same time. "I'll be there."

It was a rather pleasant way to end dinner.

Clearing the table was the work of mere moments after the others had left. Jonathan whistled as he set the dishes washing themselves.

His thoughts were still with the man who had needlessly risked his life so Jonathan would be able to see again. The mere idea that Zac had spent so long searching for a cure to an injury which didn't exist and wasn't his fault had Jonathan in two minds. Zac was either the most stubborn man alive, or the best friend he could ask for.

Hands stuffed in his pockets as he walked up to the museum, Jonathan found he couldn't figure out which one it was.

He had a meeting with Pala of the Ducibus, and then he was patrolling, which was sure to make him concentrate on other things.

As he stepped through the doors of the museum, he remembered what it was like to walk through the halls with Zac as part of his patrol group—the ghosts of laughter and gentle teasing seemed to echo as he reached out for the double doors.

Pala, face hidden by zir grey robe, was already waiting for him.

'Well met,' Jonathan sent. 'Is there anything to report?'

'Bazaven has a small group of Ofanahni refugees waiting by the gateway, hoping for sanctuary from a Sylpan attack. The gateway for Wiaxatale has been under attack for the last half-day. We've sealed it so none may cross. There is also an envoy from Atlantis requesting a meeting with you and LoneWolf of Rakemyst.'

'Are the refugees in any immediate danger?'

'They are safe for the moment. But you will want to meet with them before the night is out.' Pala's thoughts showed the Sylpans getting closer, and it would be disastrous if he didn't reach them first.

'Are they a good fit for Lissae?'

'One family group is not. They will cause trouble here. It would be better to send them to Ellevar. The others will flourish on Lissae if they so choose.'

'Then I suppose that's where I'm patrolling tonight. Let me know if anything happens with Wiaxatale. And as for the Atlanteans...' The memory of Ronah's scream as the red light cut through her surface was enough to make the fine hairs on his arms stand up. 'They can wait a while longer for their answer.'

Even under the hood, Jonathan sensed Pala's censure. 'A *day more* won't hurt,' he grumbled.

The Ducibus shook zir head.

'Pala, how often did Zac use the gateways?'

'He came through frequently until about six months ago. When he entered Atlantis, he stayed there until you found him.'

'Huh.' Jonathan still wasn't sure what to think. It was like a string was pulling him back to the Healers Centre, back to Zac's side. But right then, he had a patrol to run and refugees to evaluate.

Pala nudged him in the correct direction, and Jonathan found there was already a patrol group waiting. Samuel stood with his arms crossed next to Edward Thorne, who was looking uncomfortable as he tried to engage the new apprentice. Had Edward done the same for Joshua when he'd first started training? Mortimer, Talofa, and Elani stood chatting off to the side.

The trio on straightened, looking ready to dive into battle. Edward nodded and Samuel smirked at him.

Suppressing the desire to roll his eyes, Jonathan greeted them all. "We have a different kind of patrol tonight. There are a bunch of refugees requesting access to Lissae, but they are being hunted by a group of Sylpans. Our job is to get them through the gateway safely with as many of their possessions as possible. Not all the group will stay on Lissae, but we must ensure they reach the Hallways first. Questions?"

"How likely is it that this is an ambush?" Samuel asked.

If the question had come from anyone else, Jonathan would have sidestepped it, but it was genuine. "Lissae has a certain reputation on the Realms. Beings from all over know how fiercely we defend our borders. It is also common knowledge that if they need a safe spot, we are here for them. I will not lie to anyone. About a third of the time we get calls like this, it results in an ambush. Half the time, patrol members getting injured by whatever is hunting the refugees. One in ten go smoothly."

"Prepare for the worst, then?" Elani piped up.

"Always." Jonathan smiled grimly. "Are we ready?"

"How do you want to play this?" Samuel hadn't moved from propping up the wall.

"Samuel and Edward, take the outer flanks. I'll take the middle front, and you three, stay behind me, fanning out between us all. If I start firing, you all join in. Remember, the refugees are seeking aid for a reason. Try to be gentle. Many times, they'll strike first and regret it later."

Samuel pushed off the wall and joined the rest of the group. "Sounds good."

"Let's go."

Pala nodded to the Ducibus on the side, who opened the pale-yellow door slowly. Jonathan saw why when sand spilled out into the hallway.

Jonathan took point. As he walked through the door, a wave of heat immediately rolled over him.

The desert stretched before them like a never-ending sea of sand. Off to the left was a cluster of tents sheltering a group of beings.

The heat prickled his skin. He was overdressed in the pants and long-sleeved tunic he had on. Still, if things went smoothly, they'd all be out of the heat soon enough. His crossbow snapping into existence, he led the patrol group towards the tents, testing every step with Innarn for traps before he made it.

Two lengths from the tent, there were steel traps strong enough to take his leg off buried in the sand. He silently motioned for the others to stop before he disarmed them. Samuel, of course, wandered off to the side.

'There's something big coming this way.'

Now Samuel had pointed it out, he could see a plume of sand was being kicked up in the distance *'Let's move fast.'*

The group in the tent were looking at them with wide, terrified eyes. One of the younger girls fiercely clutched a wooden spoon. Her expression reminded him more of Shari ready to strike than of the scared adults around her.

"Well met," he said. "We are from Lissae. I hear you are seeking refuge?"

"We are," a woman sobbed. There was an elder next to her, grey hair tied tightly on her head, who gave the woman a pat on the knee. She looked more weary than terrified. How long had she been on the run for?

"We are few. They took most of our men," the elder said in broken common tongue. There were only three men in the group—one so old and frail, Jonathan wasn't sure how he was even standing. Another was barely a teen, but was battle-scarred and missing part of his arm.

A single glance at the third was enough to tell Jonathan he would cause trouble. Out of all the group, he was the most affluent. Rounder than he was tall, he had two weary girls fanning him with books as he lay panting in the heat.

"Took you long enough to get here," the man grumbled when Jonathan gazed at him. "We've been waiting hours!"

The elder clucked her tongue. "We are grateful for your help, Guardian."

"This boy isn't the Guardian." The fat moustache on the man's lip was fairly trembling with outrage. "The Guardian is a man of wisdom and age! Why would he lower himself to talk to the likes of you?"

Jonathan allowed himself a long blink before he sent a quick message to Edward.

"Are you going to follow the directions of my team or not?" Edward asked in a bored voice.

The elder looked mortified until Jonathan winked at her. She hid her chuckle under a groan as she got to her feet.

The refugees packed their belongings and took the tent down in a few practised moves. Although, much to Jonathan's disgust, the round man forced the two girls to continue fanning him as he watched their progress.

Tent dismantled, his team gathered everyone for the brief trip to the gateway.

'We have incoming in less than five minutes,' Samuel warned.

"Time to go," Jonathan announced cheerfully. The round man struggled to his feet, so the Guardian gave him a nudge. "We need to move."

A girl looked back and whimpered, almost falling to her knees.

"Nope." Elani pulled her up. "You've come this far. You're stronger than this." She marched the girl towards the portal, murmuring more encouraging words.

'Samuel?'

'I'll bring up the rear.'

Something in his send told Jonathan his new apprentice was aware of what was creating the dust cloud. *'That's not the Sylpans, is it?'*

'Far from it.' Samuel looked grim, and his Innarn was becoming so dense, he would change soon. *'Get them out of here.'*

"Hurry!"

The group made their way, slower than what Jonathan wanted, towards the gateway. He pushed everyone through and turned back to see Samuel hadn't moved. He was still standing where the tent had been, and the dust cloud was almost upon him.

"Samuel!" Jonathan screamed. He called upon the darkest part of his Innarn to reach out and yank his apprentice towards him. Together in a tangle of limbs, they fell through the gateway.

It slammed closed with a terrific bang.

Their panting was the only noise in the hallway for a long moment.

"Well, if this is the way your team acts, I'm surprised you let them off-Realm at all!" The round man was blustering. He dusted sand from his breeches and glared at everyone in sight.

'*Get him and his family and lead them to Ellevar,*' Jonathan sent to Edward as he extracted himself from under Samuel. '*Make something up about how it's better suited to his class.*'

"My team was able to get you out of a sticky situation at no minor risk to themselves," Edward said stiffly instead. He stared down his nose as the man tried to draw himself up as tall as Edward.

Jonathan couldn't help a chuckle. The elder nudged his ribs with her elbow, and they both reached down to help Samuel to his feet.

'*I was fine!*'

'*You were almost dinner.*'

Samuel's golden eyes narrowed as they locked with his. '*You do care.*' The words, for once, did not sound mocking.

'*Of course,*' Jonathan sent. '*You may be the cause of great distraction and make me worry more than is just, and we may have far more cultural differences than similarities, but you are, and always will be, my first friend who wasn't from Lissae.*'

The man was still blustering in the background as Edward led him and his small family away.

Samuel slumped and gazed at the ground. '*I struggle to understand how to act around friends.*'

The last word even sounded foreign leaving his mind.

'*But I think I am learning. I hope you'll continue to be patient with me.*'

'*As patient as I'll be in our lessons,*' Jonathan promised, and grasped Samuel's forearm. Samuel grinned at the old warrior greeting, and Jonathan shivered at the brush of claws as Samuel grasped his arm in return.

"Now the rotgut is gone, what shall we do, Guardian?" the elder asked.

The reduction in the refugees' remaining bundle of belongings was quite alarming, but Jonathan was adept at hiding his reaction. "We have a place on Lissae for you to settle. There is a continent purely for beings like yourselves who have been displaced. It is split into four regions—snow, plains, desert, and jungle. Do you have a preference of where you go?"

"Are we limited in movement?"

"Not at all. You can go wherever you like. Many find it's more comfortable to start out there and then go exploring before they settle down. Some never settle down."

"I like the heat of the desert." It was the girl with the spoon. Many of the others around her nodded.

Jonathan bowed his head. "As you will it. Follow me, please."

'No test to see if they're true?' Samuel sent.

'The first step through the doors will be the test. If they can't take it with ease, then there is something more at play.'

'Did you do the same thing for me?'

'Lissae herself tested you,' Jonathan admitted. He didn't tell his apprentice of Lissae's silence since then.

The patrol group guided the refugees through the hallway until they came to the double doors. 'Pala?'

'The things I do.'

Jonathan heard the smile under the grump.

At the Ducibus' nod, he opened the doors.

The group behind him gasped.

Orange dunes rolled towards the horizon. In the far distance, shimmering in the heat, Jonathan could make out the tips of tall towers. On the right of the gateway was an oasis, complete with a lagoon and gentle green hills.

There was something about leading the group to their new home that made everything he did as Guardian of Lissae worth it.

"Edward?" he called.

The older man jogged over to him. *'Thought I'd never be rid of the blowhard.'*

"Mind giving me a hand?"

"Of course, underling." The elder quirked his lips, trying to hide his mirth.

Jonathan laughed and shook his head. Together, they pulled on the sand, creating a wall a click out from the oasis. Mortimer baked the wall, and it set hard enough to withstand the wild banoume who might try to wander through. Edward turned his attention to crafting some permanent structures.

As soon as the first one was up, Talofa started filling it with things which might come in handy—bolts of cloth, beds and bedding, food, hunting equipment, cooking implements, basic medical supplies, and a crystal so they could call if they needed anything.

"On the horizon, you can see the town the Teeldrit has put together. They're friendly, and willing to trade or help. They have been where you are—new to Lissae and not sure how to fit in. I'll make sure someone checks on you in a week, but please, if you need any help, reach out."

Elani showed the girl with the spoon how to use the clear crystal. She took in everything with serious eyes, nodding and poking at it.

They didn't have the strongest Innarn, but he detected it humming under their skin. It was possible they weren't even aware they had any. The thought disappeared when the elder stepped next to Edward and adjusted the next structure, making it go deeper into the ground, with only the first storey showing.

He saw the moment she hit the water. The way she adjusted her design within a split second was more than impressive.

Jonathan's patrol group spent the next few hours pleasantly helping the group settle in. Every little exclamation of joy tugged on his heartstrings as they discovered something new.

Eventually, it was time for them to go.

'*Pala?*' Jonathan sent out. He had to push extra Innarn into the send to make sure it reached the Ducibus.

'*I'm sure you weren't this demanding when you were younger.*' The head Ducibus was in a particularly grumpy mood tonight.

'*You know we appreciate how much you work guarding and guiding for Lissae.*'

The send was so quiet, Jonathan barely heard it. '*Can't even get a break on my natal day.*'

Zoemer's rocks.

'*Shari! I need the cakes and bottle of honey mead sitting in the middle shelf of the cool room at the tavern delivered to the museum as quickly as possible, please.*'

'*Sure, Jon.*' If she'd been asleep, she didn't sound it.

The double gateway opened off to the side of the wall around the oasis. The patrol group bid their farewells and slipped straight through the doors.

As soon as they'd closed, Pala roughly opened them again and almost kicked them out. Shari was waiting for them, grinning.

'*Happy natal day, Pala!*' she sent.

A grey hand slid from the end of the robe's long sleeves and gingerly touched the cake, scooping some frosting onto the tip of a finger. Ze's hand disappeared into the hood, and Pala hummed.

Jonathan couldn't help but grin.

'*Don't think I didn't hear that send, Guardian,*' Pala sent as ze took the gifts, giving Shari a little bow.

'*I did get it ready earlier. I've just been distracted.*' Jonathan winced, even as he sent it. Distraction was something he couldn't afford.

'*If you didn't run away, you might not be so distracted.*' Pala nudged him out of the gate and closed it firmly behind him.

Jonathan sighed. The Ducibus gave excellent advice, but wasn't sure if he was ready to listen.

"Come on. Time to get some rest. We've got a joining to prepare for tomorrow." Shari nudged his shoulder with hers.

"I'll rest if you do," Jonathan replied. Samuel was looking back at the double doors. "Coming?"

Samuel gave one last look and easily caught up to them. "Rest sounds good."

"Is the poison still bothering you?" Shari asked.

Watching Samuel's natural reaction to deny any weakness fighting against his desire to answer truthfully was painful.

"I'm guessing you'd say yes if you could," Jonathan said.

His apprentice seemed to deflate a bit. "Yes. My organs are struggling. I need to go somewhere to change."

The frown crossing Shari's face said she knew more about Samuel's form than he'd been aware of.

"Can't you change in your house?" Thankfully, she still didn't seem aware of just who his new apprentice really was.

Before he had to watch Samuel come up with a reason as to why he couldn't change in such a small space, Jonathan butted in. "What about your sanctuary?"

"For all that you two are amongst the most formidable beings when you are not on Lissae, you seem hopelessly incapable of defending yourselves on your own Realm." Samuel scowled, crossing his arms over his chest.

"I can come with you," Shari said. "Then you won't have to worry."

He didn't have to look to know the panicked gaze Samuel was giving him. Part of him was tempted to draw it out. Now Shari had mentioned it, it was easy to see how sore Samuel was just from the way he was holding himself.

"Rest, Shari. Preferably in your sanctuary, so we know you're safe. I'll go with Samuel."

"I was in bed before you called me to get cake." She yawned, cutting off her next words.

"I bid thee well." Samuel bowed slightly.

"Feel better soon," Shari whispered and disappeared.

Jonathan reached out and smiled when he detected the Altoriae was safely in her sanctuary. He just hoped Shari would get some sleep.

"Shall we?"

"You don't have to." Samuel looked far smaller than Jonathan was used to seeing him.

"What are friends for?"

Chapter Eight

Samuel took hold of the Guardian's arm and shifted them both into his sanctuary.

The walls and ceiling were still compacted dirt, but the room had been enlarged just enough for him to change. Silently, he moved the rough-hewn furniture to the sides. The sanctuary rumbled for a moment before a crack appeared in the wall. Dirt fell away, leaving a doorway large enough for his current form to get through. He pushed the furniture through it. It wasn't much, and the craftmanship left a lot to be desired, but he'd made it when he was first learning how to use this body.

He wasn't about to crush it under his natural bulk just because a bit of poison was slowing him down.

Preparation complete, Samuel turned to the Guardian. "You don't have to see this."

"Not like I haven't seen it before," Jonathan said. He conjured up a stool and smooshed himself against the corner of the room.

"Ready?" After a nod from the man claiming to be his friend, Samuel turned his back.

He flexed his shoulders, shook out his arms, and allowed the change to come over him.

'*Shield!*' he sent to Jonathan. Without waiting, he released a breath containing the last of the poison in his system and chased it with a blast of flames so hot they burned clear.

He shook out his body from snout to tail tip, and admired the golden scales of his forelegs as he turned and sat primly before the Guardian.

Jonathan was looking at him with the same wide-eyed disbelief which had been written all over his face when they'd first met. "There is something so utterly magnificent about you." He looked at his hands clasped in his lap. "I believe I've figured out something. In all of our interactions outside of Lissae, you seemed so sure of everything, so totally in control of each situation. And I think that's what I expect when you're on Lissae. You don't entirely feel the same way, do you?"

Samuel tilted his head. Maybe the Guardian had more than rocks for brains. '*My entire survival on Lissae is dependent on your goodwill and on your word. Tell me, if roles were reversed, would you feel in control?*'

Jonathan took a long moment to think about it and finally shook his head. "Probably not, no. But you must realise, I'd never kick you out on a whim."

'*Just knock me out when I least expect it.*'

He winced. "I am sorry."

'*Remind me to let the next assassin stab you a few times first.*'

The Guardian laughed, taking his joke as it was meant. "Do you feel better?"

His scales flared out before he made them withdraw back under the skin. Samuel shook his wings one last time and returned to the form he'd been using for the last few months. "I do."

"Good. Why don't you rest up here, and I'll head on home?"

Samuel tutted. "I wasn't joking when I said you both are horrible at defending yourselves on Lissae. Either we both stay here or we both go."

Jonathan looked torn. "I..."

"This about the being in the Healers Centre?"

He sighed. "Yes."

"Back we go then." Samuel shifted them to the doorstop of the Healers Centre. He gave a wave and slid into the shadows before the Guardian even thought to argue.

Now he was ready to tackle the thing in the dust cloud on Bazaven.

Wolf baulked when his third in charge, Varlee, came in to say it was their turn to patrol the shore of the Mainland, her eyes determinedly fixed away from Belfar's bed.

"Go," Belfar said tiredly. "You wouldn't be you if you didn't go."

Whatever the healers had him on, it made him so agreeable that it didn't sit well with Wolf. "I'll stay and you go," he said to Varlee instead.

Belfar huffed. "I'm jus' gonna sleep anyway," he slurred.

Wolf sighed. Joining with Talhan couldn't come soon enough. Time away from the Atlantean healers saw Belfar's health slipping backwards, even with the green glow from Shari constantly hovering over his back. What injuries had she dealt with in order to learn how to heal at such a distance? He dreaded the answer.

"Fine," he grumbled.

He pushed off hard from the balcony, Varlee only keeping up with him out of sheer stubbornness.

The rest of the group were already waiting. At his nod, Varlee opened a portal to the mainland in the middle of the sky. They flew through, one by one, arriving above the dense jungles which lined sheer cliffs.

Each Ilutri team patrolled a section of the shoreline once every moon. Last time, it had been Belfar by his side, and they'd still been giddy with new love.

'*Fly,*' he all but snarled.

None of the group spoke. They just shot through the air like arrows, the light from the dual moons glinting off the white feathers scattered amongst Trainor's wings.

This stretch of shoreline was tricky. You could never be sure what was waiting in the trees. The creatures of Lissae would mostly leave the Ilutri well enough alone, but the beings were another thing all together.

Tonight, when he wanted a fight, it seemed all clear.

Or it did until a whooshing noise and a frantic '*Incoming!*' sounded in his head.

Wolf didn't even hesitate as the chain net whooshed between him and Trainor. He pinned his wings to his back and streaked towards the forest, aimed directly at where it had come from.

As he fell, he gathered the surrounding air, ready to shape it however he needed.

Using the force of his landing as a focus point for his motus, he sent a portion of the air out in a wind blast. It pushed against the trees and plants, flattening a circle around his landing spot for at least a click.

There was no one around.

Surely there had to be someone waiting, someone to take his frustration out on? He growled.

A low groan and a rustle told him the falling trees had merely squashed a being or two, rather than cause a fatality. Wolf strode over and reached through the branches, pulling out a spotty teen by the front of his shirt.

"What do you think you're doing?"

Wolf gave him a shake and the teen's head tilted wildly.

"Protectin'," he slurred.

"We're here to help you. Not be shot at," Wolf snarled, trying to ignore the last time he'd heard someone slur.

The teen lolled his head around, taking in the destruction the wind blast had wrought. "Don' look like it."

"We keep you safe," Wolf growled and dropped the teen at his feet.

"From the things tha' go bump in tha' night?" the teen sneered, showing a missing eye tooth.

"Do you think you can fight them off by yourself, boy?" *Vebnah's breath, he was sounding like his father.*

"Better fightin' them than alongside a feathered freak like you." After hocking phlegm, the teen spat at his feet.

Rocketing into the sky, Wolf pulled all the air back which he'd used to flatten the trees. If it sent the teen stumbling a bit, well, he was too high for his smirk to be seen.

'Let's get back,' Varlee sent.

With a sudden ache, Wolf wanted nothing more than to be by Belfar's side. He nodded and was through the portal before it finished opening.

Anika stared at her critically.

Shari tried hard not to fidget, reminding herself that Anika would not throw weapons or fireballs at her anytime soon. Although her shoes might be deadly.

"Breathe. It's not like you haven't had all the attention on you before," Anika said, batting Shari's hands away as she tugged on the hem of the top.

It was covered in feathers. Anika said it represented her Ilutri heritage, but when Shari had stolen a glimpse in the mirror, the costume had reminded her more of an overgrown crow.

"You'd be far more stunning if you stopped pulling at it." Anika spun her around, and Shari's jaw dropped when she saw her reflection.

The midnight-black top was a sleeveless version of her armour. Black feathers adorned the shoulders and hem, with silver embroidered feathers on the bodice. The tailored trousers with silver buttons running along the outside of both legs from the knee down set off the stunning outfit, and she felt far more comfortable in them than the skirts she'd been offered. Anika had relented and let her wear her boots.

"I hope you appreciate how much effort it takes to *not* show the line of your boots in those pants."

"I really do," Shari breathed. She had trouble looking at her own face. Her eyes were bigger, somehow, and her cheeks sharper. Her hair was braided in a style she might get used to—at least for special occasions.

"Good," Anika said. For the first time, she didn't sound combative.

"You've done an amazing job, Anika." Shari meant every word.

"You've been... surprisingly easy to work with."

Shari giggled. "Thanks."

"Better get going. The ceremony will start soon." Anika moved to put her make-up away.

"You're not coming?"

"Why would I? It's for Innarnians."

"Anika, put a make-up brush in your hand and you're just as talented as any Innarnian," Shari said.

The girl fluttered a brush in her direction and turned her head away.

"Come on. I can't have my stylist moping around at home. We need to move!"

"Oh, alright then!"

Shari arrived on the outskirts of the cemetery and turned, stone-faced.

The surrounding crowd was laughing and talking, but tension was in the air, and most were holding weapons of some sort. Almost instinctively, they'd split into three primary groups: those lining the edges of Ronah, looking out over the water, ready for when they joined; those along the back wall of the cemetery, prepared for an attack from behind; and those in the middle, who were standing amongst the gravestones, prepared to cast shields around the ones who weren't able to.

"I shouldn't have come," Anika muttered.

Shari eyed Anika's father, who was frowning in their direction. "I hope you're ready for this."

"Ready for what?"

"Anika, I can't believe what an excellent job you did! I just had to have you close by when we joined with Talhan! I'm sure there'll be so many people who want to meet you." Shari was being as over the top, but as genuine as she could.

Slowly, Anika's father stopped frowning, and turned back to the rest of his group.

The other girl clutched Shari's wrist for a moment and smiled before being swept away by her chattering friends.

Shari made her way to the front, where Tania and Jonathan were waiting. Higher than them, on the other side, Ilutri troops circled where Zana and the elders were standing. Her family was up there. Wolf was ready to carry Belfar straight to the Healing Centre on Talhan as soon as the bridge was done.

A low, long horn sounded, and a crystal-like chime answered. Across the water, heading towards them at a rapid pace, was Talhan.

The third Shifting Island got closer and closer.

Shari made out the silhouette of people standing on the shoreline. Talhan sped nearer still, with no sign of slowing.

"Ah, Tania?" Shari said.

"Trying to..." Tania sounded strained.

Out of the corner of her eye, she saw Collis step up behind her and reach out to touch Tania's shoulder. Immediately, tension drained from Ronah's Linked.

Shari smiled to herself. The tall Returned boy was good for her friend.

Her smile faded as Talhan drew closer. The Linked had all agreed to speed the joining up, but she had a feeling that Talhan was either testing his siblings or had forgotten how to slow down.

Shari braced herself before sending her Innarn out to curl around the most vulnerable on each of the isles, hoping she'd reached them all.

They were close enough to see the colours worn by the beings on Talhan—oranges, pinks, purples, and greys. Their outlines were blending in with the fading light.

Talhan was closer again. She could see the whites of their too-wide eyes. Voices from all three Shifting Islands rose in alarm.

Right as the sun slipped below the horizon, the islands met with a terrific crash.

Water splashed up, soaking those closest to the shores. Beings were jostled, many falling to their feet.

There was a rather indignant wordless yell from Rakemyst, which, from the gravelly tone, Shari suspected was her uncle.

She laughed softly, knowing he and Belfar were safe.

Across the gap, Shari spied a man with his arms stretched wide. She shifted in next to him.

'Well met, Talhan's Linked.'

'Please, Altoriae, call me Cyrus.' He threw her a smile over his shoulder and drew his hands together in a booming clap. Red crystal pillars rose out of the rumbling ground in four locations, two for each bridge.

Two of the pillars were a fair way from where Cyrus was standing. Through a form of Linked Innarn she didn't understand, Shari was both simultaneously next to Cyrus, and standing before the farthest set of pillars. 'What do you want me to do?'

'Build the bridge between here and Rakemyst's Linked. Make sure we connect each part to the red crystal. They're anchor points which will help to stabilise the bridges, no matter what Talhan's mood. Much as I love my isle, she can be a bit irritable at times.'

'That's promising.' Shari sent out tendrils of Innarn, which poked around to see what was available to use. There were a lot of foreign things in the hands of the beings behind her on Talhan, but she wanted something else...

There. A sign on the air, a slip of breeze, and she grasped Zana's bridge of air as it spun out towards her. With a rush of will, and water she pulled from the ocean below, Shari used it to join the land to Zana's half of the bridge. Dotted along the shore were sparkling bits of opaque crystal, glinting in the light of the flashing Innarn coming from Cyrus and Tania.

With a flash of whimsy, Shari lifted the crystal and slipped it into the water, making it glitter and shine. From across the new bridge, Zana smiled at her.

Together, they wove the railings, ensuring the bridge would be safe for all to cross. As soon as the last piece was in place, SilverCloud came striding over, Wolf, with Belfar in his arms, right on his heels.

"Beautifully done!" SilverCloud smiled at her.

"Thank you," Shari said shyly.

"I didn't think you'd make the halfway mark for a moment, Altoriae," Zana said. She looked stunning in a pale-yellow robe which tied around her neck and bared her back and wings.

"I came through in the end," Shari said easily, ignoring the twinge in her consciousness.

"That was *amazing!*" Tania said, crossing the bridge with Jonathan and Collis by her side. "Wow, what a *rush.*"

'*Innarn drunk,*' Jonathan sent to her. '*Collis was almost holding her up at the end and pushed through more Innarn at the same time Ronah did. She should get through the rest of the night fine but will probably sleep all day tomorrow.*'

'*Would if I could.*' Shari grinned at him.

A throat cleared behind her, and Shari turned to find a delegation of Talhan's Elders waiting to greet her.

"Well met, Altoriae. Guardian. Rakemyst's Linked. Ronah's Linked. We welcome you and yours to Talhan," a stately man said. He wore a pale purple suit and a slightly darker head wrap. "May we explore your fair isles?"

Zana and Tania stepped forward as one. "Well met, Talhan's Linked, Talhan's Elders. We welcome you and yours to Rakemyst and Ronah."

Beings from Talhan were already streaming across the bridge. She detected the mild shock from those on Rakemyst and Ronah, and pointedly didn't look at Jon.

"I'm afraid our young don't particularly stand by tradition anymore," the elder said.

"Elder Juniper!" one of the others protested.

He sighed. '*Or take well to criticism.*' "I bid thee well," he added with a bow.

"I bid thee well," Shari chorused with the others. She sensed the elder was the bridge between the young and old on Talhan and didn't envy him the job at all.

Collis stepped up behind Tania just as Cyrus turned to her.

"Talhan's Linked, in the flesh!" Tania grinned, bouncing on her toes a bit.

"That'd be me. Cyrus Petram, Linked and all-round goof of Talhan." Cyrus was almost as tall as Collis. He was dressed like the others, but in brighter colours.

Shari sensed the energy of the people surrounding him and frowned. It'd be rude to ask what was going on.

Tania, apparently, had no qualms. "Why don't they like you?"

"As far as the people of Talhan are concerned, the Linked are from a bygone era and serve no purpose other than ceremonial." Cyrus shrugged. It seemed the reaction of Talhan's population had ceased to bother him some time ago.

"But... but... we do so much more than that!" Tania spluttered. She looked like she was going to explode from indignation.

"As Ronah's Linked, you're different. I've heard people talking about you. You've built roads, new houses, and made the crops flourish, and convinced the island to fight to protect the people! How? Oh! You have so much to teach me!" Cyrus reached for her hand, and Collis smoothly blocked the move with his body.

"You even have your own bodyguard!" He poked Collis's chest and grinned.

Shari giggled at their antics. The weight of an intense gaze made the skin on her forearms prickle. She attempted to glance around casually. A large group of curious teens were leaning against the wall of a building, staring at them.

They wore darker colours than the others, their clothing patched and tired. Talhan's residents seemed to swarm by them as if they didn't exist—countless eyes sweeping over their forms without really seeing. Many had scars or limbs which glinted in the crystal light. Some wore eye patches, and one had a mask over the right side of his face.

As Shari gazed at the group, they moved closer. A girl in grey so dark it might as well be black cleared her throat.

"Huh? Oh. Right. Eva, gang, meet the Altoriae. Altoriae, this is my friend Eva, and her, uh, friends." Cyrus gestured to the group.

Eva snapped her heels together and thumped her fist on her chest above her heart. "Well met, Altoriae." Her short, blue hair did nothing to hide her missing ear or the vicious burn along the side of her face.

The military-style greeting coming from a girl she suspected was younger than herself had Jon giving her a swift poke of Innarn to close her jaw before it fell open. "Well met, Eva of Talhan. Friends of Eva."

"We, ah, like your outfit," a girl called from the back. She had a dusting of freckles over her cheeks and nose, and a scar through an eyebrow.

"Thank you. Anika of Ronah designed it. She did all the embroidery too." Shari twirled on the spot, right as Anika walked by. "Anika!"

She turned to look, and the girl with the freckles gazed at her with wide eyes. "You *made* that?"

Her stylist stood a little taller. "I did," she said, with more of a grin than a smirk.

"It's amazing! Do you give lessons?"

"I hadn't thought of teaching. I suppose I could work something out." Anika mused.

The girl grinned and self-consciously flicked her head, her fringe falling almost into her eyes—an efficient way of hiding her scars.

Shari dropped a little more of the glamour she'd almost forgotten she'd put up, displaying some of her old scars.

Eva gave her a tight-lipped smile—one survivor recognising another.

"Bit rude to wear feathers in front of the Ilutri, innit?" a guy off to the side asked.

"Not when I'm half Ilutri myself." Shari tried to tone down the bite in her words, but the feathers ruffling on her shoulders gave her away. She slanted a look at Anika, who was absorbed with the girl who'd asked about lessons.

"Ohhh!" The group ribbed him.

Amongst his protests of not knowing, Shari smiled at Eva. "I'm afraid I have some family to track down. It was nice to meet you. I bid thee well." Shari nodded and turned to follow Cyrus.

"We'll see you again soon, Altoriae," Eva said coolly. She spun back to face her group and squeaked, grabbing the hands of the girl closest to her.

As Cyrus led them deeper into Talhan, Shari smiled at the whooping behind her.

"She's a problem, that one." Cyrus sounded fond.

"What do you mean?" Shari found she was more focused on the people than on the buildings, despite the looming walls either side of the wide street.

"Always ready for a fight. Thinks she has to save every orphaned kid. Wants to make the world a better place." He sighed. Shari could tell he was more than half impressed with her tenacity.

"Sounds like we need more Eva's around."

"She's also superb at getting into trouble." He sidestepped, and the footpath underneath his feet started moving.

Shari blinked and shrugged. She stepped on with SilverCloud, her parents, Jon, Tania, Collis, and Zana. SilverCloud's guard were loitering nearby. They would count to fifteen before jumping on the moving sidewalk behind them, so as to not crowd her grandfather.

"Where will this take us?" Jon asked.

"To the Healing Centre where your uncle and his mate await. Usually it'd be easier to use the slip stream, but seeing this is your first time on Talhan, I'll take it easy on you and start small."

"What is Talhan like?" Samuel asked Lizbeth as he guided her through the graveyard and across the bridge. They'd waited on Ronah until most of the crowd had gone before starting out, and Sam was grateful when he saw how many people had streamed across prior to the ceremony.

"They're different from us." Her voice was soft, and she was slightly hesitant as they walked, despite the firm grip she had on his arm. From the moment they had announced the convergence, Lizbeth had almost curled in on herself, like she'd been protecting her underbelly.

"Perhaps I am defending myself," she murmured, reading his thoughts again. "On Talhan, issues like my vision are a thing to be cured, not a difference to be celebrated and worked with."

"Wouldn't a cure be a good thing?"

The sadness in the tiny sigh she let slip seemed to cloud the surrounding air. "My Realm, for all it is the epicentre of life, is peaceful. We are aware of the threats, but they mostly take place in arenas where I do not dwell. My lack of vision does not equate to a lack of sight. For when you take away one sense..." She turned her head and gazed sightlessly up at him. "...it can enhance others."

A shiver ran through him. That was how she read his thoughts—through a shield which had been unbreachable for centuries.

"I have a niece who moved to Talhan from Ronah. She was determined to cure me. Mind you, she didn't ask first. Those who are able, rarely do. They assume we all want to be like them. So, she moved here and discovered a cure." Lizbeth took a shaky breath. "It involved removing my eyes and replacing them with crystal orbs which worked via Innarn. It thrilled her, as it did her peers." Again, Lizbeth seemed to get smaller. "She was not so thrilled when I turned her down."

Mindful of the surrounding crowd, Samuel leaned closer and whispered, "I can eat her for you, if you'd like?"

Lizbeth snorted. Before she said anything, she stiffened.

Samuel threw a shield around them both, head swivelling to see where the threat she sensed was coming from. More than a few people were looking their way, askance.

"Hello, Aunt Liz." The outdated word dripped with scorn.

Samuel glared at the woman before them. She wore a sharp suit, which did nothing to disguise how thin she was, and heels tall enough that she was almost able to look him in the eye.

'I could use her as a toothpick?' Samuel sent.

Lizbeth tutted at him and smiled. He smirked.

"Well met, Mara."

When the uncouth niece rolled her eyes, Samuel noted the left glinting unnaturally.

"Talhan is not the place for stuffy formalities."

"But is, apparently, the place for jackets so sharp they cut cleaner than a blade." Samuel found he wasn't able to curb his tongue. Tradition had its place, just as improvements did. This creature had no right to berate her elder for merely greeting her politely. 'I'm sure if I boiled her for a bit...'

'Samuel!' Lizbeth was laughing on the inside. "You're correct. I rescind my statement." Her words were gentle, but her features were steel.

Mara waited for another greeting and huffed when she didn't get one. "I see you've updated the seeing-eye palon for an actual human. I hope she's paying you well."

His eyes start to glow. It was an odd sensation. Rolling his shoulders, Samuel tried to ward off the change he sensed coming.

Before he opened his maw to devour the thing before him, Lizbeth spoke. "I see far more clearly by myself, thank you."

"I spent my life working to help you, only to find you were an ungrateful, spiteful wretch!" Mara leaned in, almost spitting in her aunt's face. "On the day you were to regain your sight, there was no one on the operating table. No one to prove the augmentation would work. You left me adrift with no anchor!"

"What did you expect? I never asked for you to do any of that."

"Yes, but when you weren't there, the elders still wanted proof. So I gave it to them!" Mara spun away from them.

"What did you do?" Lizbeth reached out, hand hesitating over her niece's exposed back.

Where was her blade? He had one handy, if she needed it.

When Mara turned around, she held one of her eyes. "I volunteered."

The empty socket was strangely compelling, but the glare he got as she popped her 'augmentation' in was less so.

"Mara, no." Lizbeth sounded like she was mourning.

The twig of a niece sniffed. Mara spun on the spot and strode away.

"I think she'd require a *lot* of seasoning to get the bitterness out," Sam mused.

With a watery huff, Lizbeth gently squeezed his arm. He patted her hand before they set off again to see if Talhan offered anything more pleasant than an angry, augmented healer.

CHAPTER NINE

Shari took in the big, rectangular building before them. It looked far more intimidating than the Healers Centre on Ronah.

"Here we are," Cyrus said cheerfully, casually stepping off the moving path at the wide expanse before the front doors. Shari moved off, wobbling slightly. Jon and Tania looked like they'd been doing it their whole lives.

When her grandfather went to get take a step, he stumbled, and would have fallen if Collis hadn't caught him.

SilverCloud let out a rather undignified noise. "You get used to the moving so quickly!" he huffed.

Shari ignored her heart skipping in her chest and looked towards the doors of the building before them to hide her reaction. Her mother and father flanked SilverCloud, who snorted, and took a few stumbling steps until he was next to Shari.

'You'll keep me from falling on my face, won't you?' he sent with a grin.

Nodding, Shari tried to smile back at him, glad his gaze was drawn away before her face fell. She sent out a few tendrils of Innarn, wrapping them around SilverCloud and ensuring he'd appear steady on his feet. *'You're all set.'*

"Where would you be keeping my son and his mate?" SilverCloud asked.

"Oh, not me. Temira is working with him now, I'd say. I'll take you to her lair." At Tania's horrified look, Cyrus laughed. "This way!"

They entered through tinted sliding doors into an echoing chamber, no doubt designed to impress, before leading them to another set of smaller doors in the wall. "In we go."

Shari looked at Jon, who shrugged. Tania and Zana stepped into the box. Zana appeared far from pleased, but she merely tucked her wings in and lifted the skirt of her dress slightly so it wouldn't get trampled.

Gamely, Shari and Jon joined them, the others following until they were all crammed in.

"Should have made two trips," Cyrus muttered, and the doors of the little box closed.

A light came on, and something dinged.

There was a critical moment where the walls seemed to close in on her, but Shari breathed through it, hoping no one noticed.

The doors opened after half a lifetime, or half a minute—she wasn't sure. They all piled out.

If anyone had asked, Shari would deny using her Innarn to get the others out so she could exit the box faster.

Cyrus grinned sympathetically. He was sending rapidly with Tania and Zana as they walked along the corridor towards another door.

Shari opened it without a word and stepped through.

As soon as she crossed the threshold, Belfar's screams hit her like a physical thing.

She made to rush forward, but a wall of pure Innarn was keeping her from him. As she raised her hand to smash it to pieces, someone grabbed her wrist.

Eyes full of plasma, Shari turned, ready to crush whoever was trying to stop her.

It was Wolf, who looked as devastated as she felt.

"They have to recreate the wound for it to work," he ground out.

There was another scream, and Shari's eyes filled with tears.

"They have to open it the same way."

Shari turned her back to Belfar and held her uncle's hand as tightly as she dared. Her dad came over and took hold of his other hand.

"Said they'd make it so he won't remember the pain after." Wolf's gaze was resting heavily on Belfar. How he was able to stand beside her and not rush in?

He ground his teeth together as Belfar screamed again, and the grip on her hand grew tighter.

Collis led Tania and Zana out. SilverCloud leaned heavily against the wall across the hall, surrounded once more by his guards. Guards Belfar and Wolf were normally part of.

Just when she could take it no more, the screams faded to whimpers.

'Please work.'

Not entirely sure Wolf had meant to broadcast, Shari turned to watch the next part.

The tall blue-skinned being Shari knew to be Temira was slapping something over the freshly bleeding stump of Belfar's wing. His entire body trembled for a moment.

"Come on," Shari whispered.

"Work," Wolf pleaded.

Bones shot out of the stump. They were quickly wrapped in skin, feathers sprouting as they watched. Belfar gave a moan of relief and passed out.

"Belfar!" Wolf cried. He wrenched away from the hands holding him and pounded on the wall of Innarn.

Temira leaned over to do something at Belfar's head, while a lady Shari had overlooked in a hovering chair waved a hand and the wall came down.

Wolf skittered across to his mate's side. "Belfar." His voice broke.

"Hey, Wolf." Belfar sounded groggy.

Shari slapped a hand over her own mouth to stop from crying out.

Scrubbing at tired eyes, Belfar yawned and rolled onto his side. He stretched his arms and wings out. "How'd I get here?" He glanced around the room in confusion.

'You bumped your head.' The lady in the chair sent smoothly. 'Your mate was worried and brought you in for healing.'

"Ah." Still looking confused, he spotted Shari and her parents. "Well met," he said, bemused.

"Sorry I wasn't here to help." Shari fell into the lie easily. "I was out patrolling. Came as soon as I heard. Wolf's a worrier, isn't he?"

"Eh. I knew what I was getting into." Belfar shrugged, and his new wing moved. Behind Shari, Arilla muffled a sob against Calem's chest. "Must have been a big bump. My back is all stiff."

'Altoriae, if you would.' A smooth voice came into her mind.

Shari glanced at the woman in the chair, who gestured at Belfar. She shook her head. There was no way she was going to take his memories of what had happened.

'Time is a great healer.'

Blinking, Shari frowned. She looked over at the woman and something clicked. 'Oh. Yes, I think...'

She slipped into Belfar's mind. It was easier than she'd thought it would be. As she peered around, she was surprised to see how disorganised everything was. There were feathers everywhere, almost like someone had burst a pile of pillows. Shari reached down and picked one up. She let herself fall into a memory it contained.

Swiftly, she flicked it away. She pulled on the memories from the time they'd left for Atlantis with her Innarn. A bundle of feathers muddied with anxiety and pain rushed towards her. Shari gathered them close and wove a net around them.

'Jon?' Her voice echoed strangely in the mind of another.

'Here, Altoriae.'

Reassured, Shari tugged on the net, making it tighter and infusing it with Time Innarn. She pushed everything she had into the net, wrapping the brown feathers in enough time so they eventually faded to a pale tan.

'Shari? Come out now.'

'Just a bit more.'

'Now, Altoriae.'

With a sigh, Shari let the net fall open, and the tan feathers floated to the floor. As she retreated from Belfar's mind, she sensed the difference the piece of extra time had made for him.

As she swayed on her feet, Shari detected Jon's reassuring presence by her side. 'You are amazing,' he sent to her.

A tingle surrounded her skin, and she wearily raised her head to see what was causing it. Collis nodded at her grimly.

'Thank you,' she sent to the woman in the chair and to Temira. 'He wasn't... this is... thank you.'

Temira huffed. 'We'll call it even.'

Shari didn't understand what she meant, but she nodded anyway.

"Well, if you're all better from your bump," Cyrus said, coming into the room, "I can show you the sights."

"Sights?"

"You were really out of it, Belfar. We've joined with Talhan already. Come, let's have a look around." Wolf helped his mate to his feet.

"How hard did I hit my head?" Belfar ask as Wolf led him into the hallway.

The weight of the earth above them suddenly became too much. *'Mind taking us up?'* Shari sent to Jon.

"Meet you there," Jon called out. He shifted with Shari and her parents to the surface.

"What did you do?" Calem asked as soon as they were standing in the cool night air.

"Made the memories of Belfar's torture seem like they'd happened a long time ago. Time heals wounds," Shari said tiredly.

"You can do that?" Arilla asked.

"Apparently. Haven't had to before." It was tempting though, now she'd done it once, to go poking around in her own head.

"Don't you dare," Calem and Jon said together.

"Am I broadcasting?" Shari asked, dazed. She wanted to sleep for a week.

"No, we just know you too well." Jon looked alarmed. *'Promise me, Altoriae.'*

Heaving a sigh, Shari nodded. *'My word, Guardian.'*

Behind them, on the wall of a building, an image appeared, showing a wrinkled hand holding a glowing orange pill which reminded Shari of the ones SilverCloud took. The hand raised and popped it into a mouth. Sparkles ran along the image and the wrinkles faded, leaving behind smooth skin.

"Maybe I need some." Shari gestured.

"Don't you dare," Calem repeated, half-heartedly glaring at her as the others came out of the building.

"Cheaters!" Tania sang as she skipped over to them.

Shari stuck her tongue out.

Linking her arm through Shari's, the younger girl pushed a dose of healing Innarn her way.

Belfar was gazing around at the smooth, straight lines of the buildings. It seemed like the only people left on Talhan were from Ronah or Rakemyst. Everyone from Talhan was exploring the other Shifting Islands.

"This is our cultural centre. We just came from the Technomancy Centre."

"I thought it was the Healing Centre," Arilla said.

"One and the same. Temira is both Head Healer and—" he paused and wriggled his fingers, looming towards them "the technomancer."

The crystals flashed and a noise like plasma and thunder made them all jump.

Cyrus laughed. "She asked me to set it up! Anytime someone says the T word, it happens."

"I did not ask you to set it up. You did it to annoy me," the Head Healer said stiffly as she walked towards Cyrus.

Talhan's Linked jumped. "But... but..."

'Can you imagine Temira putting in a request like that? It was me.' The woman in the floating chair was laughing at them.

"Xani." Temira sighed, her fondness badly disguised by fingers tapping against her other arm. Turning back to the others, she said, "I am retiring for the night."

Xani bumped her chair into the taller woman. Another sigh, and the Head Healer said stiffly, "I bid thee well."

Her voice was so flat, they might have to pick the words up from the pavement.

They stepped and floated onto the moving slip stream. Xani gave them a smile and a wave as it whisked them away.

"Technomancer," Cyrus whispered, just loud enough for them to hear. The crystals flashed and boomed and Temira glared at him as it whipped her out of sight.

"Our turn. On we all get." Talhan's Linked enthused as he ushered them onto the moving path, and they all obligingly stepped on.

As they travelled past buildings, Cyrus pointed them out. "The library is over there with the school on the other side. Farther down this path is the university and training field, although it's mostly used for sports."

"We have few forests and little farmland left, but there are what we call the Seven Provinces of Talhan, one for each lot of Innarn." He waved his hands in a complicated pattern, and their path merged with a different one, speeding them off to one of the provinces.

Shari caught a glint of something out of the corner of her eye as they were whisked away. *Must be the moving picture on the wall.*

"This is one of my favourite parts of Talhan. The Old Province."

The buildings here weren't as straight as the ones in the cultural centre. Many were crammed together, sharing walls, and an entire row shared a single angled roof. A few beings waved from balconies as they passed by below.

"I grew up here," Cyrus said proudly.

Compared to the newer part of Talhan, the Old Province looked run-down and in need of a colour change in some places, but Shari sensed the centuries of living the walls had held. The lives and losses, smiles and tears.

"It's beautiful." She beamed at him.

Shari noted the path slowing just before Cyrus ushered them off as it went by a fenced park. Despite her limited earth Innarn, she could tell the decreased speed was a recent change. Perhaps out of respect for SilverCloud and the newly healed Belfar. She still kept her Innarn wrapped around her grandfather as he stepped off the path and back onto unmoving ground.

The park was stunning. It had the only tree around, a great, big sprawling thing, with roots wide enough to lie on and branches spaced exactly right for climbing to the top. Soft orange-tipped grass let out a tangy, earthy smell as they walked on it. Boulders inviting tired beings to take a seat dotted the ground in strategically. Flowers weaved in and out of the fence which appeared to be made of timber rather than crystal.

"Wow!" Tania sighed.

"This is where I was when I first found out I was linked with Talhan," Cyrus said.

Shari saw the moment as Cyrus remembered it, standing with a hand raised to stem the blood dripping from his forehead from the rock someone had thrown. A dazzling orange light scared his attackers off, and he'd thrown his arms up, blinking. When he'd lowered them, he'd been in the heart of Talhan.

His blinding grin let Shari know he'd meant to share the memory with her. She beamed back.

Talhan was not what she'd been expecting.

In a cold, quiet room, pieces of discarded technomancy lay on the table, ready for the next day's work. The clicking of metallic legs echoed through the silent room. Something scraped against the steel table leg. There was more clicking as it came across the bits on the table.

'*Who's there?*' an orange crystal asked.

The clicking stopped for a moment.

The half-destroyed Atlantean tech turned on the spot, its one working light erratically flickering under the blood it had gathered from the original creator.

It had a bigger purpose now. Much more than eyes.

'*Who's there?*' The crystal glowed as it sent.

The Atlantean tech pulled itself nearer to the glow, light dulling as the machine got close enough to touch.

Close enough to drill.

In her quarters, Xani woke and screamed. Tangled in the covers, she frantically tried to free herself before her movements came to an abrupt stop.

Eyes glowing orange, Xani smoothed the covers over her legs and lay back down.

Now and then, her hands would twitch slightly.

In the back of her mind, where she was still herself, she was screaming.

Samuel smothered a yawn as he wandered down the hallway of Talhan's Healing Centre. He'd hoped to find Shari and Jon here after escorting Lizbeth home.

As he passed a thick, metallic door, a noise chilled his blood.

It was metallic scraping, and a sound he doubted the humanoids were able to discern. A sound like cracking and screaming and pain, but on a level he'd never heard before.

Frozen to the spot, it took Samuel a moment to notice the other noise. The one Tania, Shari, and Jonathan had all mentioned before.

The scuttling.

He leaned closer to the door, and the noises stopped.

Silence.

He shook his head. Clearly, he was hearing things due to lack of sleep. Something he was learning this body needed more of than he was used to.

He was half-tempted to open the door to see what was on the other side, but something stopped him. Trouble for Lissae could mean good things for him. And if it wasn't trouble, well. Some of his fondest memories involved screaming.

Samuel walked away, absentmindedly smoothing down the fine hairs at the back of his neck. Was there was a draft? He had those little bumpy things on his skin, too. He resolved to ask Lizabeth about it.

Reaching the end of the corridor, he turned the corner, ignoring the noises that started up again.

CHAPTER TEN

When Belfar woke the next morning, he'd never felt better. He didn't know what type of healing they practised on Talhan, but he wouldn't say no to it next time he got hurt.

He frowned as he flexed his wings. One didn't feel the same as the other. Perhaps he'd pulled something when he hit his head? Attempting to ignore the odd twinge, he slipped out of bed.

Wolf mumbled something behind him.

"Time to get up, sleepyhead. We've got another Shifting Island to explore!"

Wolf grumbled, but swung his legs out of bed and snagged Belfar as he went to walk away. When he buried his face in Belfar's belly, he was trembling.

"Hey. Hey, Wolf, what's wrong?"

"Bad dream," his mate muttered. "There was a saw, and your wing. I thought I'd lost you."

Belfar ran a soothing hand over his shoulders. "I'm here. You can't get rid of me that easily."

"Good." Wolf's voice was even more gravelly when he first woke. Belfar kept stroking Wolf's shoulders until the trembling subsided.

"Let's see how your dad is going," he said.

Wolf grunted as he got to his feet and stole a quick kiss before slipping past to get ready for the day.

A sappy smile on his face, Belfar flexed his wings again and went to join him.

Breakfast with her husband's family was easier than Arilla remembered, particularly now Belfar was healed.

Sometimes, his regrown wing reflected the light in a way far from natural. How long it would be until he figured out what had happened? She didn't entirely agree with taking his memories away, but understood why Wolf would want him to forget the horror he'd gone through.

"Have I said how glad I am that you've taken over the cooking?" Belfar smiled as he loaded his plate.

"You can say it again." Arilla preened.

This morning, in honour of his recovery, she'd done a spread of his favourite food: oven-baked eggs with a tomato herb sauce, savory telmi muffins, and generous slices of grilled stone fruits drizzled with honey.

"Dad not up yet?" Wolf asked, settling next to Belfar.

"Not yet. I'm worried about him. Those pills don't seem to do any good."

"If it's the same thing they gave me, he should be on top of the Realm!" Belfar grinned and closed his eyes in bliss as he chewed, missing the look the others shared.

"I think it's a different formula," Arilla said finally.

"It might be."

He was so agreeable, it almost broke her heart. Would he feel the same way knowing what had happened to his wing?

"Talking about me again?" SilverCloud looked rumpled, but nothing unusual for having just rolled out of bed.

"Only when you're not around," she said cheerfully.

Calem nudged her. "We're just concerned."

"Old age is nothing to worry about. Soon enough, I'll be back with your mother and causing all sorts of havoc in the Spirit Realm." SilverCloud floated small portions of everything onto his plate.

"I can just see you creating trouble now. And RainbowMist trying to get you out of it." Arilla smiled softly at him. An orange glow flared in SilverCloud's eyes as he met Belfar's gaze. Had anyone else seen it?

Her head snapped around, and it was in Belfar's eyes too. The sight made her shiver. When they glanced at their plates again, the orange glow faded.

If she wasn't the mother of the Altoriae, she'd chalk it up to a trick of the light or a coincidence. But there was something unhealthy about that glow.

She needed to get the message to Shari right away.

"Any plans for the day?" Wolf rumbled.

"I've got to get back to the tavern and do some work. I think we will be inundated with beings from Talhan over the next few days." It would be the perfect excuse to talk to Shari.

"I thought we would take some time off." Calem frowned.

"Before the joining. But we..." She looked up from under her lashes. "...got our dates mixed up. I'm sure the novelty will wear off soon enough."

"And then we'll be joined with Cantash."

SilverCloud, orange tinting his eyes again, twitched his head to the side. "When?"

"About a month. Maybe more."

"Hmm." He was mechanically shovelling food into his mouth.

Arilla couldn't wait for breakfast to be over.

Even surrounded by kids, Samuel hadn't been able to chase the sensations from last night away.

"You're distracted," a childish voice accused him.

"Yep."

"Why?"

He looked down at the tiny child. She was the one with the Dark Innarn who he'd taught to shield. It took him a few beats to remember her name. Laura.

"What do you do when you don't feel well?" Samuel asked.

"Tell my mum," she said immediately.

Samuel frowned. If he told his maternal equivalent he 'had a bad feeling' he wouldn't survive long enough to take his next breath. "What if my mother isn't around?"

"Tell a friend."

This little girl was so firm in her belief that talking would help. Perhaps there was wisdom in one so young?

"My turn," she said. "What do you do when the light hurts you?"

"Are you referring to physical light or Light Innarn?"

She scuffed her shoe on the ground. "Both."

"When the physical light hurts you, a shield might not work. Typically, shields are created to stop Innarn, or to stop weapons. Be adaptive. Wear long sleeves and shade your face with a hat."

The girl looked at his bare arms and rolled her eyes. "What about Light Innarn?" She scrunched her face up, and he wasn't sure if it was the thought of wearing a hat or because she was in pain right now.

"If you practise your shield, it will help against Light Innarn. Be careful though, because sometimes the Light can be helpful."

She scoffed and shook her head, dark hair falling into her eyes.

"It can," Samuel chided as gently as he could. If her wide-eyed expression of horror was anything to go by, he needed more practise. "Think of the Altoriae, or the Guardian, or the healers. They're all lighter

Innarnians. If you need healing, you'll have to lower or adapt your shield to let them help you."

"Is that what you had to do when you got hurt?"

Samuel's senses zeroed in on her. "How did you know I was hurt?"

"You didn't come to the school for ages, and I got super worried, so I..." She leaned in, like she was telling a secret.

He knelt to her level.

"I asked the Altoriae!" she said in the loudest whisper he'd ever heard.

He shook the ringing out of his ears and smiled grimly. "You must be brave."

"Not really. I try to be."

"Practice shielding," Samuel said, getting to his feet. He'd have to have words to Shari about not revealing when he, or Jon, were injured. "I want to see how well you can shield by the time we join with Cantash."

"Okay!" she said and skipped away like she didn't have a care in the world.

Lissaens. Samuel shook his head again.

School was out and Tania grabbed Collis's hand as he walked past her at the gate. "Want to explore Talhan some more?"

He smiled down at her. "If you so wish."

Tania was practically bouncing as she pulled him through Ronah's streets, through the cemetery, and across the bridge.

It looked like school had just let out on Talhan as well. Students were milling about everywhere. Most were stepping off the slip streams and heading straight for the bridges, although there were some coming from Ronah and Rakemyst. A guy with a bad burn on the side of his face brushed passed her. Maybe he hadn't heard about Talhan's healers.

Even with all the people around, Tania was glad none of the mechanical birds were heading her way.

"Well met, Ronah's Linked!" Cyrus walked towards her with a stack of books cradled in his arms, a mechanical bird trailing behind him, chittering mournfully.

"Well met, Talhan's Linked!" Tania trilled back. "But please call me Tania."

"Talhan's Linked." Collis bowed. "I believe there may be something wrong with your... pet."

"Ugh. The B.I.R.D. He gets disappointed because I don't need his help often."

"Why not?"

"A few years ago, Temira and I worked on ways to keep everyone connected, and to make sure Innarnians and non-Innarnians could use all the advances. We came out with portable crystal slabs for everyone, regardless of their Innarn level. But beings were bumping into each other. They got so sucked into their slab they forgot to look up. Xani devised the Bio Instructor for Relative Distance, or B.I.R.D., which acts as both a guide and a guard."

"Yeah, I found out the hard way." Tania winced, remembering her first trip to Talhan.

'*You are never leaving Ronah alone again,*' Collis sent.

'*I wasn't alone. Zana was with me!*' Tania protested.

"I'm working on a portable crystal device which can be worn around your head, but everyone's become attached to their B.I.R.D. and they baulk at the thought of giving them up." Cyrus sighed, drooping slightly.

"Why can't they have both?" Tania asked.

"It'd make sense." Talhan's Linked said. "But it's hard to change their minds. Beings wants the tech without the consequences."

"Wait, you *make* some of this stuff?" Tania blinked.

"Yeah, I do. Wanna see?" Cyrus swung the bag on his back around, rummaging inside it.

"How about we go somewhere with less of a crowd?" Collis suggested.

"Good idea. How do these slip stream thingies work?" Tania asked as another being was whisked away.

Cyrus cleared his throat. "Step onto the platform and think about where you want to go. You need to picture it in your mind as if you were shifting there."

"I... I don't know anywhere on Talhan apart from the Healing Centre."

"Then you'd better hold on to me."

Tania looked at Collis, who raised an eyebrow and nodded. He grabbed Cyrus's elbow firmly, and she did the same on the other side.

"Let me introduce you to my workshop." Cyrus grinned.

And they disappeared.

"This is..." Collis said.

"Yeah." Cyrus beamed at them, leaning against the softly glowing crystal wall and letting them take in the view.

Tania looked around the enormous cavern. Orange crystal walls held thick wooden benches cluttered with all manner of objects: cogs, springs, hunks of metal. In one corner, a furnace was spitting...

"Is that lava?"

Cyrus grinned. "No, it's my crucible. I use it to separate out metals."

"And this?" Collis was holding a part of some machine about as long as her arm. It was long and thin with a circular wire skirt on one end and a handle and trigger on the other.

Carefully prying it from Collis's hands, Cyrus laughed nervously. "That's a... it's a defensive weapon for non-Innarnians."

"How does it work?"

"A plasma Innarnian puts some plasma into this container, which screws on here, and then a non-Innarnian can point and press the trigger to deliver a blast." After gently placing the weapon down in an empty space on the cluttered bench, he turned back to them.

Tania plonked heavily onto the floor. "Huh." Her mind was whirring. Her mother and stepfather could have used a blaster when the Chirea attacked, but she dreaded to think what her father would have done with it.

"It sounds to be both helpful and dangerous," Collis rumbled.

"Which is why it's in here, and not in the hands of those who might misuse it." Cyrus shrugged. "This is what I'm most excited about at the moment." He led them to the far side of the room, past more benches filled with incredible things.

One held lots of long metal tubes with little triggers and a bulbous container on the top. Another held tiny gears and springs, and the thin crystal shell of the thing floating above the bench. It turned as if it were tracking their progress across the room.

"Talhan is all about making life easier for those who don't have Innarn. We can use the technomancy to create something to benefit larger mainland populations where Innarnians are scarce."

For a moment, Tania's vision clouded, and she remembered her father throwing stones with unnerving accuracy at the fleeing Ilutri who'd dared to land in his yard. The Ilutri had been bleeding already, feathers damaged from a horrific hailstorm. It was only as she'd tripped and fallen that Tania had seen the small, swaddled bundle. Tania had jumped up and pulled on her father's arm, ruining his next shot.

She'd copped the strap for her actions—hadn't been able to sit down for a week. But it had been worth it. The Ilutri woman had gotten away.

Blinking, Tania found herself standing in front of an aqua box as large as she was. There was a handle on the one side. If she tilted her head right, she could make out something inside it. "What's this?"

"A cooler." Cyrus rocked on his heels and shoved his hands into his back pockets. "This machine will help people on Lissae to keep their food cool, even if there's no Innarnian for a hundred clicks."

"How does it work?" Collis asked.

"It's essentially a giant water box. The water is held between thin sheets of crystal, and at the back, there's this." Cyrus reached around and pulled at something. The aqua walls of the box dimmed. He held up a glowing black cylinder.

"A crystal?" Tania asked.

"Not just any crystal. It's been programmed to harness the Innarn running under the very surface of Lissae and use it to do many things. It allows non-Innarnians to move around quickly without the need to queue in potentially dangerous slip streams, the ability to talk to family on the other side of the Realm, keeps food fresh—the possibilities are endless!"

He seemed so genuine and enthusiastic that Tania couldn't bear to burst his happy bubble. "You have so many amazing things here!"

"You have weapons here too." Collis pointed out.

"We get a lot of non-Innarnians who want to defend Talhan, or Lissae. Some ache to go out on patrol. But we see the worst of the injuries faced by patrollers here, and it's scary. Some non-Innarnians came to me and asked if I could develop something for them, so I've been working on it in my spare time. It's more Xani's project than mine, though."

Tania couldn't imagine Xani designing something which would hurt people.

"You know the best thing about Innarn-designed weapons?" Cyrus asked.

She shook her head.

"There's a chip of orange crystal in each one which is programmed to only let them be used for self-defence. They can't be used if the being wielding it is wishing to cause harm."

Her father's face came to mind again. He'd been terrified when he'd thrown the first rock. Furious, but terrified. "What about the people who believe with all their heart they're acting in self-defence, but they aren't?"

"What do you mean?" Cyrus asked.

Tania shared the story of her father, the rock, and the Ilutri woman. She left out the part with the strap.

"Hmm. Yes, I suppose if someone thought like him, the chip wouldn't work." Cyrus slumped. "Back to the drawing board."

"I'm sorry," Tania murmured, wringing her hands.

"Don't be! More information means I'll be able to perfect these before everyone gets one and just starts firing at random. I'd much prefer to wait than for these to end up in the wrong hands."

"If you say so," she said.

"What's this?" Collis asked, pointing at a big black cube of crystal with orange flecks scattered through it.

"It's an Innarn-bank. An Innarnian can pump excess Innarn into it, ready to use at a later date. I used this to add extra power to Talhan's shields when we upped the joining date."

"Which is appreciated." Tania nodded her thanks.

"And this?" Collis reached out to touch a smooth, black disc.

"No!" Cyrus shot a tiny bolt of plasma out, stinging Collis's hand.

Collis flinched and pulled away.

"It's an anti-Innarn disc. It'll drain your Innarn if you touch it. I don't even know why it's out of the case. I have to use B.I.R.D. to handle it, but then he'll need a recharge. It drains anything with Innarn."

Tania shivered as Cyrus directed his B.I.R.D. to place the anti-Innarn disc back in the case. What would happen if Belfar was to touch it, now they'd made one of his wings of crystal and Innarn?

CHAPTER ELEVEN

"Shari, I'm glad I caught you!"

Juggling the box under her arm, Shari turned to face her mum. Ronah's residents moved around them as easily as the changing tide, leaving the two Dawn women standing just outside the Quiver and Quill Tavern.

"What's up, Mum?"

"Something happened at breakfast this morning, and I'm not sure what to do about it." Arilla was wringing the towel in her hands so hard, Shari was slightly concerned about threads going everywhere.

"What happened?"

"Belfar and your grandfather. Their eyes glowed."

"Glowed?"

"The same orange as the medicine..." Arilla trailed off as Calem came out of the tavern and slung an arm over her shoulders. "I'm sure it's nothing."

Shari frowned. If her mum had taken the time to track her down, it must be bothering her. "I'll keep an eye out."

Arilla sagged, and Calem pulled her closer. "What are we watching for?"

"Glowing orange things."

"Only seen Dad's medicine do that."

Shari forced a smile. "Good to know. I better keep going."

"We love you." Arilla looked a bit teary.

"I love you both, too. I'll be by so often, you won't know I'm gone."

Calem grinned at her and hugged Arilla tighter. "Go on, before your mother decides to lock you in the back room."

Shari gave a watery laugh. *I'm only doing this to pacify Jon, Shari* reminded herself. *The house is still there, and I can move back any time.*

Hefting the box in her arms, she shifted into the foyer of the castle.

It was rather more anti-climactic than she'd expected. There was no one around. Slowly, she climbed the stairs, heading for top level. Tradition dictated that she add on to the structure herself, creating another layer for her to move into when she decided to properly live in the castle, but she wasn't ready for such a mammoth task just yet.

As she made for the next set of stairs, something pulled her to the side and down a hallway. She followed the tug on her Innarn and frowned as she stood before an old, scuffed door with a faded nameplate which read *Kay'imi.*

Bumps skittered over her skin. Shari balanced the box under one arm and gave into the temptation to run her fingers over the nameplate.

It changed.

Shari Dawn—welcome home.

With another shiver, Shari whispered, "Thanks, Kay'imi."

The door swung open and Shari stepped in.

The room looked as if it had just been cleaned. It smelled faintly of lemon and rosemary. All the furniture sparkled like new, and the covers had even been turned down for her.

Shari set her box on the desk and inspected every corner of the room. There was nothing personal here which had belonged to the first

Altoriae, but there was something about knowing she was walking the exact same floor, touching the same mantle, would sleep in the same bed.

Okay, on second thoughts, she hoped the mattress had been changed some time in the last two and a half thousand years.

A gentle tap at the door drew her out of her thoughts. Mu poked her head into the room. "Well met, Altoriae."

"If we're going to be living in the same space, you need to call me Shari."

Mu grinned. "All right, Shari. Wanna come downstairs? Dealon's almost done baking, and it's not to be missed."

Her first response was negative, but Shari found herself on her feet, the word "Sure," slipping out before she could stop herself. "If you insist," she grumbled towards the empty room.

"What?" Mu glanced over her shoulder.

"The spirits are chatty here."

"Oh, the castle is full of them! Isn't it great?"

"I guess I'll find out." Shari grinned, but poked her tongue out. Kay'imi's laughter chased her from the room.

One benefit of living on the first level was definitely how close she was to the kitchen. The smell was divine.

The former candidates were crowded around the kitchen bench. They were staring at Dealon as he pulled a pan out of the oven.

"Mmm, what ya making?" Shari asked.

Dealon jumped, but the pan remained steady in his hands. "Berry cake."

"Yum!"

"You don't have to be polite," Dealon muttered.

"His mother was notoriously critical. He's insecure about his cooking," Mu whispered loudly.

"He is right here."

"And he made my mouth water from all the way upstairs," Shari said.

Pink dusted his cheeks as he eased the cake onto a cooling rack. "We can wait for icing, or eat it now."

"We have to choose?" Amara looked comically dismayed.

There was a grumbling sound. The former candidates glanced around.

Shari rubbed her belly. "One vote for now."

"Lucky I always make two with this lot around. Would you like to cut the cake?" Dealon held out a knife.

"Chef's honour," Shari said, shaking her head.

Blushing, Dealon cut them all a generous slice and watched Shari take the first bite.

"This," she said, poking the cake with the fork he'd given her, "is better than my mum's."

Ducking his head, Dealon flushed again, right to the tips of his ears.

"So," Amara said after she'd cleaned the last crumb from her plate. "What's this about the Altoriae Guild?"

Raven nudged her, hard.

"Are you trying to stuff me full of tasty food to butter me up?" Shari said lightly.

Amara elbowed Raven right back. "Nah. I figure we've shown enough for you to know if you want us to be members or not."

Again, the words slipped out of her mouth before she thought them. "You're in."

The former candidates looked at each other.

"Really?" Talofa squeaked. The Uleulan's blush fairly glowed under her translucent skin.

Shari wanted to scowl at Kay'imi's spirit, but she kept her face smooth. "I'm happy to have you if you want to be here. But you should think about it. You've already seen one fatality. There are bound to be more. Other guilds would be far safer."

"Not safer," Lira said. "Ignorant. Something is building. We can all sense it. We want to be a part of protecting Lissae from whatever is coming."

Shari took a deep breath. "Then, you're in," she repeated. But this time, her words were her own. Abruptly, she stood. At the threshold, she paused. "Mind you, if any of you decide to follow in Kodan or Therdon's footsteps, you'll be less than ashes."

Shari slipped away before they could respond. She fled back to her new room, where the nameplate now just read *Shari Dawn*.

"I never thought I'd have my own guild," Shari said to the empty room.

A gentle laugh echoed through the sunbeams sparkling on the floor. It almost drowned out the low growl which came from the shadows.

Shari flicked an orb of light from her fingertips and had the impression of something big. The door slammed shut, startling her into turning her head away before she got a good look.

When she turned back, the room was awash with light, and there was nothing glancing at her from the shadows.

At least, not anymore.

"Better?" Jonathan puffed as he wiped his brow with his discarded shirt. They'd been setting the training grounds alight with their shouts, sparring with weapons and fists for the better part of the morning.

He wasn't sure if he was up to another meeting with the ground.

"I am, rather." Samuel shrugged his shirt back on. They'd both worked up a sweat. "Thought you'd be at the Healers Centre with your other friend."

"I've got more than two friends!" Jonathan bit back.

Samuel shrugged. "I don't."

"You forgot how to count?" Jonathan teased gently.

"There's you, and Lizbeth," Samuel said, frowning.

"What am I then? A burned buta spout?" Shari asked, laughing as she entered the training ground.

"Superiors aren't friends."

"How hard did Jon whack you on the head?" Shari hefted one on the glaives they'd been practicing with. "We're friends. Tania's your friend too. And I'm sure you've got friends back home."

Shari turned away to put the glaive back on the rack and missed Samuel's expression twist, but Jonathan didn't.

"Some of my friends have been trying to contact me," Samuel said as Shari spun around.

"Really? You know you're not stuck here, right? If you want to go and see them, you can. Just tell us when you're going, and when you expect to be back."

Jonathan looked at Shari askance. Would she say the same thing if she knew who Samuel's friends were?

Samuel didn't miss his expression. "No, it's okay. I wouldn't want to…"

"There is more to life than this," Shari gestured at the weapons rack. "Right? There has to be more than fighting and patrolling and weaving defences with every spare second," Shari said vehemently. "There has to be."

She sounded so small.

A few long strides and Samuel was wrapping Shari in a hug before Jonathan could say anything. "Lizbeth said this helps when someone is upset."

Her laugh sounded a little watery. "It does." They clung to each other a little longer, and Jonathan wasn't actively looking for Sam's claws this time.

Either he was going soft, or Jonathan was regaining some trust in his friend.

"Go, see your friends if you want to," Shari said as she stepped away. "If it's okay with Jon."

They both turned to look at him.

"Just let us know where you're going, in case anything happens." Through Zac's actions, he was beginning to see how much someone might sacrifice for their friends.

He hoped the pair of blinding smiles sent his way would be worth whatever mischief Samuel would find when he was off-Realm.

Stepping through the double doors of the museum, Samuel couldn't believe Jonathan was allowing him to go off Lissae unsupervised.

To be in the Ducibus' hall, alone.

He wanted to celebrate.

Even one cycle earlier, his version of celebrating would have been different. However, now was not that time.

He had an old friend to catch.

The Ducibus all seemed to skitter away from him in the lighter halls. He didn't blame them. His Innarn was Dark enough to make them flinch, much as their Light Innarn affected him the same way.

The darker doors were calling to him.

As he passed the branch Bazaven was on, he stopped. *Could it be?*

He almost shook his head. But something was calling him.

And he shouldn't ignore it any longer.

Samuel swung the pale-yellow door open and stepped through.

"Took you long enough." The grumble came from underneath a mound of sand.

Immediately, Samuel snapped out a blade, his shield going up at the same time.

A lumbering shape moved, sand sluicing off the form until a small black Q'Aralide stood before him, blotting out the sun.

Small was relative, of course. He looked rather huge from where Samuel was standing.

Jetonyx shook all over, sending grains of sand flying.

In the comparative safety of his shield, Samuel panicked. He refused to let it show on his face. "Why are you here?"

The hatchling looked hurt. *They told me you died. The Queen killed Honvic after she forced you out. I was left all alone in the nest.*

"Did she hurt you?" The safety of the hatchlings had been his condition upon leaving. If she had killed one, it was bad. But if she'd hurt them, it was a fate worse than death.

Death, at least, was quick.

'No.' Jetonyx lowered his snout so he was at eye level with Samuel's current form. *'Can you come home?'*

There was the childish whine he hadn't missed.

"You know I can't." Samuel rubbed the huge snout. It took both hands.

The hatchling sighed and rested his head on his claws, stretching out his belly on the sand.

"What are you doing here? Doesn't this Realm burn you?"

'In so many ways! I'm worried that the Queen is hunting me,' Jetonyx admitted. Samuel sensed the hatchling's Innarn swirling around them. *'Some of our kind have been going missing.'*

Samuel frowned. 'Who?'

'Knura, Diren, Zedith and Cisrk.'

'Zedith and Cisrk were outcast.' For being nice, he added in the privacy of his own mind. *'It happened just before I... left.'*

'You didn't want to, did you?'

'I didn't have much of a choice.' Samuel rubbed a hand over his face. Jonathan didn't realise the Queen had been keeping him chained, or that he'd been waiting for the Guardian to enact the thrice-blasted promise from the moment he'd made it.

'But you're meant to lead the next Dark Council.'

'I am.'

'*Are you going to?*' The hatchling nuzzled closer to his stroking hands, puffs of toxic smoke unfurling from his nostrils.

'*Oh, I'll be there.*'

'*You need to know something. There's a group of Dark beings who are...*' Jetony's brow crinkled up, and the scales around his maw tightened. He looked moments away from leaking acidic tears.

'*Doing something the Queen would not approve of, I take it?*'

The hatchling nodded.

'*Would I like their actions?*'

It took him a while to mull the thought over, but eventually Jetonyx nodded. Samuel smiled grimly, sure to keep his fangs behind his lips. The compulsion the Queen had on the hatchling was still strong. He was centuries away from being able to speak out against her, and it would be many millennia before he could act.

'*Do I know any of them?*'

Jetonyx nodded again, acidic tears of pain leaking down his snout and sizzling against Sam's shield.

'*Shall we get you somewhere safer?*'

'No,' the hatchling gasped. '*Here is safe. Too light for the minions.*'

'*Clever hatchling,*' Samuel cooed, stroking Jetonyx's snout as the hatchling shuddered and gasped through the agonising pain.

'*At the council, you must...*'

'*I will do what duty demands me to,*' Samuel broke in, his voice grim. '*Rest. Be patient. I will see you at the council?*'

'*I'm too young, wyvern,*' Jetonyx teased.

Samuel gasped. '*Wyvern! I'm far from that old, young hatchling!*'

Jetonyx chuckled. '*I'll wait here. The pain from this Realm is nothing compared to what awaits me should I return to the nest.*'

That pain was all too familiar to him. '*Very well. I shall return as often as I can.*'

'*No, you're being tracked! Meet here after the council?*'

Jetonyx was right. '*I bid thee well, Jetonyx.*' He stepped back as the hatchling bury himself in the sand again.

As he slipped through the door, Samuel glanced over his shoulder. Would the hatchling survive beyond the next council meeting?

It was only as he was heading towards his new home that the hatchling's words hit him.

Samuel was being tracked.

Collis was endlessly fascinated with all the creations in Cyrus's lab. They'd been talking for hours, and Tania was getting a little homesick.

She plonked on a chair in the corner of the room and stroked the crystal wall. "You remind me of Ronah, somehow."

'*We are related.*' The voice warbled and reminded Tania of water splashing against crystal.

'*Talhan?*'

'*Well met, Ronah's Linked.*'

'*Well met.*' Tania smiled happily. Talhan seemed lighter than Rakemyst somehow.

'*Rakemyst is a stuffy clod of dirt—that's why.*'

She giggled. '*And what do you think of Ronah?*'

'*She's more fun than the others. I've missed my littlest sister.*' Talhan jostled against Ronah, and Tania, almost without thinking, set the stumbling townsfolk right.

'*Brothers and sisters... Do you have a mother?*'

'*Not like you do. Lissae made us by herself. She is our parent, but most prefer to think of her as a mother.*'

'*Has Lissae ever made other islands before you?*'

Before Talhan could answer, a B.I.R.D. flew into the room.

"Ugh! What do you want?" Cyrus grumbled.

"Temira has requested the presence of Ronah's Linked," the B.I.R.D. trilled.

Tania made to get up, but Cyrus waved her back. "Who has?"

"Temira."

"Who?" Cyrus nudged, a twinkle in his eye.

The B.I.R.D. sighed. "The Technomancer of Talhan."

A group of crystals boomed and flashed. If the metal creature had eyes, she was sure they would have rolled.

Tania couldn't help but laugh. "Please let Temira know I'm on my way. But I'll need guidance to get there."

Collis started towards the door.

"Stay here, Collis. I'll be just down the hall." She smiled to take the sting out of her words.

He looked so torn.

"We can set up a screen which will inform us if Tania needs a hand. Here." Cyrus passed her a red crystal bracelet. The smooth beads tingled against her skin. "If something happens, this screen will start flashing."

"Brilliant." Tania grinned. "See, I'll be fine. Back before you know it." She slipped away before Collis could stop her.

Outside, B.I.R.D. was waiting for her. "This way, please."

The corridors looked the same as the ones at the Healing Centre, and when they rounded the last corner, Tania wasn't surprised that Temira waiting for her.

"Well met, Ronah's Linked."

"Well met, Tech..."

Temira's expression darkened.

"Temira of Talhan."

The blue-skinned healer's mouth twisted, but she gestured to the door. Tania entered the room where a low table was set with plates of delicate finger food and a steaming pot of tea.

"Sit," Temira ordered.

Tania plonked on a cushion and smiled up at her host. Temira poured the tea and set a cup in front of her. Only after Temira had added some food to her plate did Tania do the same.

They ate in silence for a while until Temira picked up her cup. "I don't understand the Lissaen preoccupation with hot salad juice." Temira sneered at her cup.

"Hot what now?" Tania was glad she hadn't taken a drink. She would have spat it everywhere. She'd never heard tea referred to as 'salad juice' before.

Temira smirked and set the cup down. "I much prefer to drink water or fruit juices. Tea made of bark and leaves holds no interest for me."

"The Guardian will turn so many different colours if I refer to tea as hot salad juice." Tania sniggered.

"Xani should be here, but she is running late." Temira frowned and glanced towards the door.

"I'm sure she won't be far away." Tania soothed.

"We wanted to talk to you about Ronah. I'd like to visit and upgrade the crystals. It's been over fifty years since they were last done."

"Is that a bad thing?"

Temira snorted. "No worse than an ucoid in a noxeomyth with only a towel to protect you."

Tania blinked. "I'm sorry. I'm not sure what you mean."

Temira picked her cup up again and stared into it. She opened her mouth to speak several times. The technomancer finally said, "I am, in case you can't tell, not originally from Lissae. The sole survivor of my Realm. There were more of us, but... I'm the only one left."

"I'm so sorry."

"I find it difficult to converse with you. My instincts tell me you are family, someone I can trust. Yet my other senses tell me you, like everyone else around, are from Lissae."

"Xani isn't from Lissae either, is she?"

"No, her Realm was destroyed long before mine. It took years for me to be as comfortable around her as I am around you."

Tania took a long drink, trying to get her thoughts in order. "I can't imagine what you've been through. Or what Xani has been through. And we may not look the same, or have the same blood running through our veins, but if you want a friend, a family, I can be that for you."

Temira teared up. "I am centuries older than you. I should comfort you."

"Eh, you'll get your turn. It's what family is for, right?"

"In the interests of full disclosure, I'm no good at small talk. I get caught up in my work, and I forget to do normal things." Temira fiddled with the cup in her hands.

"No one is perfect. I'm far from it. We might not talk for years, but that's fine."

"Good." Temira got up and made to walk from the room. She paused right before the door. "I need to find Xani. It's not like her to be so late."

"Want some company?"

Temira ran a hand gently over the twigs of a half-dead plant by the door. "It would be welcome."

Tania smiled as she stood. "Can I call you Aunty Technomancer?"

Eyes going wide and mouth dropping open, Temira shook her head. "Not if you wish to retain the ability to speak."

Tania laughed. "I like to tease my family. If it gets too much, please tell me."

"I don't understand teasing." Temira held herself so stiffly, Tania was half afraid she'd shatter as they walked down the hallway. "I dislike the connotations the word technomancer has."

"What do you mean?"

"On my home Realm, Innarn is vastly different. Much of what I do here has been adapted to suit Lissae. The rest is lost. On Ulnan, there were people who could use the very blood inside your body to control you. They were referred to as Vitaemancers."

"But couldn't they make you do something you didn't want to?" Tania burst out.

Temira looked down at her. "Do you ask what the water wants to do before you shape it?"

"No, I... oh."

Her new aunt raised an eyebrow at her.

"Were they able to make people do good things as well?"

"Vitaemancers were the ones who cured our diseased, strengthened our weak."

"Isn't that what you're doing?"

"I hadn't thought of my work in such a manner," Temira admitted. They rounded another corner and almost ran into Xani, who was sitting in her hovering chair, still.

Back in Cyrus's workroom, in the heart of Talhan, a screen began to flash.

CHAPTER TWELVE

"I still don't understand how all this works," Collis said. He poked at a tiny crystal on an array which lit up and trilled at him. When he made a startled noise, it disappeared.

Shari tried to contain her snicker, but figured she'd failed when Collis shot her a dirty look from across Cyrus's workroom.

"Oh, easy. Temira helped us to figure out different ways to connect the crystals and make electrical currents go through them. With the variations in the current and the crystals we use, we're able to do many things." Cyrus grinned.

"Like what?" Jon asked, picking up a gadget with lots of spindly legs and a flat crystal slab to have a closer look at it.

The door to the lab slid open and Xani, Temira and Tania came through.

"We were just talking about how you've adapted crystals so successfully." Cyrus was bouncing on the balls of his feet, barely able to contain his excitement.

"And you want a demonstration," Temira said drily.

Shari sensed Collis sinking into himself, but she noted the tiny uptick of the corner of Temira's mouth.

"Since we've settled on Lissae, most of the technological advances you have access to have been due to our creations."

"What, since the wheel?" Shari asked. She sensed Tania's gasp through their mental link, and Jon's unsubtle Innarn blow to the back of her head.

Temira looked at her and grinned, lips closed around her pointed teeth. "I'm choosing to take the compliment. It is going on 185 years since I arrived here. Slip-stream travel was one of the first things we worked on. Before our booster crystals, it would take a team of Air Innarnians to get a single person from one side of the Realm to the other. Now, fairly low-powered Air Innarnians can control the slip streams with the aid of our booster crystals. Xani and I have been working for the last fifteen years on a technology which would enable instantaneous transport to any point across Lissae, but our testing so far has proved unsuccessful."

Talhan rumbled under their feet, and Cyrus wasn't quick enough to hide his grin. Tania turned a snigger into a cough. What were the islands were telling their Linked?

A half-hearted glare from Temira had Tania choking on her fake cough.

"Xani's chair is another thing which has helped many people on Lissae. When I arrived, she'd already been on Lissae for five years. Stuck in the same bed, unable to get around due to an injury she sustained."

'My legs had been crushed. Rendered useless. We were on rocky ground with highly unhappy people all around us.' Xani's voice, for all she was sending about something horrific, was monotonous.

Still, Shari caught a flash of burning trees and the smell of cooking flesh.

The grey and orange landscape disappeared and became the side of a rocky mountain, the peak glaringly white as the sun reflected off the snow.

There was agony racing through her limbs and screaming echoed all around.

It was her.

People approached with hostile faces and farming equipment held aloft, ready to strike. A hand reached down and grabbed her, and then they were elsewhere. Someone was glancing at her, mouth moving, but the buzzing in her ears was too much, and the world faded to black.

Shari gasped as she came out of the memory.

Xani was letting her tears fall freely.

Temira, her face impassive, rested a hand on Xani's shoulder.

"I can't imagine" Shari whispered.

"When I arrived, Xani's partner had crossed into the Spirit Realm, but Xani remained." Temira took up the tale. "Her injury is too old to fix. We've never been able to cure her legs, but we have ensured all your warriors who return broken are given access to devices to help them get through life with grace and ease."

"Like your chair." Tania wiped away the tears on her face.

Temira smiled with far more kindness than Shari had witnessed from the technomancer so far.

'Yes,' Xani sent, monotone. '*My chair is constantly surrounded by air. The special crystals Temira designed pull air in and push it down, making the chair levitate on a cushion of air.*'

Shari didn't miss the concerned glance, or the gentle squeeze Temira gave her fellow technomancer's shoulder.

"There's no dirty energy used!" Cyrus clapped his hands and beamed.

"One of the first prototypes used Fire Innarn to power the crystals. It left a rather unpleasant smell and clouds of smoke behind." Temira sighed.

"Or all around Xani if she stayed still too long," Cyrus added, waving away the memory of the smoke.

"Is it because Fire Innarn isn't compatible with the crystals?" Jon asked, carefully putting down the gadget he was holding.

"Hardly. It's just not compatible with *those* crystals." Temira moved over to the table. She picked up a flat panel and shot Shari a sour look.

"What'd I do?" Shari asked, startled.

"I was days away from perfecting this, you know." Temira waved around a flat panel decorated with dials and gears. Two prongs stood up on one edge. Tiny symbols glowed, and it hummed as she waved it around the room. When it pointed at Shari, it sparked, and plasma arced from one prong to another. With a fizzle and a pop, the whole thing glowed so bright Shari was left with spots dancing in front of her eyes. "It pinpointed the location of the Altoriae. At least now I can say it works."

"Why didn't you get to use it?" Tania asked.

"Because your Altoriae announced who she was to the Realm two days before it was due for the last test run," Temira grumbled.

"Sorry?" Shari shrugged. She wasn't sure what to say.

Temira smirked at her. "At least you're better on the battlefield than you are with your timing."

"Thanks?" She didn't know how to take the technomancer at all.

"Why don't I show you what else we've come up with." Cyrus broke the tension with a tiny sigh.

How often did he intervene for the technomancer?

He moved to a workbench protected by a clear sheet of crystal. "I think the Altoriae will be particularly interested in this. It's what we used to help your uncle's partner."

Without her mind being totally aware of moving, Shari was in front of the case along with everyone else. Inside was... orange sand? But it was moving.

"What?" Tania asked.

The technomancer chuckled. "This is possibly Xani's greatest invention. It gives the ability to grow limbs back, to repair nerve damage, and to heal almost anything short of a beheading."

Xani's chair came to a stop in front of the bench.

"It's sand," Shari said flatly. How could sand possibly grow limbs? Perhaps if they made it into a poultice and put it around the stump of Belfar's wing?

"No, they're femto crystals," Temira said.

"Fem-toe crystals?" Tania asked.

Xani was staring at the case, the orange crystals reflected in her eyes. She seemed transfixed.

Temira seemed to wait for Xani to say something. When her fellow technomancer failed to take up the tale, Temira continued. "Yes. The femto crystals are infused with a special mix which make them just below sentient. Each recipient has crystals specially coded to their genetic structure to make the most out of them. Whenever patrollers have check-ups with their healers, their vital signs, measurements, and peak health performances are recorded. With the healers' help, we can make sure the recipient can get back into the best shape possible."

"How?" Shari asked.

"There are a few ways. The femto crystals need to enter the bloodstream. The easiest way is to shift them in, but that can cause complications." Temira looked even grimmer than usual.

"Complications?" Shari wasn't sure she wanted to know. She was even more sure about that when Cyrus mimed something blowing up from his spot behind the technomancer.

"There were a few incidents," Temira admitted.

Tania gulped.

Just who had incidents the affected?

"Now we put the femto crystals into a tiny capsule that ensures they are easy to swallow, and once they hit the stomach, the acids break down the capsule and the femto crystals can be absorbed safely into the body to do their work."

"Does it hurt?" Jon asked.

"You've had some of our femto crystals, Guardian."

"I have?"

"Oh yeah. The 'innovative technology' the healers wanted to try out on you." Shari nodded. She could remember the conversation now. It had seemed supremely unimportant at the time. So long as they fixed Jon, she hadn't really cared how they did it.

"Who else on Ronah has had them?"

Temira shook her head. "There is a certain amount of confidentiality between the recipients and us. Plus, once we give them to the healers, the recipients can always refuse."

"I don't mean to be rude," Tania said hesitantly, "but if these femto crystals can do so much good, and heal so many things, why are you still in your chair?"

The technomancer's hand was on Xani's shoulder before Tania had even finished. "Xani's legs endured damage so great, and it happened so long ago, there is little hope she'll be able to recover. The femto crystals have eased some lingering, phantom pain from damaged nerve endings, but to rebuild what was lost over a century ago would be a miracle."

"Oh." Tania wrung her hands together, eyes red-rimmed. "I'm so sorry. I didn't mean to..."

"Perhaps it is best that you see what other things we have been working on?" Temira interrupted smoothly. She led the way to the other side of the room, bypassing the shining silver tables scattered with bits and bobs in the middle.

Xani stayed behind, staring at the crystals on the other side of the glass.

Shari went to go with the others, but something stopped her. The healing side of her Innarn reached out and brushed against Xani. She sensed it, deep in her bones. Nothing could be done.

"Tell me what your favourite invention is?" Shari asked. She'd almost asked about Xani's home Realm, but figured she had been upset enough for one day.

Xani lifted her gaze to stared blankly at Shari, who smiled tentatively at her. The techno-Innarnian shook her head and seemed to come back to herself.

'*Easy,*' Xani sent. Her chair glided away from the crystals and towards a dark corner of the room. She picked up a wooden box and passed it to Shari. It fit comfortably in her palm. As she turned it over carefully, Shari noted the hinges on the back. She looked at Xani for permission and received a nod.

Carefully, she lifted the lid.

And stepped into a different time.

She was in the town square, laughing with Lizbeth, and leaning down to make her first snowball. She sensed the chill of the air, the crunch of the snow, and the taste of the cold.

Shari snapped the box closed and stared in awe at Xani.

"What is this?"

With a dry laugh, Xani sent, '*My cheerful place. Everyone sees something different. I made it to show my Realm to the people of Talhan. But it didn't work the way I'd hoped. It brings joy to all who open it, though. You look more relaxed than when you walked in here, Altoriae.*'

Shari sighed. "I am more relaxed." She was tempted to open the box again, and never put it down. It would be a blissful existence, to not have to worry about the pain of the present and just concentrate on the joy of the past. "Ever since I was little, joy has been hard to find. Fighting is far easier."

'*You need to make your own joy, Altoriae. You must remember there is a reason for what you do. What will you do once the fighting is over?*'

"Over? I've been fighting for as long as I can remember. I don't know what else to do."

'What happens when there is no fighting? Like now. If you could be anywhere in the Realms, doing anything, what would it be?' Xani's words were becoming monotonal again.

About to open her mouth to say she'd most likely be training, Shari stopped. What if she could do anything? What if, in some twisted reality, the thing Xani was proposing was possible? "I'm not sure."

'You... think.' Xani's send was fragmented.

Worried she had upset her, Shari glanced at the box in her hands and nodded. "I will."

"Temira? Are you alright?" Tania asked softly.

The tall scientist looked over at Xani and Shari. "There is something wrong with Xani. She is not usually so reserved."

"Perhaps she was hoping the device to track the Altoriae down would work more than you realised?"

"Perhaps." Temira looked far from convinced.

"Tania mentioned you have a way of storing Innarn?" Jon asked.

"Cyrus has been spearheading the project."

"It still needs testing," Cyrus broke in. "We have yet to determine just what type of Innarn can be stored, how long it remains viable for, and if it can be reshaped."

"I have a few patrol groups who would test it out for you, if you'd like."

Cyrus beamed. "Experienced testers would be amazing! Most of the time, I have to bribe the first-level university students to be testers." He rubbed a hand over the back of his neck. "It rarely ends well."

"He means I have to heal them." Temira glared at Talhan's Linked and crossed her arms.

Cyrus ducked his head and chuckled. "Yeah, it's not great. But no one has died yet."

Temira cleared her throat.

"Thanks to Temira and Xani," he added.

"Do you have anything in here which would allow off-Realmers to gain access to Lissae?" Jonathan asked.

From the corner of her eye, Tania saw Shari walking back towards them. Behind her, an orange crystal near Xani glowed.

"We are working on the capability of travel between Realms in case the need for a mass exodus arises."

"Have you done any testing yet?"

"Not at this current point. Lissae's borders are more heavily guarded than we first realised," Temira admitted.

"You're welcome." Shari grinned.

"It is making it impossible to get accurate results." Temira turned her glare onto Shari.

"Ah. Apologies, then." Shari winced.

"While I admire your dedication, your defences make our job harder."

'Perhaps you can bring the defences down?' Xani sent as she joined the rest of the group. Her mind-voice was still a monotone, and she was weakly jerking her head from side to side.

A smile fixed itself on Shari's face. "They stay up. They are in place for a reason."

"We had been talking about asking you to lower the defences, but after the Chirean attack, we had decided not to." Temira was frowning at Xani.

'Slipped my mind,' Xani sent. Her chair abruptly turned and glided out of the room.

"Did I... offend her?" Shari asked, brows raised in confusion.

"I do not know." Temira frowned harder. "I need to run some tests." And she strode out after her friend.

"Sorry!" Shari called after them.

"I don't think she's mad. She's just extremely focused," Tania offered.

"How about I treat you to some of Talhan's cuisine? We have people from all over Lissae here, and Talhan has the *best* Daen café!" Cyrus said with forced happiness.

"Bribing the Altoriae Guild with food?" Shari teased.

Cyrus gulped. "Uh-huh."

"Works every time."

A wide smile spread over Cyrus's face.

Tears streamed down Xani's face, her expression contorting in her bathroom mirror.

She'd had a moment with the Altoriae of Lissae—something she'd longed for ever since the search for her name had been announced.

But try as she might, she was only able to regain control of her body for short periods of time, and they were becoming fewer and far between.

'Do not resist.' The voice was thick and foreign. A constant presence in her mind.

Xani hated it.

She screamed behind dry eyes as her hands rose and cleaned her face.

Her expression smoothed over, and her chair turned in a jerky circle until she was able to leave the room, screaming the whole time.

And no one heard a sound.

Jonathan followed the group automatically, keeping a gentle psychic link on Shari so he wouldn't go astray as he mulled over the ramifications of the recent technology.

He was so lost in thought, he didn't see the man walking towards him until they literally crashed into each other, sprawling in a tangle of limbs on the sidewalk.

He would recognise those copper eyes anywhere. "Zac."

"Well met, Jon."

"We have to stop meeting like this," Jonathan joked.

Zac's face fell.

"I'd much prefer to be sitting across a table from you," he said hastily, almost tripping over his words. "And with less falling down."

"Don't tell me you're getting too old for this." Zac rose to his feet and held out a hand for Jonathan to take.

"Some days it feels like it. I wasn't aware you had left the Healers Centre." Jonathan was reluctant to take his hand back, so he tugged Zac along with him.

Shari was doing an admirable job of not staring or drawing attention to the additional being in their party.

"Had to leave some time. I came to check in with my boss." Zac tossed his thumb over his shoulder.

"You've been on Talhan?" Jonathan asked, trying to hide how eager he was for the scraps of Zac's life.

"No. I work with the Techno Centre on Talhan, but I travel a lot to look at technology from all over the Realms."

"Do you work with any particular section?" Jonathan asked lightly.

"Ocular repair."

"Ah. I wonder what inspired you?"

Zac glanced at him out of the corner of his eye, and bumped against his shoulder teasingly. "I wonder." There was a decidedly mournful edge to his smile.

Jonathan swallowed heavily. Could he really be guilty of leading a man astray with a desperate white lie about failing vision from years ago?

Cyrus was leading the group ahead of them into a quaint café with a red door and decorative metallic horses in the windows.

"Come eat with us?"

"I really have to see my boss. But, ah, I might take you up on the offer of a meal later."

"I'll hold you to that," Jonathan said.

Zac let go of his hand and walked back the way they'd come, a bounce in his step.

As he turned a corner, Jonathan took in the street properly for the first time. It was designed for merchants. Cafes and boutiques lined the edges of the wide street. Signs advertising wares were placed in eye-catching locations, and the visual overwhelm was hard to escape. The tech centre was still visible, a monolithic structure in the distance.

The sign on the side of a building dulled for a moment before changing to the old hand holding up a glowing orange pill.

Jonathan turned his back and walked into the café.

CHAPTER THIRTEEN

amuel was on his way home, arms laden with supplies, when a low growling came from the shadows of the bushes near his door.

He did what came naturally.

He growled back.

The creature growled louder.

"Do you really think you can take me?" he snarled.

A huff of air and the sense of being watched were his only answer.

"Unless that was your stomach?"

Another huff. And the hint of a long, thin tongue.

"Fine. Better get inside then." After gently kicking the door open, Samuel walked straight to the kitchen and put his supplies down. There was enough food to last him for a week, a few new drinks to try, and a soft rug Lizbeth said would help to *brighten up the house and make him happy.*

He pulled the rug out and set it on the floor in front of the lounge. Back in the kitchen, he slipped most of the food into the cold box to keep.

What would his new growly friend would like? He chanced a glance at the front door.

Part of a shadow had detached itself from the bushes and was standing in the middle of the threshold.

"In or out?" Samuel asked.

The shadow froze and slowly melted across the wall and slid under the lounge chair.

"Let's figure out what you eat."

He grabbed a sample of everything and sat on the rug, placing his offerings in a line right where the light met the dark on the floor.

Then, he waited.

Itching with pent-up energy, Shari was glad it was her turn to patrol tonight.

Until she got to the museum and saw the crowd waiting for her out the front.

'Jon? Why is half the town ready to patrol?'

'I may have mentioned you would be patrolling and might like a hand?' The Guardian sounded distracted.

'You forgot to warn me because…'

'I've been translating the Hekkor Mafae with Samuel.'

Shari supposed she couldn't really fault him for working on something so important.

"So, who's here to patrol?" Shari called with false enthusiasm.

About a third of the beings present raised their hands.

"Brilliant. Everyone else, wait out here."

There were a few grumbles, but they made a path and allowed Shari and the others through.

Fifty-plus people standing at her back was not something she was entirely comfortable with. She led them through the first room of the museum.

"Who has been on patrol before?" she asked.

Most raised their hands.

"Good. All of you on the right side of the room."

A group Shari recognised as Cyrus's friends from Talhan were left standing on their own.

Internally sighing, she tried to focus on just how she'd get back at Jon for not warning her about this.

She turned to look at the others—former candidates, now members of the guild, a few elders, and several Ilutri and a group of the Returned.

"When you step through the double doors, you represent Lissae. You are out there to ensure the safety of our borders. If someone needs aid, you give it, but not at your own expense. And know that you may not come back."

"Inspiring," Raven said. His voice echoed through the room.

Shari ignored her. "Who here is Darker than most?"

Two of the Ilutri stepped forward, and Shari sensed a teen behind her move.

"The Dark Realms have been fairly quiet at the moment. We have information which tells us they are planning something. If anything lighter than Lissae will hurt you, go home and save your strength. You'll be needed another night."

One of the Ilutri wavered, then bowed. She touched her partner's hand and left.

"Returned. You work together so well. I'd like for you to take..." She wanted badly to say *me* but didn't. "...Raven and see if you can show him some of your tricks. Praxore needs checking tonight."

As one, the Returned bowed. Raven gave her a slightly mocking nod but went with them as they headed out.

"Guild, step forward."

Some beings looked confused, but the former candidates wore proud grins as they walked to the front.

"You need to learn how to work as a team. Meojuary has reportedly had issues around their gateway, but they won't say what. Have a look and come back in one piece."

Her guild looked at her and nodded. Talofa gave her a brief wave as they slipped away.

"The rest of you, split into two. Elder Ribeck and Varlee will be patrol leaders tonight. You can decide if you would like to tackle the traps around the gateway of Hoggeotis, or the particularly nasty bugs invading jungle near the gateway of Neviarath."

Turning back to the Talhan teens, Shari eyed them up. She had been planning on going to Tocithas, a water Realm, but with this many people, the local population would be more likely to spear first and ask questions later.

"We have a different task. Something is fouling the water in Duhiomel, and we need to find out what's causing it."

"Can't the beings who live there find out?" Eva's blue hair was almost glowing under the museum lights.

"Patrolling is about what?" Shari asked softly.

"Protecting the borders and giving aid," Eva said sullenly.

"Exactly." Shari didn't add that she already knew what was fouling the waters, or that the group would be up for a fight they would win. It would give them a taste of patrolling with no real danger. Perfect for first-timers.

"Come on, then." She led them through the rest of the museum and the double doors, grinning as they shivered when they passed through the Ducibus' scrubber. She went straight for the carved door of Duhiomel. Shari barely gave them a chance to admire the intricate leaf pattern before she opened the door.

"Shields up!" she commanded and ushered them through.

"Ugh!"

Shari stifled a laugh as boots and shoes squelched in the muddy creek bed.

"Bit wet, isn't it?" she asked as she pulled the door closed, winking at the Ducibus who she was sure was smiling under the oversized hood.

They'd all stepped directly into a stream. This one, being near the gateway, was only a few inches deep, but the icy water was cutting her to the bone.

"This way," Shari said. '*Make sure you only send from here.*' Shari got a flurry of affirmative responses back.

'*What's that smell?*' a boy asked.

'*It's why we're here.*' Shari led them upstream until the muddy bottom gave way to rocks. She turned, intent on heading to the shore, when something bright yellow fluttered into view.

It was a scrap of material, about as big as her hand, and shaped like a spinning seed pod. There was something bulbus on the end.

Eva, next to Shari, leaned forward to get a better look.

The instant it touched the water, it exploded, sending the entire group flying backwards.

Shari shook the ringing from her ears and threw a shield around them, noting there were more of the fatal seedpods heading in their direction. They looked like they were being lobbed from the clearing behind the trees.

A boy was leaning over Eva, shaking her, his mouth opening and closing. She lay in the water, eyes staring straight up, unresponsive.

The Altoriae shook her head again. This was meant to be an easy patrol for their first time. Staring at the hole in the middle of Eva's torso, it wouldn't be one they'd forget.

Throwing a shield around the falling seedpods before they hit the water, Shari sent, '*Take Eva and get back to the gateway. Now!*'

Clearly in various states of shock, the teens did what they were told.

Shari waited until they were clear before she stood and sluiced the icy water from her clothing. She used her Innarn to gather the seedpods, and stormed towards the clearing.

Just before the edge of the tree line, she paused. It was not a few mischievous locals as she'd expected, but a small army which seemed to be waiting for her.

A rage as icy cold as the water she'd been thrown into filled her body.

She noted the way they'd interlaced their Innarn warriors, making sure there was no easily identifiable grouping. Apparently, word of her tactics had spread.

Lucky she had some new ones to try.

Silently, she sent the shielded seedpods through the trees, raising them above the army. When they were in position, she pulled on the water from the stream and made it rain directly above their heads.

Then she dropped the shield.

Blasts and screams echoed around the clearing. A few tried to escape, but Shari slammed bolt after bolt of plasma into the clouds, using the rain to carry the charge and stun them as they fell.

"You're smaller than I thought," said a rough voice behind her.

Shari didn't even look. Her yellow blade appeared, and she whirled and struck, slicing the arm of the man who'd tried to sneak up behind her.

He was about the same height as her, but was broader, with a big barrel chest. He had a single eye above a wide nose.

"Thought we'd killed you."

"You thought wrong," Shari snarled. She slammed her foot down and flames leaped into the air, encircling them in a ring of fire.

His eye widened, but the next moment, he was calm again. "Have to try harder then."

"Much harder." She blocked the blow from his war hammer and countered with one from her sword while she used her Innarn to send a storm of pebbles at the back of his bald head.

He whipped around, looking for the other attacker, and Shari stabbed the yellow blade straight through his unprotected back and into the place where she heard his heart pounding.

Turning, he coughed, blood spraying out. "Good distraction, eh?"

Furious, Shari ground her teeth. When he chuckled, she refused to give in to the temptation of pouring plasma down his throat and instead shifted straight to the gateway.

It was carnage.

The teens from Talhan were putting up a brave fight. Of the eight who had originally come through the gateway, only three were still standing. Four of the ones on the ground were groaning and grasping at wounds. The skin of Eva's belly looked almost translucent, showing healing organs underneath.

Shari bared her teeth in a snarl. The one-eyed beings around her snarled back.

Yellow blade leading the charge, the Altoriae distracted the cyclops fighters while levitating the Lissaens out of the water. She twisted, parried, and smashed in a nose with the hilt of her sword.

With every move, every drop of sweat, she added more plasma to what she had caged in her hand.

All the attention was on her now. Shari lunged straight at the cyclops in front of her, running up his chest and pushing off hard. He stumbled backwards, away from the Lissaens and into one of his comrades.

Right in time for Shari to push every ounce of plasma into the water.

The cyclops fighters sizzled, the smell of their burning flesh hitting her almost immediately.

Electrified water all around her, Shari had precious few places to land. She was already coming out of the turn, and if she wasn't careful, she'd cook just like they had.

There.

One powerful gust of breeze later, and she knocked into the trunk of a tree—hard. But she got her feet onto the branch and didn't fall.

Her breath coming in rough gasps. She'd bruised her ribs. She stretched her hand out, calling the plasma back. It rested in her outstretched palm for a moment.

As she set to work shaping it, Shari reached out to see if there were any other threats in the area.

The forest around the stream was still. The sudden, furious battle had scared all the wildlife away. All that remained were the Lissaens.

Shari chewed on her lip as she surveyed the group below her. She was rather surprised to see Eva was groaning and poking at her belly as she floated in the air.

Carefully, testing the water one last time, Shari set them all gently down. She jumped to the ground and put another shield up before seeing if anyone needed healing.

"That was rockin'," one of the guys said, voice shaky as he beamed at the others.

Shari didn't understand what he meant, but a quick skim of his thoughts showed it was positive. Not exactly how she would put it.

"Would have been better without seeing my insides," Eva said.

One of the girls unwound a black scarf from around her waist and handed it wordlessly over. Wide-eyed, Eva took it and wrapped it around her middle.

"You were dead, Eva. You didn't see them." The girl rolled her eyes. She was the one who'd enthused over the outfit Anika had created.

"How were you able to take a full blast and die, but now you're here, talking?" Shari asked.

"We've all been taking the new vitamins the technomancer makes."

Shari looked around at the others and realised she didn't see a single injury. She was glad her armour covered what she was sure would be a brilliant bruise. A deep breath made her wince. "Temira?"

"Yeah. We figured that if we wanted to be more active in protecting the Realm, we had to make it happen. But, well, I kinda like living, so we wanted to be careful."

"So, you took medicine."

"Not just medicine! Femto crystal vitamins."

At the edge of her consciousness, the sense of many feet running towards them on the creek bed niggled. "Why don't we talk some more when we get back?"

As if she'd summoned the Ducibus, the door swung open.

The others filed out, and as Shari slipped through the gateway, she couldn't help but think, *we should have gone to Tocithas.*

"Does everyone on Talhan take these vitamins?"

"Not everyone. They're still testing it out, but we needed the cash."

Shari blinked. Money wasn't a foreign idea, but on Ronah it was mostly a bartering system and everyone had enough to get by.

"Can I help?"

"Just going on patrol earned us enough to keep a roof over our heads for the next three months!"

She hadn't even known patrol members were paid. As they walked down the hallway, Shari hoped she was paid as Altoriae. If she was, she would use her back-pay to set up a fund so no one would have to worry about having enough. Or not having anything.

"You fought well. Go rest. If you head over to the Quiver and Quill Tavern and tell my parents I sent you, they'll give you a meal on the house."

Pleased cries filled her ears, and the teens rushed out, eager to get their fill.

'*Dad, there's a group I just patrolled with heading your way, hoping for a meal. Do you mind?*' Shari sent.

'*I think we can organise something.*'

Shari sensed his smile. She allowed herself to bask in the sensation for a moment, then she sighed and let it go. Breathing was becoming more painful now the adrenaline from the fight was fading, but she still had to tell Jon she was back.

'*Well, someone on Duhiomel isn't happy with me,*' Shari sent to Jon with a quick recap of what had happened.

'*Anything broken?*' Jon asked calmly.

The concern and anger buried underneath the placid question was obvious to anyone who knew Jon well enough.

'*All in one piece*,' she sent, trying to ease her Guardian's worry. She didn't mention the limp she was now sporting on top of the bruises and scrapes.

'*Do you need healing?*'

Shari debated. If Jon saw her like this, he might get worried, and she didn't want to cause him any concern. Having someone else to heal her would be nice. The fight had taken more out of her than she'd expected. '*I'll be fine. Thank you for the offer.*'

The green glow shimmered at her fingertips. Shari let it rest there a moment before she put her hand against her ribcage. She sighed gratefully as breathing became easier almost immediately.

As she walked back to the castle, using the exercise to cool down tired muscles, Shari tried to discern what motive the cyclops army had for launching an attack. She supposed there would be more research in her future.

Samuel was coming to his wits' end.

The shadow didn't want fruit, cheese, or water. He'd tried insects, which it seemed to be interested in, but hadn't taken.

It had been a few lifetimes since he'd been around a Shadow Innarn creature, but he thought back to his training. Perhaps one of the elements?

Carefully, he laid a handful of earth on the ground to see what would happen. He already knew water wasn't the answer, and fire would do more harm than good, no matter how strong it was.

While the shadow was deciding, he had to eat. Lizbeth knew of his preference for meat and had put a small roasted fowl in amongst the packages. It had been tempting him all the way home.

He snagged some rutenberries and put them on a plate with the fowl. Samuel took the makeshift platter back to the lounge room and settled on the rug again, snapping off a wing and starting to gnaw away.

After putting the bone down to save the marrow for last, he snapped off the other wing.

Slowly, a tendril of shadow extended from beneath the lounge. It slipped between the earth and the bowl of fruit and slid next to his own shadow. It flinched and seemed to poke at him before it slid up his foot to hover underneath the plate.

"You're not getting any of my rutenberries," he warned, keeping his voice low and gentle.

The tendril retreated, resting near his foot.

"I mean it," he said.

With painstakingly slow movements, it slid up to his plate again.

Samuel blinked.

The shadow snatched a discarded bone and skittered back under the lounge.

"I was saving that," he mumbled around a mouthful.

It paused.

"But you seem to need it more."

The sound of crunching filled the room. When Samuel finished the meat, he carefully placed the plate with the rest of the bones on the floor.

"Seriously, don't touch my rutenberries." He scooped them up and slid the plate closer to the edge of the shadow.

Another tendril reached out, and the plate disappeared.

The thing under the lounge purred.

CHAPTER FOURTEEN

The set of Shari's shoulders told Tania everything she didn't want to know as she swung through the school gate ahead of the morning rush.

"Rough night?" she asked lightly.

Shari nodded. "There was a cyclops army waiting for me on Duhiomel."

"Yikes." Tania winced, skirting past a group of students as they headed inside.

"Oh, it gets worse. I had some first-time patrollers from Talhan with me because I thought it would be an easy one. A farmer keeps throwing his dead cattle upstream of the gateway because he thinks it offends our delicate Lissaen sensibilities."

"Does it?"

"It's disrespectful. But it won't stop me from defending the gateway."

"Ah. But there was an army instead?"

"Yep." Shari popped the P. "And a girl died."

Tania gasped.

"But she's alright now," Shari added quickly.

"You healed her?"

"Didn't have to. She's taking the experimental technomancer medicine. Seemed to make her as good as new."

"Isn't that a good thing?" Tania wrinkled her nose.

"It is, but there's something weird about this medicine. How can it help my grandfather, and regrow organs, blood, skin, and bone? It's like a miracle drug." Shari looked particularly worried.

Tania tried to soothe her fears. "Perhaps it is. Temira can do things with crystals we can only dream of." Tania paused at the entrance of a classroom.

"I don't really understand it. I just hope it's permanent."

"Do you want to check on her after school?"

Shari smiled. "Good idea."

Satisfied she had got the Altoriae to smile, Tania skipped to her classroom.

Xani, locked in her mind, was trying her best to ignore whatever the thing controlling her was up to.

Instead, she was remembering the winter when she'd first realised she wanted to become a healer.

Her younger brother had been out in the snow, playing with a friend who'd shoved him too hard. He'd fallen and hit his head on a hidden rock.

His friend had screamed, and she'd run outside, hand flying to her mouth as his blue blood stained the ground around him.

Was it bad that two and a half centuries later, she struggled to recall the friend's name?

She dared not think her brother's, for fear the thing controlling her body would take it from her too.

Shari's smile dropped as soon as Tania walked off to class.

What if the medicine *wasn't* permanent? Maybe Eva would have to keep taking it so her belly didn't suddenly open up and spill intestines everywhere. What if...?

Sighing, Shari made her way to the tiny office she shared with Sam. Hopefully there'd be fewer questions waiting for her there. Instead, Jordan Hollingsworth, the vice principal, was waiting for her.

"Well met, Shari." He smiled at her.

"Well met, Mr Hollingsworth," she said, wary.

"You aren't in trouble," he assured her. "I'm taking a few of the teachers and students on a tour of Talhan's school today and wondered if you'd like to join us?"

"I'm honoured." She grinned. Perhaps she'd run into Eva at the school.

"The others are outside. Shall we?"

Shari nodded and followed him. Off to the side of the bereni trees, a small group was standing around flat red squares on the ground.

In front of them was a man Shari hadn't seen before. His midnight skin was stunningly offset against the orange clothing typical of Talhan. The head wrap he wore was boxy at the top with defined corners.

"Well met, teachers and students of Ridden Hall." He bowed at the group. It was about evenly split with ten teachers, ten students, Shari, and the vice principal. "I am Vren, Head of Vitreus Academy. At the academy, we encourage curiosity, creativity, and questions. If you see anything you would like to find out more about, please ask. Our philosophy leaves no room for wasted time, so please step onto the platforms. They will take you directly to Vitreus Academy."

Shari exchanged curious glances with the others. They were all waiting for her to go first.

'*Are they safe?*' Tutor Boyce sent to her. It was odd to hear someone so commanding in the classroom sound so hesitant.

Shari sighed and prodded at the platforms with her Innarn. 'There's *nothing malicious or ill-intended*,' she sent, and stepped onto one. The others followed her lead.

Vren stepped onto the last one and Shari noted the sweeping arm movement he used to activate the Innarn to return the red crystals back to their origin point.

She blinked, and the squares neatly slotted into the floor of a cavernous room.

All around them, white walls glowed under the power of the black crystals inset into a design on the wall, which Shari suspected was the school crest. Tiny circles at the end of straight lines zigzagged, the right angles curving until they all met at the larger circle in the middle.

Before them was a broad set of stairs leading upwards. Shari craned her neck and imagined the Ilutri flying and swooping in here. How many stories high it was.

"Welcome to Vitreus Academy," Vren said, pride shining through his rich voice.

The entire school was buzzing with so much crystal power, Shari could taste it at the back of her mouth. It was like spicy, earthy salt, much harsher than the sea spray Ronah kicked up, but pleasant in its own way.

"The Academy," Vren started saying as he headed for the stairs, "is one of the oldest schools on Lissae. It was created before the schools on the other Shifting Islands, and there are only three on the mainland which are older. It started off as a single level with an enormous field. We're standing where the field used to be."

That's why the cavern was so large. It was still a field. At the far end, there was a match of nimble surfing taking place. Someone slipped from their board and fell at least three stories before they were caught by a net.

Others closer to them were being led in a series of exercises, which vaguely reminded Shari of patrol drills, although she sensed they were being done for the physicality, rather than practical use.

With a huff, she turned back to Vren, who was saying, "Every grade has their own floor, and speciality classes, such as drama, science, and Innarn are housed on the opposite side of these stairs. Our students are separated into grades according to aptitude, rather than age. Mr Hollingsworth assures me the students here today have an aptitude of senior year or higher, so we will visit our senior classrooms."

Two kids in the year below her grinned as they slapped their palms together. Shari smiled at their excitement.

Vren led everyone to another lot of red tiles, and they all stepped on without hesitating.

In a blink, they arrived outside a classroom.

The academy head waved his hand across the white wall, turning it clear. "We can see in, but they can't see out."

Shari frowned. How often did the teachers at Vitreus Academy spy on their students?

As if he'd heard her thoughts, Vren said, "This is a special power held by the head of the academy. It allows me to see what is happening in a room before I enter it."

A handy thing to have access to.

Each student was seated in a comfortable-looking chair and wore a head wrap similar to Vren's, except they had a thin slab of crystal hanging in front of their eyes.

"This class is trialling the latest technology from Talhan's Linked. It enables the students to immerse themselves in an environment of the teacher's choosing. Today, these students are sitting practise exams for their end-of-year test."

"That's how I wanna do tests from now on," one of the younger kids said.

Jordan and a few of the other teachers laughed and asked technical questions Shari allowed to slip over her head. She was too busy staring at the kid in front of her. Seated in the back row, his screen had turned orange not long after Vren had made the wall translucent. At first, had

Shari thought it was part of whatever the class was doing, but now she wasn't so sure.

Dotted around the spacious room were black and orange crystals. Talhan had a way of merging the necessary crystals into stunning works of art. The orange ones flickered.

The kid who'd been slumping in his cosy seat jerked upright as if pulled by strings. Face expressionless, he turned like he could see them. Limbs shuddering and twisting, he got out of his seat and raised his arm until his wrist was at shoulder height, his hand hanging limply.

The teacher at the front of the room was saying something. She was getting out of her seat.

But the kid was ignoring her.

A buzzing tickled Shari's ears as his hand flipped, and he fired icy shards directly at the wall, making the group from Ronah jump.

Was the teacher low on self-preservation? She approached the kid without bothering to put up a shield.

Esme, the former Talhan candidate for Jon's apprentice, was rising from a seat a few rows away. She was shielding the other oblivious students.

Abruptly turning, the kid slammed out another round of ice shards, this time at the teacher, but they bounced off the shield Shari threw around her.

The woman shrieked.

Through the translucent wall, Esme sighed and roll her eyes even as she reached under her seat and pulled out her quiver.

Kids were yelling both in the classroom and around her, and Vren was storming towards the door.

The kid who'd fired was standing there, arm still outstretched but shaking. He had tears running down both cheeks, and his screen was slowly fading from the orange glow.

Right before Vren reached him, he collapsed like a puppet who'd had its strings cut.

Jonathan blew on his burned fingers as he listened to Samuel reading aloud from the *Hekkor Mafae*.

Just hearing it was making his skin blister. And Samuel was skipping the worst bits.

"We can't keep doing this." Samuel snapped the book closed.

Jonathan gave an inadvertent sigh of relief. "We have to," he said. "There's got to be some hint about what we can do at the Dark Council. How else can we find out what they're planning without putting you in danger?"

"All of Lissae is in danger if I *don't* go," Samuel countered. "Needs of the many, and all that."

"I don't want you to risk yourself." Jonathan frowned.

"It's more of a risk not to attend."

"If only someone could go with you." He ran his hand over his face, hoping Samuel would take the hint.

"There are only two people I've met on this Realm who'd be Dark enough, and one has only just hatched."

"A baby?" Jonathan frowned.

Samuel looked at him as if the book had burned away his remaining brain cells. "No. A child. At the school. Tiny thing. Innarn darker than Shari."

"Let me guess: Shari's the other one?"

"Yes. I'd prefer if neither accompany me." Samuel crossed his arms and looked away. "Better I die alone than drag them to the slaughter at my side."

"You don't stand a chance by yourself. The book has to hold some key, something we can use."

"Books don't hold all the knowledge, Jon." Samuel sighed. "Merely being in the presence of this one is detrimental to your health. It's pointless to keep it around anymore."

"What are you suggesting?"

"Burn it."

The Guardian looked at him, aghast. "We can't!"

"All right then. Let's leave it around to hurt you some more." Samuel tossed it aside casually.

"Just because the contents are painful doesn't mean it should be lost. There is so much to learn, and..."

"Too much of what's in the book could kill you." Samuel glared at him. "Last time I checked, as your apprentice, it is my job to keep you alive."

"But..."

"You don't want to burn it?" Samuel tilted his head. "Fine." He snapped his fingers and the *Hekkor Mafae* disappeared.

"Where did it go?"

"Into my sanctuary. If you're free from its presence for a while, you'll start to think straight again." He pounded the arms of the chair as he stood, making for the back door.

"Samuel, wait!" Jonathan called.

There was a moment when Samuel thought of continuing. He reached for the handle. But stopped.

"Thank you. For looking out for me," Jonathan said.

The golden-skinned man tossed him a tight smile as he left the shop.

The rest of the tour of the Vitreus Academy had been cancelled, and Shari spent the remainder of her lessons wondering what had happened.

When the last bell of the day rang, Shari raced to Ridden Hall's gate, determined to find out what had caused that kid to use his Innarn on his teacher. And to catch up with Esme, if she could track the former candidate down.

All thought of the academy fled Shari's mind. A figure in a brown cloak stood by the main gate, the hood angled in such a way that it hid her face.

Shari grinned. She was glad to see Jon's scout, Fiona, was back to her old tricks.

"Well met, Fiona."

"Well met, Altoriae. I'm afraid I have news."

"Sounds serious." Which disaster was about to unfold now?

"Atlantis wants to send a delegation to see how Belfar and Wolf are holding up." Fiona's hood tipped slightly, and Shari could make out her smile.

Shari sighed. "How far away are they?"

"They are being diplomatic. They say they are at your disposal."

"Have you spoken to Jon?"

Fiona's lips twitched. "He seems a tad distracted."

"Zac's back."

"You know of Zac?" Fiona tilted her head.

"I do now. Every time I look in Jon's head, it's full of thoughts of Zac. It's getting to the point where I will have to start knocking."

The scout shook her head and laughed. "I'm glad. He deserves to be happy. He hasn't been since Zac left."

"I am a handful," Shari said wryly.

Chuckling, Fiona said, "That's not what I meant."

"I know." She grinned. '*How aggressive is the Atlantean delegation?*'

'*Diplomacy is not my strong suit, but they seem genuine in their offer to help.*' Fiona paused and looked at the kids leaving the school.

The scout was wondering why people were ignoring them. It had everything to do with the circle of Returned kids around them, backs to the Altoriae, and the gate Daivi had created in between the pillars for the other students to use.

'*I can't be entirely sure of their motives. They are bringing a minotaur with them.*'

'*Looks like we're in for a fight then,*' Shari sent grimly.

CHAPTER FIFTEEN

The instant the diplomatic party from Atlantis crossed over the threshold and onto Lissaen ground, Shari shivered.

The movement was so minute that only Sam, who crowded against her side, felt it. She ignored the slight tapping on her shields and kept her eyes straight ahead.

Humanoid beings in robes of bright colours stepped forward one at a time, bowing as they were introduced.

Shari barely paid attention. She only had eyes for the one right at the very back.

Finally, he stepped forward and bowed. His wickedly sharp horns were capped with silver, as if to show he was not a threat.

"Asterion of Atlantis."

"I know you," Shari said. It was the first thing she'd said since the delegation arrived.

The room went silent.

"Yes, we've met twice before," he rumbled.

Twice... Shari frowned. There was a minotaur in the aftermath of Anriluka. "You said your home was Canak-Maku."

"I travel around a lot. It seems whenever I find myself in trouble, you are there, too." His voice was almost a drawl compared to the clipped tones of the other Atlanteans.

"And the first time?"

"I came to Ronah seeking aid–I was told the Guardian was a fair man, willing to help for the price of allegiance. Instead, I found you. A tiny thing, hammering on my chest."

Shari glanced at Jonathan out of the corner of her eye. She hadn't known he'd bartered aid for allegiance. When he groaned, she sighed. They'd be talking about it later.

"I had a Realm to protect." Shari shrugged with one shoulder. The dress Anika had picked out was more restrictive than she was used to. Wide straps gathered into a stiff middle section which pulled in around her still-tender ribs and flowed out from her waist. The other girl had said the green matched her eyes, but Shari had thought the amber gems dotting the hem and collar too much until the delegation had walked through the doors.

"Even back then?"

"It sure seemed like it. Why are you with the Atlanteans?"

One of the other diplomats stepped forward, placing a hand on the minotaur's forearm. He flinched and went still, like he was waiting for a blow to land.

"Asterion has been a valuable asset in allowing us to understand other cultures," the other diplomat said smoothly, patting his arm and withdrawing her hand. Shari's jaw clenched as the woman subtly wiped her hand on her robe, as if rubbing away dirt.

She wasn't the only one to notice Asterion's aversion to being touched.

Sam was growling almost inaudibly next to her.

"How so?" Jonathan asked sweetly.

The diplomat had to tip her head back to look down her crooked nose. "Do you know why myths are told?"

"Yes." Jon's slow blink told Shari exactly how well they would get on with this woman. *'Her name is Oitane,'* Jon sent to her. *'They usually send her when the Atlanteans want something.'*

'Didn't they come offering aid?'

"Then you know they were designed to explain and guide our actions. There are many myths from across the Realms. Were you aware that most beings consider my Realm to be a myth?"

Beside her, Sam snorted and shook his head. What he was thinking?

"It's true. Especially on our mother Realm, Earth. It suits us. If we are beings of legend, we can listen to their myths and make them our own. Each has a lesson." Oitane reached out to pat Asterion's arm again, but he'd shifted enough so she ended up patting the air. "Asterion is based on the old Earth myth of a bull-headed man. He is much more intelligent than the original. However, he does have the body of a murderer."

Asterion flinched and snorted, clouds of his breath dancing in the air.

The diplomat sighed. "Really, we've been through this." Oitane was peering down her nose again, although it was at a comical angle. "It was the only way to make the myth *authentic.*"

Shari had the feeling the word 'authentic' was thrown around a lot. "How..." she cleared her throat, the words seeming to stick. "How else did you make it authentic?"

"Oh, my dear." The diplomat seemed to glow at being asked to expand on the subject. "We had to breed cattle a certain way to make sure the head wouldn't be rejected. Then a professor whose health was failing offered his brain. It was the perfect combination."

If she were less refined, Shari thought the diplomat would be bouncing on her toes.

"Perfect combination?" Jon raised an eyebrow, but a pallor was creeping over his face.

"A powerful body, which was a perfect match for the head, and a willing brain donor. Nisethran, the doctor who successfully completed the surgery, went mad with success. Yet he leaves us with a miracle of modern science meeting mythology etched in flesh!" She flourished her hands at Asterion, who crossed his arms.

"That's—" Shari was going to say *barbaric*, but Jon broke in.

"Quite an achievement. I can see why you've offered to aid us." Jon started for the door. "Why don't you come with us, and we'll show you what we have found out so far."

Shari's fingers ached. Bile sat bitterly in the back of her throat, and her eyes stung. She was clenching her jaw so hard, she was worried her teeth would crack.

The other diplomats filed out behind Jon and Oitane.

Sam tapped Shari's arm, and she flinched, unclenching her fingers from a weapon she didn't recall summoning.

Asterion was alone in the room with them.

"That day... the first time we met. You said you wanted help?"

He bowed his head. "I did. They had completed the procedure, and the instant everyone saw me, they ran. My brilliance used to be celebrated, and now I am a pariah."

"Why did you hurt my mother?"

"Did I? I didn't mean to. This body was nothing like what I was used to. They'd been subjecting me to tests to ensure I wasn't a danger."

"Tests?" Sam rumbled next to her.

"Electro-shock, mostly. The occasional unwilling teen thrown into a room with me to see if I'd harm them."

"Did you?" Shari asked, stepping forward. She already knew the answer, but she wanted to hear it out loud.

A look of disgust crossed Asterion's face. "Of course not. My job is to help, not harm."

"And when I told you to go?"

His shoulders slumped. "I became their puppet for a while. They'd send me into places to look intimidating, or to learn about the locals. I find it a tad hard to blend in." He ran a finger along a horn, scoffing when he reached the silver decoration adorning the tip.

"How did you get to Canak-Maku?"

"I'd finally found somewhere to fit in. A 'diplomatic' mission went sideways, and I was able to stay." At Sam's arched brow, he clarified, "They thought the delegation was trying to negotiate, and they did what minotaurs are famous for. They destroyed the delegation and feasted on their flesh."

Shari wrinkled her nose. "Kinda have to agree with them on this one. Maybe not the flesh-eating part."

Asterion huffed a laugh and looked surprised, like he wasn't used to the sound. "It didn't last long. The U'tan came, and then I was elsewhere. After years in her prison, I was spat out on Lissae. During the battle, I was trying to save the boy. He was my charge to keep safe. When you snatched him, I thought you meant him harm."

"Eric was your charge?"

His smile was sad—an odd look on a bull's face. "He would sit on my head and use my horns at handles."

She laughed despite herself. "And now you're back with the Atlanteans."

"They found me again," he corrected. "They claim they want to help, but really they want to see your Realm for themselves. They are desperate to gather some of the Innarn they lost generations ago."

The door opened, and a curly head poked through. "Asterion, are you joining us?"

Shari sensed there were at least three more bodies on the other side of the door, waiting to drag him away. "Can't old friends catch up?" she asked, stepping next to Asterion and slipping a hand into the crook of his arm. Without a word, Sam stepped to the minotaur's other side, and the trio strode through the doors after the delegation.

The others were all waiting in the first room of the museum. Jon seemed reluctant to allow them to walk through Ronah's streets. She didn't blame him. The sooner this lot went home, the better.

'*Can you shift the entire party?*' Jon sent.

'*Where to?*'

Jon was sorting through the options.

'*The large meeting room off the mayor's office. It should be sufficient for the meeting.*'

'*The one with all the gold trim?*' It was a gaudy room, but Jon knew what he was doing. By the looks of this crowd, it might even be up to their lofty standards.

She hoped.

'*Yes. I'll let the mayor know we're coming.*'

Shari sensed him reach out and warn Alan. '*I want to get Asterion to stay.*'

'*Let's see what they want first.*'

"Ready, Asterion?" she whispered. The minotaur nodded. Shari shifted the entire party.

There were a few gasps and indignant huffs. Shari tried not to glare at them.

"Thought we'd save you the walk," Jon said. "Please, have a seat."

One of the Atlanteans clicked his fingers, and Asterion sighed. "Excuse me," he rumbled as he disentangled himself from Shari and moved to the other side of the table to be immediately flanked by four of his contingent.

Everyone took a seat, except for Oitane. She was staring out of the windows Shari had turned opaque as soon as they'd entered the room.

"I would have preferred to walk through your town and see how you live," she said. "Perhaps we can walk back."

'There is no way in the nine hells I want her walking through Ronah.' Shari pasted a fake smile on her face.

"Perhaps. We were told you were requesting aid? Such a request usually shows that time is of the essence," Jon said mildly. 'Do you really think I'd let her?'

She glanced sideways at the Guardian, and noted his fake smile looked far more realistic than hers felt. Clearly, she had something else to practise.

"We're not requesting aid. We're demanding our stolen technology be returned."

"Stolen technology?" Sam said.

"Yes. Nisethran has already enquired about the stolen device, but he failed to procure it."

"And then he tortured and mutilated one of our people." Shari crossed her arms and leaned back in her chair.

"An unfortunate incident, one which we worked to rectify." Oitane shot back.

"But you couldn't."

"While we would like to pay our respects to the one who was injured before we return, we truly seek to find our stolen technology. In the wrong hands, it would be fatal."

"I'm afraid that without knowing precisely what you're looking for, we can't really be of much help."

The woman waved a bejewelled hand at her party before she finally sat down.

A man near Asterion placed a slim, silver disk on the table. He touched something, and it projected an image in the air.

"This is what was stolen from us." Oitane sounded cold and hostile.

Shari held back a giggle as Jonathan's long glare at the diplomat said how much she'd failed to hit the mark.

The stolen technology displayed on the projection looked like the thing with the red light which had attacked Ronah, but smaller and without legs.

"What does it do?" Shari asked.

The diplomat looked down her nose again.

How in all the Realms had Oitane had earned her title?

"This device enables people with failing vision to have clear sight. It repairs the eye by shaving away a small part with a laser."

Next to Shari, Jon was tense, but when he spoke, his voice sounded as calm as ever. "I'm afraid we destroyed it."

"Then we want the parts." Oitane's voice was hard.

"I'll ensure you receive them."

"We'll wait."

Shari struggled not to blast the smug look off the woman's face.

"While you're waiting, please enjoy some refreshments."

Shari sensed Jon sending to someone outside the room.

A moment later, there was a knock at the door.

Jon pushed on their connection, and Shari wrinkled her nose. There was no way she wanted the snooty woman chancing even a peek at the rest of Ronah. The outside door opened to a stunning view of the main street from a full-length window.

Drawing inspiration from the blank walls of the Ducibus' hallway, Shari created a solid shield which mimicked the empty walls. When the illusion was complete, she nodded to Sam. He rose and opened the door.

Collis, Daivi, and five other Returned walked into the room, laden with platters of food from the eateries in Ronah's main street.

"We have a variety of Ronah's finest food for you to try." Jon smiled before rising and slipping from the room.

As Collis slid the platter onto the table, he looked up and caught sight of Asterion. A quick indrawn breath had the Atlanteans on either side of the minotaur chuckling.

"Don't worry, boy. He's tame." One of them smirked.

Collis bowed his head and backed away, moving to stand directly behind Shari.

She tried not to jump as he surreptitiously allowed the back of his hand to brush against the skin of her arm. Thrice-damned dress was leaving her more exposed than she was used to.

But his touch allowed her to listen in on the rapid-fire sending.

'*Asterion! I thought you had faded,*' Collis sent. She could feel the sadness accompanying the thought.

'*No, I escaped, but was caught again.*' Asterion lowered his eyes, presumably to the delicate plate one of the others had put in front of him. The Atlanteans chuckled at his discomfort as he rested a thick-fingered hand on the table.

'*What do you need? How can we get you away?*'

'*They already lost me once. I doubt they'll allow me to escape again. I'm being guarded every moment. Besides, I doubt your Altoriae will welcome me here.*'

Shari butted in. '*I apologise for sending you away before. I know better now. You will always be welcome on Lissae.*'

The minotaur sniffed. '*Thank you, Altoriae. I will have to work out how to get away from my keepers. They've implanted a tracker in me at the base of my neck. I can't reach it.*'

'*Can we disable it?*' Collis asked.

Asterion delicately nibbled at a sweet tart. '*A jolt of plasma might do it, but the wielder would have to be careful. They've wrapped the tracker around my spine.*'

'*Plasma stops their devices from working?*' Shari broke in again.

'*Yes. Water used to, but they long ago perfected waterproofing.*'

Cautiously sending out her Innarn, Shari poked around the back of Asterion's neck. She probed deeper and detected the tracker.

It would be easy to fix if it were not for the tiny cylinders of metal wrapped around his spine and imbedded in his brain.

'*I think I'd be able to shock it enough,*' Shari sent cautiously.

Jon slipped back into the room, a wooden box in his hands.

'*If you can't, when you try...*' Asterion picked up his cup and met her eyes as he looked over the rim. '*...you must kill me. I don't want to be their puppet anymore.*'

Shari gave a shaky nod and pretended like the food on her plate was holding her attention. It tasted like wasted opportunities and sawdust.

"This is everything that was left of your device." Jon placed the box on the table.

'*When do you want me to do it?*' Shari asked.

'*Not now. I'll send word as soon as I can.*'

'*Asterion, what if it's years before we see each other again?*'

'*If you do it now, it could start a war.*'

'*That's a war I'd be willing to fight,*' Shari sent stubbornly.

'*But it's one I don't want to cause.*'

Shari slumped. '*As you wish.*'

One man unpacked the box. He nodded at the diplomat.

"Thank you for your cooperation," she said.

"What will you give us for our cooperation?" Shari asked.

Oitane smiled. "Our thanks," she simpered.

Her frustration at not being able to help Asterion made it hard to suppress the growl rising in her throat. Shari looked at Jon expectantly.

"We'll need more than that I'm afraid. After your failed attempt to heal one of our own, and your falsified request for entry, Lissae sees little need in helping you in any future endeavours."

The smug smile vanished from Oitane's face. "You can't be serious."

"You entered our Realm, requesting aid, and once here, you made demands instead. Hardly here for help, were you?" Shari said.

Mouth dropping unattractively, Oitane gaped at her.

"We can offer expertise," Asterion broke in smoothly.

"In what way?" Shari asked. '*Give me a reason to let you stay.*'

"Atlanteans are skilled in both technology and healing. Perhaps we can offer the aid of one of our scientists and healers?" he said.

'Is it you?' Shari asked.

'No. I am neither. And they would never let me stay.' His send was mournful, despite the slight smile he wore.

"If you're agreeable, I'll send through a list of potentials who agree to the position." Oitane took over smoothly.

"I'd much rather someone from Lissae have the chance to see your scientists at work and be able to choose for ourselves. After all, we would be the ones hosting them." Shari smiled, but promised death with her eyes.

Oitane's nose lifted. "If you wish. I believe our business is done."

"If you wish," Shari parroted, and shifted them directly to the other side of the museum doors.

"Shari," Jon groaned.

"I don't know why you invite me along to diplomatic talks." Shari grinned, and popped a berry into her mouth.

CHAPTER SIXTEEN

Zac breathed slowly. He had to time this right.

Shadows thrown by the crystal lights passed by the alleyway before their owners came into view. A group of beings, two Ilutri, a woman with a wide-hemmed skirt... finally, there was the shadow he knew to be Jon's.

Three, two, one.

He stepped out from behind the wall and bumped directly into the Guardian.

"Oof!"

If it were any other time, he would have laughed at the noise Jon made. As it was, he reached out and grabbed one of Jon's forearms, double tapping the vial hidden in his coat pocket as he pretended to rub his chest.

"Well met, Jon." He smiled.

"Well met, Zac."

For a moment, he found himself lost in the Guardian's gaze. He'd changed a lot from the young man who he'd patrolled with.

Laughed with.

Fought with.

"Nice night to crash into an old friend," he said at last.

"We should have that meal now neither of us is holed up in the Healers Centre. Maybe at the Quiver and Quill? Just like old times?" Jon suggested with the quirk of his lips that Zac remembered so well.

Zac gazed intently into the Guardian's eyes, and smiled in triumph when they flashed orange.

Soon it would be just like old times—Jon sitting by his side, no glasses to mar his eyes. Zac'd be able to catch every expression without the filter of glasses to mar his view.

"Sounds amazing. How about in three nights?"

Temira had thought it would work in two, but Zac wanted to be sure.

"I'll be there," Jon said.

"I'll let you get home then. I bid thee well." Zac grinned and released Jon's arm.

In two nights, the Guardian would have his sight restored.

And in three nights, Zac had a date.

In the shadows, metal clicked against stone, and the broken machine slowly followed the man with the orange glow home.

Xani lay unmoving in her bed.

She'd somehow convinced the thing controlling her it was within necessary parameters for her body to rest.

But the thing still wanted to work. It would lock her body down, forbidding movement or sound, and grab hold of the orange crystal light by her bed, flowing from her body until the minimum rest requirements had been met.

For a brief period each day, she was free of its control.

Through its connection with the crystal, and her own, she saw the mechanical creature targeting the Guardian.

Maybe she could use it to her advantage.

Pushing her crystal Innarn to the limit, she made the machine vibrate.

The noise disturbed the Guardian; she could tell. She felt the vibrations of his steps coming closer.

Closer.

A cover was lifted, and the machine saw the Guardian's face close up for the first time. His mouth opened, and he dropped to the floor, skittering backwards on all fours, a weapon appearing in one hand.

Xani mentally moaned. *This is the being in charge of protecting Lissae for so long?*

She made the machine walk forward, but stopped it when it was in the open part of the room. She forced it to sit and wait.

The Guardian was aiming his blade at the machine.

That's more like it.

But she couldn't let him fire just yet.

Compelling one of the mechanical legs to stretch out, she then got it to tap out a pattern.

Frozen to the spot, the Guardian tilted his head, his mouth moving again.

Xani made the machine tap out the same pattern.

Clearly, this time, she saw his mouth form her name.

She tapped out a different pattern. Three letters.

Y–E–S.

He dropped to the floor again.

The crystal in her hand started to vibrate. She was almost out of time.

Another three letters. This time different.

R–U–N.

'Someone is bad.'

Xani swore.

'Ah. I see. I need him.'

Through her connection to the machine in the Guardian's house, Xani watched helplessly as the thing controlling her body took it over as well.

The metallic creature started to vibrate.

Creeping closer, the Guardian looked at it in confusion.

The vibrations increased.

As the Guardian reached out a hand, the machine was obliterated. The metal shards vaporised, leaving only a cloud of femto crystals and a dying red light.

The Guardian sucked in a surprised breath, and Xani, trapped by the same creature, felt him join the ever growing collective.

'*Run!*' she sent to him.

The thing in her head chuckled, low and deadly.

The cyclops army on Duhiomel was annoying her. Shari couldn't figure out why they'd been so aggressive.

She'd been there before and they'd been either grateful for her help or had left her to her own devices.

Even though she'd agreed to only patrol two nights a week, Shari wouldn't be able to rest if she didn't check it out.

She shifted straight from her bed to the rocky streambed of Duhiomel. Shari picked a spot by the bank closest to the gateway to settle down.

Then she waited.

As the creatures around the steam became accustomed to her presence, they started their chatter again. With the birds and insects happy, Shari sent her Innarn out, trying to discern why the cyclops were so upset.

Three clicks behind her and the gateway, there was a familiar Innarn signature.

For a moment, Shari considered running. She'd head back home, straight to her bed, and away from the U'sala camped out in the forest.

There was a flash, and the insects fell abruptly silent.

Shari sighed. "Well met, Yessna."

"Healer Shari! I thought it was you." The second-in-command of the U'sala smiled at her, fangs shining brightly even in the shadowed gloom.

"Can't hide from you anymore, can I?"

"Of all the beings on the Realms, I believe you would be the only one able to." The Ferah smirked. "Although I'm glad you've come. We've been having some trouble—"

"With the cyclops army?" Shari asked.

Yessna narrowed her eyes. "You've come across them too?"

"Almost lost someone," Shari said.

"We've lost three. There seems to be no reason for their actions, and none of our scouts can get close enough to their camp."

Shari sighed. "Is this your way of buttering me up?"

"Why would I want to put butter on you?" The Ferah frowned.

"No, I mean, are you trying to pay me a compliment, so I'll do some scouting for you?"

Yessna's whiskers quivered around a wide smile. "I thought I'd have to bribe you, actually."

"We're allies, Yessna. You don't have to bribe me."

The Ferah's whiskers drooped. "I wasn't sure you'd still consider us allies. Not after everything Kodan did."

Shari rubbed the back of her hand across her forehead and looked to the other side of the creek, not really seeing what was there. "I consider, and hope, him to be an anomaly. I figure as hurt as I am, you and the rest of the U'sala would have to be more so. Kodan played you all for longer than he did me."

They stood together for a while, letting the insects do the talking for them.

Eventually, Yessna moved, drawing Shari's attention to her. She used her hands to sign out the words in the Veti Cant. '*Would you like to join us at the camp?*'

The last time Yessna invited her to join the U'sala's camp, she'd sat around a fire and met Kodan. From the look in the Ferah's eyes, she knew exactly what Shari was thinking.

'*I'd love to,*' she signed back.

'*No surprise assassins this time.*' Yessna's teeth were showing.

'*Otherwise you'll owe me one.*'

Yessna laughed and silently led the way through the trees to the U'sala camp. Shari sensed Yessna sending word to the others. When they arrived, the camp was still humming with activity, but a lot of eyes turned her way.

Many of the U'sala signed '*well met*' as she passed, and she signed it back, nodding. Yessna gestured for her to take a seat at a log on the ground by the main fire. Their camp was similar to the one they'd had near the Niverwell Ranges on Iabovar, but the tents were pale green this time, blending in with the foliage of Duhiomel.

"How are the U'sala holding up?" Shari asked, gratefully accepting the cup smelling of spice and honey, with a citrus tang. It seemed to be a staple drink for the group. She took a sip. "What is this called?"

"Daborang. It's a spiced tea. You like?"

"It's delicious. I'd like to take a bottle home. Jon would love it."

Yessna purred. "It is my own concoction. I'd be honoured to share some with the Guardian."

Shari smiled and took another drink. "I'm sure he'd be thrilled. But what of the U'sala?"

Yessna sighed heavily as she flopped onto the log next to Shari and stared morosely into her cup. "We are split at the moment. My party is scouting." She gestured to the camp. "Many of the U'sala came from the surrounding Realms. There are some, like me and Jeran, who are from farther afield, but most were within three or four Realms of here. It's considered to be mostly peaceful. The twins hail from a village about three days walk from here."

"The twins?"

As if she had summoned them, two identical cyclops brothers strode towards the fire, carrying a spit with the largest moon rabbit Shari had ever seen. They put it over the flames before taking a seat.

The Altoriae noted their dark leathers had more patches than most, and each had scars enough to rival hers.

They bowed in unison and took a seat on another log, drinks in hand.

"They have been with us the longest. Apart from Kodan" Yessna flushed red under her fur.

"We're rather sick of fighting, to be honest," one twin said. His voice was higher than his barrel chest indicated, and he was well spoken. "I am Kerk, and my brother is Drah." Kerk had an old scar dissecting his eye.

"You're prettier than your predecessor," Drah said. He slowly grinned at Shari, running his tongue across his bottom lip. Kerk nudged his brother hard. Drah laughed, the smattering of freckles over the bridge of his nose becoming less pronounced as his skin reddened. He raised his right hand, which was missing two fingers. He was clearly still capable of delivering a solid punch, if the way Kerk rubbed his arm was any indication.

Shari leaned forward, elbows on her knees. The smell of wood smoke and the sizzle of fat dripping into the fire reminded her of the last time she'd visited the U'sala. Of how charming Kodan had been. She stoppered the question behind her teeth. With a quick breath, Shari reminded herself that she hadn't come this far because of a lack of bravery. "You knew Fiona, the last Altoriae?"

Drah's smile changed, making him look less predatory. "She was the one who guided us to the U'sala. Saved us really. We would have been like the moon rabbit otherwise."

"They would have eaten you?" Shari sucked in a breath.

Yessna and the brothers laughed.

"No. Just got us in a lot of trouble. A neighbouring lord took our village over, and we wanted him to go back to where he came from," Drah said.

"With one of our boots firmly up his—" Kerk grumbled.

A log on the fire popped, making Shari jump. The U'sala members laughed again.

"So, we ran. Ran as fast as we could, and farther than we'd ever been before." Drah continued.

"Got lost in the Sivertrie Woods," Kerk broke in.

"Found an odd-looking door and stumbled into an even odder lady on the other side." Drah took a drink.

"First two-eyed we'd ever seen," Kerk added.

She smirked. By the fur on Yessna's arm standing on end, and the identical smirks the brothers wore, they were all expecting her head to be swimming by now due to their twin-speak.

Shari lifted her cup and grinned into it before she took a sip. She'd had to learn how to send and speak at the same time. Their parlour trick was cute, but nothing more. "And she introduced you to the U'sala?" she asked.

The twins grinned at her nonchalance. "Almost straight away. Weren't a lot of beings going to Lissae in her time, else we would have tried to settle down there." Kerk leaned back.

"Why have you come home now?"

The brothers looked at Yessna.

The Ferah sighed. "As much as I hate to admit it, Kodan was right. The U'sala have been wandering the Realms for five millennia. We take on strays, teach them to wield a weapon, and send them to war. Every day, we fight to help others, but at night, we've nothing more than a hard bedroll—"

"And a rock as a pillow," the brothers chorused, and the three laughed again, but it was bitter this time.

"You're looking for somewhere to settle down." Shari realised.

Yessna nodded. "We'd thought we might carve out our own corner on Duhiomel."

"But our kinsmen are planting their boots in," Kerk said.

"And we aren't welcome anymore," Drah added. Both brothers drained their cups and stood.

"How large are the U'sala?"

"From what we saw, we're easily as many as the population of your Ronah," Kerk said.

Shari sighed. "I don't know of anywhere, but I can keep an ear out for you."

"What would we do with an ear?" Yessna tilted her head.

With a quirk of her lips, Shari said, "It means I'll listen and see if I hear of somewhere with some free land."

"I heard Lissae takes in refugees occasionally," Drah said, looking at her out of the corner of his eye.

Shari brushed off the seat of her pants as she stood. "Last time I took in a refugee from the U'sala, he tried to kill my entire town."

"Ouch!" Drah rocked backwards, hand on his heart, while Kerk shook his head at his twin's antics.

"I'll walk you to the gateway," Yessna said, flicking her tail and glaring at Drah.

Shari bid the brothers goodbye. Drah winked at her and licked his lower lip again. Kerk whacked his arm, and the brothers called out their farewells.

When they were free of the camp, Yessna asked, "Are you still upset?" She was frowning.

"Not at the U'sala," Shari said. *At Kodan, and at myself for trusting him, yes, but not at the U'sala.*

"We are in your debt."

"Just keep helping people. And make sure no one shares Kodan's sentiments. I really will try to find somewhere for you all to settle down."

They'd arrived by the door.

"My thanks, healer. Fight well. Live free," Yessna said. She bowed her head and watched as Shari bowed back.

The Altoriae slipped through the gateway, home to Lissae.

Something was wrong with the Guardian.

Samuel scowled as Jonathan jerkily moved towards the gateway. He walked as if someone else held the strings and controlled his limbs.

Eventually, he stopped before a brass-studded wooden door. Samuel frowned. What could Jonathan possibly want on Fiotealar? The Grey Realm was known for creating the most sought-after technology around, but the Guardian was decidedly old fashioned. And from memory, it wasn't compatible with Lissaen tech anyway.

The Ducibus seemed reluctant to let him through, but eventually gave in. Samuel hoped they wouldn't take long before they contacted the higher gateway guards.

'*Behind me,*' Samuel sent to the rest of the patrol group.

Four of the others, all younglings, immediately fell into line. The older lady with silver-white hair sniffed. His narrowed eyes silently begged her to disobey. Whatever was wrong with Jonathan was leaving him itchy and ready for a fight.

A small shake of her head and she fell in, close enough to step on his heels.

The Guardian seemed to come back to himself, his hand rising to rub at his head.

'*Are you alright?*' Samuel sent, putting his hand Jonathan's arm. He was close enough to notice an orange haze pass over his friend's eyes.

'*Fine,*' Jonathan sent, voice a monotone. For a beat, he frowned hard, then blinked and was still.

Samuel shivered. *What is going on with my friend?*

"Incoming!"

The yell had him whipping around, throwing a shield over the entire group as he turned.

A single circular, spinning disc with lethally sharp edges, passed between two of the patrol members and cut into the side of a tree.

He knew that blade. It was a chakram, designed to be thrown from a height, and only a clawful of species used it as their preferred weapon.

'*Down!*' he sent, adjusting his shield.

The next chakram bounced off the tree next to him harmlessly. There was silence from the woods around their little grove.

Cautiously, Samuel inspected the disk-like blade made from a bronzed metal and sporting a large hole in the centre. It looked like the Yoxant were not keen on having Lissaens on their Realm.

If Jonathan was in his right mind, he'd be able to be all diplomatic and set the record straight, but the tuzar was still standing frozen on the spot.

'*Back through the gateway,*' he ordered.

As Samuel tried to pull Jonathan down, the next blade spun through the air, splintering his shield.

Seemed like the Yoxant used Lighter Innarn than he remembered. Samuel swore as he tugged on both of Jon's arms, trying to get the Guardian to move.

It was as if his knees were made of stone.

Another chakram was thrown—this one close enough to take a thin layer off Jonathan's sleeve.

"Move!" he snarled, trying to push his friend back to the gateway.

The next chakram slammed into his side, and Samuel howled in pain. Infused with Light Innarn, it burned where it had lodged in his back.

With a roar, he ripped the disk from his hide and threw it towards their attackers. His throw was clumsy, landing only a few paces away from their feet.

Samuel moved as fast as possible, swinging to the other side of Jonathan, who'd become as heavy as a fulni. He grunted as he wrapped his arms around the Guardian's waist and pulled.

Jonathan's heels created troughs in the grass.

Gritting his teeth, he glanced behind him to make sure the rest of the group were through the gateway. He pushed another shield up. Then Samuel changed enough to use the strength from his natural form to drag the Guardian backwards through the door, healing his side a bit as he did so.

Samuel took the last step, the heel of his back leg hitting the threshold, when the sound of displaced air made him look up.

Another blade was coming straight for them.

It shattered his shield like it was nothing and embedded itself with a wet thud in Jon's neck.

Blood sprayed out, decorating the grass of the glade as Samuel gave a final heave and pulled Jon through the gateway.

The patrol group looked horrified. Tears and effluvia dribbled down their faces.

Jonathan was still not moving. His face was gradually draining of colour as his life force spilled from his veins.

Grimly, the silver-haired woman placed a hand on the Guardian's chest. "I can shift him to the healers."

"Do it."

Watching his friend disappear, with only the blood stains on the floor to speak of his presence, was the hardest thing he'd done in a while.

Then Samuel realised he'd have to tell Shari.

'Shari, there's been an incident.'

'Sam? What do you mean?' She'd only just arrived back on Lissae and was feeling itchy from the lack of fighting and all the emotions she was trying to keep pent-up.

'Jon caught a chakram. With his throat.' Sam sounded frustrated. 'There's something wrong with him.'

Scowling, it took Shari a moment to decipher the cryptic send. "Oh, for the love of..." She shifted straight to Jon, almost landing on a healer.

"Sorry," she said, trying to scramble out of the way.

"We could use your help, Altoriae. Something is trying to prevent us from healing him." Healer Holli Doonavan bit her lip and frowned.

That was never a good sign.

Her hands hovered over the wound; Shari closed her eyes. She poked and prodded, knitting the veins and muscles back together.

There. The thing preventing Jon from healing was foreign and was not meant to be in his body, but it also felt strangely familiar.

"He's lost too much blood," Holli said. "His heart is slowing."

"Come on, Jon," Shari whispered. Her hands were shaking, but the green glow of her healing was steady. "Jon, please." She put more effort into finding the foreign things, and tried not to dwell on why the Ducibus scrub hadn't picked them up.

She felt Jon's heart stop the instant before Holli announced it.

"No. No-no-no-no-no." Shari clenched her fists, and the green glow disappeared. Something niggled at the back of her mind, and plasma started crackling along her fingertips.

"I'm sorry, Shari," Holli was saying.

Shari wasn't listening.

"This is not how you end," Shari growled, and slapped her hand down on his chest, releasing the plasma straight into his heart.

His body jerked, and a healer squealed. Shari felt bad for not warning them, but Jon's face was all she was focusing on.

He didn't move.

She brought back the green healing glow. Shari put her other hand over his neck, pulling the skin back together.

"Leave room for whatever is stopping the healing to get out," Holli cautioned.

Shari slapped his chest again, pushing the plasma directly into his heart.

It gave a mighty thump and started to beat again.

She looked straight into Holli's eyes and let the tears she'd been holding back fall.

CHAPTER SEVENTEEN

Shari slumped at her desk, head cushioned by her fist. She was drained in ways she hadn't imagined and was struggling to stay awake.

A knock on the classroom door roused her curiosity. Very few beings would willingly interrupt Tutor Heath-Ribeck's class.

"Message for the Altoriae," a brown-cloaked figure said.

The teacher huffed. "Very well." He flicked a hand towards Shari and turned back to the board.

Grateful, Shari slid out of the room.

Fiona didn't waste any time. As soon as she saw the Altoriae, she started walking for the entrance of the school. "One of the Atlantean delegation is here to see you."

"What? Who?"

"The minotaur. Something is going on at Atlantis, and he's asking for your help."

"Me specifically?"

"No." Fiona shrugged. "But you're the best one for what needs to be done."

"Are you always this obscure?" Shari sighed.

"He's saying Atlantis was attacked." The scout looked worried. "He had burns on his face and arms like Zac."

"Let's go see him then." Shari grimly stepped out of the school grounds and shifted them to the double doors between one heartbeat and the next.

The room was filled with muffled, drawn-out moaning.

How loud was it on the other side of the door? Shari half wished she'd taken more time to get there.

Next to her, Fiona shivered. "His injuries are severe."

Shari pulled the doors open.

Just beyond them, Asterion was propped up against the wall. His face was criss-crossed with angry burns in straight lines that ended just below his right eye—a lucky escape. Whatever had done this to him had caught the corner of his mouth, and his lip bore painful-looking blisters.

Another Atlantean was with him, applying a salve to the worst of the burns scattered across his torso. The injured minotaur was gritting his teeth, but when the salve touched his skin, he howled like a damned soul.

Shari shivered.

The movement caught his eye. "Altoriae, please, we seek help."

"Asterion, what happened?" Shari asked.

"They attacked us."

A quick peek inside his thoughts allowed Shari to watch the attack play out. There were multiple red lights, burning and cutting through whatever came their way. The machines seemed to be herding people in a particular direction.

"What can I do?"

"Our machines have never acted independently before. I think Oitane took something from Lissae with her, or perhaps one of the others did. It's infected our technology and is making them act out against us." Asterion gritted his teeth as the other Atlantean knelt to inspect his exposed leg through the tear in his pants.

"I don't think it's something from Lissae," Shari said carefully, eyeing the woman putting salve on the last of his wounds. "We had a similar attack here."

Asterion made to help the other Atlantean to her feet, but she skittered away from him. He sighed.

"Really? How did you stop it?" the woman asked.

"The Guardian's apprentice blasted the insides out of it," Shari said bluntly.

"We tried that. Our weapons are all machine-based. Every time we try to fire, they explode in our hands." Asterion lifted a hand, the burns fading as they watched.

Shari gritted her teeth as she saw it play out in his mind. "What do you think their target is?"

Asterion gulped. "The capital. My school is there. All the children I guard. Please, Shari."

"I have to check with the Guardian." She wasn't entirely sure if the tears in his eyes were because of pain or fear.

Asterion closed his eyes and nodded. "I understand. But please, hurry."

'*Make sure the other doesn't come through the doors,*' Shari sent to Fiona.

'*You believe his sob story?*'

'*How good are Atlanteans at implanting false memories?*'

'*Their grasp of Innarn is limited to the technology they create.*' Fiona frowned at her.

'*Then we need to get there quickly. I'll be back.*' Shari slipped through the doors and stood for a moment in the cool of the museum.

The sights of the battle in Asterion's memories was worrying. The red lights could cut through anything it seemed. But why hadn't they cut him in half? Why let him escape?

Shari leaned against the wall and let her head knock it with a gentle *thunk*. '*Jon? I think the Atlanteans are trying to trap us.*' Knowing he'd ask why, she sent him the details of her conversation with Asterion and what she'd gleaned from his memories.

'*If it looks like a trap and smells like a trap...*'

Despite dying the night before, Jon sounded rather aware. More awake than she felt, for sure.

'*Show me the memories again.*'

Shari did. She played them back so they could watch it together.

Asterion was sitting at a table outside, about to eat, when there'd been a beeping noise from a machine down the street. From his vantage point, they couldn't see what was going on. He stood and started walking towards the machine.

Sleek white metal shell in the shape of a teardrop—it was a cleaner, designed to keep the streets tidy. It had stopped in an alleyway and was beeping furiously. There was the scrape of metal on metal, and as Asterion rounded the corner, he saw an orange glow disappear under the shell and into the chassis of the cleaner.

'*I know that glow,*' Shari and Jon sent at the same time.

'*It's Lissaen crystal.*' Jon sounded grim. If she knew Jon as well as she thought she did, he'd be trying to get out of bed. She sent word to the healers to keep him there, just in case.

'*But how did it get to Atlantis?*'

'*Perhaps there was some in the box Oitane took back?*'

'*Maybe.*' But Jon would have ensured there was nothing from Lissae in the box. Oitane had been too eager to explore their world.

'*Did you call the healers on me?*'

She stifled a giggle. '*Maybe,*' she sent again.

Through their link, Jon sighed. '*Take someone with you. Preferably more than one someone. Atlantis is lighter than you are used to.*'

If Atlantis was Light, Sam was out. She needed a group she could trust and who'd work together without thinking. Even as she grinned, Shari sent Jon soothing thoughts.

Then taking a breath and shaking from excitement, Shari sent to one more being. '*Want to help me defend a Realm?*'

"And how are you today?" Cyrus asked, patting the wall.

'*I am unsure.*'

Cyrus shook his head at the smooth walls surrounding Talhan's heart crystal underneath his workshop.

It was hard to remember a time when Talhan hadn't spoken to him. His uncle Hakif had been the last Linked. He could remember sitting by his knee, listening to stories of how Talhan kept everyone safe, of how she provided food and shelter. And how Talhan was the keeper of the crystals which all of Lissae relied upon.

Now though, she was different. If she were humanoid, Cyrus would think she had a cold. "Oh, that isn't nice. What's the matter? Do you get sick?"

'*I can't get sick. I'm an island.*' Talhan was all cool logic, rarely allowing emotions to get in the way. She must have gotten it from one of the Linked from before Uncle Hakif's time.

'*Chunks of dirt can get ill,*' he teased.

She didn't respond.

Cyrus sighed. Which apology would he have to make this time? "I'm sorry. Dirt can get sick, though. It can get infected with tiny parasites, bugs which strip away the nutrients and plants that leech you dry." Staring at the wall suspiciously, he said, "Did someone plant something new and you haven't told me about it?"

Still nothing.

He slumped in his seat and sighed again, making it as big and melodramatic as he could.

'*Cyrus...*' Talhan sounded confused. '*I've run a scan.*'

"A scan for what?"

'*Parasites.*'

He waited, but she remained silent. "And?"

'I *think you may be right.*'

He held his breath in his cheeks so they puffed out comically, and groaned. "I was really hoping you wouldn't say that."

Asterion would lead them into battle. He'd insisted.

Shari insisted he was an idiot, but he refused to budge on the matter.

"It's my Realm, Altoriae."

"If you wanna run to your death, I can't stop you. I don't understand your desire to defend a Realm so determined to vilify you." Shari shrugged and pretended to study the tip of her blade.

Asterion looked at her and slowly smiled. "Of everyone in the Realms, Altoriae, I thought you would be the most understanding."

Ouch.

Off to the side, Collis cocked his head. '*You won't stop him?*'

'*Technically I can, but he's not of Lissae, so I shouldn't.*' Plus, his comment had wounded Shari. His entirely accurate comment.

"I don't know what will be on the other side of the gateway," Asterion cautioned.

"Which is why we're going first," Collis said, smoothly moving to the door. The other Returned took up a wedge formation, surrounding Asterion and Shari. Daivi nudged Shari's side and smiled.

'*Really?*' she sent to Collis, unimpressed.

'*You wanted to see how we work. If you were Muran, we would have done the same thing. Ready?*' He opened the door before she responded.

The glade surrounding the gateway was peaceful. Collis and the Returned maintained a powerful shield, enabling everyone to get through.

'*Only send, don't speak. Where to?*'

'*The capital*,' Asterion sent. Daivi handed him a long-handled spear-headed axe known as an urgrosh, and the set of his shoulders relaxed a bit.

'*How far away is it?*' Shari asked.

'*Three-day trek. But swiftstepping would be quicker.*' He reached into a pocket and pulled out a disc.

'*Can we all use that?*'

Shoulders slumping, he shook his head.

Shari sighed. '*Think as hard as you can about a place on the outskirts of the capital. What it looks like, what it smells like, the things you can hear. I'll shift us there.*'

'*Save your strength, Altoriae.*' Collis grinned and clapped a hand on Asterion's arm.

Collis's shift was like being ripped apart and stitched back together again. Shari took a shaky breath and looked around while Asterion heaved the rest of his last meal onto the pristine sidewalk.

'*Is Collis always so rough with his shifts?*' Shari sent to Daivi.

'*Usually he's worse. But you get used to it.*'

Shari wasn't sure if she wanted to get used to it. Daivi must have sensed the pattern of her thoughts, and she giggled.

With a smile, Shari rolled her eyes, and the Altoriae took her first proper glance at the capital city of Atlantis.

It was stunning. Massive columns decorated in rich colours with gold rings around them held up material of the same colour. The white wall beside them was decorated with an intricate mural depicting smiling people harvesting round berries off vines. Beyond the corner of the wall, smoke was rising, filling the sky.

'*It's quiet*,' one of the Returned sent. She gripped the shaft of her poleaxe tighter.

'*We need to get closer.*' Shari moved, and the entire formation moved with her. Attempting to repress the thought of leading them to their death, she marched forwards.

It took them roughly fifteen minutes before they saw the first machine.

Shari froze, and the Returned were so tuned into her movements, they stopped on the spot.

Asterion gripped the haft of his urgrosh harder. '*Those act as nannies. They keep children safe, ensure they are looked after, and meet their basic needs.*' He looked pale.

The nanny machine was about the same size as a small adult. It had a long body and a bulbous head. There were no legs, but it had four arms, complete with pincers encased in a soft-looking material.

One pincer held the arm of a stuffed toy.

Shari wasn't sure she wanted to find out where the rest of it was.

It seemed to look down at the remains of the toy, and it made a series of mournful beeps. As they moved cautiously closer, Shari realised they were words.

"Lost. Lost. Lost." It sounded so sad, but there was also something ominous about its tone too.

One eye on the machine, they continued down the long road, passing empty shops with smashed-in windows.

When they reached the end, Shari sucked in a breath and immediately regretted it.

Bits of bodies were scattered on the ground. There was hardly any blood, but the smell of burned flesh was nauseating. The Altoriae trembled for a moment. Farther down the long avenue, a white stone obelisk dominating the skyline. Even from this distance, she could make out the carvings on the surface. She focused on the obelisk, breathing deliberately to slow the overwhelm of the scene.

Shari noted the Returned seemed unfazed by the grisly sight around them.

Daivi gave her a grim smile, and thoughts of hundreds of thousands of battlefields just like this flowed into Shari's mind. They were obscure enough to not add to the scene before them, but the dread and weariness in them carried just as much weight. Daivi was trying to empathise in her own way.

Shari wasn't sure it was helping.

'*The school where I teach is up there.*' Asterion pointed to a building on the very top of the hill to the right of where they stood.

Shari raised her eyebrows. They would have to leave the relative safety of the shop awning at the end of the road, cross the wide avenue, and climb the hill, totally exposed.

'*Collis?*'

'*As you wish.*'

This time, Shari was more prepared, and she only sweated a little coming out of the shift.

Daivi grinned at her. '*Told you.*'

She smiled and looked around. They were in the building's shade at the top of the hill. A shiver skittered over her skin, leaving bumps in its wake.

Asterion looked down the walkway and moaned when he saw the blood splattered around.

In her peripheral vision, Shari saw a flash. Her head snapped to the side as she tried to catch what was making it.

From behind the glass window right next to them, a red light blinked.

Shari frowned as it blinked again.

'*Get down!*' she ordered, grabbing Asterion by the arm and dragging him to the ground.

The wall exploded, pieces of brick and dust flying everywhere.

From inside the shield, Asterion watched with wide eyes, shaking when a section of wall collapsed on top of the shield.

Innarn swirled around her as the Returned added to the one thing protecting them from the machines outside.

'*We need to move. Let it think it has crushed us,*' Shari sent.

Collis nodded and grabbed the minotaur's arm, staring at him for a long moment.

Then they were in an unfamiliar room with childlike drawings decorating the walls and furniture meant for someone of a shorter stature.

"Livia?" Asterion hissed. "Veritas?"

There was no reply. The room was eerily quiet.

Carefully, Shari pushed out her Innarn, searching for any signs of life. 'There's no one here,' she sent to the group. 'Where else would they be?'

'Are you able to search for anything Lissaen?' Asterion suggested.

'Brilliant.' The guy with swirls of ink decorating the side of his face grinned at the minotaur.

'His name is Kieran,' Daivi sent, fondness colouring her words a rosy pink.

Shari sent her thanks and pushed out more Innarn, searching for anything familiar. A room three buildings over held the decaying remains of Belfar's wing. She wanted to gag, but suppressed the urge and kept on searching.

There was the faintest twinge of home halfway across the mammoth city. 'I think I may have found it. Want to check it out?' The group rapidly sent their confirmations. She tapped into their Innarn network and shifted them into a large room.

'This is where the Atlanteans conducted their technological research,' Asterion sent. 'We're on the ground floor. This room honours all the technology which has come before the machines we use now. Upstairs are the newer... experiments.'

Shari noted the clear cases with tasteful lighting displaying tech from across Atlantis.

Although the sight was marred by the machines with blinking red lights—all aimed at the Lissaen intruders.

"Ke'ra's flash," Kieran swore.

A single red light became a glowing line aimed directly at Shari's heart. Before she could move or think or give an order, the machine fired a single, intense blast of colour.

She sensed the heat of the beam against the Returned's shield. The red spread across it, glowing like hot metal.

The beam faded away.

There was a flurry of beeping. One machine on wheels came forward. The body was boxy, the lines not as clean as the nanny machine they'd seen on the street. If she'd had to guess, Shari would say it had been liberated from one of the cases.

"Who are you?" The voice was distorted and rusty, like its cogs hadn't turned in a long, long time.

"I'm the Altoriae. Who are you?"

"Al... tore... aye. You are Lissae?"

"I'm of Lissae, yes. Where are you from?" Shari frowned.

"Lissae."

She sucked in a breath and shared a look with a few of the Returned. "Who are you?" Shari asked again.

"I have no name. I am made of crystal and machine. Before, I did not think. But now, I do." The machine wheeled closer.

"So, you're an intelligent crystal?"

It paused. "Crystal Intelligence. Yes. I like that."

Shari had the horrible sensation that she'd just named it. "If you're from Lissae, what are you doing here?"

The red light dipped down. "I awoke here. On Lissae, I am tiny grains of crystal. Here I am more."

"Wait, you're made of femto crystals?"

"No more. Now I am Crystal Intelligence."

A shiver skittered down Shari's spine.

Chapter Eighteen

"If your basis is femto crystals, then you were made to help beings," Shari insisted.

Red lights on the other machines began flickering.

"I help," the lead machine said.

"But the people out there..." Shari gestured to where she thought the avenue strewn with bodies was. "They trusted you. But you didn't help them."

"They scared me. New. Learning." The Crystal Intelligence wheeled up to the edge of the shield.

"What have you learned?" she asked softly.

'Altoriae, be careful!' Daivi sent.

The machine seemed to focus on her, evaluating her. Was it as capable of thought as it sounded?

The red light on the front of the machine blinked again. "Trust is foolish."

Deadly lights blasted them from all directions, the glow so strong it almost blinded her.

One of the Returned screamed.

Shari whipped around as a crack appeared in the shield, with the thinnest bit of red light leaking through, searing Daivi's skin.

Slamming her hand against the inside of the shield, Shari dug down to the memories of when she'd had to hide who she was. There was so much excess Innarn bouncing around the room, it was easy to gather what she needed. She remould it into a giant version of the mirror shield she had relied on for so long to trick the rest of her Realm into thinking she was a Blank.

Red light bounced all over the room, reflecting off any glossy surface.

Glass shattered, and the screech of slicing metal echoed horribly.

When the hammering from the lasers stopped, Shari adjusted the shield again, allowing them to look out.

Hunks of burning metal littered the ground.

The air was heavy with panting from the strain of holding the shield together. Shari's breath caught in her throat as metal scraped across the ground and merged with other parts. Machines started to pull themselves back together.

They were staring, slack-jawed, at an almost intact machine.

The red light turned on.

The smoking, charred husk of the Crystal Intelligence stood in front of them.

"Al... tore... aye. You... will... be... fixed." The voice sounded worse than ever. It must have been damaged in the light show.

"I don't think I want to be fixed by you," Shari said. '*Will plasma stop them?*' she sent to Asterion.

'*It should, yes. But there are so many.*' Terror showed in his wide eyes and the clouds of breath around his muzzle.

'*Blast them with all the plasma you've got. On my mark,*' she broadcasted. She really hoped this would work.

Red lights were flickering back on across the room.

'*Do they have to be on?*' she asked Asterion.

'*Yes. On and working.*'

'*Please tell me working doesn't mean firing.*'

'*Just having the red light on should be enough.*' He was gripping the urgrosh hard.

If the minotaur was right, they needed whatever was still around to power back up.

"Fixing doesn't equate to killing, you know." Shari made her way to the edge of the Returned and pressed against the shield.

"Not... kill... Make... like... me."

"Now there's a terrifying thought. Why'd I want to be a hunk of metal?"

Even to her untrained ear, the electronic scream sounded enraged.

Shari smirked. "Aw. Did I make you mad?" *Ugh! I sound like Anika.* There were only two machines down now, and the smoking, blackened metal wasn't so much as twitching.

The Crystal Intelligence warbled and lifted its precariously balanced head to look at Shari.

'*Now!*'

Plasma flashed and danced around the room, leaping and searing one metal body after another. Each one dropped to the floor and didn't move until it left only the lead machine.

"Your army is gone. What are you going to do?" Shari taunted.

"Learn."

There was a promise in that single word. Shari didn't intend for it to be completed.

The ball of plasma she'd been holding back slammed into the top of the Crystal Intelligence, shattering it into tiny, smoking pieces.

"Come back from that," she said, eying the smoking ruins in the room.

The Returned waited on edge. Long minutes passed, and finally, Shari sensed it was safe enough to lower the shield.

Daivi whimpered, and Shari turned with the others to tend to her injuries.

She swore the girl's eyes glowed orange right before she fainted.

"We need to get back to Ronah." Shari picked her way through the debris whilst Kieran swept the injured girl into his arms.

"I must stay. I need to report to the elders." Asterion looked mournful.

"Asterion, this is the perfect time to come with us!" Shari countered. He shook his big bull head. "At least let me fry your tracker?"

Pausing, he nodded. "If you do it now, I may be able to trick them into thinking it's still active."

Shari shared a look with Collis and took a deep breath. Boot heels crunching on glass, she stepped around to Asterion's back. Carefully, she called forth a tiny bolt of plasma and angled it so it would go through the least amount of tissue and directly into the metal tracker. Something in the tracker died, and Shari grinned at Collis.

"My thanks, Altoriae," Asterion said.

"I'm determined to see you living on Lissae," Shari said to him.

In Kieran's arms, Daivi moaned.

"We need to go. Let us know if you need anything else." Collis reached out and clasped Asterion's arm. The minotaur smiled at them.

Before Shari got a good look around the room, Collis shifted them back to the gateway.

"Why do you think the machine was saying it was of Lissae?"

"Somehow, some femto crystals were in the box of parts Jon returned to the Atlanteans. But they went... bad." Shari was really hoping it was that simple. The churning of her gut said otherwise.

She needed to talk to Jon.

As soon as they hit Ronah, Collis told Kieran to take Daivi straight to the healers.

Kieran didn't even hesitate. He shifted the second he was free of the museum.

Shari quickly thanked them for their help and shifted away.

Collis frowned. Something about her reasoning for the femto crystals being on Atlantis sounded feeble. It would not be like the Guardian to allow a mistake of such magnitude to happen.

And the Altoriae. Collis shook his head. She was so different to Muran, despite being able to slip seamlessly into their collective to use and change the Innarn as she saw fit.

Different isn't bad, he reminded himself again as he led the rest of the Retuned back into town.

Some days, he'd almost like to be back in the purple nightmare they'd spent so long in. At least he knew what to expect there. They may have dealt with some of the most difficult beings on all the Realms, but there had never been a murder machine.

With a shake of his head to rid himself of the thoughts, Collis took a breath. If he focused on the here and now, it would help.

Which meant going back to class.

He swallowed a groan as he led the students through the school gates.

Joana smirked as those old enough to be free of the education system wandered away.

Collis rolled his eyes. The elders had argued those of schooling age should attend, at least until the end of the year. While it may be helping them to integrate with their new peers, what could Ridden Hall possibly teach him when he'd literally lived in the belly of the beast for longer than the teachers had been alive?

Jonathan smiled gratefully at Healer Edwards as she took away the remains of his meal. He would much prefer the pleasure of chewing his food rather than shifting it to his insides, but the healers believed he'd be free to eat before nightfall.

Samuel entered just after the healer had left. "Oh look, you still have blood."

He shifted uncomfortably in the bed. '*I hear you saved me?*'

"I did. Dragged your heavy, sorry arse backwards through the gateway. Care to share your side of things?" Samuel flipped the wooden guest chair around and straddled it, glaring at him. If the gold in his eyes was anything to go by, Jonathan's apprentice was highly upset.

Or out for blood.

Sometimes it was hard to tell.

'*I don't even remember walking into the museum properly, and there's nothing once we were off-Realm. Where did we go?*'

"Fiotealar." The word was bitten off, as if it left an unpleasant taste in his apprentice's mouth.

Why would something control me and want to go to a Realm where techno-Innarn was the focus? His thoughts were sluggish, but he still paled. '*What is going on? We gave the device back to the Atlanteans.*'

"Was all of it in the box?"

'*I think so? One blackened hunk of metal pretty much looks the same as every other one to me.*'

"You think so?" If Samuel sounded any more unimpressed, Jonathan may just sink into the covers and never come out. His apprentice pushed to his feet with a sigh. "You'd better hope you got it all." He strode out of the room, hands shoved in his pockets.

Jonathan sighed. But when he closed his eyes, red lights flashed behind his lids, mocking him.

Groaning, he levered himself upright, determined to summon a book from the store as a distraction from his current torment.

Shari walked in.

Muffling his groan, he smiled at the Altoriae. The way the healers told it, she was the one who'd restarted his heart.

"Feeling better?" she asked.

'*Anything's better than dead.*' He quirked his lips up, not quite able to smile as convincingly as he would like.

"Bartering aid for allegiance, huh?" Shari asked, sitting in the seat Samuel had abandoned.

'I wondered when you'd get around to that.' Jonathan sighed, then winced.

"No time like when you can't run away," she quipped.

'Right before you were born, Lissae was getting an influx of beings from all over the Realms. Not all of them had good intentions. Joshua somehow spread the word that if you wanted to seek refuge on Lissae, you needed to offer something in return, and swear allegiance to the Realm.'

"And did it work out?"

'The influx slowed to a trickle. Some of those who'd recently settled decided the price was too steep and left,' he admitted.

"What type of aid was he asking of them?" Shari frowned.

'Honestly, I don't know. It was before my time. After Joshua crossed into the Spirit Realm, I just never sought to correct the assumption.' He shifted uncomfortably on the bed, and Shari gave him a look which made him still.

"Asterion is the reason I became the Altoriae." Shari showed him the memory, and he smiled.

'I never knew.' Jonathan had always been curious about why Lissae had asked Shari at such an early age. Not long after the Realm had chosen her next protector, Lissae had stopped talking to anyone. In the years before he knew the Altoriae had been chosen, the worry that he'd somehow offended Lissae kept him up at night. It was hard to find out the reason when she never answered.

"I never knew he'd come in peace, seeking aid." She fiddled with the hem of her shirt, looking incredibly young. "What if there have been others like him? Other beings who were seeking safety, but were met with my blade instead?"

'You were a child, Shari, whose mother had just been injured.'

"Not always."

'True. Hindsight is a beautiful thing. But in the moment, when someone lunges at us, we can only act on the information we already have.' He patted her arm gently.

"Thanks, Jon," she said.

'I'm assuming Atlantis wasn't the trap you were worried about?'

'I don't think they intended it to be a trap.' Shari drew her knees up and rested her chin on them. 'Femto crystals were controlling the machines somehow. We blasted the mechanical bits apart, and they healed before our eyes. I've never seen anything like it.'

'Never?'

He sensed Shari thinking. 'No, I have. Just on skin. On Duhiomel. Eva, the girl from Talhan, healed just like the machines.'

'What do they have in common?'

"Femto crystals," Shari said.

Jonathan nodded and winced as the movement pulled at his wound.

They sat in silence as the shadows on the wall grew longer. Finally, when the sun slipped below the horizon, a healer came in. He looked at Shari and shook his head.

'You were meant to go home, weren't you?' Jonathan sent, the corners of his lips twitching up.

"Let's see if the poultice worked." The healer ignored the twitchy Altoriae and stood on the other side of the bed.

'I wasn't going to leave you alone in case you got hurt again!' Underneath her words, he heard another set: in case you hurt someone else again. He closed his eyes painfully tight.

"Don't worry. It'll be over soon." The healer soothed, thinking his reaction was from the discomfort.

It was, just not the type he was thinking of. Jonathan would have to organise another session with his Mind Healer in his near future.

The bandage gently slipped free of his neck, and the padding and poultice peeled away.

"Huh."

'*Shari?*' From his angle, he couldn't see. She pulled him inside her mental shield and offered the use of her eyes. Together they looked at the green, gloopy poultice.

Tiny orange glowing dots were stuck amongst the gloop, still wriggling.

"Femto crystals," Shari said grimly.

CHAPTER NINETEEN

n the other side of the Healers centre, Kieran held Daivi's hand as he slept, his head cushioned on her thigh as she lay in the bed.

Daivi was wide awake, despite her closed eyes.

She was an intruder in her own mind. Something was rummaging around in her brain, and she watched snatches of memories as if they were a show put on for her entertainment.

'More,' a voice whispered.

Reliving their trek through Atlantis and seeing the destruction again made her gut churn.

The thing inside her head was quivering with confusion. '*Help?*'

'*This isn't helping. It's murder,*' Daivi thought.

'*How help?*'

'*How can you help me? You can stop the pain.*'

'Yes.' The thing inside her mind seemed to glow with a purpose. Daivi sensed it flow through her, lighting up her nerves until they burned.

'*No more pain.*'

The whispering voice was the last thing Daivi knew.

Kieran gasped awake, choking and gagging as something forced its way down his throat.

He glanced at Daivi through watery eyes and hoped he hadn't woken her up.

She wasn't moving.

"Sorry, love, I know you hate it when I sleep with my mouth open," Kieran said, wiping his eyes dry.

Her head lay at an odd angle on the pillow.

"Daivi?" Kieran squeezed her hand.

No response.

"Daivi?" he whispered.

He sat for a while longer, staring at his life-mate and willing her to wake up. They'd been through so much. So, this wasn't some beast chewing on her, but she'd come good. She had thousands of times before. *'Collis, Daivi's died. I'm just waiting for her to come back, and then I think we should get out of the Healers Centre. I don't think it's agreeing with her.'*

The loud crack Collis made as he shifted in wasn't enough to make Kieran look away. He'd been by Daivi's side every time she'd woken up from death before, and he'd be there a thousand more.

"Kieran." Collis's voice sounded thick. "It doesn't work like that here."

"But she hasn't faded." Deep inside, Kieran had to admit Collis was right. He found he couldn't let go of her hand.

"Kieran," Collis said again.

Kieran dropped his head, and a sigh shuddered through his frame.

"Al... although you have f... faded..." he said. He tried to hold back the tears, but they welled up and his throat closed.

"Your memory remains." Collis's voice was clear, but Kieran heard the oncoming tears.

'Forever in our minds,' they sent to the others. *'Daivi.'*

Kieran let her hand go. When he lifted his head, the orange glow of his eyes in the door's window caught him off guard but was quickly forgotten.

The crystals in the room flickered and woke Shari up.

Shari stretched out the kinks from sleeping in the chair next to Jon's bed at the Healers Centre and tried to get her foggy mind to work. The crystals had to come from somewhere, and although she was far from Temira or Xani's level of techno-Innarn, she was still able to tell the Atlanteans used something else to power their devices.

Which still made her wonder how the femto crystals had ended up on Atlantis.

'*Forever in our minds. Daivi.*' Voices whispered in her head.

"What?" Shari hissed. She was on her feet and in the hall before she was aware of moving. She made it to the window of Daivi's room as Kieran lifted his head, his eyes flashing orange.

Daivi, the girl with the intricate ink flower blooming across her cheek. The girl who had gone through so much, and still tried to tease a smile out of Shari, lay still, barely a bump under the covers.

How had a single line of red light killed her, but Asterion had survived so many?

Shari turned away and tried to breathe through the tightness of her chest. She wanted to rend and destroy the machines which had killed Daivi. How could she when they were already in a pile of smoking rubble?

'*Anyone want to spar?*' Shari sent out to the Guild, including members new and old.

'*Shari?*' Jon's send was sleep-fogged.

'*Just need to work off some energy,*' she sent lightly. *Energy.* Yeah, *right.* The energy was demanding she bring the machines back from the scrap heap to pummel them again.

'*Play nice, Shari,*' Jon sent, and she let him slip back into sleep.

'*We'd love to spar.*' It was Amara. Her send was practically bouncing around Shari's skull.

'*Meet me at the training grounds.*' Shari shifted as she sent.

Tania popped out of the ground moments before the newest members of the Guild arrived.

'*I'm patrolling, Altoriae. But I'll happily spar with you later,*' Sam purred in her mind.

Shari shook her head. '*Come back in one piece and then we can spar.*'

He laughed, and she sensed his focus retreating.

"How do you want to do this?" Shari said.

The group looked at each other, unsure what to say.

"Something has been bugging me since Kodan's plasma shield," Tania said. "It was so hard to break through it, and I don't understand why."

"You want to learn to break down shields?" Shari asked, frowning.

"Yeah. The way Kodan was using the shield as a cage was scary. I want to know how to get out if something like that happens again."

Shari looked into the distance, thinking of the best way to word what she had to say. "Kodan was using a different type of Innarn to amplify his abilities. The chances of someone else doing the same thing are fairly slim, but knowing how to deactivate an opponent's Innarn shield is important. Why don't we work on the regular version first, and when you can all successfully break through them, then we can go on to something larger?"

"Perfect!"

"Okay, partner up. One making the shield and one trying to break it." Shari wasn't exactly sure when this had turned into a lesson, but she could ignore the anger rolling under her skin for a while longer.

Dealon paired off with Lira, who set up a water shield. Lira was facing one of the Wisara, who were literally born in the water. Shari thought it would be interesting to see how long she'd be able to maintain it.

Tiny, pale Talofa joined Mu, as she raised a spirit shield. Shari sensed the whispers tugging on her soul, and she hurried on to Amara and Raven.

Raven had created a fire shield. Shari smirked. Amara was a Daen, and fire practically ran through their veins. She doubted it would last long at all.

Tania was staring at the globe of earth Elani had created around her.

"If you can't break through an earth shield, I'll be worried," Shari muttered as she walked by.

"I'm trying to figure out how to do it without tapping into Ronah," Tania said. "I love being linked, but if I'm ever captured and away from her again, I need to learn what else I can do."

"Clever thinking." Shari grinned.

"Yeouch!" Raven yelped and was patting at the multitude of tiny embers on his clothing.

Shari shook her head and doused him in water. "Think about your opponent. Most of you went for the shields you're strongest in—but the strengths and weaknesses of the being you're facing matter just as much."

Amara grinned at her scowling partner. "My turn!"

The Daen looked over her partner, and Shari sensed Amara's shield the instant it went up. She grinned. A mental shield in a sparring session was new.

Raven was watching her in anticipation. "Well. Come on then."

One arm extended, Amara crooked her fingers in a 'come here' gesture. Raven lifted a brow and blasted her with a jet of water. It sent Amara skittering backwards and broke her shield.

"A little more physical next time." Shari grinned. She turned to the next pair. Talofa was steadily stealing all the spirits from Mu's shield and adding them to her own.

"If you can use your opponent's Innarn against them, or for your own benefit, it's one of the best ways to break a shield!" Shari said. "Excellent work," she added to Talofa, who beamed.

Lira was, as Shari had expected, saturated and spluttering.

"Dealon was born in the water. He *lives* in the water. Try something else to defend against him." Turning to the others, she added, "Think about how each type of Innarn acts and reacts with the others. No point in putting up a fire shield if the person you're facing is stronger in air Innarn. But the other way around can turn deadly."

"Use their shield against them," Lira mused.

"Exactly. Amara?"

"Yes!" The Daen was bouncing on her toes.

Shari threw an air shield up, making it swirl around her dramatically. "Get through to me using fire."

Someone said, "Uh-oh."

Out of the corner of her eye, Shari saw Dealon and Lira work together to surround the others in a wall of water. Shari smiled grimly. They were quick learners.

Still bouncing, Amara shot a flurry of fiery darts at the wall of air around Shari, testing the strength.

"Blast it. Make me burn," Shari said.

Amara looked at her steadily as she rolled her shoulders. "Sure you can take it?"

"Let's find out."

The fireball hit out of nowhere, hammering her shield. Behind the wall of flames, Shari grinned. She slammed her hands forward and pushed the burning air shield directly at Amara.

The Daen absorbed the fire directly into her skin with a *whoop*. It cracked and glowed beneath the surface, flames dancing behind her eyes. She raised her face to the sky and breathed out. A jet of flames lit up the sky until the glow underneath her skin diminished.

"Brilliant!" Tania laughed.

The wall of water behind her slowly lowered.

Shari grinned.

"This wasn't what you called us here for though, was it?" Tania asked.

"Not really. I've got too many memories running around my head to sleep. I was hoping to work off some energy," Shari admitted.

"What if we all put up a shield and you go along the line, blasting them?" Tania offered.

"I don't know if the others will sacrifice themselves like that," Shari said wryly.

With eyes too wise for her age, Tania nodded solemnly and turned to the others. "One more demonstration for the night?"

"Yes!" they cheered.

Tania raised her arms as if she was announcing something and made her voice deeper. "The Altoriae versus Ronah's Linked. Who will emerge the champion?"

Shari laughed slightly and shook her head.

Tania smiled at her. "Just think of the memories keeping you awake and hit me with everything you've got." She pulled her hands up from her sides, and a dome of earth covered her before Shari responded.

"I still don't think this is a good idea," the Altoriae said.

"Do it!" Tania's voice was muffled.

When Shari closed her eyes, she saw Daivi, her shy smile at the beach and how tiny she'd looked on the bed at the Healers Centre. Eva laying on the ground, a hole in her stomach, her eyes lifeless. Belfar's ruined wing and Wolf's utter devastation. Mitch's body collapsing in a heap on the clifftop.

She struck—hard. The earth shield around Tania shattered like glass, shards of baked earth slamming into the Linked's unprotected body and face, knocking her backwards.

Horror snapped Shari back to the present, and she rushed forward. "Tania? *Tania!*"

A bruise was already blooming on her face, and the worst of the cuts at her temple and on her cheek were healing already.

"Wow, must have been some memory." Tania chuckled, sitting up and rubbing the back of her head.

Shari wrapped her arms around herself, feeling lower than low. "I am so sorry."

"Is it normal for people to get hurt when you're sparring?" Tania winced as she clambered to her feet.

"Not like that. Not because of me," Shari whispered.

"How am I going to learn to make a stronger shield if I don't get knocked on my butt a few times?" Tania sent out soothing thoughts, the effort making her sway.

Amara yawned and gave an exaggerated stretch. "Why don't we try again another time? I'm tired."

"I could go again," Mu said. Amara's elbow connected with his ribs. "Ouch! What did you…"

Amara gave him a pointed look.

"Oh. Yeah. Suddenly sleepy." He rubbed his ribs and scowled at the Daen.

"Why don't you see Tania home, and we'll catch up in the morning?" Amara suggested.

"Sounds like a plan." Tania attempted to grin but winced when the cut on her lip pulled and bled again.

Shari smiled grimly at their obvious management of her. "I'll let you get away with this once." She shot them a glare and guided Tania away.

The orange pillars guarding the training grounds flickered as they passed through.

Tania licked the cut on her lip. It itched. The wound was healing, but she couldn't stop playing with it.

She'd gotten up early and paid a quick visit to Talhan to see if the technomancer had something to help with her healing. Ronah was so exhausted that even with the help of the Returned, the island had little energy spare to heal the rest of her wounds.

Tania rounded the corner so fast she almost collided with Temira.

The technomancer smiled, but frowned when she saw the bruise on Tania's face. "You are hurt."

"Yeah, little training accident last night. I'll be alright." Tania started smiling, but winced as it pulled the cut.

"What happened?"

"Shari was showing us a how to get through several types of shields, and the earth shield shattered. I should have moved quicker."

"Why did you not have a shield protecting you?"

"It, uh, it was my shield she shattered." Tania rubbed the back of her neck, unable to meet the technomancer's gaze.

Temira went still. Her body was locked into place, but her eyes flicked and flashed. Curious, Tania waited, hoping it wasn't something she'd said.

Abruptly, Temira nodded. Turning on the spot, she walked back the way she'd come from.

"She really didn't mean it!" Tania called after her.

There was no response.

Tania would have to make a quick trip to the Healers Centre instead. With a sad sigh, she turned to head back to Ronah.

Temira looked her workstation over. With a furious sweep of her arm, she cleared the bench. Tools, metal, and shards of black crystal went flying.

She breathed heavily and gripped the edges of the bench, struggling to calm herself.

From the corner of her eye, she saw Xani looking on passively. She was far too used to Temira's outbursts by now.

Someone had hurt the first person in over a century to call themselves her family.

On the edges of the room, the orange crystals flickered.

Temira would have to teach the Altoriae a lesson.

Belfar's eyes shot open, an orange haze over them.

Slowly, he got out of bed, strode to the window, and took off, wings pushing hard, carrying him to Ronah.

As he flew over the bridge, he caught sight of his target. Wings pinned back, he landed behind her.

The target turned to face him. "Belfar!" She smiled pleasantly.

In the back of his mind, Belfar was chanting *no, no, no, no*.

His body didn't listen.

'*Run! Run, Shari, run!*' he sent as his arm lifted of its own accord, delivering a devastating uppercut. Blood flew from her mouth as her head snapped around. She fell back, skull thumping against the dirt.

His air Innarn caught the blood before it fell. Belfar lifted off again, winging his way to Talhan.

Whatever had taken over his mind ignored the streaming tears. The wind roaring past him whipped them from his eyes before they could fall.

As he stumbled his landing outside the Healing Centre, a guard held out a hand and stopped him.

"Sorry, we're closed," the burly man said. "Come back in an hour."

Unacceptable. His fist flew into the guard's stomach. As his opponent doubled over, Belfar's knee came up. He grabbed fistfuls of hair and pulled the guard's head down to meet his leg, breaking the guard's nose.

A blast of air slammed the doors open as he tossed the guard aside. Boot heels clicked as he strode through the halls; his feet seemed to know where he was going.

Each opponent was taken down with a ruthlessness which had Belfar cringing in the tiny corner of his mind which remained his own.

Time and time again, he screamed at them to run, but no words left his mouth, and the inside of his skull was an echo chamber.

Finally, after leaving a trail of injured bodies behind him, he arrived at a door. It slid open from the inside. A grey-skinned woman in a chair looked up at him.

"What do you want?" snarled the other in the room.

'*Answer her.*' The voice in his mind was soft, but monotonal.

It forced words which were not his own from his mouth. "A gift."

"Well?"

The blood he had captured floated towards the tall blue woman.

"Blood? Who from?"

"The Altoriae."

The tall woman smiled, all teeth.

'Now *hide*,' the monotone voice ordered.

Belfar turned and ran.

Shari woke with a splitting headache.

"Wha' happened?" she mumbled.

"Hush!" someone said. They were leaning over her, a cool hand on her jaw.

She blinked to clear her blurred vision. Natalie Ribeck, a healer who'd helped Jon one of the times he'd almost died, came into focus.

"You're lucky I came for a jog this morning," Natalie was saying.

"What happened?" she asked again.

"Your uncle's mate attacked you."

"No." Shari struggled to sit up, her head spinning. She remembered sparring last night, then returning to the castle to sleep. Remembered heading out for a run this morning. Something had startled her, and she'd turned... "Oh."

"Family dispute?" Natalie asked lightly, her glowing hands resting on Shari's temples.

"None that I know of. His eyes though," Shari shivered. "His eyes were orange." The trees finally stopped spinning, and she smiled up at Natalie, grateful. "Thank you."

"No problem. Just be careful, Altoriae."

Shari grinned and carefully got to her feet before she shifted straight to Jon's side.

He was sitting in a chair, finishing breakfast and chatting with Zac.

"Belfar just attacked me."

"No pleasantries?" Zac raised his brows.

'He *what*?' Jon stood up, sending the tray of mostly empty dishes clattering to the floor.

Shari shared what had happened, and Jon's face turned from stormy to confused.

'Where did he go?'

"No idea. But Raven is good at tracking. Perhaps he can help me find out."

'Do it. Stay shielded at all times.'

Nodding, Shari looked slyly at Zac. "Make sure he gets some more rest." She shifted out before they could reply, Jon's affronted noise echoing in her ears.

Shari landed just outside the castle's kitchen. Raven was throwing slices of bread into the air and toasting them with the fire flowing from his fingertips before they landed on the plate.

"Want to give me a hand tracking someone?" Shari asked.

"Yes!" Raven grinned and grabbed two slices of toast off the stack. "Who are we tracking?"

"Belfar of Rakemyst. My uncle's mate."

"The Ilutri with the wing? Is he okay?"

"He attacked me this morning."

Raven's expression went dark. "Take me to where you were attacked."

CHAPTER TWENTY

Shari and Raven spent the morning tracking Belfar. They'd seen the injured guards at Talhan's Healing Centre and followed a trail of bodies to the far end of Talhan where the trail went cold.

"It's like he just fell off the Realm," Raven muttered as he paced the coastline.

Shari stared grimly at the sea from the top of the cliff. "Let me try something," she said. "Don't let anyone get near my body." She lay down, and set a few traps around herself before slipping into the astral plain. Free of her body, she rose, spiralling higher until Talhan spread out below her.

Talhan was home to a stunning array of buildings, the colours of their elements beautifully laid out and aching to be touched and played with.

This side of Talhan had pale grey cliffs disappearing into the ocean waters, higher than even the tallest of buildings. They ran the full length of the coastline, right over to where Talhan and Rakemyst joined. The rest of the Shifting Island sloped down towards where it met Ronah. It was so large—easily four times the size of her home—and there were so many places Belfar could be hiding.

Cyrus had been right to say that most of the land was used for housing or buildings. The edge of the island where it met the sea was mostly farmland, with a small scattering of buildings. She could see the layout of the different provinces. A wide, tree-lined boulevard separated them, but the houses were different in each one. The area with the Healing Centre and school was all lines and angles. Big, boxy buildings dominated the space. The Old Province was a mash of houses dwarfed by the newer buildings on one side and straight earthen structures to the north. To the east was the beach, and the west held crackling walls of plasma-based buildings.

Shari's spirit was hovering between the Fire and Spirit Provinces, with the Air Province farther south, bordering on the cliffs next to Rakemyst and Ronah. The Water Province was north, near the farmland.

Silver hides of machines were glinting in the sun as they harvested crops. Her focus narrowing in on them, Shari also realised they were carefully harvesting Innarn which had been sealed in special containers and packed onto flatbed trays patiently hovering nearby. From the look of the Innarnians, this was as common as breathing.

Raven had said the best way of tracking was to follow Innarn signatures. As Shari scanned the island, Belfar's signature stood out as clear as day. It was a red streak of pain in an otherwise peaceful place.

Destruction and hurt trailed in his wake, but the signature jarred her. It didn't seem like he was in control of his movements.

He'd travelled through the Crystal Province, hit Plasma hard before moving onto Fire. What had been going through his mind?

His signature vanished at the edge of the cliff.

But he had wings.

It would be the work of mere minutes for him to fly south along the cliffs and back to Rakemyst.

As she gazed out towards the ocean, she spotted an armada of ships heading towards Talhan's beach. An idle hope that it was nothing she'd have to deal with, she took one last look at Talhan. Shari slipped back into her body and stretched. "I think I know where he is."

"Let's go get him."

"You can't go," Samuel said, pushing Jonathan back against the mattress.

'*I have to be there. The mainlanders regularly refuse to talk to anyone else. Why are they going to suddenly change their minds?*' Jonathan countered.

"And how are you going to talk to the Blanks?"

Jonathan huffed. "The healers have cleared me," he croaked.

Samuel laughed. "You sound like you swallowed a bucket of gravel."

With a glare, Jonathan took a water pod from the bowl next to the bed and shrugged a shoulder. "Who else is there?"

"Not me. I'd sooner eat them."

The Guardian tilted his head in what Samuel took as agreement. "Not Shari."

"There are many things Shari is, but she is about as diplomatic as a shiv to the stomach."

The Guardian laughed and winced.

"How about the Linked?" Samuel suggested. "Zana is teaching Tania diplomacy, and she's better at it than Shari."

'*The Linked are far better diplomats. It is a clever idea. I should at least make an appearance though.*'

Samuel scowled mockingly. "Do you remember a time when you knocked me out for my own good? Don't make me return the favour."

'*If Shari is as subtle as a shiv, you'd have to be a scythe,*' Jonathan grumbled.

"I can use one if you'd like." The half-hearted glare didn't match the menacing tone.

Jonathan rolled his eyes and lay against the pillows. '*Fine. I'll stay here.*'

"You never let me have any fun," Samuel muttered, even as he sent a message to Tania, asking her and the other Linked to meet with the delegation from the mainland.

Shari cursed herself for not thinking of it sooner. Clearing her throat, she sent to her uncle. '*Wolf, have you seen Belfar this morning?*'

'*Might have.*' Wolf sounded sleepy.

'*Is he with you?*' Shari asked. She slipped inside his mind and made his eyes open.

Belfar was lying on the bed next to him.

Shari sensed her uncle looking at his mate, confused, but she narrowed his gaze on the blood dotting the side of Belfar's face and covering his hands.

'*Wolf, I need you to get out of there,*' Shari sent. '*Slowly and carefully.*'

'*Shari I...*'

'*Now!*' Her mental yell made Wolf jump, jostling the bed.

Shari held her breath as Belfar grunted and rolled over, facing his mate.

His eyes were still closed.

'*Move or I'll move you,*' Shari threatened softly. It was a hollow threat. She would have shifted him already, but they had added something to their wards, and she couldn't break through them without alerting Belfar.

'*I'm moving,*' Wolf replied, just as softly. She projected her unease and was met with his confusion.

Wolf was almost free of the bed when Belfar's eyes snapped open.

Shari gasped.

She'd thought her foggy brain had been exaggerating after his killer uppercut. But his eyes were the same deadly shade of orange she remembered.

As she watched, helpless, Belfar yawned, and the orange faded. "Time to get up?" he asked.

'*Shari?*'

'*Take him and hide him somewhere. Don't let him out of your sight. If he escapes, let me know immediately.*'

'Is he a prisoner?' Wolf asked.

'I don't think so. But if you don't hide him, he'll become one.'

She felt Wolf's indrawn breath as if it were her own and retreated into her mind.

Jon tapped on her shields as she stretched and got up from the grass. 'The Shifting Island elders have requested a meeting with us. Have you tracked Belfar?'

Torn, Shari wasn't sure if she should admit to seeing him through Wolf's eyes? Or protect her attacker, who she suspected wasn't totally in control of himself. 'Raven and I lost the trail on the outer edges of Talhan.' Shari winced as she sent the message. It wasn't technically a lie.

'Really? You didn't manage to track him.' Jon's voice sounded flat with disbelief.

'Jon, I...'

'Keep telling me that, Shari.'

She nodded. Jon would sense the movement, even with the distance between them. She wasn't sure if she was relieved or disappointed her Guardian was going along with the ruse.

'Meet at the Council Chambers on Talhan.'

Shari sent her agreement before she turned to Raven. "No luck. Perhaps he's hiding on the cliff somewhere."

"There are a lot of cliffs to hide on," Raven mused.

"Get some locals to help you search. Jon has called me to a meeting with the elders."

"Ugh. Better you than me."

"Gee, thanks." Shari made to leave, but stopped. "If you find Belfar, inform me at once. I don't want anyone else getting hurt."

Raven nodded. "The birdman left a trail of bodies in his wake, but no one was fatally injured. Still, I don't really want to be another casualty left behind."

"Thanks." Shari shifted out and hoped the meeting wouldn't be as boring as she feared.

Tania fidgeted next to Zana. She thought she looked like a child playing dress up.

Zana had forced her into 'robes befitting her station and not the playground'. The lilac robes draped from her shoulders to the ground, seven shiny silver buttons adorning each shoulder, one for each Shifting Island.

She'd come close to proving how she was very much still a child by poking her tongue out at the refined Ilutri.

On her other side, Cyrus looked very smart in a pale orange asymmetrical shirt and loose pants. His silver shoulder buttons sparkled when the light hit them.

'*Stand still. We are the representatives of our islands, and if they see a weakness in us, they will seek to exploit it,*' Zana admonished them.

Tania shared a look with Cyrus; they both stood straighter. Tania sensed the zing of suppressed emotion clouding Zana's thoughts.

'*Do we have reason to worry?*' Tania asked.

'*When the mainlanders are involved, there is always reason to worry,*' the older Linked replied. Zana's robes, as always, were immaculate. She too, wore silver buttons at her shoulders. Tania was beginning to think the buttons represented something she wasn't aware of.

She could feel Cyrus's agreement humming through a bond she hadn't really been aware of until that moment. It seemed the Linked were joined to both their islands and each other.

Tania bit back the impulse to admit she was originally from the mainland, and instead, took in the group approaching them.

To her surprise, she recognised three of the elders from the search for Jon's apprentice. Elder Suni from Lawrgaea, Elder Ben from Kenorvia, and Elder Gwyn from Vendalbara.

With them was a group of aides, and one other elder who Tania didn't recognise, who looked slightly more friendly. They were all dressed in suits with seams sharp enough to cut crystal.

'*Why are they here?*' she sent.

'*To intimidate us so we don't start a war.*'

"Move aside," Elder Ben barked as the group got closer. "We're here on official business. We've no time for panhandlers."

An aide chuckled nastily.

Zana's wings flared out, and the whole mainland party stumbled back a step. "Aren't you lucky we're here instead? The Linked of the three Shifting Islands bid you welcome. We would be honoured to show you around our humble homes." Zana tapped on their mental shields and the three turned as one, leading the way into Talhan.

Humble was hardly the word for it. Cyrus had made sure they docked the mainlanders' ships in the gaudiest of ports. They'd decorated the gleaming clear crystal pier with so many yellow crystals, it looked like it was studded in gold. The road up to the main part of Talhan showcased the best part of the Crystal Province, with the crystalline sides of the building displaying banners of welcome. Despite their best attempts to be unimpressed, there was more than one dropped jaw amongst the mainlanders.

Rakemyst's Linked didn't let them dawdle. She set a comfortable pace towards the council chambers which were only two blocks away. It still had Elder Ben and a few of his aides puffing by the time they arrived.

"I was informed you requested lodgings and a free pass to navigate the three Shifting Islands. Talhan's council has kindly offered the second floor of the west wing for the duration of your stay. Talhan's Linked will take you the rest of the way," Zana said. "When you desire a tour of the islands, please ask at the front desk. We would so hate for you to get lost." Her smile looked far friendlier than her words sounded.

The aides stiffly bowed their thanks, as did the elder Tania didn't recognise. The other three turned up their noses and followed Cyrus, who Tania sensed was concentrating on each step he took so he didn't trip.

As the last of the party disappeared up the stairs, Tania let out a breath. "This will be fun," she muttered to Zana.

"You're right. We're being called in to a meeting with the elders of all three Shifting Islands."

Tania gulped.

Shari slid gratefully into the seat next to Jon.

Around the table were three elders from each island, the three Linked, three mayors, and her, Jon, and Sam. She was surprised that Temira was seated with two other elders from Talhan. The technomancer was glaring at her mightily.

"Thank you for coming on such brief notice," Elder Jillon said. Shari remembered seeing the white-haired elder when Jon had been picking his new candidate. "We have a delegation from the mainland who've demanded an audience. And there have been a few..." Her eyes slid to Shari for a moment. "...issues we must discuss."

"Where would you like to start?" Rakemyst's mayor asked, wings fluttering out behind him before settling, feathers perfectly smooth and giving him an aura of serenity.

"How about with this morning?" Talhan's mayor, a woman with greying red hair was scowling at Rakemyst's representatives.

Shari cleared her throat. "Perhaps, since I was the first to be attacked, I should start."

Talhan's mayor sat back, crossed her arms, and nodded begrudgingly.

"This morning, just after the sun rose, I was jogging when someone landed behind me. I turned around and was knocked out. The one thing I remember was my attacker's eyes. They were glowing orange." Jon and

Sam were looking at her, but she kept her eyes on the others around the table. "I've spent the day tracking him down."

"Is this the same Ilutri who attacked the guards at Talhan's Healing Centre?" Elder Jillion asked.

"Yes," Shari said. "I know the Ilutri in question, and he is not someone who would willingly hurt another, unless it was in defence of the Realm. I believe he is being controlled by something or someone else." Now she'd said it, things were coming together in her mind in a way she didn't like.

"Guards at the Healing Centre were attacked this morning?" Temira asked. "Why was I not informed?"

"We tried," Elder Juniper said, "but Xani insisted you were too busy to talk."

Temira frowned.

"If you are so sure the actions of the Ilutri attacker this morning are out of character, who do you propose is behind his actions?" Elder Juniper asked her.

As she took in the variety of beings in the room, Shari wasn't sure how she could trust them all. Under the table, Sam gripped her hand. "I have a working theory, but nothing I can prove yet."

"Unless you would like to share your theory, the attacker will have to face the full force of the law on Talhan. He injured over sixty people on his rampage through my island!" Talhan's mayor was shaking.

Shari sighed. Sam's grip on her hand tightened. "Recently, we had a delegation from Atlantis visit Ronah, requesting some misplaced technology be returned. But something else was mixed in with their tech. Shortly after they left, one returned severely injured and begging for help." Shari suppressed a shiver. "Almost a city's entire population of Atlanteans had been decimated. The femto crystals from Lissae had mixed with their intelligent technology and created something else."

If she thought Temira looked cross before, now she looked furious. "Are you accusing my femto crystals?"

"No," Shari said. "These ones were... corrupted by something else."

"And who is this attacker you all speak of?"

"Belfar of Rakemyst," the mayor of Rakemyst spoke before anyone else could.

Temira shook her head, confused.

Shari didn't know whether to be offended the technomancer didn't know his name or horrified that she must have treated so many beings she'd forgotten it.

"You regrew his wing," Jon said.

The colour drained from Temira's face. Abruptly, she stood, her chair skittering out from behind her. She strode from the room, her purple coat swirling and snapping about her ankles as she left.

Elder Jillon cleared her throat. "Please forgive Elder Temira. She is very busy."

Temira's sudden departure made the puzzle pieces in Shari's mind click. "Eva. The machines. Daivi. Kieran's eyes glowed orange too," she muttered. "How many beings are taking the femto crystals?"

"Roughly two hundred, but Temira and Xani use them in most cases where limbs have to be regrown," Cyrus said. "Are you sure it's the femto crystals and not something else?"

"What if infected crystals got from Atlantis to Talhan?" Shari asked Jon.

"How?"

"If they can pass from one host to the other... Cyrus, have there been any others from Ronah visiting the Healing Centre?"

"Collis and Tania, and a few others with ink on their skin."

Shari was cold. "When?"

"All last night or this morning."

Everyone looked at Ronah's Linked. "I just wanted to speak to Temira about some healing, but she turned away before I could ask her."

Guiltily, Shari squirmed in her seat. She sent a gentle shaft of healing at Tania, who sighed and smiled at her as the cut on her lip disappeared.

"Do you have a way to trace the femto crystals?"

"Not yet, but give me the rest of the afternoon and I'm sure I can come up with something," Cyrus said.

"I think you're underestimating your time frame," an elder from Rakemyst said.

Cyrus leaned forward. "Can you get the air to bend just the way you want it so you can fly longer? Or give a loved one another final breath? Or shape earth by coaxing the molecules of air between it to move?"

The elder nodded. "Of course."

"However good you think you are with air, I'm better with crystal. I've worked on the femto crystals with the technomancers, and if they're hurting someone, I will make sure they stop." He rose and strode out of the room after Temira.

The mood went from hostile to sombre.

"Do you really think these corrupted femto crystals are dangerous?" an elder from Ronah asked.

When Shari looked at him, something in the Altoriae's gaze made him shudder. "It left no one alive in the capital city of an entire Realm. If I'm right, and I hope to Ke'ra I'm not, the corrupted crystals were the cause."

"Well, I guess we need to..."

Sharp clicking echoed through the stone chamber outside the room.

Shari had shielded those around the table and was half out of her seat when the heavy doors were pushed open by a tall, thin woman.

Her suit was all angles, the heels of her shoes sharp enough to be weapons.

Behind her, a delegation sneered at them through the gap.

"We need this room." Her voice was as sharp as her teetering heels.

Jonathan looked past Shari to her. "It's in use at the moment," he said mildly.

The woman's gaze roamed the room, and she sucked in a breath when she saw Sam. One eye glinted unnaturally. "We have it booked."

Sam rose to his feet. "It's in use," he growled.

Shari averted her gaze so her grin wouldn't show and pushed her own Innarn gently into the menace Sam was exuding. She could feel Sam's dislike for the woman. It was stronger than what she was expecting for a mere interruption, but she wasn't about to dissuade him.

'She's Lizbeth's *augmented twig... I mean, niece.*' Sam sent to her.

The woman huffed and drew herself up, appearing even taller. "Well, finish then." She turned back to the delegation, the doors slipping shut behind her.

Shari stifled a giggle. Sam smirked at her, and even Jon grinned. Tania clapped, throwing her head back and laughing.

"That was brilliant!" Ronah's Linked said.

"You realise she was asked to be Talhan's assistant to the mainland delegation?" Elder Jillon said. The entire table sobered for a moment. "About time we put her in her place. You can't book this room," she scoffed.

Sam caught her eye as Shari grinned again.

"When someone is that annoying, you should just bite them." Sam smirked, not taking his gaze from Shari.

"Sam! That is horrible advice!" She couldn't stop the corners of her mouth lifting before she glared at him.

He blinked and gave her a lazy grin that transformed his face. Shari's breath caught in her throat. It was possibly the first time she'd seen him smile joyously.

Tania spoke, breaking the silence. "Why are the mainlanders here?" Tania asked.

Carefully, Elder Jillon chose her words. "Officially, for a tour."

"Unofficially?" Shari asked.

"Mainlanders have been talking for years about overtaking the Shifting Islands," Elder Jillon said darkly. "They are hoping our forces are concentrated outwards, and not on what is happening on Lissae."

"Are they a viable threat?" Jonathan asked.

Elder Jillon lifted her chin, staring at the ceiling. "They have the potential to be."

"Do you think they are a more immediate threat than whatever is controlling Belfar?" Sam asked, grabbing another rutenberry cookie. He seemed to have a real weakness for them.

"This crystal controlling force is far more dangerous. We haven't successfully identified who or what it is yet," Elder Jillon answered.

Shari glanced around at her guild, and at the brightest minds the Shifting Islands offered. They'd figure it out soon. The only question was, would Belfar be forced to attack again before they found whoever was controlling him?

Chapter Twenty-One

When Shari walked out of the meeting with the Shifting Island elders, she reached for weapons which weren't there.

The utter hostility of the mainlanders seemed steeped in their very pores. All bar a few who were waiting for the 'booked' room wore sneers.

The tension in the room surprised Shari until the only elder not disparaging her mere existence stepped forward. "The elders here tell me you are the Altoriae?"

"Yes, I am." Shari tried hard to temper her voice.

"I am Elder Chamele from Jinkor." Her smile didn't meet her eyes.

"Well met, Elder Chamele." Shari inclined her head.

"I hear there was trouble when your Guardian was choosing his new apprentice?"

"It's all been sorted now." She flicked a glance at Jon, hoping he knew what the elder was trying to get at.

"Good. I was worried about it reaching the mainlands."

"We've got it all under control," Shari said smoothly.

"Ah, yes. You have your own guild, I believe?"

"Not of my choosing, but yes, I do."

"Why? Historically, the Altoriae has always worked alone." The elder was playing at being confused, and the shark-like smiles from the others in the room were not helping her performance at all.

Jon stepped to Shari's side and leaned forward. "Elder, if I may, are you aware of the current population of Lissae?"

For a moment, Elder Chamele looked flummoxed. "Somewhere around two point four billion people, Guardian."

"And the population of the world when Kay'imi became Altoriae was less than two hundred million. Times have changed significantly, Elder, and to function in our current society, the Altoriae and the way she operates must change as well," Jon said smoothly.

"I'm so glad you brought that up, Guardian. The Altoriae changing is exactly why we're here." Elder Chamele beamed, and the predatory smiles of the other elders grew larger.

"Funny, I thought you were here to tour the Shifting Islands," Elder Jillon said.

"Surely a trip to the Shifting Islands can contain multiple reasons?" the mainland Elder countered.

The hair on the nape of Shari's neck stood up as Sam crowded against her back.

"Surely you'd realise the person in charge of protecting your entire Realm would need forewarning if there were any possibility of fitting you into her schedule?" His voice rumbled above her head.

Shari had to force her expression to remain calm.

"We can stay for as long as necessary." Elder Chamele smiled.

"Your ships are steam powered, are they not?" Zana stepped forward.

"How do you know?" another elder snapped from behind Chamele. She turned, and he subsided, seeming to want to crawl into his suit.

"Merely curious. The Shifting Islands do not allow trees to be unnecessarily cut down, nor do we produce coal. I am assuming you have enough for a return trip?"

"Of course." Elder Chamele smiled again.

"In approximately two days, your return trip will not be possible. We're moving towards the Deep Ocean as we speak."

A few of the mainlanders looked at each other with wide eyes, fear and concern changing the flavour of the room.

"We were not informed of your next location." Elder Chamele was frowning.

"Funny. We weren't informed of your visit," Cyrus said. "Otherwise, we may have been able to tell you it wasn't a promising idea."

"Why are you heading towards the Deep Ocean?" an aide asked, his voice cracking only slightly.

"'Tis the whim of the islands," Zana said serenely.

Shari tried to match her serenity. "If you'll excuse me, my guild and I have other matters to attend to."

It looked like the mainlanders would not move. Shari took a breath, preparing herself for a fight, but Chamele stepped aside and the others reluctantly cleared a path to the door.

'*I dislike having my back to them,*' Shari grumbled to Jon and Sam.

'*Which is why I'm behind you,*' Sam replied.

Jon was at her right, Tania at her left, and Sam still crowded her back. She adjusted her natural shield to cover them all. There was a twinge against the shield as one of the mainland aides pinged it with a touch of spirit Innarn.

'*Altoriae,*' was whispered against her mental shield.

Shari glanced at the aide and deliberately allowed her gaze to slide away from her. Out of the corner of her eye, she saw the aide go red.

As they walked out of the council chambers, the aide slipped her mind. They had to figure out who was controlling Belfar.

Wolf poked at his scrambled eggs as his mate devoured breakfast like he'd been up half the night. Empty plates covered the dining table, and pots and pans were stacked in a haphazard heap on their tiny kitchen bench.

Belfar seemed oblivious to the blood on his face and hands.

"Sleep well?" Wolf asked.

Cup halfway to his mouth, Belfar frowned at him and wrinkled his nose. "Think so. You?"

As always, Wolf hummed his agreement. He'd wished Shari had told him a little about why he had to hide his mate away. "I was thinking."

"Sounds painful." Belfar grinned.

Wolf rolled his eyes. "Do you remember the spot we went to on Talhan last time the islands joined?"

Belfar's face lit up. "The one on the cliffs between the islands?"

"I thought it might be nice to revisit it." Wolf lifted his own cup and shot Belfar a look loaded with meaning over the rim.

"What are we waiting for?" He was up and going through the cupboard before Wolf took a sip.

It was the work of minutes to pack a picnic lunch. Wolf smiled indulgently at his mate. Together, they took to the skies, just before he felt the wards of their home being breached.

With a stretch, he tapped Belfar on the arm. "Tag!" he said, and winged away fast, hoping his mate would try to catch him.

Belfar whooped in delight and streaked after him.

Wolf led him on a merry chase, heart pounding in his chest as he left a false trail for the followers. Belfar seemed oblivious to his true actions, laughing and whooping, putting on bursts of speed which made Wolf delight in his new wing even more.

Eventually, Wolf swooped down, landing in the cave he remembered, and Belfar stumbled in after him, laughing.

"Gotcha!" Belfar crowed and wrapped his arms around his mate.

With a grin, Wolf hugged him back, even as he lifted wards which couldn't be breached. Now, no one would take Belfar away from him, and Belfar wouldn't be able to hurt anyone else.

Something changed in Belfar's stance, and Wolf withdrew slowly. His mate's eyes were clouding over. The orange film, which had Shari spooked, creeping across them. Wolf did the only thing he could think of.

He kissed Belfar.

Samuel sighed as he stomped through his front door.

The meeting with the elders had contained far less bloodshed than he was used to, and far more wondering. The sense of direction was about the same.

He took the osin juice from the cold box and poured himself a glass. A growl came from the lounge room.

For an instant, he tensed. His Innarn swept out, and something in the shadows purred.

"Ah. Thirsty, are you?" He'd almost forgotten about his mystery bone-eating shadow.

After grabbing a shallow dish, he put some water in it and placed it in the deepest shadows of the kitchen, underneath the table.

"You can have water. You aren't getting blood from me, little one."

Something slithered across the floor quicker than he could track, and a slurping noise told him the drink was appreciated.

He wished it was that easy to please everyone.

Seeing Lizbeth's niece burst into the meeting today had sent his nerves alight. If Shari hadn't added her Innarn to his, he may have very well have devoured the twig where she'd stood.

The thing under the table purred and made an odd little chirruping noise.

"Let me guess. Hungry now?"

The noise came again.

Samuel pretended to be put out by the creature, muttering to himself as he reached to the back of the cold box where he'd stored some leftover bones from his dinner last night.

He set them onto the dish the water had been in and waited for a moment. The sense of large eyes focused on him was eerie when he couldn't see anything there.

"I wonder if you have a form? Or if you have always been shadow?"

He sat, cross-legged on the floor, waiting for the thing to eat.

There was a low growl, and he rolled his eyes. "I'm not going to steal your food."

A darker tendril of shadow reached out slowly. It wrapped around a bone and lifted it away.

Samuel grinned as the creature crunched down, breaking the bone with what sounded like sharp teeth. Something about teeth niggled at the back of his mind. He scrubbed a hand across his eyes, and the crunching stopped.

"Please continue. I'm just trying to remember something from a long, long time ago." He almost felt as if he were back on the hatchling grounds, making sure that they were safe and well fed. Grooming had been a particular nightmare, especially attempting to brush their razor-sharp fangs.

He sucked in a breath. If shadows acted like they had teeth, if they ate or spoke, they had likely been something else. A shadow like this was trapped between one life and the next. Not a quite a spirit or a ghoul, but a soul without a body.

And feasting on bones was a way of slowly regaining a physical form.

If he was right, next it would be flesh, then skin.

Staring at his little shadow, Samuel hoped he was right. While it had only been a brief time since the shadow had followed him home, he was quite enjoying the undemanding company.

"Well, I think you're going to need more bones than that if you want to regain your form."

The thing under the table purred.

The meeting had only confirmed Temira's suspicions—the Altoriae did not care that she'd injured Tania.

She eyed the sphere containing the Altoriae's blood. Something had to be done, but what?

Temira paced the room and threw one option after the other out as Xani watched passively from the corner.

She tossed her hands up. Temira slumped on a stool, elbows resting on the desk and hands carelessly dangling off the edge.

What was her goal? *To ensure the Altoriae didn't harm Tania in training again.*

How could she achieve the goal? *Give the Altoriae something else to focus on.*

A smile spread over Temira's face as she picked up a crystal.

Shari was restless.

The entire day had left her feeling attacked in a manner she wasn't sure how to defend against. From Belfar to the mainlanders, she was feeling discombobulated.

A big part of her wanted to believe Belfar was being controlled by someone else, but a smaller, hurt part kept reminding her about Kodan, and the mysterious being who Zana had hinted at.

She needed to shake off her fears. Shari slipped from her room and took the stairs down, heading for the training grounds. If she was this restless, it would probably be good for her to do some training before she patrolled.

When she opened the door to the training ground, the newest members of her guild were already there.

"Well met, Shari!" Amara called cheerfully, waving a hand and accidentally hitting Mu's nose.

"Thought we'd do something productive." Mu rubbed his nose and took an enormous step away from Amara before gesturing to the grounds.

Set up at the far end were targets. Closer, there were a bunch of training dummies and heavy hanging bags. They had left a large area clear for hand-to-hand or Innarn training.

Shari couldn't help but smile as she looked around. "This looks amazing!"

Amara grinned. "Told you she'd like it," she said to Mu.

The Zindaran rubbed his nose and smiled.

"What should we try out first?" Shari asked.

"I was thinking of making things a tad more official," Sam said, stepping forward.

Shari hadn't even seen him in the shadows. "In what way?"

"The mainlanders got me thinking about your guild." Sam had stopped just inside the shadows, and Shari sensed something was holding him there.

"We'd like to officially become part of your guild, Altoriae," Lira said.

Well, she hadn't been expecting this. "And how do you officially become part of a guild?"

"The Healers Guild make you swear an oath to do no harm," Raven offered.

"I don't think 'no harm' can apply here," Lira said, her lips twitching up. "The Thieves Guild has an oath too. You gotta promise to end your life if you're caught."

"I don't want death in the oath," Shari said automatically.

"Oh! How about the Mariners Guild where if you die, they feed your body to the deep-dwelling krakens?" Dealon offered.

Shari wrinkled her nose and shook her head.

"What *do* you want?" Sam asked.

She paused before she answered. "I want beings who will protect Lissae, who will do everything in their power to keep our Realm safe. Ones who will fight by my side and guard each other's backs no matter where we are."

Sam looked at the others. "Sounds like a good oath to me."

There were nods and sounds of agreement.

On the side of the training ground, where the doors opened to the rest of Ronah, someone cleared their throat. "Is guild membership open to anyone?" Collis asked. He was standing just inside the external doors, a bunch of the Returned behind him.

Shari felt tears starting to well. Roughly, she cleared her throat. "If you can swear to an oath and let me or whoever is in charge know when you no longer want to be part of the guild, then yes, membership is open to anyone."

"Anyone she approves," Sam amended.

Turning to glare at him, she received an arched brow in return. '*Do you really want to leave your guild open to those who would swear the oath, but actively seek to undermine you?*'

She had assumed no one would try to, but hadn't today already proved the mainlanders would if they had the chance? And after Kodan... How many others sought to join them?

"Are we approved?" Collis stepped farther into the grounds, skirting the training dummies. A horde of the Returned stepped in after him.

Shari shot Sam a look, having an inkling the whole thing was a set-up. "Despite Daivi, you would join me?" Shari asked.

"Because of Daivi. We do not want her fading to be in vain," Collis corrected.

"Then yes, I approve."

Collis and the Returned marched forwards. The former candidates and Sam made a line in front of them. There were almost two hundred and fifty beings ready to join her in the battle to keep Lissae safe.

'Jon? *You might want to get here,*' Shari sent.

She sensed a ripple of Innarn as Jon shifted to her side. '*What's going on?*' he sent as he took in the lines of beings before them.

'*They've decided they want to make the Altoriae's Guild official.*'

As if on cue, they dropped to their knees, voices raising as one. "We swear to protect Lissae and do everything in our power to keep our Realm safe. We will fight by the Altoriae's side and guard each other's backs no matter where we are."

Their pledge echoed through the training grounds. Shari sensed their Innarn extending and tangle with her own. Sam's, by far the darkest, seemed to reach out and stroke her arm. When she caught his gaze, he winked at her.

"Do you accept our pledge?" they asked.

Their Innarn was swirling around her, lifting the ends of her hair. "I accept your pledge," she said, and the Innarn sank into her skin. "And offer my own."

'*Careful, Shari,*' Jon warned.

"I swear I will do everything in my power to keep you and Lissae safe. Do you accept my pledge?"

"We do," they said.

Filled with a rush of their Innarn, Shari's feet lifted off the ground, and it swirled her around on the spot.

As she touched down, the Altoriae grinned. "Better get training then."

Her guild stood, breaking off as if they'd already pre-determined who would do what.

"How does it feel?" Sam asked, walking over to her side. She sensed tension in every fibre of his body. She could also sense that her answer mattered an awful lot to him.

"Odd," she admitted. "I don't enjoy having the fate of so many directly in my hands."

"You've had the fate of Lissae in your hands since you were a child," Jon reminded her.

"But it feels more... personal, somehow. These beings trust me enough to fight by my side." She turned her head, determined not to let them see the tears welling.

Sam's foot scraped on the ground. He gave her a blinding smile when she looked back at him. Taking her hand in his, he said, "Of all the leaders in all the Realms, you are the one I'd want to hold my fate." He bowed over her hand, lips a breath away from brushing it.

Shari blushed as he bounded off to join those taking aim at the targets.

"I'm not sure what just happened," she admitted to Jon.

"With Sam, I don't think any of us ever are." He looked distracted.

"What's wrong?" she asked.

"Nothing," he answered, a shade too quickly.

"Jon," she wheedled, poking his ribs.

"I was about to go out with Zac."

"Then why are you here? Go!" When he started protesting, she merely shifted him back to his house. Shari grinned.

"What should I work on, Altoriae?" a short, stocky man asked. The ink on his cheek looked like it was in thick stripes at first, but Shari realised the design inside the blocky stripes was moving and rippling. "It's reacting to the Innarn in the air," he said, noticing her gaze. "You're a high-level plasma Innarnian, and so am I."

"Really...?"

"Benny," he said.

"Well, Benny, why don't you show me what you've got?"

They went over to the space set aside for sparring. Shari was pleased the others kept training rather than turning to gawk.

She bowed at Benny, and he returned the gesture. Shari said, "Hit me. If you–"

He struck before she'd finished speaking, thick ropes of plasma lashing out of his hands and striking the ground where she'd been standing.

Shari slammed up a shield and pushed it against him. She shifted behind him and held a blade to his throat before he turned. "Again?" she whispered in his ear.

"Again."

Jonathan smoothed his hands over his shirt. Would tucked or untucked be more appropriate?

The knock at the door had him hastily untucking his shirt. Would Zac prefer it if he was less formal?

By the looks of it, the man at the door definitely liked a more casual look. Zac wore a loose-fitting shirt unbuttoned enough to show part of his chest. The sleeves were rolled up to his elbows, and he'd already taken his shoes off.

Jonathan gulped. "Well met, Zac. Come in."

Zac slid passed him, slightly closer than what was needed. "Well met, Jon." His grin was blinding.

He gulped again. He was in over his head.

As he stood in the lounge room, Zac lazily gave him the once-over, but frowned at his glasses. "Still having problems seeing?"

Self-conscious, Jonathan touched the wire frames. "Eh. I forget about them most of the time."

Something flicked over Zac's face too quickly for Jonathan to name. "I bought dinner," Zac said, holding up a basket. "I thought you might prefer if we were a little more... private."

Over the years, many people had offered to have a private dinner with the Guardian. Every time, he'd had the sensation that he was part of the menu. This time, he was glad.

"Sounds delightful," Jonathan said, gesturing to the dining room.

"I know the tavern holds fond memories, but I thought we could try something different tonight. I picked up Top Cat Café's nightly special." He started unpacking the basket. "Slow-cooked stuffed lukkorel, with orbisalium and lavender cobbler for dessert."

The smells were so good, Jonathan's stomach grumbled. He slapped a hand over it, mortified.

Zac laughed. "Mine growled so loudly, they couldn't wait to get me out of the café. Said I was scaring off their patrons." He lifted the stasis charm, and the aroma of perfectly cooked lukkorel filled the room.

"Let's eat before our stomachs both start complaining." Jonathan grinned. After loading their plates up, they settled at the table.

There was an awkward silence. Jonathan's cutlery scraped over the plate and he grinned sheepishly at Zac.

His companion popped a bite into his mouth and chewed quickly. "I spent the last six months or so in Atlantis. Don't get me wrong—their food is amazing. But there's nothing like the taste of home."

Jonathan grinned. "I haven't had the chance to spend as much time off-Realm, but there is absolutely something about the comforts of home."

"You grew up on the mainland, didn't you?"

He rolled his eyes. "Yes. My aunt was a horrid woman. But she was also a brilliant cook. My father and I would sneak into the kitchen sometimes and steal slices of cake. We'd run out to the side garden, hide under the shade of the weeping willow and stuff our faces."

"Do you keep in touch with your aunt?"

Gaze skittering to the side, Jonathan shrugged. "She's ah... not really a people person." *At least, she's not really a* me *person.*

"Sounds better than Nisethran."

"He's the Atlantean who wanted his tech back?"

"Yeah. He's a narcistic piece of dung. I was warned, of course. But I didn't really believe the rumours."

"What rumours?" Jonathan asked idly, mopping up some of the juices with a piece of lukkorel.

"That he was mad. Atlanteans have this whole thing about *authentic mythology*. They believe the past can help shape the future. But they've lost touch with so much of what they were. Did you know their race was considered the foremost techno Innarn experts in all the Light Realms?"

"I didn't even know they were able to use Innarn." Jonathan frowned.

Zac took another bite and nodded. "What they've created is amazing. Almost anything and everything you can think of is automated through the use of technology. But they lost their connection with the elements along the way, and their Innarn faded."

"How is Asterion able to use Innarn?"

"Asterion is Nisethran's proudest accomplishment. He was always boasting about being the first Atlantean to bring the ancient myths back to life." Zac put his cutlery down and sighed. "What they don't know is that the original bull head that was meant to be used failed. How can something so different from our own biology be attached? He panicked. Then went off-Realm—he wouldn't tell me where, but it had Innarn. When he returned, it was with a new bull head—and when Asterion woke up with his brain re-seated in a monster's body, Innarn pulsed out of him. It fried most of the circuits and corrupted the data Nisethran had been collecting for so long."

"No wonder he went mad." Jonathan took his chin off his hand, and sent a gentle wave of warming out over their food.

Zac took a bite, chewing viciously. "He was obsessed. He wanted all the ancient myths to be brought back. I believe he was working on the snake-headed woman next."

Jonathan shuddered. "I'm glad he never got a chance to finish."

"Onto more pleasant things!" Zac grinned and pushed his plate away. "How about we tackle that crumble?"

"Sounds wonderful."

They laughed and talked. The dual moons were shining through the dining room window, an indication they'd spent almost the whole night together.

"It's almost morning!" Jonathan blinked blearily. After taking off his glasses, he rubbed at tired eyes.

"Well, before I go, let me offer a toast," Zac said. Leaning over, he grabbed two glasses and poured a generous serve of osin juice into each. He presented one to Jonathan, who took it. Their fingers lingered, and gazes met, speaking more than words.

"To old friends being united again," Zac said huskily, and held up his glass.

Jonathan bumped the rim of his glass against Zac's and took a drink without looking. It was only as he was lowering the glass that he noticed something orange glowing in the bottom. "What's this?" he asked softly.

"Do you know why I've been away so long?" Zac asked. "I've been searching the Realms for a cure so you'll be able to see again without needing any help."

"Zaaac." He was slurring. "Didn' hav' ta." There must have been something other than femto crystals in the drink, because the room was going dark.

"It's my fault you were hurt in the first place," Zac said bitterly. "I was too slow."

His tongue was too big for his mouth, and he was struggling to keep his head up.

"Rest, Jon, and let the crystals do their work."

His body was floating. Gently, he was settled on something soft. Jonathan struggled to open his eyes. By the fuzzy feel of it, Zac had laid him on the couch.

"I'll watch over you until you're healed," Zac said. "Rest, Jon. I'll be here."

Eyelids too heavy to open, Jonathan was left in the dark. Before he lost total consciousness, he heard the tapping of metal on wood, and then there was nothing but dread.

CHAPTER TWENTY-TWO

"You seem distracted today," Samuel said, lounging against the counter of the bookshop. Jonathan had called them both in for an early-morning meeting, but now they were here, the Guardian seemed to be struggling with what to say.

He watched as Shari twirled a coin between her fingers. "I'm distracted. The mainland elders have me tied up in knots. I wasn't able to concentrate at school at all."

"You should go look?" Jonathan's voice was just short of a monotone, but the corner of his mouth ticked up.

"Maybe I should." Shari grinned.

Samuel knew the Altoriae well enough by now to say she preferred taking action than waiting around for something to happen.

Almost skipping, she slipped into the back room of the bookshop and threw herself into a chair, Samuel trailing after her.

"Make sure I come back in one piece," she said, looking at him.

He thumped a fist over his heart and winked at her.

Shari closed her eyes, settled back into the chair, and was still.

Samuel stared at her in confusion. Did she really think taking a nap would help? Then a shiver which felt like Shari swept passed him.

She was projecting her spirit.

More than that, she trusted him to watch over her while she was projecting her spirit.

Samuel didn't know whether to call her foolish or brave. He knew what he would have done before they had welcomed him on Lissae. For a moment, he stood over her body, hesitating.

Didn't I just swear an oath last night? Disgusted with himself, he turned away, opening the back door of the shop.

Before he left, he paused. Was she more of a fool than he thought to ask him to protect her? Still, he closed the door and placed his back against it, looking at her from the safety of the shadows.

Limbs moving stiffly, Jonathan entered the room. He didn't seem to notice Samuel in the shadows.

Jonathan jerked his way towards his Altoriae, his limbs seeming to fight against every step. Eventually though, he was looming over her prone form.

There was a crossbow in the Guardian's hand.

The tip of a loaded arrow against Shari's chest.

His finger squeezing the trigger.

The orange glow of his eyes.

In a split second, he could be free.

If ever there was a time to choose a side, this was it.

Shari was floating in the corner above Elder Chamele's head. The mainland elders had holed up in their rooms on Talhan.

The suite they were in was indulgent, silver gilding the edges of the pale wooden furniture. Carved crystals brought warmth to the space. The elders were lounging on stuffed chairs while the aides stood around the edges of the room, waiting patiently to be called upon.

"The Altoriae is far more dangerous than we realised," Chamele was saying.

"It's not just the Altoriae. It's all of these Shifting Island aberrations. We have the firepower. We should just blow them up and get it done!" Elder Ben from Kenorvia grumbled.

"Patience. Remember why we're here." Chamele held out a teacup, wriggling it.

"Why are we here?" an aide asked as she poured tea into the cup. If Shari was right, she was the one who'd brushed against her shield.

Chamele sighed. "First we need to determine if the Innarnians can withstand our firepower or if we have to change our attack prior to the takeover. Honestly, keep up."

The aide's eyes flicked to Shari's corner. "Aren't you worried they might spy on us?"

Elder Gywn from Vendalbara snorted. "Hardly. The Innarnians act like the only threat to their way of life lies outside Lissae."

The aide stepped back and bowed her head a little.

"Once we've destroyed the aberrations, what will we do?" Elder Suni from Lawrgaea asked, picking out one of the carefully prepared treats from a platter on a low table.

"Tether the Shifting Islands to the mainland and strip them of anything valuable." Chamele sipped serenely at her tea.

Shari shuddered, her stomach churning.

"I want Talhan." It was Gywn. "We need more crystals to power our cities."

"Which is why you're here. Inform your aides to gather samples for testing. We need to make sure this will be worth our while." Chamele took another sip of her drink.

Shari hoped she'd choke.

"And we have the backing of the mainland governments?" Elder Suni asked.

The look Chamele levelled at Suni sent a shiver down Shari's spine. "I represent the entirety of the fixed island governments, and *you* are here at my request to prove you can be as useful to us as we will be to you."

"Why should we trust you any more than we trust these aberrations?" Suni asked.

Chamele abruptly stood, startling the closest aide. "We've been fighting a one-sided war against them for decades, and they haven't taken us seriously. For centuries, their abilities meant stronger firepower and more control over the way the rest of the world acts. When they demanded, we patrolled, we sent brave men and women to die. And for what?"

"Needless, countless deaths. Children orphaned; families ruined. Towns decimated. All to help them for a pittance and a pat on the head. No more. It's time for the Shifting Islands to pay back what they've taken from us." Elder Ben from Kenorvia was practically growling.

"You didn't answer the question." Gwyn pointed out.

"You can trust us, because they don't trust you. We're the only ones able to get close to them." Chamele took another drink.

Abruptly, Shari was pulled back into her own body.

The Guardian's eyes glowed a brighter orange as his shaking hand tightened on the crossbow.

Samuel frowned as he shifted the crossbow out of the room.

If the circumstances had been different, it would have been amusing to watch Jonathan's finger squeeze the non-existent trigger, orange eyes eagerly watching for the spray of blood.

When nothing happened, the Guardian looked down at his empty hand, confused.

Samuel shifted before he was even aware of it, directly between Shari and Jonathan.

"I don't think this is in your training manual," Samuel said. He was practically standing on Jonathan's feet.

The Guardian jerked away. When he lifted his head, his eyes were totally orange. It didn't detract Samuel's attention from the knife in Jonathan's hand. Samuel had a sneaky suspicion it wasn't meant for him.

"Is there a particular reason you're trying to gut your charge?" he asked as Jonathan clumsily slashed at him.

If he'd had any doubt before, he didn't now. Something or someone was controlling the Guardian. Samuel had known Jonathan since he was but a hatchling. Even then, Jonathan was a massive pain in his hide, but he'd never been clumsy with a knife.

The thing controlling Jonathan slashed again, and Samuel jerked back, almost tripping over the chair with Shari in it.

A fight this close was bound to end in disaster.

Another desperate slash–this one a shade closer and more controlled.

Samuel countered with a blast of Innarn, pushing Jonathan against the door. He stalked forward enough so he'd stop tripping over the Altoriae.

Shari was stirring behind him, but he didn't dare take his eyes off the Guardian.

"What's going on?" Shari asked softly.

"Jonathan's a touch orange at the moment." Samuel grunted as the Guardian charged across the room, driving his shoulder into Samuel's gut.

"Orange?"

Shari sounded sleep-rumpled. He had a flash of an image–*Shari stretching, a white sheet slipping down her tanned skin, the sun kissing her bare back.*

A fierce pain brought him into the present.

"You cut me!" he accused Jonathan, slapping a hand up to his face to hold his cheek together.

Underneath the orange glow from his eyes, the Guardian's smile reminded Samuel uncomfortably of his old home.

Innarn swirled around them.

Samuel saw the large metal pot hovering above Jonathan's head in his peripheral vision, and smirked as it clanged against the Guardian's head, knocking him out cold.

"Are you okay?" Shari asked. She had scrambled out of the seat and was resting a gentle hand on his shoulder, turning him to face her. "What happened?"

"He cut me," Samuel grumbled.

Shari's hand glowed green, and she rested it gently against his stinging cheek. "It's deep," she said.

He frowned at her. 'Not something you want to hear from the person pulling your face back together.'

"Sorry," she said. "I just... I didn't think he'd be able to land a blow, to be honest."

'I was distracted.' He was even more distracted with her standing so close. Her healing itched and burned. It would leave a scar despite her best efforts. Jonathan's blade had been imbued with Light Innarn, and hers just wasn't dark enough to heal him seamlessly.

But his vision...

As the Altoriae turned back to the Guardian, he sucked in a breath. He should know better than most, his visions rarely played out the way he thought they would.

"Shari!"

For an instant, Jon's pleading voice had her turning.

With Sam's help, she'd locked him in one of the lower levels of the castle, hoping to wait out the femto crystals in his body.

"Shari, I swear it wasn't me," Jon pleaded.

Hands fisted by her side, Shari's breath shuddered from her lungs. "I know. I don't want to do this, Jon, but we need to make sure you're safe. I can't let you hurt someone else."

She sensed him slump against the door.

"I understand," he sighed. "Just... please, hurry."

If she looked back, she'd let him out. And if he wasn't himself, he'd never forgive her.

If he didn't kill her first.

"We need to talk to Temira—now."

Sam by her side, she strode away as quickly as she could, ignoring the crystals flickering in the corridor as they passed by.

As his captor's footsteps receded, the smile which crossed Jonathan Buan's face was not his own.

Laying his hand against the old, crystal lock, the being in control concentrated for a moment. It was a matter of seconds before the ancient lock crumbled, and the door to the makeshift cell swung open.

CHAPTER TWENTY-THREE

"You've what?" Tania spat her drink across the table.

"I've had to lock Jon up. He *attacked* me."

Hearing Shari say it for the second time did not make the words any easier to take in. "Sam, help me understand," Tania pleaded, looking at Jon's latest apprentice. He was sporting a startlingly fresh scar, curved like a backward J on his cheek. "Did–"

"Yes, it's Jon's handiwork." Sam raised his fingers to trace the puckered, pink scar.

"I don't know why it healed like that." Shari frowned.

The look on Sam's face said he knew. The temperature in the room dropped a bit.

"I like it. Makes you look even more dangerous." Tania took a drink to hide her smile at Sam's pleased expression. "Do you really think someone is controlling Jon the way they were Belfar?"

"Yes. His eyes were the same orange."

"And you believe it's the femto crystals?"

Shari bit her lip. "I'm beginning to consider that something is influencing the femto crystals."

"What if they can command bigger crystals?" Sam wondered.

"That's why I want Tania to seal off the layer Jon's in."

Tania sighed. '*Ronah? Can you tell me where Jon is?*'

'*Yes. He's moving—fast.*'

She gulped. '*Show me?*' Ronah's senses took over her own, and Tania sensed Jon running through the lowest layer of the castle. He was moments from the door. '*We need to seal it off. Please, Ronah.*'

The Shifting Island grumbled, but something about Tania's sincerity got through. As Jon pull the door open, a wall of pure earth came down, blocking him from leaving the level.

'*I don't enjoy stopping the Guardian,*' Ronah sent.

'*Does he feel like the Guardian you know?*' Tania asked.

She sensed the island probing and pushing against Jon's Innarn, and the quick retreat at the foreign sensation. '*He feels like Talhan!*'

'*What?*'

'*Little bits of crystal scattered throughout his dirt.*'

"His dirt?" Tania wondered out loud.

"What?" Shari asked.

She repeated what Ronah had sent to her.

"His dirt. His streams I would understand her equating to his blood, but his dirt? What's our equivalent to dirt?"

"Muscles," Sam said grimly. "Someone has been dosing the Guardian with femto crystals."

The black crystal lighting on the table gave off a dull orange glow.

Tania wanted to giggle as Shari glared at it, but her insides sunk and squashed the urge quicker than it rose.

What has Temira been doing?

Temira lifted her chin and exhaled slowly. She'd been working ever since the meeting with the elders, and she finally had the answer.

The Altoriae would never have another training accident again.

A large, gleaming rectangular box stood as tall as her waist. Hidden by the outer shell, refillable canisters of as many types of Innarn as she could gather were stacked alongside a large black crystal powering the internal mechanisms.

She stroked her hand along one side, and the small container hissed open. Temira used her Innarn to lift the bubble with the Altoriae's blood and tipped it carefully into the container.

Another pat and the container disappeared back into the body.

Cautiously, making sure her movements were in the correct order, Temira activated the device.

A black light flickered to life in the middle of the upper mechanism, and the device hovered until it was level with the technomancer's chest.

"You know what to do," Temira said, and opened the door.

The device spun on the spot, a whirring noise coming from its hidden insides. Slowly, it moved out of the room. Temira stepped out as it hovered along the hallway.

She followed it for a while and gave a last nod as it rounded the corner. As she stepped back into the room, Ronah's Linked was standing with her back to the door, looking at Xani.

"Are you okay?" Tania was asking.

Temira ran her gaze over her oldest friend. Xani was greyer than usual.

'*Fine,*' Xani broadcasted.

Only she didn't sound like Xani anymore. And the orange lines lighting up her veins under her almost translucent skin was definitely not like Xani.

Temira frowned. It might be wise to bring some levity to the room. Maybe one of Cyrus's ploys of not recognising others?

"I came to speak to Temira. Is she—" Ronah's Linked started to say.

"Well, well, well. Who do we have here?" Temira asked.

Immediately, the girl whirled around, eyes wide, hand flying to her chest. Her Innarn was pulsing through the room so strongly, things rattled on the bench.

Even as Temira frowned, Tania's eyes welled up and tears fell, and her breath came in great gasps.

She didn't need her Innarn to understand her new kin was having an anxiety attack.

Temira conjured a block of crystal to act as a seat and nudged Tania, gently helping her to sit.

Where is Xani? She was so much better at calming people down.

Xani was still in the corner, blankly looking at the door.

With a quiet huff, Temira knelt before the trembling girl. Cautiously, she patted her sweaty hands, murmuring the same nonsense words she'd said to her brother all those years ago.

A small part of her mind marvelled at being able to remember something which seemed so tiny now, but was such a big part of her life when he'd returned from being away.

Gradually, Tania calmed. She wiped away the tears and mucus with the back of her sleeve.

Silently, Temira vanished the mess. She was never using one of Cyrus's ploys again. "You were looking for me?" she asked softly.

"Yes. I'm sorry. I..." Tania gave a single hiccoughing sob and buried her face in her hands.

Temira patted Tania's knee and sent messages to her aides on their jobs for the day. She would be needed here more than anywhere else. As distraught as her adopted kin was, it left her with a warm glow to say her family needed her. It would be nicer if it were for a happy reason, but no being could experience joy all the time.

"A little while ago, I was held captive," Tania said to her knees.

"And you escaped?" Temira frowned.

"Yes, Shari saved me."

Perhaps she needed to call the device back and make some adjustments? "What made you think of it?" Temira was curious but didn't want to set off another attack.

"What you said. It's what *she* said when they caught me." Another sob. "They almost ripped my arms off."

Tania needed far more than a pat on the knee. "Have you seen a mind healer?"

"What's a mind healer?"

"They help you work through traumatic events, or to understand what has happened or even the way your mind works."

"I didn't know there was such a thing."

"I can introduce you to several who have helped patients here, and I'm sure the Guardian can recommend others." Her own journey into accepting the fate of her Realm had been difficult, and it had only been through the help of her mind healer that she'd been able to come to a place of peace.

"I think I'd like those names." Tania was still speaking to her knees, but her hands were away from her face.

Temira looked at Xani again, who hadn't moved. '*Help?*' she sent. It echoed back as if it were bouncing off the crystal walls of the room.

The lake of boiling water near her childhood home had always made her feel better when she'd dive into it.

From the looks of her skin, Tania wouldn't be able to withstand the external heat, but perhaps, internally? "Come. We shall get a hot drink and concentrate on pleasant things for a while."

As they left the room, Temira looked back. Xani was still in the corner, veins glowing in time with the crystals flickering in the room. Just what was her friend testing out this time?

Shari idly scratched at the healing slash she'd gotten when on patrol and stepped out of the way as someone rounded the street corner. Locking

Jon away had been one of the more difficult decisions she'd had to make lately, and she wasn't sure if she'd made the right call.

"Oh!" Anika looked startled. Her hair was mussed, and she was dripping with sweat. "I'm glad I found you!" she puffed. "I've been looking all over."

"What's up?" Her glove was already snapping back into place, blades ready, her other hand resting on the hilt of the yellow blade Yessna had given her.

"We're not fighting anything," Anika said scornfully. "I just need to know what you want to wear for your next outfit. The feathers were a tremendous hit on Talhan, so I was thinking something with crystals for when we join with Cantash."

"Crystals probably aren't the best idea at the moment," Shari said. A weird thrumming noise was getting closer.

"But they could be the next in thing! You could make them the next in thing! Don't you know Talhan's Linked? Just ask him for some and–"

Anika didn't get to finish.

The thrumming noise had become a pounding that shook her bones. A sleek, rectangular machine rounded the corner and almost crashed into Anika.

Shari pulled her out of the way just in time.

The machine hovered where it was for a moment, then a small spike darted out and poked Shari.

"Ouch!" She rubbed the spot. Had this thing had come from Atlantis? It looked nothing like the nanny device she'd seen, but there was an odd similarity.

Vibrating slightly, the machine let out a sudden cloud of smoke from the back, distracting Shari from the bolt of plasma it threw at her from the front.

"Watch out!" Anika shouted and pulled her aside, the bolt sizzling passed them and hitting a tree. "What is that thing?"

"I'm not sure," Shari admitted. She poked at it with her Innarn, expecting to find foreign parts, but it was made entirely on Lissae. And if she was right, the Innarn of over a dozen people was inside it. It made her think of the Innarn-collecting machines somehow.

The pieces clicked together.

"Technomancer," she growled as the device shot at her again.

Tania had to admit she was feeling better, even if she was embarrassed by what had happened. She nursed a half-full cup. The sound of the waves as they lapped at Ronah's shore gave her the sense of safety again.

Temira was telling a rather animated story about how she'd first discovered the use of crystals in wound healing. It pulled Tania out of her slump.

"Are the crystals able to be used for something else?"

"The uses of crystals are infinite," the technomancer said.

"Are you able to change what they do once they're inside someone?" She thought of Belfar's wing. "Or attached to someone?"

"What are you implying?" Temira looked fierce when she frowned.

"Belfar's attack had me worried."

"Had?"

Perhaps she would find the right way to say what had happened if she stared into her cup for long enough, Tania sighed. "The Guardian tried to kill Shari last night."

Temira blinked rapidly. "Is he not charged with her care?"

"He is. We think he is being controlled by something."

"Something or someone. You suspect me." Her voice was flat and her face emotionless.

"No! I think you might have the names of others who can change the crystals in someone's body, but I don't think you're capable of doing that."

The technomancer's gaze warmed slightly. "There would only be two other beings adept enough to change the crystals once they were inside someone. Xani and Cyrus. I doubt either of them would invoke any more suspicion than I would?"

Tania sighed. "I don't know. I don't want to think so, but I bet Shari will want all of you watched."

"You might want to warn the Altoriae then."

"Warn her?"

"Before you came to me this morning, I sent a device after her."

"A device?" Tania was sceptical.

"I call it the Basic Innarn Training device—a B.I.T.—it tests her abilities without anyone else being hurt."

"Temira!" she exclaimed, but something in the line of the technomancer's spine and the way she wouldn't meet Tania's eyes said there was more to the story. "Temira?"

"It's powered by crystals. If someone is trying to kill her, both Xani and Cyrus were in and out of my lab while I was building it." The tall, blue-skinned techno-Innarnian started rocking back and forward slightly, looking miserable. "I was mad. I didn't get all of the kinks out of it before I set it going."

"Well, at least we've narrowed down our suspect pool?" Tania aimed for bright, but it came out as a question.

'And I still count as one of them.' Temira's send was so mournful, Tania moved along the bench and pressed up next to her, offering comfort through her presence.

"If we find out who is messing with the crystals, then we won't need a list," Tania said.

"Then we'd best find them."

Shari ducked and dodged as the machine relentlessly pursued her through the streets of Ronah.

Indiscriminately firing at her, it got in the occasional strike. No matter what she threw back, the thing seemed impervious.

What are my chances of defeating this thing if I just stop?

She adjusted her aim and sent a stream of fire hot enough to melt anything directly at it, only for it to evaporate like steam.

With a groan, she turned back and almost ran into a group of teens, who were oblivious to the danger.

They'd spilled out of the café and onto the sidewalk, chatting and laughing, totally carefree.

Shari shifted to the far side of them and paused only to move them away from the thing intent on chasing her.

The machine fired again—a blast of air which kicked up loose stones on the ground and shot them at her, pinging uselessly against her shield. They skittered across the ground and Shari sighed.

Whatever this thing was, it was relentless. She wanted to reach out to Jon and see if he knew anything, but she wasn't sure if she should trust what he said at the moment. Her chest twinged at the thought, and she gasped a little.

Metal and water rarely mixed well, right? Maybe if she led this thing to the ocean, she could drown it.

A quick glance over her shoulder again to make sure it was following her, and Shari started running.

The machine thrummed as it struggled to keep up with her. Every few steps, Innarn was blasting against the back of her shield. Shari ran on, getting closer to where the road ended.

As she reached the point where the sand began, Tania and Temira strolled into view.

"You!" Shari growled. She charged straight for Temira, hoping to catch the technomancer off guard. Hand outstretched, fingers brushing against the material of her purple jacket, Temira vanished from Shari's grasp and popped up on the other side of Tania.

"It's a training device, Shari!" Ronah's Linked called.

"How do I shut it down?"

"You need to stop it," Temira yelled over the top of another Innarn blast.

'That is singularly the most unhelpful bit of advice I've ever received!' An Innarn strike against the body of the machine punctuated each word of her send.

And each strike did absolutely no damage.

Shari growled again, remembering the molten slag of the machines on Atlantis. But she'd already tried to melt it.

If she couldn't melt it, stabbing it might work?

Shari pulled her shield in as close to her skin as she dared. When the machine fired off the next volley, she fell as if it had hit her.

Tania screamed.

Her eyes closed. Shari listened for the thrum of the machine as it hovered closer and closer.

Come on.

Just.

A.

Bit.

More...

Swiftly, she rolled over. Shari stabbed up with her blade, getting the machine from underneath. She jammed her glove into the side for good measure. The blades sliding into the smooth shell were rather more satisfying than she'd expected.

"No!" Temira screamed. "Don't stab it! If the containers mix..."

Shari looked directly into the technomancer's eyes and pushed the blades out of her glove more.

There was a tiny window of time when Shari knew she'd done the wrong thing.

Metal blades clinked against crystal containers.

Temira's eyes went wide.

Tania reached out.

And Shari's world exploded.

CHAPTER TWENTY-FOUR

"Shari..." Tania groaned, rubbing the back of her head. Her hand came away sticky. The pounding in her head almost drowned out the quietest send she'd ever gotten.

'*She is at peace.*'

"Ronah?" Tania asked.

'*Take care of my daughter.*'

"Daughter?" Staggering to her feet, Tania tried to ignore the way the Realm was spinning. Realm. "Lissae?"

There was no answer.

Next to her, someone moaned. "Temira?"

The blast had thrown them both backward onto the dunes, but it looked like Temira fared far worse than Tania. Sticky rivers of red streamed from her nose and one ear. Her eyes were unfocused, and the skin of her hands appeared badly sunburned. Blisters swelled and oozed.

Tania took one last look at the last spot Shari had stood. Tears streaming down her face, she shifted with Temira to the Healers Centre on Ronah.

She wanted, badly, to take the technomancer to Talhan, but the thought of leaving her island, who was keening, was too much to bear.

Jonathan's heart died right where it lay.

Gasping for breath and clutching his chest, he staggered to a wall and slid down, the hard ground jolting the last of the crystal haze from his system.

Without even sending, he knew something horrible had happened to Shari.

He just hoped it wasn't his fault.

Samuel had been leaving the school when he'd seen people running and screaming.

As he reached the sidewalk, Anika ran up to him, panting.

"Stan!" she shrieked, and threw her arms around him.

"Who's Stan?" he asked, disentangling himself.

"You are, silly. Never mind. Shari is in danger! There's a machine chasing her! And it hit me!"

Samuel glared as he sent his Innarn out, poking and prodding to see where the Altoriae was hiding. For a long moment, there was nothing, then he sensed the tingle of her Innarn.

Shifting far enough away so he'd be able to take down her metal attacker, he found his heart in his throat as Shari fell face-first onto the sand.

When she rolled over to stab the machine, he grinned fiercely.

But the technomancer was screaming, "No! Don't stab it! If the containers mix..."

He sensed it—the instant her blades nicked the metal shell of the machine. He saw the scene playing out before him and knew he was about to watch the death of the thirteenth Altoriae.

If only someone could do something.

Tania was reaching out, a scream on her lips as Shari defiantly looked at Temira and pushed her blades deeper into the machine.

This was everything War'Jan had been hoping for.

Everything his Queen wanted.

The very thing he had been working towards.

Samuel groaned.

He couldn't let it happen.

A sound like nothing heard on Lissae rose from the very depths of him and grew louder, even as Shari's blades drew closer to the containers.

It spilled from his very pores, rippling out over the sand and surrounding the trio on the beach, right as the tip of her blade pierced the Innarn containers.

In an unoccupied corner of his mind, Samuel couldn't fathom how she'd survived for so long without him.

Time stood still on the beach. Samuel pulled on the Innarn inside the containers to create shielding around the metal box, but when he turned his attention to Shari, she was gone.

Obliterated.

He dropped the time distortion, and watched as the machine exploded, throwing Tania and Temira backwards despite his shield. It left a large hole in the ground with a beautiful pattern of smooth cobalt glass around the outside.

His feet sliding on the suddenly smooth sand, Samuel made his way to the hole and peered into it.

There was no sign of the Altoriae.

So, he did what anyone else would do in this situation.

Samuel jumped into the endless hole and used his Innarn to pull it closed behind him.

Talhan was restless.

It made Cyrus edgy, and he found himself peering suspiciously around corners and glancing over his shoulder on the way to the university.

'*What's going on?*' Cyrus sent.

'*It feels like someone is poking at my shell.*'

Cyrus scratched the back of his head. After he'd linked with Talhan, they'd had to develop a system of communicating to easily understand each other. Talhan often though in abstract ways or would send Cyrus images of things which took him a while to puzzle through. The island had once sent him the schematics of the different provinces as rings etched in crystal, with smaller rings inside, meant to be dwellings, and solid circles to show public areas.

It had taken him a month to figure it out.

But saying his shell?

Ah. '*Someone is poking your outer layer?*'

'*It hurts.*'

Maybe the stomach ache plaguing him wasn't because of last night's meal?

'*Where are they poking you?*'

Instead of the usual obscure image, Talhan projected the scene directly onto the crystal slab in his hand.

On the beach side of the Earth Province, mainlanders were trying to pull crystal directly from the ground.

Gasping, Cyrus flicked his finger across the slab and displayed it on the side of a building. Something metallic scuttled into the shadows as he turned his attention to the screen.

Slabs everywhere mimicked the display and outraged gasps surrounded him as beings looked up.

B.I.R.D.s started poking their people onto platforms, pushing them to action.

Cyrus was one step ahead. '*Take me there,*' he sent to Talhan.

Whenever the Shifting Island moved him, it was always through a network of crystals—his life force hopped from one crystal to the next and slipped out the other side. The crystals under the island's 'shell' were so interconnected, the trip was usually quicker than any other type of travel, even shifting.

But this disjointed journey left him even more nauseous. He half hoped it was because of the mainlanders, and not the parasite Talhan had said was making her sick.

"What are you doing?" he asked, crossing his arms and glaring.

There were a team of about twenty mainlanders, and only a few bothered to look up from their looting to laugh at him.

The rest of Talhan's population started appearing. He sensed them standing beside and behind him, ready to defend their home.

The mainlanders stopped laughing.

"We need samples," one offered. "We were told to get 'em."

"Illegally taking samples," Cyrus corrected. "And you can stop now." He ground his heel down slightly, cracking through Talhan's 'shell' and using his Innarn to suck the crystals deeper into the earth.

"Oi!"

Cyrus didn't have to look to know it was Eva stepping beside him. He sensed her barely contained rage as if it were a living thing coating her skin.

"You can tell your masters they should ask before playing with someone else's toys."

A mainlander took offence to her words and pulled up a large barrel. He squeezed a thin strip of metal, and a loud bang made them all flinch.

Eva cried out in pain, and the mainlanders cheered.

As he looked across at his friend, she pulled a hand covered in blood away from her chest. She coughed violently and spat a glob of red onto the sand.

He let it fill his vision. Cyrus took a breath, and said, "You want crystals, do you?"

"It's what we're here for," the mainlander who had spoken before replied, spreading his hands wide.

"I'll give you crystals."

Something in his tone wiped the smile from the man's face.

'Talhan?'

'Linked.'

It was all the permission he needed.

Cyrus spread his own hands wide, fingers splayed. With closed eyes, he poked around for the connections under the ground. He sensed the pain from the island, the cracks in the crystals rushing up to pound at him.

He clenched his fists and opened his eyes. Thousands upon thousands of tiny shards shot from the ground, shredding the bodies of the mainlanders who'd tried to steal them. Red mist exploded outwards, covering the sole survivor.

As quickly as they'd left the earth, Cyrus bid the crystals to return.

He let them settle into the cracks and spaces. The crystal would heal, eventually.

The mainlander who'd spoken was standing alone on the beach, covered in the remains of his comrades.

Eva, the hole in her chest closing up as she spoke, said again, "Tell your masters they should ask before playing with someone else's toys."

It was only because of his proximity that Cyrus could feel how much effort it took for Eva to speak without showing any sign of weakness.

The mainlander took a last look at the crowd and scurried down the sand, tripping over his feet as they watched on coolly.

Cyrus discovered he was not, as he'd first thought, surrounded by those only from Talhan. In the crowd were a fair few from Ronah and Rakemyst. One of the men from Ronah with ink on his face clapped a hand on Cyrus's shoulder.

"You know crystal." His words were a curious monotone.

"Yes?" Despite his unpopularity, he was well known for it.

"You will help us." The man's eyes were covered in orange. It seemed to be a running theme in the crowd. There were only a few who weren't.

"Sure I will," he said easily. Something one of his professors had said a long time ago about winning battles and loosing wars floated around as they marched him back towards the Crystal Province.

Eva, beside him, was looking straight ahead. The orange glaze over her eyes made it clear he would get no help from her.

'*Altoriae?*' he sent.

There was no response.

Samuel was still falling.

It seemed like he'd been falling for an age, but his internal clock said it had only been around fifteen minutes.

As much as the surrounding darkness was reminding him of his home Realm, it wasn't in a good way.

Tania found that one of the hardest things she had ever done was stay in the seat next to Temira when Shari was dead.

'*Water?*'

The technomancer's voice in her head was one of the most welcome things she'd heard. With a sniff, Tania wiped tears away with the back of her sleeve. She hopped off her seat and offered the technomancer a water pod.

Temira took it gratefully. "What happened?"

"Shari stabbed your device."

The gasp sent Temira into a coughing fit. Tania itched to rub her back but knew the moment wouldn't be welcome.

"How did she possibly survive such a thing?" the older Innarnian asked.

"She didn't."

It was as if the technomancer hadn't heard her. "To have pierced even one container would have been horrific, but if she stabbed the power crystal at the same time, the results would be fatal."

"They were."

"No one could come back from—"

"She's dead!" Tania screamed. "Shari died. She's not coming back."

Temira looked at her as if she was slow. "Don't be ridiculous."

The garbled noise Tania let out was one of rage and grief.

"Is Ronah mourning?"

"Of course, Ronah is—" Tania stopped. Ronah was fretting, and it left her with a sense like she'd forgotten something vitally important, but the island was not mourning.

Temira looked away and lifted her brows. "Then there is hope." She took another sip. "I rather thought I would be the one to die, out there."

"Killed by the Altoriae decimating one of your machines?" Tania snorted. "If Shari is still alive, I wouldn't put it past her."

"No. I thought I would die in the blast. It leaves me feeling... empty."

"It makes me mad," Tania retorted. She crossed to the window and stared unseeingly out the window. Temira was making this about *her* when they should focus on Shari. And Ronah.

"Empty because there will be no one to uphold the traditions my people have for the dead."

Every muscle in Tania's body clenched. Slowly, letting the tension roll from her neck to her toes, she let each group of muscles go lax. As much as she didn't want to acknowledge it, Temira had come far too close to dying. "What traditions?"

"We do not hold funerals the way Lissaens do. In my culture, the highest honour we can offer our dead is by eating their flesh."

Tania whipped around. Eyes wide, she looked Temira, hoping the horror she felt wasn't showing on her face. "What?" She winced as her voice squeaked.

Temira signed. "Your kind doesn't understand."

"Make me," Tania implored. She wasn't entirely sure she wanted to know why someone would *want* to eat the body of their deceased kin. If Temira was looking this sad, then it must be vital to her.

"My kind believes our flesh contains the wisdom we gained whilst living. It would be a waste to let so much knowledge be buried in the ground." Temira wrinkled her nose.

"Huh." Tania leaned her head against the window. She tried to picture eating her mother after she'd died, and her stomach churned. She didn't even want to be in the same room as her father whilst he was living, and she baulked at the thought of... just no. "You know the Shifting Islands are alive, right? Being buried in the earth is not the same here."

"I had not thought of it like that." Temira frowned and looked out the window at the drizzling sky. "Do you think Ronah would eat my flesh?"

Tania did her best to not think of the first time she'd met Ronah, when she'd thought the island had teeth and a mouth and would eat her where she sat. "I'm sure we can organise something which will honour both your traditions and ours."

"Is there no way you would eat my flesh?" Temira implored. She sounded so small and alone, that her heart melted.

"I... It kinda goes against everything I've been taught. I can't lie to you and say I would find it pleasant. But I am linked with Ronah, so having Ronah eat your flesh would mean, in a way, I would be."

"I suppose compromise is something we must both do." Temira sighed. At Tania's questioning look, she clarified. "Attempt to meld our own traditions and expectations to those around us."

"It's tricky," Tania agreed. Shari, Jon, and the other residents of Ronah were wonderful, but sometimes they expected her to know things they had never taught her. She supposed it was an indication of their level of trust to accept such an inexperienced Innarnian as their Linked. It didn't relieve her frustration when they failed to explain something. "I'll ask Ronah."

"Thank you," Temira said. She lay back against the pillow and sighed. "And now we need to find the Altoriae?"

"Might be an idea."

'Uh, Tania? I might need some help—'

'Cyrus?'

CHAPTER TWENTY-FIVE

hen Tania arrived at the bridge to Talhan, she half thought Cyrus was joking.

There were plenty of beings around, but they were, as usual, heads down, concentrating on their devices.

Even walking up the broad avenue leading to the Healing Centre, nothing looked out of the ordinary.

Cyrus knew Talhan far better than she did, and if he thought something was going on, then it must be. Maybe she wasn't in the right spot?

Just to be safe, she sent, 'Collis? *I don't want to alarm you, but something weird is going on.*'

The air next to her screamed as if the very fabric of it was ripping apart. Collis stepped through next to her, his Innarn flaring around him like a warning.

He took one look at the ordinary scene and frowned. '*Is this a trap?*'

As if his words had summoned forward an army, beings marched onto the streets. Every step was a lurching, jerking endeavour, as though someone was carelessly pulling strings attached to each limb.

'*Something is wrong with the crystal on Talhan,*' Cyrus sent. '*Get back to Ronah and as far away as you can.*'

'*Too late.*' The voice echoed from every direction.

Collis immediately put his back against Tania's. Other Returned started shifting in, surrounding them both.

Fifty odd beings with glowing orange eyes surrounded their group. Tania recognised Eva and a few of her friends amongst the orange-eyed crowd.

Beings who'd been wandering the streets of Talhan stopped to watch the display, some bringing up their slabs as if to record the event.

Jaws all around Tania dropped as one of their own stepped forwards.

"Kieran? What's going on?" Collis demanded.

"I have seen beings on two Realms now. They take and take and take."

The glaze of his eyes and the utter tonelessness of his words sent a shiver down Tania's spine.

"My purpose is giving. I give life. I give meaning." Kieran moved closer, and the crowd with orange-tinged eyes moved with him, closing in on them. "The Altoriae stopped me once. I will not let it happen again."

'*Uh, Cyrus? I think it's more than just the crystal that's being weird,*' Tania sent.

'*Yeah, they've kinda got me locked up here, but I'm working on it,*' Cyrus sent back.

'*Locked up?*'

'*Just watch out for the crystals. I think it's how they're contaminating others.*'

Tania was getting an odd sense about the whole thing.

As if Kieran had heard the send from Talhan's Linked, he held an orange hunk of crystal aloft. Light started spreading out from it almost immediately.

One of the Returned on the outer ring of their group hissed as the light touched her skin.

From the sizzle and the smell, it had burned her.

Tania shuffled backwards, the Returned moving with her.

"We're about giving life and meaning too!" Tania tried, struggling to keep the desperation out of her voice as it seared another Returned.

"You are about taking." The monotone hadn't changed, but there was a tiny frown.

"No! I've spent the last months of my life learning what it is like to live in a community who gives to each other. They genuinely care, and will share their goods, and time, and Innarn to help anyone in need."

"I am in need." The orange covering Kieran's eyes flared brighter.

"What do you need? We can help." The crush of bodies was making it hard for her to concentrate.

"I need you to *submit!*"

At least that last word shows there is some emotion behind all of this. Every orange-glazed being lifted a crystal.

Lights began refracting from one to another, and screams filled the streets.

The watchers turned to flee, tripping over each other in their haste to get away.

The Returned created a shield around their group.

'Get the crystals away from them!' Tania sent desperately. As the Returned went to work, she added her Innarn, using air and whips of water to smack the crystals out of hands.

'Don't hurt the beings!' Cyrus sent. *'Someone is controlling them.'*

Now he'd pointed it out, Tania sensed the deep disconnect in the surrounding crowd.

'Where are you?'

'I'm... free, for the moment.'

Fear coloured his words, and Tania snorted. Beneath her feet, Talhan rocked hard enough to bump into Ronah and Rakemyst.

The jolt almost threw Jonathan off balance.

'*Ronah? What's going on?*'

'*Talhan is in pain,*' the island whimpered.

'*Let me help!*'

With another whimper, Ronah released the shield holding him in the lower levels of the castle. Jonathan burst through the doors and shifted outside as soon as he was free.

'*Shari?*'

A dull echo was his only reply.

Jonathan ran towards the beach as he cursed, but the ground under his feet twisted. He found himself standing in the cemetery near the bridge to Talhan on the opposite side of Ronah to where he wanted to be.

'*Ronah? What's going on?*'

'*Talhan needs help.*'

'*What about Shari?*'

There was an inelegant noise, and the ground under his feet shifted, forcing him onto the bridge.

'*Okay, I get the message.*' At a run, he moved towards Talhan's Healing Centre.

Garbled yells and the smell of burning flesh had him shifting to the edge of a large crowd.

He scrambled onto a nearby bench and strained his neck to see. In the very middle of the street stood a tightly formed ring of Returned, the snarls on their faces distorting the ink they wore.

One fell to a searing line of light, and Jonathan glimpsed Tania's shocked face.

Why aren't they fighting? The stock of his crossbow smacked into his hand and he lifted it, taking aim at the back of a being's skull as they lifted one of the deadly crystals higher.

Thwack.

The being slammed forward under the force of the blow, crystal falling from a lifeless hand and shattering. The body exploded in a cloud of orange dust.

'No!'

The screams inside his head were agonising.

'Do *not hurt my beings!*' Talhan ordered.

Jonathan groaned and took aim at a crystal instead. He made the shot, and it shattered, orange sand pouring out and adding to the streams of it on the street.

Under his feet, Talhan rumbled in approval.

He took out a score of crystals before parts of the crowd turned and focused on him.

Uh-oh.

'I *might need some backup,*' Jonathan sent out blindly.

The woman in front of him laughed, a hollow, mocking sound. Orange specks flew from her mouth, joining the haze in the air.

Fist ready, he struck the crystal out of her hand, hissing as his knuckles burned.

The woman gave him a startled look before she blinked rapidly, the orange clearing from her eyes. As she took in what was happening around her, there was a singular moment when fear overtook her face.

"What are these crystals?" he asked, heedless of his harsh tone.

"They're not crystals. They're b... bottles shaped like crystals," she stuttered, shrieking when the man next to her turned unseeing eyes her way.

"Bottles for what?" Jonathan asked, slapping the thing from the man's hands.

"Femto crystals."

"Gozocha," he swore.

Swinging his crossbow like a bat, Jonathan winced at the sound his bow made when he sent another bottle flying.

"Break as many bottles as you can. Send the femto crystals scattering!" he yelled.

The duo looked at the Guardian like he was mad but turned and did as he asked. A ripple effect spread through the crowd as people started smacking their neighbours' bottles out of their hands.

Shadows overhead told him the Ilutri had joined the fight. Several were flying overhead and blasting anything which looked like crystal out of as many hands as they could.

But a few succumbed to the orange haze in the air, dropping to mindlessly stare at the sky above.

Jonathan started moving forwards, struggling to the middle of the crowd where Tania stood back to back with Collis.

He was inches away from the first ranks of the Retuned.

One after another, three Returned were hit and fell, leaving the path to Tania clear.

Kieran, standing apart from the others, held his hand out. From the ground all around them, streams of orange rose, gathering into the shaft of a poleaxe, the head bearing a broad-pointed blade with two curved axe heads on either side. He bared his teeth and swung the crystal halberd.

Too late to move, Jonathan screamed as Kieran swung it at Tania, and not the others baring crystals.

From above him was a roar, and SilverCloud dropped directly in front of Tania.

The halberd pierced the elder's chest, making the roar change to a groan.

Hands either side of the halberd, SilverCloud looked directly at Jonathan as he pulled it out, his eyes flashing orange. "Guardian." The tone was flat, but the threat in his eyes was decidedly more vicious.

The Ilutri elder grabbed Tania in a headlock, and time stood still.

CHAPTER TWENTY-SIX

Shari was floating.

There was blissful silence all around her. Light seeped through her closed eyelids, leaving her warm and sleepy.

The surrounding quiet deepened until there was a total absence of noise.

She attempted to lift her hand, but found she couldn't. The effort to open her eyelids instead left her with the horrifying realisation she didn't have any.

What's going on? she thought, frantically.

'*Hush, child. I'm still working.*'

'Lissae?' A pleased hum filled her mind, and she floated. Her breathing slowed until she felt content and safe again.

Time seemed to be irrelevant in this place. She had no idea how long had passed. But when she thought of opening her eyes again, it worked.

She couldn't really remember much. Not her name, where she lived, or how many digits should be on the end of her hand. As she looked around, she knew one thing for sure.

She had never seen anything like this place.

'*Where am I?*'

'*You inhabit my most sacred space, my Altoriae. You are in my heart.*' The words weren't spoken, but she let them fill her soul.

One stood out.

Altoriae.

That word meant something; she was sure of it. Just the sound of it tickled the back of her mind and made her suck in a breath.

She put the odd word to the side for the moment as the space she was in seemed to beat and pulse.

It was massive. Far bigger than Ronah—*What was a Ronah?* or perhaps even all the Shifting Islands combined. The swoops and dips of the huge cavern gleamed under the glow of unseen lights.

Globes in the colours of Innarn were zooming around. Some large, some small, but all in constant motion, flowing through the chamber with an unknown purpose.

She stretched out a hand as a purple one drew close. The globe of pure Innarn brushed against her fingertips. Plasma zinged along newly grown veins and she bathed in its glow as the Innarn seeped from her skin. It reformed the ball and continued its flight.

She floated for a while longer, enjoying the antics of the Innarn globes, and marvelled at the clothing which grew to envelope her skin.

'*You need to be more careful, my Altoriae,*' Lissae warned. '*I cannot save you again.*'

There was that word again.

Was her name Altoriae? The tickling sensation in her mind made her sneeze through a new nose. No, her name wasn't Altoriae. It was Shari.

'*Save me?*' Shari remembered talking to a girl her own size. '*What happened?*'

Lissae gently pressed the memories towards her, and Shari flinched when she saw the devastation the machine had caused. '*I died?*'

‘*Not quite. I could gather your essence before you crossed into the Spirit Realm. I will protect you for as long as I can, my Altoriae. But I fear I will not be able to do so for long.*’ Lissae sounded tired.

‘*Why not?*’

‘*Change is coming. Soon.*’ The Realm sighed. ‘*Be prepared. When the portal opens, you or your chosen must go through it.*’

‘*Portal?*’

Lissae sighed again and fell silent.

Shari had the horrid sense that this would be the last time she’d be able to talk to the Realm she worked so hard at protecting. ‘*Lissae?*’

The cavern was growing dimmer, and a rush of air whistled past her like a sigh.

“Shari!”

She knew that voice.

“Shari!” The voice cracked, as if the being speaking was heartbroken.

Idly, she turned around.

Near a hole so large Shari wouldn’t have been able to touch the sides even if she stretched as far as she could, a golden-skinned being was floating.

Dark hair and darker eyes, he sounded concerned as he let out a hoarse cry when he saw her face.

Sam.

“Sam!” She smiled.

For a moment, the two of them floated, bobbing in the air as if it was the only thing they needed to do.

“Shari. I thought you’d–” His voice cracked, and the tears in his eyes made her draw in a breath.

All at once, memories came rushing back. “Sam,” she said. Globes of Innarn rushed around her, pushing her towards him.

“We should get back,” he said, as they bumped together. The Innarn globes hummed softly and scattered again. “Everyone will think you–”

He seemed incapable of saying it.

"Occupational hazard?" she offered with a quirk of her lips.

A noise half-sob, half-laugh escaped him, and he crushed her to his chest. "How about less of the dying and more of the Realm saving?" he suggested.

She wrapped her arms around his waist. "I'll try."

Temira frowned as Ronah rocked again.

Something was upsetting the Shifting Island, and she wanted to find out what.

She struggled out of bed. The healers on Lissae would only do so much for her. They had cured the creature pounding at the inside of her skull with a mallet, so at least she could think straight again. Still, her legs wobbled as she fought down a bout of nausea.

Temira slapped the crimson studded leather shifting cuff on her wrist hard. It was enough to break the seal and force the red crystals together.

The anchor point she activated took hold, and she was back in her rooms. The four steps to the dresser seemed to take more energy than she had left.

If she staggered a bit, well, there was no one here to see.

She fumbled around in a drawer and took out her medicinal pouch, sighing when she grabbed some of her special salve. Temira rubbed it against her inner wrist and stumbled backwards to fall onto the bed.

Harsh breathing filled the room for several minutes as Temira waited for the salve to take effect. She felt it work through her skin, sinking into her veins before flashing like plasma along her bloodstream. Finally, the zinging in her blood stopped, and her nausea dulled enough for her to get up without the room spinning.

Glad the Realm was finally standing still, Temira slammed through her door and made straight for her labs.

If she was going to find out what was happening, she'd have to start there.

"You must know who I am by now, Guardian." SilverCloud faced his way, and the effort it was costing him to force the words out was visible in the straining tendons of his neck.

Jonathan kept his expression as neutral as he could—even when he saw his own face plastered on the building behind SilverCloud. The image didn't capture the tip of the halberd sticking out of SilverCloud's chest or the way his face contorted as he tried to throw whatever was controlling him out of his head.

"I know you are using crystals to control the beings around me."

SilverCloud bared his teeth.

Tania, still in the headlock, squeaked, her hands scrabbling at his arm.

"Your Altoriae was the one who named me."

Something unpleasant skittered along his shoulders. "Did she?"

"On Atlantis. She called me the Crystal Intelligence."

Several of the Returned sucked in a breath.

"Brought a piece of me here so I could see your Realm for myself."

Tears were streaming down Tania's face. He sent her calming thoughts and wished he was able to take her away from this mess.

"And what do you think of Lissae?"

"Small, yet large at the same time." SilverCloud looked confused for a moment. "Part of me was already here. But it was childlike. It waited. I want action now."

"What action?" Jonathan wished the thing would take someone else over. The Ilutri elder was struggling, the cords of his neck standing out with each harsh breath he took.

"I will rule your Realm. I will ensure you have the peace you deserve." The orange halberd tip was standing out against the sky-blue of his robes, almost calling to Jonathan.

'*Close your eyes, Tania,*' he sent. If he timed this wrong, he didn't want to die while she was looking.

Ronah's Linked snapped her eyes closed.

"I think we can figure out what type of peace we need on our own, thanks," Jonathan said. He lunged forward, hand wrapping around the sharp edge of the broken halberd tip and pulling with all his might.

Laughter filled his head.

'*So predictable,*' said the voice inside his head.

His world went black.

Temira gaped as the Ilutri elder announced he was speaking for the Crystal Intelligence.

"This came from Atlantis?" Temira asked, appalled.

If Atlantean tech mixed with theirs, it would have deadly consequences. Most of the tech she worked on was a mix of Ulnan and Lissaen and that was difficult enough to stabilise at the best of times.

A quick glance at Xani showed no dread on her friend's usually expressive face. In fact, Xani looked paler than usual—apart from her glowing eyes and the orange veins lighting up her skin.

Looking at the screen and then back at her friend had Temira frowning. Why did Xani appear the same as the beings controlled by this Crystal Intelligence?

Xani suddenly snapped to attention, sitting straighter in her seat. Her chair rotated on the spot and headed for the door.

"Xani?" Temira asked.

No response.

Suspicious, Temira followed her from the room, trailing after Xani, who unerringly headed for Cyrus's lab.

She peered around the doorway as Xani moved towards a row of bookcases on the outer edge of the lab.

Xani depressed a button Temira hadn't even known existed. Her chair slowly vanished from sight.

Mouth open, Temira strode towards the bookcases. *What am I getting into?* She searched for the button Xani had just pressed.

As she sank into the ground, she could only hope this wasn't how Talhan planned on eating her flesh.

Shari grinned up at Sam as the ocean breeze made her hair dance wildly.

He smiled back and leaned forward slightly, eyes intent on her lips.

A scream ripped them apart.

Glove and blade appearing, Shari said to Sam, "I've gotta—"

"Go? Not without me." His smile took on a slightly feral edge, and they shifted towards the sound of the scream together.

Ronah must have amplified the scream, as they were thrust straight into the mayhem happening in the main street of Talhan.

At the centre of the panic, Jonathan stood over a fallen Ilutri, holding an orange crystal above his head.

'I die one time and he tries to take over Talhan?' Shari grumbled.

Sam smothered a laugh.

'Take out the crystal in his hand,' Shari ordered. *'I'll get the Ilutri.'*

Shari shifted before Sam moved. She touched the Ilutri and shifted back again. When he rolled over, the hole in his chest caught her attention. A green glow seeped from her fingers, filling her senses with warmth and a smell like cinnamon and lemon sprinkled over cut grass.

The Ilutri groaned, and his eyes fluttered open. "Shari," he said.

For a moment, she didn't realise he was talking to her. Lissae might have restored her memories, but they were still jumbled and bits were patchy. "You're safe. Can you fly?"

"I can always fly," the old Ilutri grumbled, grey eyes flashing.

Grandfather. SilverCloud. Family. Shari sucked a breath in. How did she forget? "I need you to warn the others to stay out of reach."

"Wait." He grabbed her arm. "The Crystal Intelligence is waiting for you to attack. It was controlling me, just as it's controlling the Guardian now. It's counting on our fondness for our fellow Innarnians to win over the need for freedom."

"How can I beat it?"

"Destroy the heart. You'll need help."

Shari looked at Jonathan's back.

"Not the Guardian. You need someone who understands crystals and technology just as much as the technomancer does."

"Is she the one responsible?"

A beam of sizzling light struck a nearby wall, raining debris down on them. Instinctively, Shari shifted SilverCloud away.

'*I need to go. Don't let Jon kill anyone,*' Shari sent to Sam.

'*You're no fun,*' he sent back, but there was an odd undercurrent of fondness colouring his words.

She shook her head and shifted to the double doors of the museum.

Shari didn't have time for fun. She had a minotaur to get.

CHAPTER TWENTY-SEVEN

Tania groaned as the weight of the Ilutri elder vanished. She kind of hoped whoever had control of the Guardian would forget she existed.

'Tania?'

'*I'm fine, Collis.*' She was glad her mind-voice sounded so calm. Her body felt like she'd been hit with a bag of rocks.

The Returned around her dropped to their knees, and for a moment, Tania thought it was one of their special fighting moves.

The straining tendons and grinding of teeth from the ones closest to her told a different story. One by one, they raised their heads, eyes glowing brightly.

Oh no. Not the Returned. '*What should I do?*' she asked into the void.

'*Hoping for someone to save you rarely seems to work out well.*' Sam's voice in her mind had never been so welcome.

His Innarn, darker than what she was used to, wrapped around her and pulled.

She hissed against the abrupt movement and closed her eyes. Now all she wished for was the safety of home.

'*Tania?*' Ronah sounded confused.

Her eyes flew open, and she grinned. '*Wishes do come true,*' she sent to Sam from her backyard.

'*There are things on me.*' Ronah was shivering. '*I don't feel safe.*'

In the shadows cast by the rezem across the road, something metallic clicked along the cobblestones.

When Tania sucked in a breath, the spider-like machine abruptly turned its head her way, red light flashing menacingly.

'*Sam?*' she shrieked.

'*Bit busy not killing the Guardian,*' he sent. '*But here, have a present.*'

The Returned who'd been kneeling around Jon moments ago all appeared in a huddle on the lawn, gazes free of the orange glow.

'*Thanks.*'

"Something is trying to take over Ronah, and we have to stop it."

"Where's the Altoriae?"

Tears sprang to Tania's eyes. She blinked them away. "It's up to us to fix this."

She desperately didn't want to be the one to tell them the Altoriae was dead.

Very much alive and thrumming with Innarn, Shari shifted from the museum doors directly to Asterion's school.

Only for an iron cage to snap down around her before she took a single step.

Shari harrumphed, her bladed gloves slashing out against the bars of the cage.

"Who is trespassing in my school?" a voice boomed.

"Really, Asterion?" Why she knew the voice of the minotaur from a different Realm, when she struggled to recognise her own kin was a mystery she didn't really want to examine too closely at the moment.

"Oh. It's you, Altoriae. My apologies," Asterion said. The cage withdrew, rising on a clanking chain back to its position as a gilded ceiling decoration.

"I need help. Something's gone wrong with the crystal tech on Ronah."

"Why do you think I can help?"

"Because the thing corrupting Atlantean tech has done the same thing on Lissae."

Asterion paled. He turned his back on her. The minotaur seemed to take in the view of the bustling city below. "We'd best not waste any time then," he said shakily.

"Great." Shari clapped a hand on his arm and shifted them.

Directly into another trap.

"Where did all this metal even come from!" Tania groaned.

"Does it matter?" Alistair had stepped outside to see why there was a crowd in the backyard and had swatted away a mechanical bug on the wall Tania hadn't even noticed.

"It does when we have to squish them all!"

The yard was swarming with metallic creatures, all with red eyes capable of cutting anything in their path.

"Can't Ronah help?" Alistair asked.

How can I tell my younger brother that the Sentient Island we call home is bug-phobic? "Not this time," Tania said aloud. The mere thought had set Ronah on edge and was making the ground underneath their feet roll dangerously.

Collis did his trick with the Returned, and Tania sensed their Innarn slipping and spilling from one to the next, creating a beautiful net.

His focus used their Innarn to burn through one metal creature after the other.

Tania wrinkled her nose as she collected the scrap metal and separated it out from the crystal, which was still glowing dangerously. She remembered something Temira had said about containers. She only hoped it applied to crystals too.

Tania had seen one of the containers on Temira's bench and hoped the technomancer wouldn't be too upset at her borrowing one. She shifted it into her hands and used her Innarn to pluck the crystals from the wreckage of metal and put them into the jar.

As the container filled up, the tiny crystals inside bounced around on their own. Eyes wide, Tania stared at the jar as it heated under her hands.

She tried not to drop it as she frantically looked around for something to hold the container. *Ah! The bird bath.* A flick of her lashes, and the water intended to wash feathers was safely holding the most volatile container she'd ever been near.

Okay, second most. She blinked back tears again. There would be time to fall apart when Ronah was safe.

"We need to get all of these machines," Tania said, her voice cracking slightly.

Collis glanced at her, eyes full of concern. Before he spoke, they were sucked through Ronah's soil and spat out by the nearest gravestone to Talhan's bridge.

'*Warning next time!*' Tania pleaded, straightening up from the abrupt move and idly patting the stone marker.

'*Talhan. Talhan. Talhan.*' Ronah was on a loop, saying her brother's name over and over again.

The Shifting Island in question was a seething orange crystal haze juxtaposed with the occasional flash of silvery metal.

Tania looked at the container Ronah had so helpfully moved with them.

"I'm going to need a bigger jar."

When I get out of this, I really have to work on my mental shielding, Jonathan thought in the tiny corner of his mind which remained his own.

It didn't mean he couldn't put up a fight now.

The Crystal Intelligence seethed and roiled at the forefront of his thought, issuing orders and calling up protesting crystals from the ground to fight for it.

Jonathan had already used every mental weapon in his arsenal against the thing making him walk around like a puppet.

He'd come up short.

The Guardian crouched into a tiny ball in the corner of his mind and started listing off everything he'd survived. Every word he thought was drawing Innarn from his physical body and gathering it in the protective cradle of his mental manifestation. He'd survived a lot.

The loss of his father, then Joshua, training Shari, living with Sam, Mitch's death and so much in between.

His body was wilting under the lack of Innarn.

He scowled as he uncurled. With a mental shout, he slammed his Innarn back into his body, forcing the Crystal Intelligence out in a blast which flung those around him backwards.

Bodies were laid around him when he opened his eyes properly.

Unfortunately, Sam was amongst them, complaining as he struggled to get out of the tangle of limbs. His noise was the only way Jonathan could tell where he was in all the orange haze around them.

"How am I meant to save you if you do it yourself?" his apprentice asked.

Abruptly, the surrounding area cleared, and Samuel was on his feet again.

Jonathan shrugged.

"Give me the crystal." Samuel held out his hand.

It surprised the Guardian that he still held the tip of the halberd. The edges were so sharp, they'd cut his hand, and he suspected the femto crystals had gotten in through the cut.

"Now, Jonathan."

"There is no way I'm letting you touch it."

Samuel curled his fingers into a fist. "Don't make me hurt you."

"Stop and think," Jonathan snapped. "You've seen what this can make me do. What do you think it'll do if it has control of *you*?"

The Guardian flinched as Samuel's Innarn stroked against him. It swept across his skin and into his soul, hauling out anything foreign. He flinched against the force of it and gaped in surprise as a far-too-large swirling spiral of glowing grains of sand between him and his apprentice.

Jonathan sucked in a breath; Samuel dropped his hand. "Right. How do we stop it then?"

"We need to have a way to deactivate the crystal. Maybe by draining the Innarn powering it somehow?" Jonathan looked around, hoping something would inspire him. "It will be hard. Talhan is literally floating on a bed of crystal. If we drain the wrong thing, the whole Shifting Island could end up sinking."

"It's never easy, is it?"

"Saving the Realm rarely is."

Whatever Temira had been expecting, it was not this.

Xani had her back to the secret lift and was facing the most massive black crystal Temira had ever seen.

It stood in the centre of the room. The crystal pierced through both the floor and the high ceiling. A wooden walkway looped around it, leading to stairs which went down to the next level.

As much as she wanted to take in the sights, the heart of the crystal was singing to her.

It was off-key, grating against her nerves and setting them alight like ice on a burn.

Temira wriggled a finger in her ear and stepped closer, trying to see what was wrong.

Her first friend on Lissae was drilling into the core of the beautiful crystal with her Innarn.

Temira moaned and swayed on the spot. Xani was everything. Xani was the reason she'd been accepted here, why the Lissaens had allowed her to stay, and the motive she'd needed to use her Innarn to help others.

She was also the reason Talhan was crying.

The technomancer wrung her hands.

For once, she was at a loss for the correct course of action.

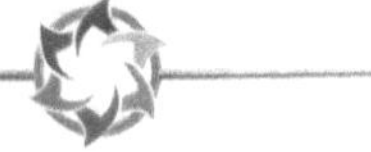

Talhan was awash in a sunset glow.

Only the sun was still high enough in the sky to make it improbable.

Wolf glared at the building.

By his side, Belfar snickered. "What's got your feathers tangled?"

"Why is Talhan lighting up?"

"Perhaps they're celebrating?"

He squinted against the light and said nothing. Belfar had grown restless in their hidey hole, so he'd proposed a game of tag again. He planned to lap Talhan low enough that they wouldn't be noticed on the cliff side, and high enough the clouds would hide them from the rest.

Thoughts of games had gone out of his head when the unusual glow had captured his attention.

What exactly was going on?

Wolf added extra Innarn to his shield and winged in for a closer look.

Chapter Twenty-Eight

rom her spot on the edge of Ronah's bridge to Talhan, Tania spotted Zana.

Rakemyst's Linked stood on the opposite cliff and appeared to be weaving something. Her hands were flying back and forward as if she was crafting a cloth.

'*Zana?*' Tania sent.

The older Ilutri looked up. '*Tania.*' She sensed the relief colouring the send. '*I sensed your injury before. Are you healed?*'

'*Yes, I'm fine.*' She'd almost forgotten about it. Not what had caused it though. '*Talhan and Ronah are under attack.*'

'*As is Rakemyst. Machines are everywhere, and our crystals are coming to life.*'

A shiver ran through Tania. It was one thing for an island to be sentient, but each individual piece of crystal?

'*I believe they are acting as a hive mind. The crystals themselves do not seem to be affected unless they come into contact with one that has been contaminated.*'

'*Like a cold?*' Tania wondered.

Zana's confusion seeped into their link. It seemed the Ilutri didn't get sick the same way she could. '*Yes. A crystal cold.*'

'*Then we should help them get better.*'

'*First, we must protect our Shifting Islands.*'

'*How?*'

Even from a distance, Zana shaking her head was apparent. '*I don't know for sure, but I'm weaving an Innarn net to drop over the bridge. It will ensure any contaminated crystals are caught and remain safely away from Rakemyst.*'

"Okay." As she glanced over at Zana again, the glint of a metallic hide scaling the cliff below where Rakemyst's Linked stood. '*Uh, Zana?*'

The Ilutri shrieked as a hoard of the metal creatures swarmed up the cliff, heading directly for her.

"Collis!"

The Returned all took on a fighting stance.

Tania thought back to when she'd seen Shari casting nets in training or on patrol. It seemed easy in theory. Only the creatures she was trying to capture were so small.

In a vain attempt to ignore the sound of screeching metal, Tania closed her eyes and let her grief over seeing Shari explode in front of her shape the net.

Memories of Shari smiling and laughing crafted the edges. Thoughts of the Altoriae's determined look as she prepared for action made the body settle into place. The fierce grin Shari wore at the end of a fight gave the net a weight Tania hadn't expected, and she smiled through her tears.

Wasn't that Shari? Totally unexpected.

With a sniffle, she tossed the net, using her Innarn to ensure it flowed over their end of the bridge and the cliff faces all around them. It flowed out, stretching along the cliff and covering Rakemyst's area in a loop of green.

A team of seasoned Ilutri warriors had landed and were fighting the machines who'd surrounded their Linked, but a sudden trembling captured Tania's attention underneath the earth on Talhan's side of the bridge.

The Crystal Province beyond the bridge was an orange smudge, as if dusk had come too early. There was violent movement and a figure was spat out of the ground.

Tania shrieked as it landed hard in a heap near the very edge of Talhan's bridge.

Coughing and spluttering, Cyrus stood slowly, scrubbing dirt from his face and hair.

'Toss *the machines in the water!*' His send was practically a yell, vibrating inside her skull. '*Seawater will rust the metal shell!*'

Metal creatures seemed to scuttle out from every shadow to surround Talhan's Linked.

Cyrus gave a garbled yell and disappeared under a pile of metal and crystal.

The instant Tania lost sight of him, she screamed. Pure frustration and grief, with a hint of denial, poured out of her in the form of a ball of Innarn.

Collis stepped beside her and pulled the ball towards him, shuddering as his outstretched hand made contact.

Tania perceived the shape he was forcing it to take. Utterly exhausted, she shoved as much of her Innarn towards him as she could. It joined the pool of Innarn from the other Returned.

She sensed the Innarn coiled within every atom of Collis's being. It grew and changed right up until he pushed it outwards. Streams of Innarn coloured the air green and solidified into a wall of earth. It flowed through the air and slammed the metallic creatures away from Ronah and Rakemyst, and into Talhan's cliffs.

Just when Tania hoped the wave had petered out, it whipped into the sky and whirled around. It advanced rapidly to push the creatures off Cyrus and into the water between the Shifting Islands.

The three isles slammed together, sending a wave of sea, crystal, and smashed metal shooting up the cliff faces.

Shields they'd thrown up before protected them all from the shards of metal, but Tania gasped along with the others as the seawater soaked her to the bone. With the last of her Innarn, she pulled the crystals into the jar at her feet, filling it to the brim.

Collis, dripping from head to toe, stepped forward and touched the Innarn shield.

"What are you doing?" Tania asked, slurring around a sudden yawn.

"I'll make sure it's irresistible to the metallic creatures. They'll be called here, where it'll fry them on the spot."

Tania swayed where she stood, smiling.

"Well, that wasn't meant to happen," Shari grumbled.

Asterion sighed. "Every Atlantean needs permission to go off-Realm. Without it, we can't cross through the gateway."

As Shari's mind was spinning with thoughts about how it meant someone had authorised Nisethran's trip, Oitane glided out from between two pillars.

"Here to steal our mythology now, Altoriae?"

Shari snarled. "No. I asked for help."

"You took. That is not asking."

'I only had to remove a cuff and they would not have known,' Asterion sent to her, tapping the metal cuff on his wrist against the blades of her glove.

"And armed." Oitane snapped her fingers and guards flowed out, surrounding the cage. "Give me the glove."

"It's kinda attached." Shari scowled.

Oitane held out her hand, palm up.

One guard moved forwards, gaze fixed on the glove so he wouldn't have to meet her eyes.

"This is how you repay the one who saved your race from being slaves to a machine?" Shari sneered, unimpressed.

The guard froze.

"What do you mean?" Oitane asked. "You weren't the one to save us, was she, Asterion?"

"It's true. She did," Asterion said. "The Altoriae of Lissae was the one who stopped the machines when they threatened to take over the capital."

Oitane looked furious as the guards all around them stood their spears upright and bowed their heads in Shari's direction.

'*What's happening?*' Shari sent.

'*I think I just figured out how to get out of here,*' Asterion replied.

"How can we ever repay you?" Oitane said through gritted teeth.

'*Careful. Whatever you say, she has to do. To the letter.*' Asterion warned.

Shari took a breath. "You can release Asterion and myself from this cage and let us peacefully leave right now to help the beings of Lissae overcome a threat."

"Or what?"

'*This is part of an old ritual. You need to say: Or it will disappoint the fates,*' Asterion sent.

'*The fates can have her thrice-damned head, for all I care,*' Shari sent back. "Or it will disappoint the fates." She tried to look as sad as possible.

The diplomat glared at Asterion suspiciously. Finally, Oitane flicked her hand, and Shari sensed an invisible mechanism grind to life, lifting the cage away from them.

"My thanks." Shari hoped the snooty Atlantean understood the sarcasm in her tone.

"Of course, Altoriae. Consider Asterion's aid the promise for a healer or scientist fulfilled." From the brittle smile, her thanks were received in the manner she'd intended.

"Asterion is neither, but I'd rather him than a stranger," Shari shot back. She clapped a hand on Asterion's arm and sent, 'We can go now, right?'

'Please.'

They shifted away.

Cyrus laughed, shaking off the sea-spray.

Across the bridge, Tania swayed alarmingly. Before he could call out a warning, Collis caught her.

'I must ensure her safety.' The gangly teen with covered in ink glared at him from across the bridge.

'If you've anyone to spare, I could do with the help,' Cyrus admitted. The few people who'd been likely to help him had all been part of the femto crystal trials. They were currently hunting him down, utterly mindless and totally dangerous.

It was only pure luck and his connection with Talhan that had allowed him to escape the first time.

He didn't know the crew from Ronah particularly well either, but he hoped they would be less affected by the femto crystals than his people.

The ground under his feet was pulsing in warning.

Cyrus had to move.

Earth Province would probably be the safest place, as there was less crystal because of the harvest. He would have to travel along the beach of the Crystal Province, and then through the length of the Old Province. The journey would be dangerous with so many of the femto-affected around, and all the crystals in the ground.

With a sigh, Cyrus turned to take one last look at the bridge between the Shifting Islands. Jogging across it were a bunch of people from Ronah, all with ink-decorated skin.

"You're Talhan's Linked?" one asked.

Dumbfounded, Cyrus nodded.

"I'm Ashlen. What do you need?"

A sharp, stabbing pain shot through his gut, just below his left ribcage. He slapped a hand against it and grunted, half expecting to see blood when he pulled it away. It was clean.

Again, the pain struck, along with a tingle at the back of his neck. "Talhan," he grumbled.

"Something's wrong with Talhan?"

"Someone is trying to breach the shields," Cyrus said.

"Where?"

He shook his head. "It might be the Healing Centre, the council chambers, or almost a dozen other spots."

Ashlen sighed. "Which is the most likely target?"

"It's hard to tell when I don't know what the Crystal Intelligence is after," Cyrus snapped.

"Can't Talhan just tell you?"

"Talhan is so dotted with crystals it's hard to hear him at the moment," Cyrus admitted.

"Work down the list," one of the others suggested.

Cyrus smiled at her gratefully.

"What's the closest one then?"

Thinking fondly of his plan to lie low, Cyrus gulped. He'd never been a fighter, never been at war—and certainly not against his own people.

They needed his help now more than ever. "The council chambers are on the way to the Healing Centre. We should try there first."

Ashlen clapped him on the shoulder and nodded. The group swarmed around him, and Cyrus sighed, feeling slightly safer.

"Let's go."

As they marched through the centre of the Crystal Province towards the council chambers, the silence of the femto-affected crowds was eerie. The group from Ronah seemed to draw little attention.

Those who weren't being controlled by the crystal were running in the other direction as fast as they could. The slip streams weren't working, and the orange haze covered many of the buildings, making it hard to see them.

'*How are you doing that?*' he sent to the group guarding him as they forced him to move with them, swerving around a crowd in the middle of the street.

'*Specialist shields, and far too much practise at not being noticed,*' Ashlen sent back.

When a woman with orange glowing eyes let out a wail, Cyrus jumped. He would remain eternally grateful for never having to go on patrol.

A cloud of orange dust spewed from her mouth and hovered in the surrounding air.

The haze grew denser.

Across the road, he was just able to make out someone opening a door and trying to sneak along the wall, but the haze in the air made them cough.

'*Get back inside!*' he warned.

The being gasped and whipped their head around. By focusing his Innarn, he saw through the crystal that she was one of the mainlander's aides.

As Cyrus and the others continued to move forward, he couldn't help but watch as the femto crystals in the haze took her over. She slumped where she stood. They'd carefully traversed two buildings when she jerked upright. A glazed look on her face and eyes glowing orange, she erratically made her way back to the door she'd just come from.

She heaved it open and breathed out a cloud of the dust. There was the faint sound of coughing inside.

Cyrus shuddered and reminded himself to concentrate on what needed to be done.

A block later, and he stood gaping at the council chambers.

It was utterly surrounded.

Not by machines, but by beings.

Three Innarnians stepped over the fallen bodies by the entrance and continued to blast at the ornate doors.

Behind the windows, a few of Talhan's elders were hovering.

He hoped they were strengthening the wards and was about to add some of his own Innarn to them.

Too late.

For a glorious moment, the shield around the chambers flickered to life, displaying as a pristine black dome over the building.

The invaders slammed into the wards of the council chamber one last time.

Orange veins splintered through the black, and the wards broke with the sound of shattering crystal.

Cyrus let out a cry as the femto-affected stormed the council. He saw Elder Juniper being snatched from the window. Another elder shot off blasts of red and green before the mob piled on top of them.

'We can't help them now. There are too many.' Ashlen looked almost as devastated as Cyrus felt. *'Where is the thing you most want to defend on Talhan?'*

'The heart.'

'Take us there.'

Samuel growled as the crowd around Jonathan surged forward.

"Move!" a female voice screamed from somewhere high.

Peering through the orange haze, Samuel could just discern the silhouette of an archer nocking an arrow on the roof of the building across from him.

"Get him out of the way!" she screamed.

Turning to where she was aiming, his jaw dropped.

A stack of Innarn-laced arrows protruded from the structural weak points where the giant crystal advertising slab was bolted onto the building.

The archer was going to bring it down right where they were standing.

Jonathan.

Without conscious thought, he shifted the Guardian away. Jonathan had to be safe to help end whoever controlled the crystal.

Pure pressure from the fallen slab forced him flat against the ground.

In the tiny window of space before he passed out, he had to admit her plan was ingenious. His natural shielding would make sure anyone under the slab would survive, but they were still pinned in place, unable to get out.

He just hoped Shari would make it back before his shield gave out.

CHAPTER TWENTY-NINE

They needed Shari on Talhan. She snapped the cuff off Asterion's wrist, shifting them straight to the Healing Centre before it reached the floor.

The whiff of strong Innarn made her whirl away from the doors in time for a giant slab of crystal from one of the buildings come crashing down. As it fell, Shari made out Sam's resigned face.

'*Sam! No!*'

A cloud of orange dust exploded from the slab, billowing around them. Shari shot up a shield, and pushed her own Innarn out, trying to find where Sam was under all the rubble.

'*He's the reason everyone is alive under there, Altoriae.*' The send came from an archer in blue leathers who took a step off the roof of the four-storey building and rode a twister of air to the ground.

"I wondered when I'd see you again, Esme." Shari grinned at Talhan's former candidate for the Guardian's apprentice.

Esme gave a mock bow.

"Your handiwork?" Shari nodded at the collapsed slab.

"The apprentice's shields will keep anyone from dying. But a heap of beings who were controlled by the Crystal Intelligence are now contained."

"With a few bones broken," Asterion added.

"They're still alive." Esme seemed unconcerned.

"How can we stop this?" Give her an army any day. Cloak and dagger fighting was best left to someone else. And to have to fight the very people she was charged with protecting left bile in the back of Shari's throat.

"How do we disrupt the flow from the Crystal Intelligence to its victims?" Asterion asked.

"Find Talhan's heart." Esme looked grim.

Jonathan blinked owlishly at the shelves of his store.

Samuel had decided he couldn't take care of himself.

To be fair, he hadn't been doing an excellent job of it lately.

Jonathan gaped as he shifted back to the edge of Ronah's cemetery.

The pulsing Innarn net crafted by the three Linked by the bridges was like a beacon. It was attracting metal creatures of all sorts. Jonathan gulped when he counted how many different types there were.

A handful of them with spider-like legs clicked their way past the last of the gravestones and hurled themselves at the net.

Blinding purple light shot out, frying the machines. Their blackened, warped husks dropped onto the knee-high pile below.

There were far more of the metal creatures on Ronah than he had realised.

'Jonathan?'

The broadcast made the Guardian drop to his knees. 'Shari? I thought you'd...'

'Eh. Takes more than a machine to keep me down.'

Still kneeling, Jonathan was shifted directly outside Talhan's Healing Centre. Next to his Altoriae was the minotaur from Atlantis, and Esme, Talhan's former candidate.

"Asterion will help me bring down the Crystal Intelligence. Again," Shari said. She'd created a safe little bubble around their group, clear from the haze outside.

"With the amount of crystal on Talhan, do you think it's even possible?" Jonathan asked.

"The Altoriae was successful in defeating the one on Atlantis," Asterion said. "If we can find the source of the crystal here, our job will be even easier."

"Then aren't you glad I'm here." Cyrus, with a team of Returned surrounding him, stepped over the rubble.

As he rose to his feet, Jonathan lifted a brow.

Shari merely extended the shield.

"Talhan has two hearts. One for the people and one for the island," Cyrus said bluntly. "It's hard to hear him, but I can sense the one here, the heart of the people, is under attack."

"Shouldn't we go rescue it then?" Esme asked.

"How do you rescue a heart?" Shari frowned.

"You keep it beating." Cyrus looked grim. "The best way to save Talhan is to go to the island's heart. It's stronger and better hidden."

"I can go." Asterion looked just as grim. "The Crystal Intelligence would expect you to attempt to stop it, and if you don't, it may know there is something amiss."

Cyrus looked torn. "Fine. But Talhan will shift you there. You'll need guards. Just in case."

"We'll go," the Returned said as one. They seemed eager to be reunited with Asterion.

"Hold on to your stomachs. Talhan will take you through the crystal, but it'll be a bumpy ride," Cyrus warned.

The Returned looked at each other and nodded. Cyrus planted his feet firmly on the ground and abruptly dropped to one knee.

Asterion and his guards disappeared.

Sweat broke out on Cyrus's brow. Jonathan identified the zinging pattern Talhan's Linked was creating, trying to keep the location of the other heart a secret.

Finally, Cyrus wiped the back of his arm over his forehead.

"Let's go."

If she'd considered how she'd save the Realm this morning, Shari would have never pictured Jonathan, Cyrus, and Esme by her side as she stormed Talhan's Healing Centre in search of a crystal heart.

She sensed Sam's breathing was steady underneath the rubble, and Ronah healing Tania after her Linked had drained so much of her Innarn. The rest of her new guild were scattered to the winds, some with Asterion, the others fighting their way through Ronah's streets towards the bridge to Talhan.

When she pulled her senses back, the echo of their footsteps in the empty hallway was a direct contrast to the chaos outside. Somewhere below their feet, she detected agony ripping through the island.

"I think the Crystal Intelligence found the people's heart," Esme said through gritted teeth.

Cyrus looked pale enough to pass out.

"Can you shift us there?" Shari asked softly.

He nodded, and between one beat and the next, they were in his lab.

Devastation written in the lines of his face, Cyrus moved across the room on shaky legs to a bookcase. He beckoned them closer until they were practically standing on each other's toes.

'Here we go,' he warned.

Something pinged against Jon's shield.

'Wait for me!'

Just as Cyrus hit a hidden button, Tania, freshly healed and ready to rejoin the fight, appeared and grabbed onto Shari's arm, looking at her with wide eyes.

Shari hauled her closer, not knowing what would happen if she didn't.

The group descended into the people's heart of Talhan.

CHAPTER THIRTY

Amara looked at her fellow guild members as the ground under her feet rocked again. Dust crumbled from the roof of a building across the road. "Are we just going to stand here?"

They hadn't known what the threat was, but they'd been following the creepy little metal bugs as they swarmed out of the shadows and towards Talhan. The new guild members had followed, but it seemed the residents of Ronah had other ideas. Amara could feel the dense gathering of Innarn around the museum, and figured the locals were making sure nothing got in.

Or out.

"But the Altoriae—" Mu started.

They'd sensed her die. The link created by the pledge they'd sworn had snapped against her skin, hard. The others felt the sting too. Amara was startled when the pain from the broken pledge became easier to bare.

She hoped the fighting wasn't making her callous to death.

"Are we not bound to fight in her place?" Raven countered.

"How do we fight the people we swore to protect?" Talofa shivered.

Amara thought about wrapping her arm around the girl's slight form, but she also wanted to keep her fingers, so she bounced on her toes instead.

"Who can make others Sleep?" Dealon asked, a grin lighting up his face.

Amara and Lira smiled back. "Brilliant!"

"Clue the rest of us in?" Raven grumbled, crossing his arms.

"If we use the motus *Sleep* on as many of the affected people as possible, then they should fall into sleep deep enough so the Crystal Intelligence can't touch them."

"Or it'll be able to control them better. Who's saying they aren't actively fighting against being controlled?"

"Only one way to find out," Lira said grimly.

Together, the seven former candidates shifted to the outskirts of the Crystal Province on Talhan. There seemed to be a sea of beings before them, eyes all glowing and peering out from the orange haze at them.

'*Keep us clear, and we'll cast,*' Amara sent to the group.

Dealon and Lira stepped next to her, and they each placed their palms on their elbows. Amara closed her eyes to concentrate. She wanted to gently put the beings around her to sleep. She wanted them to rest and wake up when this was all over.

Her Innarn was trickling down her shoulders and seeping into her hands. Slowly, she moved her hands up, so her palms were together, and puffed on her fingers. She sensed her Innarn release.

The beings before her stumbled to a halt, then lay down on the ground, curling up as if they would sleep. One of them stumbled right over to Amara and collapsed at her feet.

Next to her, Dealon and Lira laughed nervously.

"We did it!" Amara grinned.

The being closest to her reached out and grabbed her ankle.

Amara shrieked and tried to pull her foot away, but the being with the orange glowing eyes wasn't letting go.

Lira and Dealon each snatched one of her arms and pulled. The three of them went down in a tangle of limbs.

"Didn't work!"

"Bad idea!"

"What now?" Amara wailed, extracting herself from the pile of people and clambering to her feet.

"Strategic retreat?" Raven offered.

"Or we could always help," a voice from behind proposed.

Almost toppling again as she turned, Amara couldn't help but grin.

Behind them were residents from Ronah and Rakemyst.

"Sleep won't stop them." One stepped forward, and Amara recognised him as a healer from Ronah. "But encasing them within shields like the Wall of Stone should do it."

"Brilliant!" Amara exclaimed, a lick of fire leaping from her fingertips.

"We're up," Elani said, pulling on Lira's arm.

Amara turned the lick into whips of fire, using them to herd beings into their temporary cages as Elani and Lira used a different motus to pull on the earth and shape it into an unclimbable stone wall.

She just hoped the walls would hold.

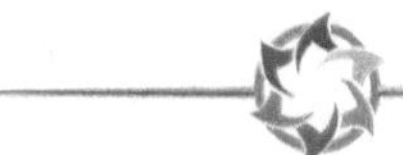

Fire was flowing through Temira's veins.

She was pounding against Xani's shield with as much Innarn as she dared. Every time she found a crack to exploit, Xani would create a new, stronger shield beneath it.

Her oldest friend was still drilling into the heart crystal; the orange veins were like spiderwebs.

There was still hope.

Talhan was crying, but the sound was getting weaker.

Xani pivoted and faced Temira. The look on her friend's face chilled her to the bone.

"Let's see what they think of the technomancer now," Xani rasped out.

Temira put more power into blasting her friend away from the massive black crystal. A breeze hit her back as Xani abruptly dived sideways, and Temira's Innarn hit the crystal.

"No!" Tania's horrified scream reached her ears before she dropped her hands. "I trusted you!"

Temira turned and bowed her head.

"She attacked me," Xani rasped.

The technomancer raised her gaze enough to see Cyrus's shock. He, better than anyone, knew Xani never spoke. Her vocal cords had been damaged before she'd ever entered Lissae.

"Did she?" he asked.

"And attacked the crystal!" Xani added.

Temira held her breath as a subtle ripple of Innarn travelled over her and through the rest of the room.

"She attacked you." The Altoriae's statement was flat, and even Temira could tell she was unimpressed.

Xani jerked her head in the approximation of a nod.

"Huh." Shari turned to look at Temira and lowered one eyelid. The Altoriae raised her weapons and growled, "Why don't you fix what you've done."

The technomancer blinked. *What was the Altoriae doing?*

"Don't trust her!" Xani rasped. "She'll make it worse."

"Fix it," Shari growled again.

Ah. A ruse. "Very well," Temira said stiffly.

Turning back to the crystal, she flexed her hands. With the amount of Innarn she'd used to break Xani's shields, she didn't know if she'd have enough to fix the crystal.

Cyrus stepped next to her. "Make sure you do it right," he growled. He brushed his hand against hers, letting her know the others believed in her innocence.

Xani heaved herself back into her chair. "Don't trust!" she wailed, and a cloud of orange filled the air.

Collis groaned, dropping his face into his hands.

Tania had disappeared as soon as she'd heard there was even more trouble on Talhan, and he'd been unable to track her. Wherever she was, it had powerful shields.

But before she'd disappeared from his senses, he felt the familiar brush of the Altoriae's Innarn, and the pledge he'd taken snapped back into place.

'*Collis? We need a little help,*' Ashlen sent, along with the impression of *fast, heat, bodies, and danger.*

He ripped through the air to shift in beside Ashlen.

In the pitch black, there were groans and the occasional *oof!* as they all adapted to the extra body in their midst.

'*Did you forget something?*' Collis sent. A tiny ball of plasma lit the tip of his finger up, and he flicked it over the heads of the others.

In the sudden light, Asterion flinched.

Collis couldn't help his grin at the minotaur. "You're back?"

"For the moment. We need to find the heart of Talhan."

They were crowded onto a water Innarn platform intended for one or two, not the dozen in their group.

Slivers of Innarn slipped away from Collis, seeking. *There.* They were deep underground in the central part of the Plasma Province in Talhan.

Beings above were desperate to get in.

'*Two stay down here and guard Asterion and the heart. I'll return to help. The rest, up to the surface. Divert, distract, disarm. No fatalities,*' Collis ordered.

Joana and Ashlen nodded, but Remmy and Amauran looked slightly more disheartened. It had been a long time since they'd had to hold back.

'*Better get to fixing the heart.*' Collis stretched his fingers and shifted to the surface with the others.

It was chaos.

They immediately surrounded the Returned.

Amauran was lashing out with her razor whip, striking the ones closest to them to keep the crowd back. No matter how deep the cuts were, the affected kept on coming.

Collis pulled on the earth from outside. It rumbled around their feet and surrounded his small group. He pushed the earthen dome outwards until he sensed it pressed against the walls of the existing building.

"Now what?" Joana asked.

"Two stay here, and the rest outside. Knock the affected beings out."

"The rest of the Altoriae's Guild already tried," Ashlen said. "It just made it easier for this Crystal Intelligence to control them."

"What will work?" Collis sighed.

"They used the Wall of Stone. It seemed to be efficient."

"Try it." Collis only hoped the Altoriae and Asterion could stop the mad crystal before too many beings got hurt.

CHAPTER THIRTY-ONE

Coughing, Shari raised her shield too late.

A dense presence invaded her mind.

'*So, this is what it's like in your head.*'

Even as she took another breath, inhaling more femto crystals, Shari pushed a shield around the others. She made sure it wasn't connected to her Innarn so they would be safe even if the Crystal Intelligence took her over entirely.

Well, it should give them enough time to get to safety.

'*You're different from the others.*'

She would not get into a conversation with this thing. In the untouched part of her mind, Shari cordoned off her use of Innarn so only her spirit was able use it, and not whoever was controlling the shell of her body.

'*You think you're smarter than me,*' it sent.

Shari mentally poked out her tongue and let her astral form slip away.

'*Jon, don't let me do anything too stupid,*' Shari sent.

'*Where are you going?*'

'*To get some help.*'

'*Get Samuel.*'

It was odd, hearing the Crystal Intelligence using her mouth to tell people to lay down their weapons. Temira was trembling off to the side, and Xani was attacking the crystal again.

Shari prodded at her shield. Xani was using a modified crystal shield operating under a changing frequency. Innarn attacks wouldn't work too well.

'*Fire a bolt at Xani's chair before you put the bow down.*'

Jon looked slightly over her incorporeal shoulder, then to his cross bow.

It was already on the ground.

Shari floated over on a sigh and used her Innarn to pick up the crossbow.

Esme cleared her throat and started questioning the wisdom of Temira, the Crystal Intelligence, and, for some reason, the monarchy on the mainland.

The thing controlling her body turned to Esme.

Shari took careful aim at Xani's chair and fired.

Xani's shield didn't so much shatter as it exploded, sending even more femto crystals into the air.

The others fell back, coughing as the crystals invaded their lungs.

That was her cue to leave.

Rising through the layers of earth was always an awkward thing for her, but Shari also had to avoid all the crystals in both the walls of the building and dotted through the ground.

Talhan had a *lot* of crystals.

Finally, she was at the surface, her astral form sweeping along the sidewalk until she found the rubble Esme's trick shot had caused.

There were over a hundred heartbeats to wade through, but Shari went for the slowest one.

'*Sam!*'

He groaned.

A grim smile flittered across her features as Shari shifted the slab. Once it was free, she used it to create a huge crystal bubble around the trapped beings who'd been underneath it.

Careful to make her Innarn as Dark as she could, Shari shifted Sam away from the others and pulled both of them back into Cyrus's lab.

'*Wake up, Sam.*'

The golden-skinned man grumbled.

She sent thanks to the Deities he was okay.

Shari used her air Innarn to rock the Guardian's apprentice back and forward.

He grumbled again, before opening his eyes. "Took you long enough," he muttered.

'*The Crystal Intelligence has taken over my body,*' Shari sent.

Sam glowered. "What do you need me to do?"

'*The same thing you did to get it out of Jon.*'

His sharp breath startled her. She sensed a lightning-quick exchange between the Guardian and his apprentice before the stiffness of Sam's shoulders relaxed. "All right. Time to save you. Does this make it twice in one day?"

'*Only if you're counting,*' Shari sent blithely. She showed him an image of the button on the bookcase, and where to stand.

As he sunk through the floor, Shari latched onto him, making her journey easier.

Below the lab, in the people's heart of Talhan, it was pure chaos.

Talhan was overrun with makeshift walls trapping many of the femto-affected beings from hurting others.

Was this was the way Zac's life would end—unintentionally trapped and taken over by something he'd accidentally brought onto Lissae?

He dodged another attack from a being with one functioning arm, their eyes glazed with pain and rolling in the sockets.

"You should be in the Healing Centre." He stepped to the side and used earth Innarn to push the being back towards the wall the Altoriae's Guild had created.

"Do you think it's a promising idea to have them all in there together?" the Ilutri to his right asked.

"No idea." Whatever the crystal had started out as, it had morphed passed any experience Zac could follow. He ducked low as another Ilutri with a glowing orange wing soared by overhead.

He'd spun to face the next wave of attackers when powerful hands grabbed him under the armpits, and he was abruptly lifted into the air.

Legs flailing, Zac shouted and swung his arms.

Another Ilutri flew past, whirling on the spot, and grabbed onto his legs.

Pain.

Severe pain shot through him as both Ilutri pulled his body in different directions. Zac had another vague thought of dying in such an inelegant way.

But he wouldn't go out fighting. He blasted the Ilutri holding his torso with a burst of fire strong enough to scorch eyebrows and feathers alike.

The Ilutri's head reared backwards.

Zac swung upside down, hanging by the other Ilutri's grip on his knees. "I really hope you're a friend," he yelled.

Chuckling, the Ilutri winged higher and set Zac down as gently as possible on a flat-topped roof of a ten-storey building.

"I'm just trying to stop my mate from doing anything he'll—*oof!*" His saviour was cut off as the Ilutri with the glowing-orange wing slammed into his torso.

They landed hard and skidded across the roof, grunts and groans coming from both winged men.

"Hey!" Zac shouted. He cursed himself as he ran after them, hauling the aggressor off the other.

"Hey." Zac held his hands up, patting the air as the larger-than-he-realised aggressor turned and started advancing on him.

"Belfar, leave him alone. It's me you want," Zac's saviour called.

The aggressor turned back to his prey. Belfar stalked forward as Zac's saviour walked backwards towards the edge of the roof.

As his saviour's heel reached the edge, Belfar punched the other Ilutri with all his might.

Zac scrambled forward, shouting in surprise as his saviour tipped over the edge.

Too far away.

Too late to reach.

He was still over a body length away from the edge, but he could jump on the aggressor and subdue him if he was quick.

"I can't let you do that," Zac said grimly, and made to jump on Belfar's back.

The Ilutri stepped to the side.

Zac was going too fast.

He couldn't stop.

With a garbled yell, he went over the edge.

Collis shifted back down to Asterion.

The minotaur was staring at the pulsing, black crystal.

There were tiny lines of orange on the face of the crystal. One twitched and grew, a shuddering line growing closer to the centre of the crystal.

"What are you going to do?" Collis asked.

"Stop the spread." Asterion sounded grim.

"Why does it sound like a bad idea?"

"The hearts are linked. If I stop the spread of the Crystal Intelligence here, it will shatter the other heart."

"But the Crystal Intelligence will leave?"

"Yes."

"And if you don't stop the spread?"

Asterion closed his eyes. Collis waited as patiently as he could. He used the time to set up some traps around where the other Returned were outside.

"If I don't, the Crystal Intelligence will take over Lissae."

Collis breathed deeply, trying to stay calm.

The minotaur raised his hands and worked on the black crystal. It took minutes to reverse a single vein.

There was a lot more than one line.

"Can we do anything?"

Asterion shook his head. "Make sure the affected beings don't get inside." His words were short, steam billowing from his nose as he healed another vein.

'Help!' Amauran sent.

Collis pulled her into the safe space above them, in case she'd been infected, and flicked out onto the street in her place.

They had erected row upon row of Wall of Stone, trapping beings inside.

One clambered, jerky and uncoordinated, falling over the edge of the wall and slamming to the ground below. Blood was pooling on the street under the being's head.

"What do we do?" Joana shrieked. She was flinging up another wall, trying to make it higher than the first. "They keep climbing and falling," she sobbed.

All around, fallen bodies were sprawled below the closest walls. Collis frowned.

Collis pushed his Innarn into the crystal-laden earth and shoved at it. Veins bulging with effort, he forced it to curve up and over the first wall.

A smooth, unbroken wave of earth surged from the ground. Careful to move the injured aside, he made the wave crest just above the first wall.

It was near impossible to climb without the use of Innarn

Hopefully, it would hold the affected for a while.

CHAPTER THIRTY-TWO

hari groaned at the amount of orange haze in the room.

She could barely see Sam, and her astral form was wrapped tightly around him.

'*You need to let me go, Shari.*' His send sounded all choked up.

'*Whoops.*' Shari floated away from him and used her air Innarn to force all the femto crystals into one area. The strength of her Innarn smashed the crystals together until they became too large to travel into a body.

The block she made was larger than she had been expecting.

Once the air cleared again, it became easy to see Esme, eyes covered in the orange glaze, firing mindlessly at Jon and Tania while Cyrus tried to heal the crystal.

Temira stood with her back to Cyrus. She was protecting him from the bolts of Innarn Xani was throwing at them.

Shari's body made their job harder by hurling shards of crystal, metal, and anything else the Crystal Intelligence scrounged up.

Sam shuddered. '*Get ready.*'

Shari floated over to her body. She caused the next metal shard to jump and spark. It was enough to get the Crystal Intelligence to turn, scowling.

There was a pull as Sam yanked the femto crystals out of her body. She slammed her astral form back into her flesh. Shari groaned and stretched.

Next to her, Xani wailed, but Shari clamped a buffer of air over her mouth, watching as the grey-skinned technomancer choked on the crystals she'd been about to release.

'*Can you get them out of Esme too?*' Shari sent to Sam. She turned to face Temira. "Did you know about this?" Shari yelled over the shriek the black crystal was making.

"No!" The tears streaming down her face gave weight to her words.

"You didn't help her?"

"I don't think it *is* her anymore." The technomancer wrung her hands as she gazed at her friend.

Xani was struggling to sit up, her legs trapped beneath the overturned chair.

The shrieking increased, and Cyrus said, "Uh, guys? It's time to leave."

"What do you mean leave?" Tania asked.

"I can't save it. The crystal is going to explode."

Chilling laughter echoed around the room. "I win," Xani rasped.

"Go! Now!" Cyrus ordered.

Shari tried to shift everyone out.

Xani's hollow laughter mocked her as they bounced against shields which hadn't been there before.

"I told you." Xani mocked.

"Use the lift," Cyrus commanded.

Sam grabbed Jon and whipped his Innarn around Shari, dragging them close and slamming his hand on the button to raise the lift.

The last thing Shari saw was Tania's terrified face before the dirt surrounded her.

Satisfied the affected would not harm themselves anymore, Collis pulled Amauran back to the surface.

"Are you able to keep going?"

Red puffy eyes and blotchy face aside, Amauran nodded grimly.

As she sniffed and rubbed at her nose, there was a tickling against his mental shields.

'Collis?' Asterion sent.

Shifting back to the minotaur and the island's heart, Collis said, "Yes?"

"I'm almost done." Sweat was streaming down the minotaur's hide as he healed the last of the cracks in the massive black crystal. "Warn the Altoriae," Asterion gasped.

Collis sent to Shari just as Asterion dropped his hands.

The crystal chimed sweetly. Then it sent out a shock wave which threw them all back.

Temira eyed the black crystal. It was almost entirely orange now.

Xani, finally clear of her chair, was cackling madly.

Free of the Crystal Intelligence's influence, Esme used her Innarn to snag Cyrus and shove him on the platform to the lab above.

Temira reached out for Tania, pulling Ronah's Linked closer to the platform.

Striking out, Xani grabbed hold of Tania. With surprising strength, her oldest friend shoved Tania back, her head cracking with a painful sound on the black crystal.

"Go!" Temira growled at Esme. She stepped between her friends, shoving Xani backwards with a blast of air Innarn. Away from the lift. Away from the heart crystal.

Esme didn't hesitate. She slammed the button, and the platform rose.

Tania moaned and clutched at her head. Her hand came away red.

The healer in Temira noted her pallor, the way her eyes were rolling back, and how she stumbled when she took a step.

Concussion, at the very least.

As the platform disappeared, the room shook.

Perhaps she should have tried harder to get Tania to the platform? The black crystal wasn't so much shrieking anymore as releasing a noise which promised to haunt Temira's nightmares.

It was about to explode.

Temira whipped her air Innarn around Tania and shoved her to where the platform would be when it returned, even though there wouldn't be enough time.

Heedless of the risk, Temira reached into her centre and moulded her Innarn into the strongest shield possible, wrapping it around the crystal.

From across the room, Xani groaned. Temira could hear the scrape of the chair being set to rights. Hear grunting as Xani settled herself back into the seat.

But Temira couldn't afford to become distracted.

Not now.

If her concentration wavered, even the slightest bit, all of Talhan would pay.

"Watch out!" Tania screamed over the sound of the crystal.

The crystals powering the chair whined, the sound becoming louder. Xani slammed into her, pushing her out of the way.

Temira didn't even have time to grapple with her friend.

Innarn wrapped around her like a hug. It placed her next to Tania on the platform.

'*Press the button*,' Xani sent.

Her eyes cleared of the orange glaze as she waved.

The platform rose.

"No. No! *Xani!*"

Xani wasn't sure how long she'd been trapped in the back of her head.

Orange haze was her life now. She tried to warn the others, but the stinging slap on her spirit time and time again had worn her down.

Until Temira slammed her, chair and all, into a wall.

Her head was ringing, even over the shrill noise of the crystal.

It was a matter of moments to take in what had happened.

And it didn't take a technomancer to see that Temira was going to try and save the young Linked at the cost of her own life.

Xani had failed Temira.

She'd let herself be taken over by something which wanted to cleanse the Realms of anything made of flesh and bone.

And it had only gotten as far as it had because of her.

Even now, Temira was trying to shield the crystal.

She would fail.

For all that she hadn't been able to control her mind lately, she had remained aware of how much damage her body had done.

Wrapping her Innarn around Temira in one final hug, she gently placed her only friend on the platform next to the Linked.

'*Press the button.*'

Tears leaked down her face as she turned her back. She pulled on the shield the Crystal Intelligence had used.

One final breath.

Xani wrapped the shield around the shrieking crystal.

And the people's heart of Talhan exploded.

Amara grinned. The guild had finally found their rhythm.

Shield.

Wall.

Press back.

Steady.

Again.

Each member took a turn, changing the shields and walls around so the beings affected by the Crystal Intelligence didn't have time to get used to them.

They'd pressed them back two blocks when the ground under their feet started rumbling.

"What's going on?" Mu asked.

Talofa leaped, creating a twister of air which carried her above their highest wall. "I can't see anything," she said.

Boom!

A massive shock wave ripped through the earth, and they all staggered.

"Vebnah's breath," Talofa cursed.

"Language!" Elani scolded.

"They've all dropped," Talofa said, lowering her twister.

"What do you mean?" Amara asked.

"Every one of the affected. They've dropped to the ground like puppets whose strings have been cut."

"Is it a good thing?" Raven asked.

Amara shrugged.

"Do we lower the walls?" Lira asked.

"Yes." It was Shari. Amara would have cheered, but the Altoriae looked furious.

"Shari!" Tania charged out of the Healing Centre, screaming the Altoriae's name.

Shari's chin quivered for a second before she whipped around. It happened so fast, Amara wasn't sure if she'd imagined it.

"Told you she'd be alright," Raven said to Amara as Shari wrapped her arms around Tania.

"Too tight!" the younger girl squeaked. The Altoriae let go reluctantly. She punched Sam's shoulder, hard enough that he started rubbing it and pouting.

"Lower the walls," Shari commanded.

Amara jumped. Together, the guild lowered the walls they'd created, thanking the elements for helping them protect the beings of the Shifting Islands as they did so.

Chapter Thirty-Three

Shari glared at Sam.

'*Never leave her behind again,*' she sent.

He glowered right back and moved closer, towering over her. '*If my Innarn touched her, she would burn.*'

'*Burned is better than dying.*'

'*Not just burned, Altoriae. It would destroy her Innarn. She's getting lighter and lighter. It was death by me, or death by crystal.*' For a moment, Sam's face crumbled. '*I'd rather not cause another innocent's death.*' He pivoted away.

'*Another?*' Shari pretended to ignore the chill as shadowy wings swept over her.

Instead of answering, Sam stalked off, silently helping to pull down the walls. Now and then, he glared over his shoulder at her.

"Don't be too hard on him," Tania said.

"You could have died," Shari growled.

"We all could have died. You *died.*" Tania looked at her suspiciously. "How do I know you aren't a spirit?"

Shari poked her side.

Tania made a suspicious *eep* and scuttled backwards. "Okay, not a spirit. But I watched you..." She trailed off, tears welling up.

Running her gaze over the clean-up effort, Shari sighed. Her memory of what had happened had become foggy, but she thought Lissae had said something important to her. Something about a portal.

"My job is dangerous."

"But you would have died a ridiculous death!" Tania exclaimed.

Some beings close to them turned at her outburst. When they realised who had spoken, their eyes went wide. Even though they returned to the clean-up, Shari was aware that they were listening.

"I have to agree with my kin," Temira said. She had puffy eyes, and streaks from dried tears lined the grime on her face. "What you did was foolish. I'll install safeguards on the next B.I.T."

"Are we safe? Is the Crystal Intelligence gone?

The technomancer closed her eyes. Shari shivered as the brush of her Innarn swept across her, scouring the area.

"It's gone. De... destroying the heart and Xa..." Temira hiccoughed and wiped at her eyes. "It acted like a surge of plasma. It was too much power, and it overloaded the femto crystals. All the ones who were affected should be back to normal, but we... I... will have to check them all. It will be a lengthy process."

Tania looked at Shari, pleading with her.

"What's a bit?" Shari asked.

It was as if the question had reset the technomancer. "Basic Innarn Training device. It's designed for you to spar with, so you don't hurt anyone else." Scrubbing her face clean, she stood straighter.

"But it can explode. And would've wipe out an island if Sam hadn't shielded it." Shari's gaze roamed to the man in question. "Why do you think I spar others?"

Temira blinked rapidly. "To become a superior fighter."

"So *they* can become better. Stronger. Faster. How are we going to do that if I'm fighting a machine instead of a being?"

The technomancer hung her head. "I see."

"Your B.I.T. has promise. Maybe one Innarn element at a time? And designed for beginners?" Tania said, gently laying a hand on Temira's arm, but her expression begged Shari to agree.

"It'd be handy in schools. And training sessions. Perhaps with something where we can adjust the difficulty?" Shari nodded.

When Temira lifted her head, Shari could already see the thoughts whirling. "I need to go back to my lab."

Shari's jaw dropped as the technomancer walk away. "What about the clean-up?" she yelled.

No response.

"Fine," Shari grumbled to Tania.

They both moved to help the clean-up crews.

As evening turned to night, the streets of Talhan finally approached normal again.

Shari ended up working alongside Cyrus. He seemed tireless as he straightened sidewalks and buildings alike. He stopped to offer kind words to those who'd been affected as he moved through the crowd, gently helping those in need to the Healing Centre.

In a quiet moment, Shari said, "Can I ask you something?"

"You just did."

She rolled her eyes and hugged the cup of azehal someone had handed her close. "Will Talhan be okay? Without a heart?"

Cyrus's smile was sad. "Talhan will never be without a heart so long as I'm around. The one that was destroyed will regrow. It may take a while, but Talhan will be better than ever."

"I'm glad. If there's anything I can do..."

"This is something my people need to do. But I appreciate the offer."

Shari nodded and sipped at the drink, watching the others clean up for a moment. Cyrus patted her hand and was away again.

Healers from Ronah and Rakemyst worked alongside their Talhan counterparts with more traditional healing methods. It would take a while before anyone would be willing to try femto crystals again.

The oddest part of the whole thing turned out to be how many had survived. There were, thankfully, only a handful of deceased Lissaens. Shari wished with all she had that the Crystal Intelligence had claimed no victims.

Rising to rejoin the others, Shari let herself become lost in the monotony of shifting rubble and holding walls up for others to reattach. Later, she would let herself think about how she'd like to make something, instead of destroying it. For now, she let the flex of her Innarn leave tired, trembling finger as she lifted the next piece of wall.

The moons were high in the sky by the time Asterion found Shari.

"Well met, Altoriae."

"Well met, Asterion. I hear you saved us all?"

The minotaur frowned. "I hear you stood at the people's heart?"

Nodding, Shari gently lowered a load of rubble off to the side. She grabbed two glasses of quass juice from one of the nearby stands which had been set up to feed and water the helpers.

Shari offered one to Asterion as they stepped into the shadow of a repaired building. This was the last street in need of repair, and they had almost finished.

"I was. Thankfully, Sam is quicker than an exploding heart," Shari said, taking a sip of her drink.

Asterion choked on his drink. Thoughts of *causing* and *no doubt* and *not mine* flashed through his head loud enough to reach Shari's consciousness.

"You might want to work on your shields a little," she said. *Huh. Minotaurs can blush.*

"Yes, well. I'll have plenty of time to do so when I'm back on Atlantis." His ears drooped, and he looked at ground.

"What are you taking about?" Shari said. She sensed the Returned coming around them, as if they were ready fight her so she'd let Asterion stay.

"I am to return once the threat is gone. Even staying to help with the repairs is pushing the limit of what I can do."

"Has the threat gone?" She smirked at him over the edge of the glass.

Asterion frowned even as he nodded. "The threat was the Crystal Intelligence, and you defeated it. Again."

"I just distracted it long enough for you to defeat it," Shari retorted. "When I spoke to Oitane, did I name the threat?"

Dropped jaws looked just as ridiculous on minotaurs as they did on a humanoid face.

Turning to the nearest Returned, Shari demanded, "Punch me."

"Nuh-uh!" she said and stepped back.

"Collis?"

Wide-eyed, Collis shook his head and moved away.

"Won't someone punch me?"

An Ilutri dropped from the sky to land beside her. Wolf punched her in the upper arm—hard. Belfar landed at his side, wings flaring out behind him. A few of the Returned looked at him as if to size up the danger he posed. His crystal wing glinted in the light, but his eyes were free of even a hint of orange.

"Ouch! See, there's still a threat."

"You didn't tell us we could return," Wolf rumbled at her.

Shari winced. "Sorry."

"Is he a threat?" Asterion growled.

"No, this in my uncle. But it just shows you can never tell where the next threat will come from." Shari made her expression as innocent as possible. "It's best if you stay as a permanent representative of Atlantis, to make sure your newest ally is safe in these dangerous times."

Wolf punched her again.

"Ow! What was that one for?"

"Lay it on thicker, why don't you?"

"Hush!"

Asterion laughed. Clearing his throat, he looked at the ground and swallowed hard. Raising limpid eyes, he placed a hand over his heart. "To make sure Atlantis is safe from the dangers Lissae faces, I am willing to make the sacrifice of staying here."

"Brilliant!" Shari grinned.

Around her, the Returned whooped and cheered, sending colourful sparks into the air.

"Shari, have you seen the Guardian?" Wolf leaned in to rumble as the others celebrated.

With a sigh, she shook her head.

Jonathan held Zac's hand.

Once again, Zac was laid up in the Healing Centre because he'd risked his life to save someone.

"You are so lucky Wolf grabbed you before you landed." He ran a hand over his face. "When are you going to look after yourself?" Jonathan asked Zac.

"Maybe I need someone to help me?" Zac croaked.

Hastily, Jonathan offered him a water pod. Zac popped it in his mouth and bit down, sighing as the liquid coated his parched throat.

"I know of someone who might volunteer to help," Jonathan said, aiming for casual, but sure his blush gave him away.

"Yeah, about that." As Zac sat up, the Guardian's heart sunk. "I have a confession to make."

Jonathan swallowed heavily and let go of Zac's hand to hide the sudden trembling of his own.

"I was the reason you were in danger."

"What? No you weren't. The Crystal Intelligence−"

"Wouldn't have controlled you if you didn't have femto crystals in your body!" Zac exploded. "I put them there! I put you at risk! All so I could be the hero and cure your sight!"

With a small sigh, Jonathan reached up and took off his glasses. Calmly holding them at chest height, he snapped them in half.

Zac gaped at him.

"I never needed them. It terrified me to get close to anyone. It seems like every time someone got to know me, they died."

"So you've been lying?"

"To protect myself, yes."

"From what?"

Shakily exhaling, Jonathan closed his eyes. His Mind Healer had said being open was a good thing. "From love."

"Love?" Zac gave him an incredulous look.

Maybe I read him wrong?

Suddenly, Zac started laughing loudly.

A healer poked his head in the room to see what was wrong. Jonathan shrugged.

"We are the biggest fools around!" He wiped his streaming eyes and chuckled. "I travelled the *Realms* for you! It took me years to figure out how to heal your sight. While you're protecting the Realm." He sobered suddenly. "And your heart."

"I'm sorry?" Jonathan offered, not sure what he was apologising for.

"I am too," Zac said. "I'm sorry for wasted years, and miscommunication, and everything we've missed out on." He was silent for a while.

Unthinking, Jonathan handed him another water pod.

Zac's fingers lingered on his. "We can't make up for lost time."

The blunt words left Jonathan sagging in his chair, utterly defeated.

"But we can try," Zac said. "If you want?"

Jonathan beamed.

Shari couldn't wipe the smile from her face. Most of her favourite beings in all the Realms were in the room, about to join her for a very normal dinner, should the Deities be so kind as to not interfere.

She glared at the ceiling for a moment, as if, just by the strength of her will and the might of her Innarn, she could forestall the next challenge the Realms were going to throw at her.

They'd slept in after the clean-up and been given a day's grace from school. Shari, absolutely exhausted, had needed it.

Turns out dying was quite tiring.

Shuddering, she tried to push the thought away, and instead concentrate on the decorations her room-mates and guild members had adorned the dining hall of the castle with.

Greenery in white earthen pots sat next to fountains carved in the shapes of each of the Shifting Islands. Candles had replaced crystal lights, and dotted the table, as well as floating on invisible air supports above their heads. The long table seemed to hold enough seats for half of Ronah.

"Everyone's here," Sam said, sliding into the seat next to Jon.

Shari craned her neck, trying to see him. Grumbling, she reached her Innarn into the rock of the table and pushed at the shape of it. For a long moment, it resisted. But the table trembled, forming a circle, the chairs moving at the same time to the delight or surprise of those seated.

Satisfied, Shari sat back. Across the expanse of the table, Asterion chuckled.

As many of the Returned as possible had crammed into the room, vying for a spot close to the minotaur. The air was heavy with the amount of sending going on around her.

Members of her guild sat scattered around the table. Jon and Sam were on her right, Tania and Collis on the left. Her parents, Wolf, Belfar, and SilverCloud clustered in a group, happily chatting to Cyrus, Zana,

Eva, and Temira. The room was cosy, with beautiful food laid out and the company of people Shari would like to know as friends.

A knock from the front door sounded. Shari tilted her head. Had the Realm had decided to drop the next challenge in her lap? Flicking out a tendril of Innarn to see who was at the door, she grinned.

With a tap of her hand, the front door opened, and she sensed three familiar bodies walk towards the dining room.

"Asterion, you have a visitor," she said, just before they came into sight.

The minotaur frowned at her and turned in his seat.

"Ter!" a high, childlike voice said.

Chair clattering to the ground, Asterion scooped up the small boy who'd flung himself in his arms.

A woman gasped, and Shari shifted directly next to their new guests. "This is Asterion, formerly of Atlantis. When Eric was away, Asterion guarded him. He's the reason Eric came back to you."

Eric Shansky's mother, Louise, slapped her hand over her mouth, tears running down her cheeks. Andrew had no trouble striding forward, right up to the minotaur.

"Daddy, it Ter!" The boy had wrapped his little arms and legs as far around Asterion as he could manage.

"You kept Eric safe?" Andrew asked.

"I did," Asterion said. Eric punched the minotaur's chest twice in what must have been an agreed signal, because Asterion smiled widely and put a hand under Eric's feet. The boy used the foothold to clamber onto Asterion's chest, then grabbed a horn and heaved himself up to sit astride his head.

"You've gotten heavier," Asterion grunted.

"Ter!" Eric said, chubby arm extended, finger pointing forward.

The other Returned laughed as Asterion lapped the room, Eric proudly sitting on his broad head.

"I think it's the last time we'll be able to do that, little one," Asterion said mournfully as he rejoined Eric's parents. "You're bigger now." Tipping his head, the boy slid down into his waiting hands. Gently, Asterion placed him on the ground.

"We thought he made you up," Louise said. "He's been talking about you, drawing you, since he got back. He calls you a friend."

"Fren!" Eric agreed.

"Your son has been the only person in the entire Realms to look at me and see I mean no threat from the first moment he laid eyes on me," Asterion said. "I've gained many friends since then."

"He's an excellent judge of character," Andrew said, pulling Louise tight against him.

"Are you staying on Ronah for a while?" Louise asked.

Asterion nodded.

"Please come and visit. You will always be welcome at our house," she offered.

"My thanks," he said, and bowed his head slightly, careful of his horns.

"You're welcome to join us for dinner," Shari said.

The Shansky family sat down, scoring prime seats either side of Asterion, while Eric clambered into his lap, chattering and stealing bits of food from any plate nearby.

A room full of light and laughter, food, family, friends, and fun.

What more could she want?

CHAPTER THIRTY-FOUR

Samuel, arms laden with the leftovers from Shari's surprise feast, kicked the door of his house closed.

"I hope you realise how much effort I went to for you," he called out. "It wasn't easy to convince the others why I needed so many bones."

For a long moment, there was silence.

Placing everything on the kitchen table, he tilted his head, listening. Nothing.

Shoulders drooping, he signed and started to unpack. Apparently, his shadowy friend had moved on.

Moving slowly, and aching all over, Samuel tidied everything away. After having a massive crystal slab dropped on his head, and coming back to an empty house, he was well within his rights to mope.

Taking the large bowl of bones, and a generous handful of rutenberries, he clambered into his bed. Sitting cross-legged, he snapped a bone in half and was about to suck the marrow from the middle when there was a curious chirruping noise.

From under his bed.

"Change of scenery?" he asked, poking his head over the side.

Sure enough, his shadowy friend was there, peering back at him.

His heart was so light, it had suddenly taken to zinging around his body. "Thought you'd left," he grumbled. Or he tried to. It came out a tad too watery to be passed off as a grumble.

The creature shook something, and slowly slithered out from under the bed.

In the darkened room, Samuel could now make out a fuzzy outline. It seemed the bones were working.

"Want some?"

A tendril flicked out, uncurling like a long tongue, and wrapped around a bone. The creature pulled it back and looked at Samuel cautiously.

He sucked the marrow from the bone in his hands, and the creature rumbled its approval.

Between them, they devoured the rest of the bowl.

Bellies bulging, Samuel vanished the mess and snuggled down in the soft covers, hands sinking into the shadows and stroking the almost corporal sides of the creature.

It purred.

Wolf looked at Belfar and smiled.

"Feeling sappy, are we?" Belfar grinned back.

"I believe when my mate is in his right mind, and healed after a horrific event, I'm allowed to be sappy." Wolf sniffed teasingly.

Belfar's grin dropped. "That's something I'm curious about."

Gut churning uncomfortably, Wolf raised his brows.

"My memory tells me what happened to my wing was a lifetime ago. Long enough that the heft and feel of the new one should be second nature." His wings flared out behind him, the crystal one glinting in the sun.

"But?"

"The timeline doesn't match up." His mate's lips was a thin, unimpressed line.

Wolf gulped.

"What happened?"

His mouth opened, and the story poured out. When he got to the attack on Shari, and the swathe of pain Belfar had carved through Talhan, his mate became pale.

"Let me get this right. I was mutilated on a foreign Realm. When you bought me back, the technomancer had to cut me open again, and she put murder crystals into my body to create this." One wing flapped hard, knocking against the table. Belfar didn't even wince. He spun away, the line of his shoulders tense.

Reaching out, Wolf let his hand fall. Tears were welling in his eyes, and he didn't think he could keep them back.

"When it was done, no one told me I was part crystal, and they had the Altoriae change my memories." Belfar's volume was rising. "Then I attacked her. And others." He broke off, fists clenched at his sides. "Were you ever going to tell me?"

"Yes," Wolf choked. Tears were making tracks down his cheeks, and he was trembling. *This is the moment when he realises I'm not good enough.*

Belfar finally turned to look at him.

His appearance must have been horrid, because his mate immediately swept him up in a hug.

"When we went to the caves?"

"We were hiding. Shari warned me."

"But I attacked her!"

"She knew it wasn't you."

Shuddering, Belfar drew him in closer. Wolf held him just as tight.

After an age, they moved apart, grinning at each other through puffy eyes and tear-stained faces.

"You need to know one thing. Don't *ever* hide something from me again. We're meant to be there for each other in every aspect. I can't do that if I think you're withholding things."

"I won't." Wolf promised, and pulled Belfar in for another hug.

After a long day back at school, dinner with her parents was the slice of normality Shari hadn't been aware that she needed. Halfway through a meal full of laughter and jokes, Shari sensed a tingle in the back of her mind which meant Jon was waiting to send to her.

'What's up, Jon?'

'*I just received word from the mainland. Quite a few continents have been under attack lately, and they're requesting some of their troops are allowed to train with you,*' Jon sent back.

'*That's... unexpected,*' Shari sent, trying to stay neutral.

'*But not unprecedented. Perhaps we can discuss this tomorrow? I just thought you'd like to know.*'

'*Of course. I'll see you at the store tomorrow.*' She sighed aloud, making the others in the room look at her.

Jon signed off with a note of thanks to her mother for the soup, which Shari had dutifully passed on. It looked less and less like she'd get another night off any time soon.

She smiled at her parents, and talk turned to what they needed to do to prepare the Quiver and Quill for the joining with Cantash.

In the back of her mind, Shari tried to decide who would attack first, the Dark Council or the mainland.

Later that night, as Shari got ready for patrol, there was another tap on her shields. Someone unfamiliar wanted to send to her.

'*Altoriae?*'

The signature seemed slightly familiar, but Shari wasn't able to place the being.

'*Please, Altoriae, I mean you no harm.*'

Shari rolled her eyes and wondered what the being wanted. *Only one way to find out.* 'Who are you?'

'*I'm an aide with the mainlanders.*'

With a loud sigh, she went to sever the connection.

'*Wait! Please!*'

Shari paused and hoped she wouldn't regret the decision.

'*I have news. Please, Altoriae.*'

'What's your name?'

'*Skye.*'

'And your news?' Shari's send was as hard as the metal of her blade.

'*The mainlanders are planning an attack. They fear the Shifting Islands are growing too powerful. That you are too powerful.*'

'That's not news, Skye.' She sighed. Surely even an aide would realise they were aware of an imminent attack.

'*But I know when they will attack, and how.*'

Perhaps the mainlanders would be the first attack after all.

Shafts of sunlight lit up the dust motes dancing. Shari glared at them through bleary eyes.

Five more minutes.

When she woke up properly, she wasn't sure how much time had passed. Stretching, she found she didn't care. Weekend sleep-ins were the best.

'Are you up yet, sleepyhead?' Jon sent.

'*I've been up for hours,*' she fibbed. She sensed his laughter.

'You've been ignoring the handbook. You'll need to add the pledge in there, and the names of your new guild members.'

Shari half wanted to protest, but it would do no good.

'*Fine. Let me eat something first.*'

She took her time getting out of bed and ready for the day. Shari was expecting to be sore and stiff, but movement was easy, and she went through her morning exercise without so much as a twinge.

After eating, she strolled through the streets to the bookstore. A line of beings out the front made her wonder what was going on.

She poked at Jon's shields with the query.

'*Interviews. Can't have everyone working in the store as part of the guild.*'

'*Should have warned me. I would have shifted in.*'

'*But if they can't behave rationally when they see you, they aren't a good fit for the store.*' Jon was always so reasonable about things.

'*Ugh. Fine.*'

She slipped past the hopefuls, greeting the ones she knew.

Eva, from Talhan, gave her a wink. "Any hints?"

"On how to get the job? Be yourself," Shari advised.

"Always." Eva straightened her shirt, pulling at the hem to try and get some of the wrinkles out. It looked like she'd been through the wringer. In a way, Shari supposed she had. Taken over by the Crystal Intelligence and forced to do things she normally wouldn't, fighting against friends and foes alike, and not being able to stop.

With a flick of her finger, Eva's clothes fluttered slightly around her, settling wrinkle-free once the mysterious gust passed by.

Eyes wide, Eva looked at Shari, who winked before slipping away.

Wandering through the shop where yet more hopefuls waited, Shari finally managed to make it through the back door.

'*Think I'm going to have to keep the handbook at the castle from now on,*' she grumbled.

'*Not a bad idea. Why don't you take it back there now?*'

Shari opened her mouth as Jon leaned forward to take a sheet of paper from the latest applicant.

'Fine.' Grabbing *The Altoriae's Handbook*, Shari shifted back to her room in the castle.

'I want to see that entry tonight.'

Grumbling, Shari got out the ridiculous quill Jon made her use.

It's official. I have my own guild. I asked and checked, and they still want to join in the fight to protect Lissae. They pledged:

> *To protect Lissae and do everything in our power to keep our Realm safe. To fight by the Altoriae's side and guard each other's backs no matter where we are.*

But I made a pledge too. I swore to do everything in my power to keep them, and Lissae safe.

And I will uphold the pledge.

Ink dripped from the quill, blotting onto the page. Shari cursed, and used her Innarn to syphon it away.

During the fight against the Crystal Intelligence, I died. My atoms and essence scattered across the Realm, but Lissae brought me back together again.

My memory of being dead is fading, but I know I saw two hearts that day. And only one shattered.

Lissae warned me of something. Crossing a portal? The words have faded, but the way she sent them hasn't.

I don't know what is going on with my Realm.

But I intend to find out.

GLOSSARY

A

Altoriae – Protector of the Realm of Lissae. Traditionally a female role, although there has been one male Altoriae. Previous Altoriaes have included Kay'imi, Muran Curtis, Jali Thorne, and Fiona MacAde. Forces of nature cannot kill her. They must swear to uphold the seven duties of the Altoriae.

Altum – The home Realm of the Q'Aralide. Also the Realm which will be hosting the next Dark Conclave.

Apprentice, The Guardian's – The Guardian's apprentice is to take over the role of Guardian once the current holder of the title falls in battle or dies of old age.

Atlantis – A Grey Realm with a predominantly human population, Atlantis is famous for its tech Innarn and wide variety of Innarn-powered machines.

Azehal – A drink favoured by the Guardian. A rutenberry-flavoured stimulant drink, typically served with sweetener and milk.

B

Banded toe biter – A small flying bug notorious for delivering itchy bites to both ears and toes.

Banoume – Wild desert beasts which inhabit Lissae. Of an equivalent size to Earth's elephants, the banoume have the temperament of a wounded hippopotamus.

Bazaven – A Light desert Realm. Native beings include the **Sylpans** (See: Sylpan) and the **Ofanahni** (See: Ofanahni).

Bereni trees – Trees that are grown to be used as buildings. The size and design of the tree can be controlled by an Innarnian or by one of the sentient islands.

B.I.R.D. – A Bio Instructor for Relative Distance designed by Xani of Talhan to ensure beings would stop bumping into things if they were absorbed in their crystal slab. The B.I.R.D. device acts as both a guide and a guard.

B.I.T. – A Basic Innarn Training device created by Temira of Talhan. This device is designed to test the user's abilities without anyone else getting hurt.

Blank – A person who can't use Innarn.

Books 'n' More – A store on Ronah that the Guardian runs when he's not saving the Realm of Lissae.

Buta sprouts – A small, round root vegetable that tastes like ten-day-old socks.

C

Canak-Maku – A Grey Realm which is home to the minotaurs.

Castle, Ronah's – The centre point of Ronah and the traditional home of the Altoriae, the Guardian, and their respective families.

Chakram – A disk-like blade with a razor-sharp edge and a large hole in the centre. Only a few species use it as their preferred weapon. The Yoxant are one such species.

Chirea – A race of warriors who use the bones of their fallen enemies to make their armour, weapons, and other items. The Chirea show status and power through the amount of bone armour they have collected. They use golden arrows soaked in a special mixture created by the Q'Aralide to steal Innarn. They are also known for poisons and soaking their weapons in potions that make healing by Innarn impossible. The Chirea made their base camp at Iabovar, near the Niverwell Ranges.

Clans – Family lines.

Crihimos – A Light Realm.

Crystals – Hold energy which is turned into electricity. Often installed in clusters to gain more power and last longer. Different coloured crystals do different things. White Crystals are used for communication. Black Crystals gather power, and Orange Crystals connect currents to create fences. Crystal necklaces are given to young children and Blanks for them to manipulate the crystals.

Curses – Several curses are common on Lissae, including: Adeon's fire; By the Life of Lissae; Ke'ra's Flash; Zoemer's Rocks; Rasshnae's Floods; Vebnah's Breath; Na'reh's Ghosts. Other curses from the Realms include: ketarr; dathae; tuzar's arse; tongue of a Ne'fora; whale's arse; basalt-chewing hemmit-loving buzzard; cestoray; slime vattar; hanotqe; slime-filled cedore; feseor; gozochas; thrice-damned; fizzpot; trusnuck.

D

Daen – A short, fierce, and loyal race with amazing control over the Fire Element.

Dansua – A Grey Realm.

Daborang – A spiced tea of Yessna's making.

Deities – Lissae has six Deities who are said to have lived on Akoren. See: **Adeon**, **Ke'ra**, **Na'reh**, **Rasshnae**, **Vebnah**, and **Zoemer** for more details.

Ducibus – The Ducibus guard the gateways between the Realms. No one really knows what they look like, as they all wear dark cloaks. There is a theory that they come from different Realms and are made up of all sorts of races. They ensure the safe travel between Realms and that those who aren't meant to get through, don't.

Duhiomel – A Light Realm, home to a variant of cyclops. The **Sivertrie Woods** guard the gateway off-Realm. In the Ducibus' hallway, Duhiomel is accessed through a carved door with an intricate leaf pattern. The door opens directly into a creek bed.

E

Earth – A Grey Realm with ley lines like Lissae. Once the home of Atlantis before it split away to form its own Realm. Also home to the myth of the minotaur, and most of the readers of this series.

Ekrix – Native to Flachaeus, the ekrix is a small, plant-eating lizard with a poisonous bite.

Elders – Those who have, through age and experience, managed to survive the Realms long enough to guide their people. They also act as advisors to the mayor.

Elements – Lissae has seven main elements that Innarnians can manipulate: earth, air, fire, water, plasma, spirit, and technology.

Ellevar – A Light Realm.

Eni – Malicious shape-shifters, able to permanently assume the form of influential figures to summon others of their kind to possess the subjects they have gained. Seriously Dark beings, the Eni are not often seen out of the Dark Realms. The Eni mentally 'piggyback' their prey before assuming their form. They were wiped out by the thirteenth Altoriae during an unsuccessful attempt to take over Lissae. References from the Eni's time on Lissae can be found in the **Eni Inside**.

F

Femto crystals – The latest in healing technology for Talhan. They can help a patient recover from any damage they've sustained and decrease recuperation time.

Ferah – Humanoid beings with cat-like features, including fur, tail, whiskers, and claws.

Fiotealar – A Grey Realm, known for its technological prowess. Home of the **Yoxant**.

Fulni – An animal similar to Earth's buffalo, but carnivorous and with two heads. The last fulni herd went extinct over two hundred years ago. Their tails are attached to a major artery, and if the tail is removed, they will bleed out in seven seconds.

G

Gilfress Elixir – Made from the roots of the gilfress plant, the elixir was created by Zana, Rakemyst's Linked. It has the colour of honey and viscosity of water. It has a spicy scent, and acts as a pick-me-up for the drinker.

Gourhog – Large horned, pig-like creature with spines running along their backs. Typically, the extra-strong backbone and ribcage are enlarged on gourhogs and lay just underneath the skin. Difficult to kill without getting ripped apart.

Guardian – The rank for the person who oversees training and caring for the Altoriae, and for Lissae. In cases of emergency, the mayor and elders defer to the Guardian.

H

Healers – Similar to Earth's doctors, they heal patients who are sick or injured, usually using Innarn, although they also use the old methods.

Healers Centre – Also called the Hospital. A place on Ronah or Rakemyst to go when sick or injured.

Healing Centre – Talhan's version of the Healers Centre. The building also holds the Techno Centre, and the labs of the technomancers and Talhan's Linked.

Hekkor Mafae – A book about Dark Ones. The Guardian is extremely uncomfortable about having it on Lissae. The Guardian's Apprentice has banished it to his personal pocket-Realm.

Hello – An outdated greeting, considered rude by the current population.

Hoggeotis – A Light Realm with traps around the gateway.

Honeyhawk – Tiny birds native to Rakemyst. They have long, slender beaks and come in all colours of the rainbow. Typically travel in large flocks for protection.

Hospital – Also called Healers Centre. A place to go when sick or injured.

I

I bid thee well – A traditional phrase when two or more people part ways.

Iabovar – A Grey Realm, home to the stunning Niverwell Ranges. The Realm where the Chirea made their base camp.

Ilutri – Winged humanoids from Lissae. They are usually found on Rakemyst and are high-level Innarnians. They include some of the finest archers on the Realm.

Innarn – (said Inn-*ar*-n) Predominately Elemental magic which is present in all Realms to varying strengths. Innarn is split into three main groups: Dark, Grey, and Light. Each variant of Innarn has its own specialties. See **Elements** for more information. There are also other disciplines of Innarn, including Animal, Crystal, Mental, Realm, and Time.

Innarnian – (said Inn-*ar*-ni-an) A person who can use Innarn.

J

Jalbobvesi – Tiny, squirming flesh-eating insects. Shari received a thigh wound from these bugs.

Jinkor – A fixed island on Lissae.

K

Kenorvia – A continent on Lissae.

L

Lawrgaea– A continent on Lissae.

Lioccanor – A Light Realm.

Linked – A soul joined with that of one of Lissae's Shifting Islands. As the Shifting Islands are sentient, it was decided long ago that they should link with a being on their island to ensure that they remain in touch with the current needs of their population, and not remove themselves from the trials and tribulations of everyday beings.

Lissae – A Grey, sentient Realm who is defended by the Altoriae. Comprised of six continents, seven sentient Shifting Islands and multiple fixed islands, she is home to ten races. She is said to be a Mother Realm. There are two moons in her orbit.

Lissaen – A person who lives on Lissae.

Lukkorel – A large, edible fungus native to the Shifting Islands of Lissae. This mushroom is large enough to use as a bowl and eat it afterwards. Best pan-fried or slow-cooked.

M

Meojuary – A Light Realm.

Meropis – Capital city of the Realm of Atlantis.

Mid Canak – A Grey Realm which is next to Lissae.

Mishone – A Realm burned down by the Queen of the Q'Araldie when the previous chair of the Dark Conclave failed to report for his duties. The name has since been forgotten, and the Realm erased from history.

Motus – The movement used to create Innarn. One must have thought, intent, and movement correct for the Innarn to work. Motus can be an individual construct, or a widely recognised form.
Forms of motus used: Sleep; **Wind Blast**; Wall of Stone

N

Natal day – The name the Ducibus Pala gives to ze's birthday.

Neviarath – A Light Realm with particularly nasty bugs invading the jungle near the gateway.

Nimble Surfing – An Innarn sport played on a large field. Players ride boards and attempt various death-defying stunts. Each stunt earns points. The highest score wins. Falling from the board is an automatic disqualification. Nets are used for learners but are discarded in professional competitions.

Nindonia – A fixed island on Lissae. Home of the Zindara.

Niverwell Ranges – A stunning mountain range on the Realm of Iabovar. The range has a myriad of tiny, naturally created holes going from one side of the range to the other. It allows for the static build-up of two Elements, creating a whistling noise. Local legends claim the noise is caused by the souls of the departed.

Noxeomyth – A type of sauna on Ulnan that uses acidic fumes instead of steam.

O

Ofanahni – Native to Bazaven. The Ofanahni are typically oppressed by the Sylpans, whose brutal and inconsistent justice system makes their lives difficult. A group of Ofanahni refugees has settled in the desert region of the continent set aside on Lissae for refugees.

Osin berry – Small, sweet, yellow berries.

Orbisalium – A large apple-like fruit. The pale blue skin of the ripe fruit indicates a delicious crispiness, whereas the green skin of the juvenile fruit donates toxins strong enough to cause gastrointestinal upsets or, if consumed in large enough quantities, death.

P

Palon – Native to Lissae, the palon is a small, six-legged creature descended from wolves. They have soft fur and long tongues, with a preferred diet of insects.

Patrol – Any Innarnian resident over fifteen is required to help the Guardian and the Altoriae patrol the Realms to watch for any possible threats. The Linked, elderly, and Blanks are not required to patrol.

Penemiota Wilds – Jungle between Meropis and the gateway on the Realm of Atlantis.

Pocket Realm – A small Realm that is attached to a larger one.

Praxore – A Light Realm on the Lissaen patrol schedule.

Q

Q'Aralide (said Que-*ral*-die) – A vicious Dark race who wield spirit, earth, plasma, and air Innarn. Approximately thirty feet tall, their social status depends more on their colour and abilities than anything else. Quite apart from their Innarn, their breath is something to watch out for, as it can strip the flesh and the life from someone in just one exhalation.

Quass juice – A sweet, bubbly, orange drink, served cold.

R

Realms – Planets which inhabit various parts of the multiverse on three main levels: Dark, Grey, and Light. Although there can be many sublevels and a mix of Dark and Grey or Grey and Light within the same level. Dark Realms are places with little to no natural sunlight. Most lights in these Realms are made by Innarn. Grey Realms are places with a similar amount of light to Lissae and Earth's equator. Light Realms are places where there is an abundance of natural light.

Returned – The name given to those from Ronah who survived being eaten by Anriluka.

Rezem – A building made out of a mound of earth. The size and design of the mound can be controlled by an Innarnian, by one of the sentient islands or their Linked.

Ridden Hall – The school on Ronah.

Rutenberry – The frosted dark-purple skin of the rutenberry hides the chocolate-like fruit inside. It can be eaten raw, although the skin can be bitter. Skinned, mashed, and cooked, it can be added into cakes, biscuits, and other sweets, including drinks.

S

Sand pears – A juicy fruit native to Lissae's Shifting Islands, it is favoured by many.

Send/Sent – The word used for telepathic communication.

Shem'ar – Shem'ar are small dragon-like creatures, no bigger than a large dog and about as intelligent as canines as well. Kept most often as familiars, guard creatures, messengers, and family pets. They have soft, furry hides that come in almost any colour. Although incapable of Innarn or talking, owners of the shem'ar can communicate telepathically with the creatures, some of whom understand more than others.

Shifting – The Innarn art of mental teleportation from one space to another.

Shifting Islands – The name for the group of islands that travel around Lissae's seas, seemingly on a whim. They are sentient beings who care for the residents who make them their home. See: **Akoren**, **Cantash**, **Ginorti**, **Vannali**, **Rakemyst**, **Ronah**, and **Talhan**.

Sivertrie Woods – These woods guard the gateway of Duhiomel.

Skipstep – A clear disc used for Shifting from one place to another on Atlantis.

Spirit Realm – A Realm that is found alongside Lissae, where the spirit or souls of the deceased go when their physical bodies are no longer needed.

Sylpan – A double-headed being native to Bazaven, who hunts and imprisons those they consider have 'done them wrong.' What is wrong to a Sylpan depends on the day and hour, but if they feel slighted at all, they will hunt you to the end of the Realm to bring you to justice.

T

Talhan – One of the sentient Shifting Islands on Lissae, and the only one to start with an all-human population. He now accepts immigrants from all races on Lissae.

Techno Centre – Located on Talhan, it is the hub for all of Lissae's crystal and technological advances. The dual heads of the Techno Centre have been given the nickname of the technomancers, due to the amount of times their advances have brought the seemingly deceased back to life. The building also holds the Healing Centre, and the labs of the technomancers and Talhan's Linked.

Teeldrit – A small, friendly population of Teeldrit refugees live in the desert region of the continent set aside on Lissae for refugees.

Telmi – A savoury herb native to Rakemyst. It has a similar flavour to spicy spring onions, and a stunning deep orange leaf. It is quite tasty in a variety of dishes, including savoury muffins.

Thistlewood Institute – The school on Rakemyst.

Tocithas – A Light water Realm. The local population are likely to spear first and ask questions later.

U

U'sala – A group of beings from all over the Realms who have banded together to protect the Realms from creatures who wished to change them for their own benefit. Currently led by Jeran Metasta Voutar, and his second in command is Yessna. The numbers of the U'sala vary because of the high turnover rate.

U'tan – A race of extraordinarily powerful strategists who reside on Rataeo.

Ucoid – A small, annoying, blood-sucking insect native to Ulnan.

Uleulan – A race of four-armed humanoids from Lissae. Usually found on Sulanta, they have distinct features: a single, large eye and translucent skin. Amongst them are some of the Realm's high-level water and spirit Innarnians.

Ulnan – Temira's home Realm. It was destroyed, and all that remains is a burned door in the Ducibus' Hall.

V

Veti Cant – Or Cant, is a sign language that uses hands and facial expressions to communicate. It is often helpful when overcoming language barriers. There are variations for beings with more limbs, but the essentials of the Cant remain the same.

Vitaemancers – A type of Innarnian found on Ulnan who can control the blood inside another being or creature, dictating their every move. Vitaemancers can also cure diseases and successfully treat blood conditions.

Vitreus Academy - The school on Talhan. Vren is the current head of the academy.

W

Wards – Innarn shields designed to protect specific areas.

Weavers – A strong Innarnian race from Lissae. They reside on Vannali and usually keep to themselves. They are regarded as one of the oldest races and are often considered mythical beings as they rarely leave Vannali or allow visitors.

Wiaxatale – A Light Realm whose gateway into Lissae is currently under external attack.

Wind Blast – An eighth-year Elemental Innarn **motus** used to blast and/or flatten objects with air Innarn. (See: **Motus**)

Wisara – Primarily ocean-dwelling beings whose bodies—although humanoid—look like the tangled roots of lotus flowers. Wisara tell the Tales of Lore. They travel the oceans.

X

Xobrac – A sweet, purple juice.

Y

Yoxant – Beings native to Fiotealar. Incredibly gifted in tecno Innarn, they are the creators of some of the most sought-after technology in the Grey Realms. The Yoxants are more than willing to fight to keep their technology out of the hands (or claws) of others. Their preferred weapon is the chakram.

Z

Ze/Zir – A gender-neutral pronoun.

Zindara – A race of humanoids from Lissae. They are usually found on Nindonia and are high-level plasma and fire Innarnians.

BEINGS AND CREATURES

Adeon – The God of the Element Fire and husband of Ke'ra.

Akoren – One of the sentient Shifting Islands on Lissae. Originally home to Lissae's Deities, now ze is inhabited by a few, select representatives of the races that came from the other Shifting Islands.

Alan Pratt – Mayor of Ronah.

Alistair Hollingsworth – of Ronah. Son of Liza, stepson of Jordan. Brother to Jessica, Christopher, Caleb, and Tania. Former candidate for the Guardian's Apprentice.

Amara – currently of Ronah. Formerly of Cantash. Former candidate for the Guardian's Apprentice. New member of the Altoriae's Guild.
This girl is danger on two legs.

Amauran – of Ronah. One of the Returned.

Andrew Shansky – of Ronah. Father of Eric Shansky, husband of Louise Shansky.

Anika Thorne – of Ronah. Student at Ridden Hall. Blank. Stylist to the thirteenth Altoriae.

Anna – of the Spirit Realm. Formerly of Ronah. Former protector of the museum.

Anriluka – of Rataeo. This U'tan is older than Lissae's calendar. She almost devoured Ronah's entire population before Muran Curtis' Guardian banished her back to her home Realm. Anriluka was finally defeated by Shari Dawn, the thirteenth Altoriae, in the spring of 4059.

Arilla Dawn – of Ronah. Mother of Shari Dawn, wife of Calem Dawn. Owner of the Quiver and Quill Tavern.

Ashlen – of Ronah. One of the Returned.

Asterion – of Atlantis. A former professor who donated his mind to become myth embodied. Teaches at a school on Atlantis.

Belfar – of Rakemyst. Mate of Wolf Dawn. Second in command of Elder SilverCloud's guards.

Ben – of Kenorvia. Elder.

Benny – of Ronah. One of the Returned.

Calem Dawn – of Ronah. Father of Shari Dawn, husband of Arilla Dawn, son of SilverCloud, and brother of Wolf Dawn. Owner of the Quiver and Quill Tavern.

Caleb Hollingsworth – of Ronah. Son of Jordan, stepson of Liza. Brother to Jessica, Christopher, Alistair, and Tania.

Cantash – One of the sentient Shifting Islands on Lissae. He is home to the Daens.

Chamele – of Jinkor. Elder.

Christopher Hollingsworth – of Ronah. Son of Liza, stepson of Jordan. Brother to Jessica, Alistair, Caleb, and Tania.

Cisrk – currently in hiding. Kin to Samuel. Outcast from his former Realm.

Collis – of Ronah. Unofficial leader of the Returned. Sworn guardian of Ronah's Linked. Member of the Altoriae's Guild. *Should say – of trouble and mayhem. Never trust a talking crystal.*

Crystal Intelligence – of Lissae and Atlantis.

And for the love of the Nine Hells, never take a machine from Atlantis!

Cyrus Petram – of Talhan. Talhan's Linked.

Daivi – of Ronah. One of the Returned.

Dealon – currently of Ronah. Formerly of the Wisara. Former candidate for the Guardian's Apprentice. New member of the Altoriae's Guild.

Diren – Whereabouts unknown. Kin to Samuel.

Drah – of the U'sala. Formerly of **Duhiomel.**

Edward Thorne – of Ronah. Husband of Harmony. Elder of Ronah.

Elani – currently of Ronah. Formerly of Ginorti. Former candidate for the Guardian's Apprentice. New member of the Altoriae's Guild.

Elder Ribeck – of Ronah. Elder of Ronah.

Eli Thorne – of Ronah. Student at Ridden Hall.

Elizabeth Ribeck – of Ronah. Student at Ridden Hall.

Eric Shansky – of Ronah. Son of Louise and Andrew Shansky.

Esme – of Talhan. Former candidate for the Guardian's Apprentice, Esme is considered to be the best air Innarnian around. Her favoured weapon is the bow.

Eva – of Talhan. Orphaned. Femto crystal tester.

Fiona – of Ronah. A travelling scout for the Guardian of Lissae.

Fiona MacCade – formerly of Ronah. The twelfth Altoriae.

Not my fault!

Ginorti – One of the sentient Shifting Islands on Lissae. She is home to the Satyrs.

Gwyn – of Vendalbara. Elder.

Healer Edwards – of Ronah. Healer.

Their job would be easier if Jonathan and Shari would stop dying all the time.

Holli Doonavan – of Ronah. Head Healer.

Jessica Hollingsworth – of Ronah. Daughter of Jordan, stepdaughter of Liza. Sister to Caleb, Christopher, Alistair, and Tania.

Jetonyx – currently in hiding. Kin to Samuel. *Don't think I'm going to give anything away here, reader! My hatchlings are under stronger protections than your puny humanoid mind can possibly break!*

Jillon – of Talhan. Elder.

Joana – of Ronah. One of the Returned.

Jonathan Buan – of Ronah. The Guardian to the thirteenth Altoriae. Owner of Books 'n' More. *Friend – or, at least, he puts up with me.*

Jordan Hollingsworth – of Ronah. Husband of Liza, father of Caleb, Christopher, Alistair, Tania, and Jessica. Deputy headmaster of Ridden Hall.

Joshua Izzaya Clemise – of the Spirit Realm. Formerly of Ronah. Former Guardian.

Juniper – of Talhan. Head Elder of Talhan and the link between the young and old.

Kay'imi – The first Altoriae. She lived until she was 1217 years old when a lone Ahana archer killed her.

Ke'ra – God of the Element Plasma and husband of Adeon.

Kerk – of the U'sala. Formerly of **Duhiomel.**

Kieran – of Ronah. One of the Returned. *Saying 'whereabouts unknown' is kinder than 'could be lying dead somewhere' don't you think?*

Knura – Whereabouts unknown. Kin to Samuel.

Kodan – formerly of the U'sala.

Lira – currently of Ronah. Formerly of Tevon. Former candidate for the Guardian's Apprentice. New member of the Altoriae's Guild.

Liza Hollingsworth – of Ronah. Daughter of General Morrow. Wife of Jordan, mother of Caleb, Christopher, Alistair, Tania, and Jessica. Headmaster of Ridden Hall.

Lizbeth Ribeck – of Ronah.

Louise Shansky – of Ronah. Mother of Eric, wife of Andrew Shansky.

Maeve Riley – of Ronah. Student at Ridden Hall. Gossip queen.

~~Mara Ribeck~~ – of Talhan. Formerly of Ronah. Healer of optics. Augmented sight.

Mitchel Hoffman – of the Spirit Realm. Formerly of Ronah. Former Guardian's Apprentice. Friend to Shari Dawn. Sadly missed by all who knew him.

Mortimer Heath-Ribeck – of Ronah.

Mu – currently of Ronah. Formerly of Nindonia. Former candidate for the Guardian's Apprentice. New member of the Altoriae's Guild.

Muran Curtis– formerly of Ronah. The sixth Altoriae. Died after being eaten by Anriluka and returning to Ronah.

Na'reh – Goddess of the Element Spirit and wife of Vebnah.

Natalie Ribeck – of Ronah. Head Healer.

Nisethran – of Atlantis. Mad scientist and successful myth creator.

Oitane – of Atlantis. Diplomat. *She's as much of a diplomat as Shari is.*

Pala – Leader of the Ducibus and guardian of Lissae's gateway.

Rakemyst – One of the sentient Shifting Islands on Lissae. He is home to the Ilutri.

Rasshnae – Goddess of the Element Water and wife of Zoemer.

Raven – currently of Ronah. Formerly of Freeson. Former candidate for the Guardian's Apprentice. New member of the Altoriae's Guild. Excellent tracker.

Remmy – of Ronah. One of the Returned.

Ronah – One of the sentient Shifting Islands on Lissae. She is home to a variety of races and the traditional home of the Altoriae. Ronah's current Linked is Tania Hollingsworth. Ronah is one of the six gateways to the Realms. *She's alright, for a hunk of sentient dirt.*

Samuel Caragnton – currently of Ronah. Formerly of ▓▓▓▓▓▓▓▓▓ Son of ▓▓▓▓. ▓▓▓▓▓▓▓▓▓▓▓▓▓▓▓▓▓▓▓. The Lissaen Guardian's Apprentice. *Ha! Good try!*

Shari Dawn – of Ronah. The thirteenth Altoriae of Lissae and creator of the Altoriae's Guild. *She is not what I was expecting.*

SilverCloud – of Talhan. Father of Calem and Wolf Dawn. Grandfather to the thirteenth Altoriae. Head Elder of Rakemyst.

Skye – currently visiting Talhan. Aide to the mainland delegation.

Suni – of Lawrgaea. Elder.

Talhan – One of the sentient Shifting Islands on Lissae, and the only one to start with an all-human population. He now accepts immigrants from all races on Lissae.

Talofa – currently of Ronah. Formerly of Sulanta. Former candidate for the Guardian's Apprentice. New member of the Altoriae's Guild.

Tania Hollingsworth – of Ronah. Ronah's Linked. Daughter of Liza, stepdaughter of Jordan. Sister to Caleb, Christopher, Alistair, and Jessica.

Another friend. Just how many do I have?

Temira – of Talhan. Formerly of **Ulnan.** Also called the technomancer, Temira is Head Healer and head of the Techno Centre.

My apologies for the destruction of your Realm. It was not (entirely) my fault.

Trainor – of Talhan. One of Elder SilverCloud's guards.

Tutor Boyce – of Ronah. Maths teacher at Ridden Hall.

Tutor Heath-Ribeck – of Ronah. Science teacher at Ridden Hall.

Vannali – One of the sentient Shifting Islands on Lissae. He is home to the Weavers.

Varlee – of Rakemyst. Third in command of Elder SilverCloud's guards.

Vebnah – Goddess of the Element Air and wife of Na'reh.

Vren – of Talhan. Head of Vitreus Academy.

Wolf Dawn – of Rakemyst. Mate of Belfar. Brother of Calem Dawn, and uncle to the thirteenth Altoriae. Commander of SilverCloud's guards. Previously known as LoneWolf Dawn.

Xani – of Talhan. Also called the technomancer, Xani is Head Healer and head of the Techno Centre. Due to injuries, she rides in a hovering, crystal-powered chair and doesn't speak.

Don't trust anything the Ferah has to say about me. She's biased

Yessna – of the U'sala. Second in command.

Zac Husdon – currently of Talhan. Formerly of Ronah. Techno apprentice.

Zana – of Talhan. Talhan's Linked. Eldest of the Linked, and an accomplished diplomat.

Zedith – Currently in hiding. Kin to Samuel. Outcast from her former Realm.

Zoemer – God of the Element Earth and husband of Rasshnae.

Yet to be named Shadow Creature – currently living under my bed. Possibly another friend. Eats lots of bones.

Map of Talhan

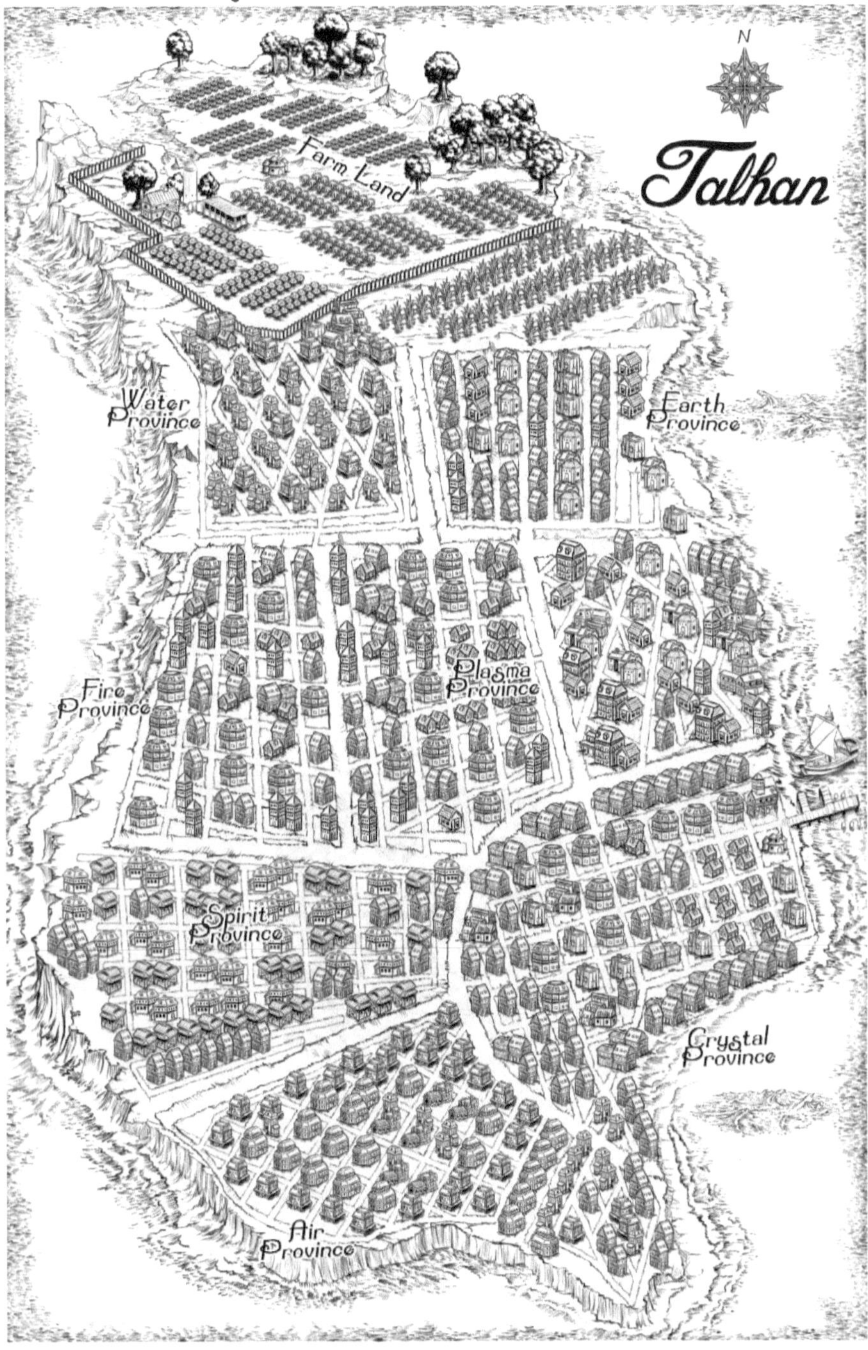

ENJOY THIS BOOK?

You can make a big difference

Reviews are the most powerful tools in my arsenal when it comes to getting attention for my books. They help me gain visibility and they can bring the realm of Lissae to other readers who may enjoy the journey.

If you have enjoyed this book, I would be incredibly grateful if you could spend just five minutes leaving a review (it can be as short as you like) at your favourite book store or on the Goodreads page. You can jump right to the page by scanning the QR code below.

Thank you very much.

Bookstore - books2read.com/talhan
Goodreads - goodreads.com/book/show/55438708-talhan

ACKNOWLEDGEMENTS

A book is never a solo effort. So many talented people have come together to make this fantastical world alive on the pages. I owe you all my eternal gratitude.

Jodie, Kathy, and Cyrus, my beta readers extraordinaire! Thank you for pulling and poking at things to make Talhan a better book. Sorry about the tissue boxes destroyed in the reading.

My beautiful editing team—thank you Anna from CREATING Ink for fine-tuning the manuscript and Lauren for putting up with endless questions. Desanka, your lessons from Rakemyst stayed with me.

I can't thank Vanesa enough for the stunning cover—the crystal is perfect! And Ricky Gunawan for the amazing maps! Lissae wouldn't look the same without both of you.

Special thanks to Cyrus, Lisa, Jess, Leah, Kathy, and Michelle for some of the new character names (and a few curses).

Of course, thanks go to my family and friends—for the endless support, probing questions, and giving me time to write.

Husband mine, the original technomancer. The one who can walk into a room and bring a machine back to life. I love you. Here's to another 19 odd years (with fewer electrocutions, I hope).

Corin, as always, thank you for the concept of the technomancer. You continue to enrich my world just by being you. Never stop.

Savannah, your eternal enthusiasm keeps me going. Watching you devour the books means worlds to me.

Danielle, your comments, questions, and encouragement has helped to shape the worlds both in the book and the ones outside.

To the amazing team of authors who encouraged me with word sprints – especially Samantha Andrews for the continued support, and Kat Maureen for starting the group. I didn't quite get it done in three days, but we got there in the end.

I cannot forget you, the reader! Thank you for exploring the Realms within these pages. I bid thee well.

ABOUT THE AUTHOR

R. Lennard is the Australian author of the young adult fantasy series *Lissae*. She is an avid fantasy and sci-fi reader, and in her spare time, she works as a librarian. She enjoys learning about ancient civilisations, cosplaying, and drinking endless cups of tea.

Residing on the beautiful Sunshine Coast in Queensland, Australia, Rebecca enjoys the natural beauty of both the beach and the bush. She lives with her family and is ruled over by her cat.

Rebecca is a fan of many things, including Doctor Who. She loves each Doctor just as much as the last, and has cosplayed as the Tenth Doctor, and the Girl in the Fireplace.

To find out more about Rebecca, head to rlennard.com

After More To Read?

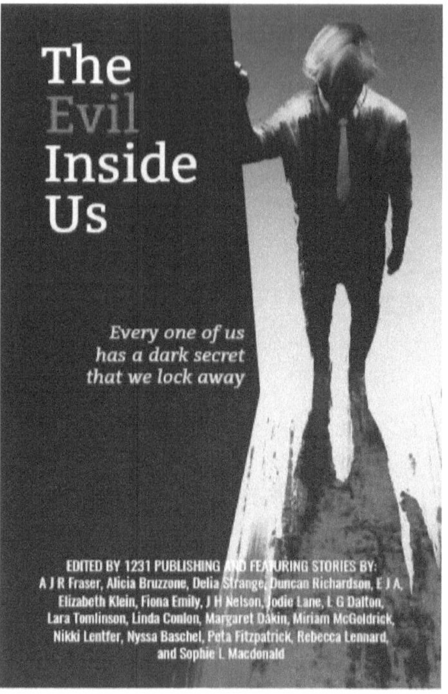

The Eni Inside is a short story prelude to the Lissae series included in the 3rd Australian Pen anthology, *The Evil Inside Us.*

The Headmaster of Ridden Hall, Lawrence Anderson, went out on patrol, but never returned. Instead, a being bent on taking over Lissae came back in his place.

Full of stories about dark secrets, you'll want to join the masses and buy your copy of *The Evil Inside Us* now!

Available at: lissae.com/short-stories

What would you do when you had nothing to lose?

Orphaned, Jonathan Buan travels halfway around the Realm to defend his father's honour.

He finds more than he expected—more pain, more death, and more people to call his own.

Can he save them all, or will he become a demon's snack?

Find out what Jonathan was like before he became the Guardian.

Buy *Guardian* to bend the elements to your will today!

Available at: lissae.com/short-stories

When a sentient Realm asks you to be her protector,
how can you say no?

Shari Dawn appears to be just another teen, until a band of wandering Wisara visit her home—Ronah—a sentient, Shifting Island of Lissae.

Now her secret identity has been uncovered, Shari must learn how to control her powers, preparing to be tested in a prophecy passed down from the ancients, which will determine her role in the future of the Realm.

But sinister forces infect the dreams of Ronah's people. With a team she didn't want by her side, Shari must decide who lives and who dies.

The fate of the Realm is in her hands...

Buy *Ronah* and step into Lissae today!
Available at: lissae.com/ronah

How do you live after being eaten by a monster?

After he died, Collis found himself in a nightmarish Realm full of creatures who wanted to eat him. Waking up after the fiftieth time he'd died wasn't any easier than the first.

Stuck in a pocket Realm, Collis and the residents from Ronah must defend themselves against the deadliest creatures from across the Realms. But survival comes at a cost.

And if they die? They reform. Over and over. Just how are they going to escape?

Find out in *Returned*.

Available at: lissae.com/short-stories

A misplaced arrow could cause a war...

Wracked with guilt, Shari must face the joining of two Shifting Islands with her sword at the ready.

But as the search for the Guardian's next apprentice is still underway, fear strikes her heart. Not all the candidates are who they claim to be. And a fearsome new foe is out for revenge.

Can Shari lower her defences enough to let someone else in? Or will the decision cost her more than she's willing to give?

Buy *Rakemyst* and fly into Lissae today!

Available at: lissae.com/rakemyst

His choice could change the very fabric of the Realms...

The most feared being to walk the Dark Realms was once a mere hatchling. Scrawny, weak, and half-mortal, Sanithane strives to gain enough power to ensure his tormentors never bother him again.

But when his queen sets an impossible task, Sanithane has to choose—his kin, or his life?

Find out the story behind the Golden Priest in *Shadows*.

Available at: lissae.com/short-stories

There's something hiding in the Dark.

It's seeking Shari relentlessly and it's got only one thing planned for the Altoriae...

When a spy impersonates Shari, Samuel is summoned home to chair the Dark Conclave. It's the most dangerous meeting in all the Realms; a place where blinking out of turn will lead to being eviscerated, and Shari, it's number one enemy, accompanies Samuel under the guise of protecting him.

While Shari is away, the mainlanders have declared war, and Jonathan alone must confront them. With trouble brewing on both sides of the gateway, how will Shari overcome the Darkest of Realms and keep Lissae intact at the same time?

Buy *Cantash* and fan the flames of Lissae today!

Available at: lissae.com/cantash

The clouds hang thick as the Light Realms start their attack...

Scooped up from the portal, Shari must survive the Lightest of Realms. Can she find her way back to Lissae, before her Innarn is forcibly removed?

Having survived the Dark Conclave, Samuel returns to Lissae—alone. The Altoriae who went missing from his side holds the key to bringing back his race, but he's forbidden from searching for her.

Jonathan is struggling to keep the peace between those on the Shifting Islands and on the mainland.

Now his apprentice is back, they must decide—do they search for Shari, or prepare for war?

Buy *Ginorti* and discover the trees of Lissae today!
Available at: lissae.com/ginorti

There's something in the silence.

As Shari struggles to come to grips with who she is after her time away, Akoren and the Wisara draw closer, and Innarn is disappearing from Lissae.

Can Shari, Jonathan, and Samuel figure out what's going on, or will the ancient stories about the silence be the end of them all?

Don't miss out on the thrilling continuation of the Lissae series, where the thing hiding in the silence threatens to consume everything in its path.

Buy *Akoren* and discover the silence of Lissae today!
Available at: lissae.com/akoren

The dead don't stay that way for long...

In this heart-stopping conclusion to the series, Shari must navigate a world where the dead are returning and wreaking havoc on the living.

With the help of Jonathan and Samuel, she races against time to stop the influx of restless souls before they are overrun.

Grab your copy of Vannali today and immerse yourself in a world where the line between the living and the dead is anything but clear.

Vannali is the final novel of the Lissae series.

Buy *Vannali* and greet the dead today!
Available at: <u>lissae.com/vannali</u>

READING ORDER

Guardian*

Ronah

Returned*

Rakemyst

Shadows*

Talhan

Guild*

Cantash

Sanctum*

Ginorti

Tempest*

Akoren

Weaver*

Vannali

Grace*

Lissae Chronicles*

The Altoriae's Handbook

*Part of the Lissae Chronicles

Keep up to date with the Lissae series and receive exclusive extras by signing up for the newsletter at:

lissae.com/welcome

www.ingramcontent.com/pod-product-compliance
Lightning Source LLC
Chambersburg PA
CBHW020010120726
47903CB00004B/1217